Mackay's Cliff House

Book One

Mackay Series

NORA WEIRICH

Triger Warnings

Contains:
Non Consent
Graphic Sexual Assault
Explicit Domestic Abuses
Mentions of a Miscarriage

Book Wrap/Cover by Nora Weirich
Illustrations by Nora Weirich/Christina Lupo

ISBN: PB 979-8-9917834-3-9
ISBN: HB 979-8-2728767-9-9

10 9 8 7 6 5 4 3 2 1
1st edition 2025
New Cover and New Name

For my mother.
Thank you for always believing in me, for being my editor, for being my biggest fan. I wouldn't have published a single book without you, I love you mom.

&

To all hospice workers past and present, your compassion and dedication is worth more than you will ever know. Thank you for all you do.

&

Christina L. I was unable to give you credit or thank you when Cliff House was originally released in 2023. Thank you from the bottom of my heart, thank you.

Nora Weirich

Chapter One

*T**his is ludicrous*, she thought, *and I'm getting a headache.* The noise level in the boardroom sounded like an elementary school lunchroom on the last day of school. With the amount of talking, sniping, and yelling, all the proposed ideas for expansion were lost in the din. As a result, none of the suggestions made much sense. Thirty-two-year-old Madison Danaher sat calmly and waited for the right moment to speak. She looked around the large room at all of her subordinates. This was an especially important meeting, therefore Patient Care Managers, which had been shortened over the years to PCM's for ease, from the larger offices and all of the higher-up executives had to be in attendance. Tender Care Hospice had more than one hundred offices around the United States, and because of this, there were a lot of heads in the room. Madison was seated beside the owner and president of the company, Mr. Samuel Goldblum. He was known as a shrewd and hard businessman, whose blue eyes could and would turn to steel when needed during business dealings. Yet those who knew him personally knew Samuel was a caring, loving grandfather who protected those who mattered to him. However, it was quite useful not to contradict the image Samuel portrayed. Samule sat in his chair leg crossed quietly observing the chaos that was his boardroom. Picking some phantom lint off his soft gray wool suit shaking his head.

Madison sat in silence, her patience wearing thin, decided it was time to call a halt to the annoying racket before she lost her composure as Chief Operating Officer. She leaned toward Samuel.

"Samuel, we're not accomplishing anything. However, I do have a proposal that I think you might like and could be lucrative."

Samuel looked at her and nodded. He'd come to rely heavily on her ideas. Thus far they had all been very beneficial. After all, she was the reason they were now the most sought after and most successful hospice company in the US. And to think, when she first came to work for Tender Care, she was hired as a part-time administrative assistant in one of the New Jersey offices fifteen years ago. She was now the most successful woman in the company and his right hand. He was very proud of her.

"Alright, go ahead, whatcha got, girlie?" Eye's twinkling.

That's your cue, Maddy, she thought. She scooted her chair back, swung her long slim legs from under the table, smoothed the front of her powder blue suit jacket, and walked to the front of the room. She stood by the door, but no one took any notice of her. So, she reached over and turned off the lights, much like an elementary school teacher would do when their class became unruly and needed to calm down. However, Madison found it to be quite useful when dealing with adults in a boardroom as well. *If they are going to behave like children,* she mused, *then they might as well be treated as such.*

When the room slowly came to order, she turned the lights back on. As she walked to the head of the table, she noticed Samuel, chin tucked to his chest and his hand rubbing his beard trying very hard not to laugh. Having been in meetings with her before when she had applied the same technique. Not to mention he, too, had had teachers who did the same thing. Once Madison neared the table, her nerves began to rise. *I wonder if I will ever stand here and not be nervous?* she thought to herself.

"Okay, now that I have everyone's attention. As we all know, you've been asked here to come up with a way to expand the business. Unfortunately, the only thing you've done thus far is yell, scream, and snipe at each other, and we won't get anywhere that way. Now, I have an idea that I think would work." She looked around the room to make sure she had everyone's attention. "I think expanding more in the states would be a mistake. Other hospice organizations are struggling because of our expanded services, and to an extent, this is good, but monopoly is not an acceptable concept in our line of work."

"Well why not?" muttered most of the room.

"Because if we put everyone else out of business, we become the bad guys. We no longer look like the company who cares, but the company whose main concern is to be on top. Part of hospice is to have a choice. If we put other organizations out of business, the patient will no longer have any choices. And sure that's great for us, but maybe we aren't what the family down the street wants. Maybe they will want another hospice. It is their choice if they want to pick us or someone else. Besides, you should never be the only bitch in the pack, or you'll never get any sleep."

Everyone looked at each other. Those who worked with Madison on a regular basis and were familiar with her work ethic lowered their heads to hide the growing smiles. Finally, the PCM from the Chicago office spoke.

"So, you think we should do nothing?"

"No, I think we should expand; however, I don't think it should be in the states." She took a deep breath. "I think we should go global." Once the initial shock of her comment was over, she continued, "I have been thinking about this for a while, we all know that other countries have hospice, or they want hospice. So, why not give them ours? We could start in one country first and see how it goes. When, not if, we become successful, we move on, just like here. I'm not saying it will be easy, but it *will* pay off in the long run."

Samuel leaned forward in thought for a moment. "Where were you thinking about going?"

Madison beamed. "Scotland."

"Scotland?" Samuel wasn't the least bit surprised she had a place in mind. I was a little taken aback by her choice. "Why there?"

"Because it's a small country, mostly rural and that's the type of area where we could have the biggest impact."

Samuel sat back in his chair and looked at Madison for a long while. Finally, after what seemed to be an eternity he spoke. "I think this could work. I'll give it much thought. I'll let you know by the end of the day." He smiled at her before turning his attention to the rest of the room as he got to his feet. "As for the rest of you, thank you all for coming and I will be in touch with you and let you know what the decision is." And with that, *Elvis has left the building,* she thought while she thanked everyone, gathered her thing and started back to her office.

Madison glanced at her watch on the way back to her office, *Three hours, that went on for three hours.* Rubbing her forehead, *Thank God it's Friday,* she thought. When she reached her outer office she noticed her assistant wasn't at her desk. This wasn't at all unusual, when she opened the door to her own office, Madison also wasn't the least surprised to find her assistant behind her desk at the computer.

"Margaret? What are you doing?" Madison chuckled as she walked in.

"Hi Maddy, I hope you don't mind, my computer died *again,* and I needed to get this done." Margaret looked up and saw her boss.

"Okay, don't worry about it. I need to get you a new computer; this is happening entirely too much." Madison chuckled as she sat down on her sofa and glanced at her office. She still couldn't believe it was *hers,* it was spectacular and built to impress. Yet the muted color of the walls, soft carpet throughout and a conversation area with plush charcoal blue sofa and two matching winged-back chairs, the room was restful and relaxing, in a stressful business.

"So," Madison leaned her head back on the sofa and closed her eyes. Listening to the rhythmic tapping of Margaret's nails on the keyboard for whatever reason she found soothing. "What are you working on?" She and Margaret had been together for many years and were friends as well as coworkers, though they had always maintained a business attitude in the workplace.

"I can't tell you," Margaret said, without looking away from the screen.

"What do you mean you can't tell me?" Madison lifted her head off the back of the sofa. "You tell me everything."

"I'm sorry, but I can't tell you this," Margaret insisted mischievously. By this time she was off the sofa and moving toward Margaret.

"You know," She grinned, "I'm your boss. I can demand that you show me what you're working on."

"Yes, you could," Margaret looked up and smiled. "but you won't." Just then there was a knock at the door.

"Come in." Madison was still laughing when Samuel, and Dean Michaels, the chief executive officer came through the door. "I hope you don't mind if Margaret stays, her computer has crapped out again."

"Not at all." Samuel answered as gestured Madison to sit while he took one the matching winged backed chairs.

Madison took the sofa and smiled at Dean as he joined her. He was a good-looking man in his early forties, tall with a medium build. It always impressed her how he was always impeccably well-dressed, everything including his attractive silver hair neatly in place. There was a friendly affection between the two of them, but nothing more. Sometimes she'd get an impression that he might want something more, but Madison made sure never reciprocate.

"Well?" After a few seconds of silence she couldn't take it anymore. "What did you decide?"

"After giving it much thought and talking to Dean..." Samuel sighed and then smiled. "We've decided to let you go ahead with your idea."

Madison, shocked and unable to hide the expression on her face. Both men grinned as Madison leaned back into the sofa.

"Oh, wow." She was a little shell-shocked. "Really?"

"Yes, but there's a catch." She turned her attention to Dean as he continued. "You'll only have six months to pitch the idea. At the end of the six months, you'll have to give us a report. Oh, I almost forgot you're going in person to make the pitch."

"What! You want *me,* to go to Scotland, for six months?"

"You don't want to go?" Samuel asked in mocking disappointment, yet he couldn't keep the twinkle from his eyes; Madison looked like a kid on Christmas morning.

"Are you kidding? I can't wait!" By the time they finished with all the details, it was five o'clock and time for the office to close for the night.

Since she was to be on a plane no later than Friday of next week, Madison would be staying late to make all the flight and hotel arrangements. She knew that this was the kind of thing her assistant was *supposed* to do; and Margaret wanted to stay and help her, however, she liked doing it. Besides, it was late and a Friday to boot. Margaret should be going home to her family not staying late to take care of something she could do herself.

By eight o'clock, Madison was still sitting at her desk working, and after staring at her computer for almost three hours her eyes had begun to sting. She leaned back in her chair, kicked off her shoes, stretched, and decided to have a drink. On the far side of her office was a mini bar, she started to pour a glass of Irish when there was a knock on her door. Leaning on the doorjamb with his ankles crossed, coat thrown over his shoulder, and one hand in his pocket was Dean.

"Dean, you scared me. I thought I was the only one left in the building." The company CEO stood in his gray suit pants, a baby blue shirt with red suspenders and matching red tie loosened at the neck. *God he's good-looking,* she mused, *He would look terrific on the big screen, a modern-day Cary Grant.* Over the years she'd often wondered why she wasn't strongly attracted to him. Other women in the office and out of it for that matter, found Dean exceedingly attractive. She had seen women make fools of themselves trying to get his attention. Did he have any idea how much he affected most women? *He must*, she decided.

"Can I make you a drink?" She was a little nervous. She'd been alone with him many times over the years, and there'd been times when he would look at her a certain way, like now, that she felt the need to put her guard up. She wasn't sure why.

"No, I don't want anything to drink. Thank you, though." He walked into the room throwing his coat on the chair next to him and shut the door behind him.

"Why are you here so late?" he asked, never taking his eyes off the woman standing in front of him. She was standing perfectly still on the most gorgeous legs he had laid eyes on in years. He glad she was wearing a skirt to show them off for him. His eyes moved up to her small waist then settled on her full breasts. Her chestnut hair, which she normally wore up during the day, cascaded around her shoulders. Her ivory skin and eyes of the Caribbean Sea made her, in his eyes, perfection. His gaze settled on her mouth, or more specifically her lips, which he most desperately wanted to taste. As he moved closer, he could tell she was breathing rapidly as if she was nervous.

"I needed to start making plans for the trip to Scotland. Why are you here so late?" Her heart pounding in her ears. *What the hell is going on here?* She was frozen, like a deer in headlights. He stopped in front of her, in her stocking feet, the top of her head came to the middle of his chest. He took her drink from her hand and placed it back on the counter of the bar behind her. Resting his hands on her shoulders.

"Had some work of my own to do and I saw your lights on my way out. So, I thought I'd stop in." she kept her gaze on a button in the middle of his shirt, trying to regulate her heart and rationalize his strange behavior. He crooked his finger under her chin and brought her eyes up to his. "You know you really shouldn't be here alone this late." Alarm bells sounded in her head. He bent down and touched his lips to hers. "But I'm pleased you waited for me."

Waited for him? she thought. *What the hell is he talking about and where is this coming from? And how do I get out of this gracefully?* "Dean, what are you—?"

With his hand still under her chin, he took mouth again. She was stunned, as he became more aggressive, Madison pressed her palms to his chest in an effort to escape and tried to turn her head away. He moved one hand around to the small of her back and pulled her against him while the other grasped the back of her neck, effectively trapping her. When she heard him moan, it sent her heart into overdrive beating so hard it was in her ears. She pushed harder on his chest but couldn't budge him. *Why is he doing this?* Her head was reeling. He'd kissed her many times over the years, always small brotherly kisses, but never like this. She pushed and pushed but he was an unmovable wall of determination. When the shoving had not effect she would've brought her knee up, but the pencil skirt restricted her.

His hand moved down her back and over her buttocks, she tasted better than he ever imagined, and he wanted more than this kiss. God, how he wanted her, his arousal, and his need for her was becoming more than he could handle. His hand moved up to the side of her breast, he wanted to see what was under her clothes. After years of waiting, he was going to have her at long last. Dean broke away from the kiss, running his lips down to her neck. His breath hot on her neck, as he moved down to the base of her throat. He wanted so much to make love to her, and began to unzip the back of her skirt. Her breathe and the way she was wiggling told him she was just as affected as he was.

My God, she thought. *What the hell does he think he's doing?* She pushed hard on his chest and tried to step back.

"Dean, please stop." He continued his assault, *The hell with graceful,* she decided "Please...STOP this!" With a massive hit of adrenaline she was finally able to shove him completely away, and took a solid three steps back from him. The whole incident lasted no more than sixty seconds, but felt like an eternity.

He saw it in her eyes, the sexual heat. *God, she wants this as much as I do,* he thought. *How could she stop?* She stared at his normally brown eyes, that were, in that moment, almost black with desire and to see actual bewilderment on his face at her breaking away filled her with anger and dread.

"I'm sorry, but I can't do this." She read the unspoken question on his features, well, she was also baffled by this change in him.

"I don't understand. I see in your eyes you want this as much as I do," Dean whispered as he watched her move further away from him and put her desk between them.

"Dean, I'm sorry, and to be honest I have not idea where this came from, but if that's what you see, you need stronger glasses." *He thinks I want this?* "You and I have never explored a romantic relationship and to be frank, I never sought one with you."

"Can you at least give me a reason?"

Are you learning impaired? she wondered. *Did he not just hear what I said?*

Dean circled the desk, placing his hands on her shoulders, and turned her to face him. *He,* apparently didn't want distance between them. "After all, we've known each other for fifteen years and it's obvious there is a mutual attraction here." He crooked his finger and forced her to look up at him. He bent his head and tried to kiss her again, tender, and gently. When Dean lifted his head and looked at her eyes, he saw anger and couldn't understand why.

"Dean," keeping her voice as calm and even as she could, "I cannot and *will* not do this." She stepped back from his touch. "I do not want an intimate relationship with you. You are my boss, and I want our relationship to remain professional." Because of the professional dynamics, she wanted to reject him as calmly and clearly as she could.

"What are you afraid of?" he whispered as he reached out and traced his fingers down her cheeks. She began to tremble with anger. *What is wrong with him?* she thought. *He's obviously not listening to what I am saying.*

"Shh, never mind, you don't have to tell me now. Come here." He tried to pull her to him, but she backed away again.

"Dean, did you hear what I said? I am not interested in an intimate relationship with you." *Holy crap on a cracker, can I be any plainer?* she wondered.

"Why don't we go to dinner and talk about your trip?" She smiled, "We haven't had dinner together in a long time. Not since our last date." He spoke as if she never opened her mouth.

She looked up at him in frustration. *He is learning impaired,* she thought as he smiled at her.

"I promise nothing will happen that you don't want to. No matter how much I want it too," he told her as she backed away from him for some distance.

"Date?" she asked. Warning bells were blaring in her head again. "We've had business dinners." Madison moved farther from Dean. "Not dates." Turning her back on him made the hair on the back of her neck rise, but in doing so she removed him from her sight, even if only for a few seconds. She rounded around the front of her desk to put a piece of furniture, once again, between them.

"I guess you don't want to go to dinner?"

"No, I do not," she answered bluntly. "But I do want to go home. Now." She began to quickly gather her things.

Dean smiled and went to sit on the sofa to wait until she was ready to go.

"ALONE!" she emphasized. "Do you need any help that's work related?" she asked, annoyed that he was still there.

"I thought I would walk you to your car." He smiled his megawatt smile as he settled back in the sofa.

"I do not need, nor want you, to walk me to my car." She no longer cared about being polite to her so called boss. It took her another twenty minutes to gather everything she would need over the weekend and closed her office.

Dean walked with her to the garage, all the while trying to convince her to go to dinner with him. He knew that if he could get her to go to dinner she would come to her senses about making love with him.

"Well, why don't you come to my place, and I can cook something for you?"

"NO, Dean!" Feeling her temper rise again, she took a calming breath. "Thank you, but no." *I think I'd rather go home, eat worms and have a tooth pulled,* she wanted to say. "I'll see you on Monday." she said as she got into her Jeep Wagoneer.

"Sure! Hey, wait." He placed his hand on her car door before she could close it. "Why don't we get together for dinner tomorrow night?" He watched her think for a minute, not knowing she was visualizing the tire iron on the floor of the back seat.

"No, Dean. Like I said, you're my boss and I don't want anything but a *professional* relationship with you." She tugged her door from his grasp and drove away without another word.

On the twenty-five-minute trek home from Philly to Cherry Hill, New Jersey, Madison thought about her day, that she was going to spend six months in Scotland, but what mostly filled her mind was what went on between her and Dean. Their relationship had always been one of professional and mild friendship, with no more than the occasional hug or sibling peck on the cheek. This complete change in him was more than unsettling, it was boarding on scary. One thing was for sure; she would never allow it to happen again or be alone with him, if at all possible. Although she was the COO, he was still her boss, so she felt the need to tread lightly. Not to mention she had other personal reasons for not starting anything with him or any other man for that matter.

"Stop it, Maddy," she told herself as she started to shiver. She flicked on the radio and sang the rest of the way home. It was almost ten o'clock when she pulled into the driveway of her townhouse. As she walked up the pavers to her front door, she looked at the drab dark gray siding, with burgundy shutters of her home. It was January, so her grass, although not brown, was still very short and frosted, her flower beds were empty and seemed a little sad. She bought this house four months back, and hadn't given any thought to the outside yet. Her front door was oak with a long oval-etched window, and in the window with her paws pressed up against the glass was Madison's beloved cat, Julie. She adopted the pure white kitty who sporting one green and one blue eye as a kitten four years ago. Once she reached the door, Julie could be heard screaming at her. She rarely came home late and knew she was in trouble and as she opened the door sure enough she was getting an earful from white ball of fluff. She put down all of her things and bent to pick up her soft, furry friend.

"Instant purr." She smiled. "See? I'm home," they bumped heads making her smile. "I'm sorry I'm so late, but I had to work." She walked into the living room that, for the most part, was set up and unpacked. The far wall of glass sliders opened out to her backyard and in the far-left corner of the living room was her entertainment center. She placed Julie on the back of the large gray microfiber sectional before she walked into her least favorite room in the place, the kitchen. Not being much of a cook it wasn't that much of an issue. This room was nothing more that the place to house Julies food and water bowls, wine, and the occasional frozen food in the freezer. Mostly she had takeout or went out to eat. However after the night she'd had, she picked up the phone and ordered pizza. Afterwards she collected her briefcase and laptop from entry hall, and set them on the table in the dining room. Since the house was still in the decorating stages, her home office was buried in boxes so, the dining room table was dubbed as her temporary desk.

Feeling fur on her calves she glanced down finding Julie, chuckling, she bent down and gave her a pat and a scratch behind the ear.

"Come on, sweetie. Let's go upstairs and change clothes."

Her bedroom was her favorite, and it was a mirror image of the living room with one spectacular except. Instead of a backyard off the wall of sliders, the bedroom had a balcony she screened it so Julie could go out there with her. As Madison walked into her closet she stripped out of her suit, she considered throwing it away, but since it was a favorite of hers she decided not to let Dean ruin it. So instead she put it in the dry clean bag and threw it in the corner. With her pajamas and slippers on she felt more centered and cleaner somehow. She went back downstairs to the living room with Julie hot on her heels. The minute she sat down on the sectional, Julie hopped onto her lap demanding attention. She leaned her head on the back of the sofa, closed her eyes and a few minutes later the doorbell rang.

"Damn, that is some fast pizza delivery. Stay here, Julie."

She patted her cat's head and went to the kitchen and took cash from her purse and answered the door. Except, the man standing on the other side of the threshold wasn't carrying a pizza box.

"Dean! What are you doing here?" Dean stepped in, shut the door behind him never taking his eyes off her.

She stood at the door for a minute, at a loss for words, then walked to the kitchen slammed her money back in her purse. She turned to face Dean from the kitchen reading his body language and could tell that he was angry. Well, dammit, so was she!

"I will ask again, what are you doing here? I've made myself perfectly clear, you have *no right* to be here." She crossed her arms over her chest. "I told you how I felt about this."

Deans eyes roved over her, she looked so goddamned good in the baggie flannel bottoms and a snug fitting tank top. He began to advance toward her, she'd known that look and backed away, but she was not fast enough. He grabbed her arms so hard Maddy knew she'd have bruises. Then he seized her mouth with his, this was no gentle, tender kiss, no it was rough, hard, and hurt. As she began to struggle against him, he took her arms, yanked them behind her back, and slammed her roughly against the wall trapping her. He broke away from her mouth and with a free hand began to tear at her top.

"Dean, please, stop! STOP!" she screamed, tears streaming down her cheeks.

Just than the doorbell rang, Dean wrapped his hand around her throat, bored into her eyes and said, "Papa John's Pizza, ma'am!"

She jolted awake, heart racing, panting with oily sickening feeling in the pit of her stomach and realized she'd fallen asleep. When doorbell sounded again, she stood on shacky legs and slowly made her way to her purse, retrieves the cash, and went to the door. But, before she opened the door, she peeked through the curtain to make sure it was the delivery guy. With the pizza in hand she went back to the living room, put the box on the coffee table, sat back on the sofa and pulled Julie into her arms and continued to shake. Trying desperately not to have a full-blown panic attack.

"What the hell is wrong with me?" Julie purred and meowed, she looked down at her kitty and gave herself a mental shake. After a few minutes she decided to lose herself in a movie and went to the bookshelf to pick one. As her fingers flipped through the choices she came to her favorite section and choose one of Ian Mackay's films. The Scottish actor was fairly new and she thought was an absolute dream.

She spent the rest of the night and the weekend lounging around and calling hotels in Scotland to see if any of them would take pets. It was proving to be a frustrating task.

"Do all of the hotels in Scotland hate pets?" she asked aloud. "I can't even come home late one night without getting in trouble, I'm certainly not going to leave her for six months!"

Finally, on Sunday morning, she was able to get ahold of an older woman who thought she might know of a house for rent. She crossed her fingers and decided to start the packing while she waited for the call back with news. Later that night her phone rang, and scared the hell out of the cat causing her to laughed so hard she tripped over her bag getting to the phone.

"I guess I deserved that," she told Julie and picked up the phone. "Hello?"

"Aye, might I be speakin' to the young lass who was wonderin' aboot the house?" The old woman's brogue was so thick, I was difficult to understand her.

"Yes, Mrs. Stuart, this is Madison."

"Oh, that's wonderful, I'm sorry, but I dinna seem ta recall what yer last name is."

"My last name? Oh, well it's Danaher."

"Danaher, is it? Tha's Irish, is it no'?"

"Yes, ma'am, it is."

"Oh, that's nice. Well, I suppose ye'll be wantin' ta know aboot the house, then?"

"Please." Madison had her fingers crossed once more. *Please, I hope the owner said yes,* she prayed.

"Well, the owner doesna use the house like I said, and he would be happy ta let it ta ye for the time ye'll be stayin'."

"Oh, that's wonderful! He is aware I will be bringing my cat?"

"Aye, lass, he knows."

"Oh, this is so great. You have no idea what a load this is off my mind." She sighed as the weight lifted. "When will I be able to speak with him regarding the rental fee?"

"I'm ta give ye directions ta fer the house and he'll be meetin' ye there ta sort oot the details." Mrs. Stuart gave her the directions from the airport.

"Thank you so much, Mrs. Stuart. You've no idea how much I appreciate all you've done. Oh, can you remind me where the house is located?" *That's right sound like the brain-dead ditz you are.* She scolded herself. "I've called some many places over the last few days, and I've done poor job keeping track."

"It's on the tip o' the Isle of Skye, near the small village o' Lusta." They said their goodbyes, and as soon as the call ended, she did her happy dance around the room, then continued to pack. The next morning she called the office and told Margaret she'd be working from home for the rest of the week. She had a lot to do, that was true and what she told her assistant. But if she was going to be honest, she didn't want to have to deal with Dean as well, that little tidbit, she kept to herself.

The rest of the week went by in a flash. On Friday, she woke at three o'clock in the morning, showered, and dressed. About ten minutes before her four-thirty pickup, she crated Julie, who related her displeasure by hissing and screaming as she wooed her into the carrier. By four thirty the limo driver arrived and loading the car. On the way to the airport Madison called Margaret's voicemail at the office and reminded her to have everything, but the heat and water shut off in the townhouse and to be sure to forward all her personal statements in the weekly express packet.

"I'm flying into Inverness," she told Margaret's voicemail. "It's about a hundred fifty miles, give or take, the village of Lusta where I'm going to pitch hospice. I've arranged to rent a house somewhere outside the village. Take care and I'll call you when I get to the house."

Madison sat back and rested her eyes for the remainder of the drive to Philadelphia International. When they arrived at the airport, she and Julie took the electric cart to their correct gate and boarded. Once settled in the roomy first-class section, she was glad she had listened to Margaret and not stuck by her original plan to fly coach. The plane started to shudder with movement, once the plane was in the air and at the correct altitude, the passengers were allowed to remove their safety belts. Madison leaned down and picked up Julie's cage and peered in.

"Well, sweetie, next stop Scotland."

Chapter Two

After a six-hour flight, even though everything went smoothly, Madson couldn't wait to get off the plane. When they landed, the passengers had to wait another hour before they could deplane. Once again, since the first-class passengers got off first, she was grateful to Margaret's seating suggestion. When she walked into the terminal, she gave a sigh of relief upon seeing a driver holding up a large card with her last name written across the front.

"Are you waiting for Madison Danaher?" *Dear God please say yes*, she wasn't sure she could handle the roads. It may be noon her time, but it was after six in the evening in Scotland. Not to mention she'd been up since three-thirty in the morning.

"Aye, would that be ye, then?" He was an older man, probably in his late sixties, snowy white hair, and a *very* thick accent.

Madison smiled. "Yes, that's me. What's your name?"

"Me name is Shawn, Shawn Conner, Miss. And it's a pleasure ta be meetin' ye." The broad smile he offered, accentuated the wrinkles around those friendly grey eyes. "Welcome ta the land o' mists and green hills."

"It's very nice to meet you as well, I've to go and get my bags. Do you know where the baggage claim area is?" she looked around the trying to get her bearings.

"Ah sure, but there be no need for that, lassie. I've gotten yer begs already." He chuckled at her bemused but lovely face. "I've only one question to ask o' ye, though."

"What might that be?" Madison was stunned, surely he hadn't collected her luggage by himself. And if that be the case she felt terrible. She wasn't known for packing light.

"When we get ta where we're goin', would ye mind given me a bit of a hand wi um?" he chuckled.

"Of course I will." Smiling, she handed Shawn the directions to the house and followed him outside.

It was every bit as bitter cold in Scotland as it was in Philly and just as dark. Unfortunately, with the misting and night sky, she couldn't see any of the landscape. Her eyes followed Shawn as he walked to the car she would be traveling in and nearly fell over. She couldn't believe it, never in all her life had she laid eyes on a 1955 Classic Rolls Royce in person. It was gorgeous! The surface was so shiny it looked like black liquid lacquer poured over the chassis. In a daze she just stared at Shawn as he held he held open the door. Julies soft meow brought her focus back, she thanked him quietly, slid in and put Julie on the floor. The rich interior was dark red leather and the inside was so large she felt like she could stand up if she wanted to.

Before pulling away from the curb, Shawn read over the directions, then he looked up and they were off. Looking out the window, was pointless since the further they traveled from the airport and its lights the more opaque the dark became, and the icing on the cake, the mist turned into a driving rain. She leaned down to Julie and whispered, "This seems like a good time to grab a short nap."

"Would this be yer first time ta Scotland?" came Shawn's aged, raspy voice from the front seat.

"Yes. I'm here on business, but I've always wanted to see Scotland." She stifled a yawn, not wanting to be rude to Shawn.

"If it wouldna be nosey, what might yer business be?"

Madison smiled. "It's not nosey in the least," she assured him. "I'm the Chief Operating Officer of a hospice company in the United States, and we're interested in starting a branch office here."

"A hospice? I'm no' familiar wi them. Dinna know that I can say we've got any in these parts."

They both drifted off into their own thoughts, and since it was a long drive to the house she decided to take her own advice and catch some sleep. Before she completely dozed off she remembered she was to call Margaret. She pulled out her cell, dialed the number and got Margaret's voicemail.

"Hi, Margaret, it's Maddy. It's after, well I don't know what time it is. It's dark and I'm tired, but I'm here safe and sound and just leaving the airport. I'll call you from the house tomorrow."

She pressed End and leaned back in the seat. She asked Shawn how much longer until they reached the house.

"Oh, should be no more than three hours or so," he told her. "Ye might wanta take the time fer some sleep, lassie." He smiled when his passenger nodded her head trying to keep her eyes from closing.

She couldn't believe how sleepy she was, rolling up her coat and laying it on the far end of the seat, she lay down, rested her head on her "pillow" and closed her eyes.

As Shawn drove he began to recognize where he was going, and looked toward his now sleeping passenger in the rearview mirror. This place was never used, he wondered who she really was that would make the owner open the house. Shawn was very friendly with Mrs. Stuart. *Maybe I could wheedle somethin' oot o' her*, he thought.

"No likely." He chuckled. As he drove, Shawn smiled at the thought of hunting up good old Mrs. Stuart and haven a crack at the wheedling.

A soft voice and a gentle shake awakened Madison from her deep sleep. Groggy eyed she looked up and saw Shawn peering in through the open car door at her. She sat up and looked around.

"What time is it?" She yawned and stretched.

"It's after nine o'clock lass."

"Nine o'clock, holy sh—! Well," she climbed out of the car and stretched. "why don't we go in and turn on some lights, then I'll help you get the bags inside." She reached in to grab Julie, but Shawn beat her to it and led her to the door.

"Might ye have the key, then?"

"No, Mrs. Stuart said she would leave it unlocked. I'm supposed to meet the owner tomorrow, I hope. He'll give me the keys and any instructions I might need."

When they got in the house, they found a light right by the door. Shawn put Julie on the floor, and they started unloading the bags. Madison said that she'd take them upstairs in the morning, so they put everything just inside the door. When all the bags were unloaded, she thanked him and asked what she owed him.

"Ah nothing, lassie. The young lady who called and ordered the car paid already."

Margaret. She smiled, that girl was one in a million.

"Thank you again." They shook hands and she trudged back into the house. She was too tired to explore the inside, all she wanted was to let Julie out and go to bed. The only thing she did notice, the front door was a straight shot to the stairs, and at the bottom, was a litter box, food, and water for Julie. Her heart warmed, for she knew Mrs. Stuart had been there. She took Julie out of the carrier and showed her where the food, water, and litter box were, at least until she found a better spot to house them. Julie rooted around in the box for a minute and then made a beeline for the food and water.

She picked up her overnight bag and climbed up the stairs. The second floor had two bedrooms so, Madison just picked the closest one. She could explore tomorrow. She opened the door and found the room as dark as the rest of the house, she moved carefully in the room until she found the lamp and flicked it on. The bedside lamp and gave the room a soft cozy glow, especially the beautifully handcrafted king bed. The hewed log bed with its white fluffy linins looked soft and inviting, she couldn't wait to sleep in the luxury that bed offered. She opened her bag, took out her pajamas and laid them on the bed, just as she heard Julie downstairs screaming.

"I'm up here, Julie; come on, sweetie." She stood at the railing a moment and sure enough Julie made her way up the stairs. She stripped off her blue fleece-lined leggings and white cowl neck sweater, put on her pajamas, and turned her attention to the bed. Taking all the shams off the bed she looked a place to set them down for the night. At the foot of the bed along the wall was a bench, not wanting to throw the pillows on the floor Madison piled them on the bench. Satisfied, she pulled back the covers, sat on the edge of the bed, pulled the pins from her hair and turned out the light. Once she settled under the covers, Julie jumped up nosing her way under the covers and lay as close to her person as possible. Both of them were sound asleep within a matter of minutes.

The next morning she woke feeling better than she had in a long time. As she opened her eyes, and the sight of the vaulted ceiling, with its exposed logs, greeted her, *Gorgeous.* She sat up and the most breathtaking view met her eyes, in front of the bed was a very large picture window overlooking the landscape. Flanking both sides of the solid glass, were two huge double-hung, divided light windows with no screens. She sat up a little farther in the bed and to her delight there was a balcony and the large double-hung windows? They were her access to it!

"Oh that's spectacular!" she wasn't sure why she felt the need to whisper. It was still foggy from the rain the night before, but there was no mistaking the beauty that was painted before her eyes. Far in the distance were gorgeous green mountains with silver-streaked crevasses that looked like possible streams. The land closest to the house was pasture of some kind with the most beautiful emerald, green, frosted grass she had ever seen. All she could do was sit and take in the view. Finally, after drinking her fill of the beauty, she pulled her eyes from the windows and looked at the rest of the room she occupied.

It was quite large with an armoire in the far-left corner next to a closed door. It hadn't escaped her notice that the wall like the ceiling were of the same exposed logs, bringing her to the logical conclusion the place was some sort of log cabin. *Neat.* She shoved the covers back and started to step out of bed, but when her foot touched the floor, she felt fur and immediately drew back. Julie was still on the bed, so she looked down to see what furry animal had stolen into the room overnight. No furry animal, it was far worse. On the floor was a large deerskin.

"Oh my God, roadkill." She rolled her eyes, and shuddered. "How the hell did I not notice that last night?" She asked her cat who was now staring at the floor as well. "Well, be that as it may, *that* will be the first thing that gets put out of sight."

The rest of the floor was wide, aged hardwood planks. She stepped out of bed, avoided the deerskin rug, and saw that Julie was batting one of her discarded socks across the wood floor. She looked down at her feet and sure enough, she was missing a sock. Mystery solved, she took the sock back and walked to the door by the armoire. When she opened it, she found a bathroom. It was a nice size with a shower and round sunken bath that, on closer inspection, appeared to be large enough to accommodate four people. Behind the tub was another picture window with the same breathtaking view as the bedroom. Retrieving her toothbrush and toothpaste out of her overnight bag, she had to admit, it was to look somewhere, other than the mirror, while cleaning her teeth. Teeth cleaned and face washed, she made the bed and noticed another closed door.

"That has to be the closet," she told Julie, who was sitting on the bench in front of the picture window, doing the cat chirp as she watched the birds fly. Madison opened the door, and sure enough this was the closet. It was not a very large closet, but big enough for her needs, she put on fresh socks and remade the bed. Even though she'd seen the rest of the house yet, she had already decided that this was going to be her room,. "Come on, Julie, let's explore."

The pair went to look at the rest of the upstairs. There was only one other room and figured it was probably the guest room. Although it had its own bathroom and view of the front entrance drive, it was not nearly as large or as pretty. She went back out to the hall or more accurately the landing, and noticed the upstairs had kind of a loft feel. The downstairs was completely visible, with the old hardwood floors throughout the entire house. The railing and stairs were made of logs, truly solidifying the log cabin. *I must have been tired,* she thought. *I didn't even notice the live-edge woodwork as I climbed the stairs last night.* As she walked down the stairs, she appreciated the very open floor plan, to her left was the kitchen, which was huge, with polished flagstone flooring. There was an island with a grill and gas stove top occupying the center, the cabinet doors throughout were etched glass with reclaimed chestnut framing. The countertops were bright copper that flowed around the kitchen like built-in sunshine and dipped into a deep molded sink under the large window on the far side of the room. The view from the kitchen was the same as that from the guest room. Madison knew she wasn't much of a cook, and as a rule really didn't care for kitchens, yet, *this* kitchen was an absolute dream and begged to be used. She loved it.

She turned her focus to the living room; the first thing she saw was a large stone fireplace, big enough to stand in. Above the fireplace, hung a framed blue, green, and black tartan. She could only guess it was the tartan of the owner's family.

"Is it a tartan or a tartan?" She wondered aloud while she roamed the large space. On the far left there stood a desk which overlooked the view in the back of the house. The center of the room was dominated by a cozy conversation area with dark green upholstered sofa and two love seats bookended with side tables and lamps. It was then she noticed the lack or nonexistence of overhead lighting throughout the house, with the exception of the kitchen. Madison glanced around and observed, the place was by no means, lacking in windows. Now this meant no matter where you were, you were guaranteed to a spectacular view. The caveat of this however was, no privacy.

"Course who's gonna stare at you? Wildlife?" she wondered aloud while she wandered back to the kitchen to see if there was anything to eat. When she opened the fridge, she was amazed at how full it was.

"Thank you, Mrs. Stuart!" She pulled out the bagels and cream cheese, opened every drawer until she found the silverware. After she ate and got everything cleaned up, she started to move her things to her bedroom and began the long arduous task of unpacking. After she had been at it for what seemed like hours, Madison looked at the clock for the first time since she's woken up at nine o'clock, and couldn't believe it was already noon, and she was still in her pj's. Once she was completely finished with her unpacking, she took a shower and got dressed in jeans and a baggy sweatshirt. On the way out of the room she grabbed her boots and went downstairs.

The view through the windows was so inviting; she decided to go and have a look at the grounds. She grabbed her coat, which was still slung over the banister, and opened the closet by the door to find a scarf were she spied some coats hanging. Upon closer inspection, she decided that these were more suitable than her dress coat from last night, so, she swapped. Finally Madison had everything she needed, and went outside.

About twenty yards from the front door was a split rail fence and the ocean in the distance. As she got closer to the fence, she saw that sharp sudden drop of a steep cliff. And resting on the bottom of the cliff, was a secluded beach to the bay surrounded by tall mountains.

She looked to the left and saw what appeared to be a set of natural stone stairs leading down to the beach. The fridged air and with wind whipping, she was glad she switched her coat and snuggled further into the warmth the pilfered coat and scarf offered. As she walked down the stone steps, the strong rising wind made holding the handrail a necessity. When she finally reached the bottom, she turned to look back and was already dreading the return walk up the steps. The beach was much larger than she thought, it was the size of two football fields end to end. She started to walk to the water when she heard a man's voice coming from the top of the cliff. She turned and saw him coming down toward her.

"This must be the owner." She surmised, but as he got closer, she realized it couldn't be, for he didn't look any older than herself.

"Hello." His heavenly brogue carried over the wind.

"Hello." Madison started to walk to him, he looked somehow familiar, but couldn't put her finger on why. "May I help you?" she said.

"Actually, I was figurin' on askin' ye that question. What are ye doin' here?"

He had the most gorgeous green eyes she had ever seen. He stood an easy foot taller than her, and she was no slouch at five foot six inches. Couldn't exactly make out his build because of the bulky coat he wore, but decided it was either a very large coat or he had the shoulders of Adonis.

"Oh, well, I live here, at least for the next six months anyway. I'm the new tenant, I just got in last night. As a matter of fact, I was hoping to meet the owner, so we could go over everything." *Why in Gods name did I just tell a perfect stranger all that?*

He was stunned, when Mrs. Stuart told him a woman wanted to rent the place, he was expecting an old woman, not this pretty young lass in front of him. Thanks to the bulky coat and scarf covering her head he couldn't get a good look at her.

"Ah, well what's yer name?"

She decided she'd already told him to much about and wasn't about to give her name to a perfect stranger. She didn't care how good-looking he was. "I'm sorry, I don't mean to be rude, but who are you?"

Ian smiled. It was nice to meet a woman who didn't know who he was. "Och tis me who's sorry; I'm the owner from whom ye're renting." He chuckled at her dropped jaw.

"Oh! Excuse me. I didn't realize." *Holy crap on a cracker!*

"Please dinna worry. I should've told ye as soon as I got doon here. But I couldna remember yer name."

"Madison, Madison Danaher. Your accent, it doesn't seem quite as thick as what I've heard so far."

Ian smiled. "Nay, I've traveled a lot and I suppose it's lost something, and I've been asked to practice at curbing the accent." he smiled at her wide eyes.

She couldn't get over this. He was so familiar and now his smile was perfect.

"Why donna we walk back ta the house and we can talk inside where tis warmer?" Ian suggested as he took a step backwards.

"Sounds wonderful." They turned and headed back up the stone stairs. When they reached the top, she was out of breath and snow had begun to flutter down. "I'm so out of shape. I work in an office for heaven's sake." Ian smiled and opened the door for her. After they had taken off their coats, Ian got a closer look at the scarf she was wearing and chuckled a little, she looked good in his scarf. She went to the kitchen to look for coffee.

"You know I still don't know your name," she said from the pantry as she searched for the coffee. "Ah! There it is." He watched her move and decided under that big bulky sweatshirt was a wonderful figure.

"Ian." He looked down at the cat Mrs. Stuart told him about who was rubbing against his leg. "Ian Mackay. What's yer cat's name? She's cute." He looked up and saw that Madison was no longer moving. "Are ye okay?"

Chapter Three

S he was dumbfounded, is what she was. She couldn't believe it; she was renting a house from Ian Mackay, the Scottish actor! She turned and looked at him. Now she could see it, he was even more gorgeous in person. Black hair cut short to his head, but when the sun hit it, you could see the red tones. His skin was tan really set off his green eyes. She remembered when she found out his eyes were green, it surprised her because they almost always appeared blue on the screen. Oh lord, the tight-fitted black sweater he was wearing showed off his build perfectly. She walked closer to him as he had bent down to pet Julie, when he looked up at her again, her heart leaped.

"I'm sorry, what was your question?" was all she could say.

He smiled and picked up the cat, which was unusual. Julie never let anybody, but Madison pick her up.

"I asked what her name was. Are you okay?" He watched her as she seemed to give herself a mental shake.

"Oh, yeah, I'm fine." *Act normal.* "I just realized something that's all. Her name is Julie, and she's never allowed anyone but me to hold her. She must like you." *Act normal, act normal,* she repeated over and over again in her mind.

"I love animals, especially cats. That's one of the reasons I agreed when Mrs. Stuart called about rentin' the place. I hope I got the right kind of food for her." Madison's eyes widened.

"*You* got the things for her? I just assumed Mrs. Stuart did all of that."

"Well, she had the kitchen stocked and made sure the place had a go over, but when I asked her if there was anything for a cat, she said no and told me she wasna goin' ta get anything either." He saw the surprised look on her face. "Dinna, misunderstand. She's a dear old woman, but she can be vera cantankerous. Are ye sure ye're okay? Ye look like ye've seen a ghost."

Madison figure she better explain her behavior, otherwise she'd likely make a fool out of herself. She sighed, walked to the living room, and leaned on the back of the sofa facing him.

"Well, I guess I'm embarrassed." He looked confused. He was still holding Julie and came into the living room and sat on one of the love seats forcing her to turn and face him.

"Why in heaven's name should ye be embarrassed?"

"Because I should have recognized you right away and I didn't. As a matter of fact I had no clue who you were until you told me your name." Ian now understood. There was silence for a minute and then he spoke.

"Dinna worry about it. I never get recognized." Even though it wasn't true he decided to spare her feelings. "It's kind of nice actually. Why donna ye sit doon." As he watched her, he appreciated the way her jeans formed to her lovely frame, they weren't tight, but he could see she had a great lower body. Unfortunately, she had on a huge sweatshirt counseling the top portion. Julie was still in his arms and looked as though she was going to sleep.

"So, have you decided on a fee for the house?" She was trying to not stare at him, but at the same time felt his eyes on her. Oddly, it didn't make her uncomfortable like she normally would've been.

Ian looked up and smiled. "Straight and ta the point, huh?" The quick smile she shot him was absolutely captivating.

"No, it's not like that, just a change in subject." Her gaze fell to the cat. "You know, if she is bothering you...." Julie was now on his lap, and Ian looked down at her.

"She's no bother at all." He watched her squirm. "Why, is it bothering ye?"

"No." She looked down at her hands. *Why is Julie sitting on him?* she thought. He looked at her and began to smile even more, it was becoming apparent that it *was* bothering her. He didn't want to upset her, so he gave Julie a very small nudge, small enough that Madison wouldn't notice. Julie jumped down and looked up at him and then at her owner. After a few stretches and yawns she jumped back onto Ian's lap and went back to sleep. She slumped back into the sofa. *Traitor.* "So how much will I owe you a month?"

Ian decided to let the change of subject happen. He was very careful not to pet the cat on his lap and upset the owner even more. "How aboot fifteen hundred dollars a month including utilities?"

"Sounds good to me." She was doing cartwheels. She was prepared for a much higher price tag.

"I understand ye're here on business." Ian wanted to keep her talking.

"I am, but I think I'm going to lounge for a couple of days. Oh, by the way, is there a phone or TV here?"

"No phone. No TV." When she didn't say anything, he asked, "That's no' goin' to be a problem, is it?"

"Oh no, actually it will be nice. Oh shit!" She jumped off the sofa as if it had bitten her and ran up the stairs and into the bedroom. Ian was surprised by her language, not put off, just surprised. Julie woke immediately and became alert by the loud voice of her owner. Ian continued to watch the bedroom doorway, a few seconds later she immerged with a cell phone in hand. She sat down on the floor at the top of the stairs, and dialed a number.

"I can't believe I forgot to call her back. Hi, Sally, it's Madison, let me have Margaret please." She waited on hold; she and Ian locked eyes for a moment and her heart skipped a beat. As soon as she heard a voice, she snapped out of her trance-like state, but that voice wasn't Margaret's.

"Tender Care Hospice, Madison Danaher's office." Madison was silent for a second and then spoke.

"This is Madison Danaher, who is this? Dean?"

"Madison, hello. Yes, it's Dean. Hey, I'm sorry I didn't call you about our dinner date last weekend, I got tied up."

"Dean, we didn't have a dinner date last weekend, I said 'no,' remember." She rolled her eyes. "Where's Margaret?"

"She's out sick. So, how's Scotland?"

"Well, I'll talk to you later. I'm going to call Margaret and make sure she is alright."

"Sure, hey I was thinking of coming to visit you over my vacation in the beginning of February. What do you think?"

Madison didn't want him to come there, he wanted something she could not and *would* not give.

"Dean, I've told you, repeatedly, I'm not interested in anything you have to offer in that respect. Why do you keep persisting?" She pinched the bridge of her nose and tried to remain calm. "I'm here on business and I'll be very busy. Have to go, I'm losing my signal. Bye." She tapped the End so hard she was afraid she would crack the screen. *Thank God for screen protectors*, she thought. "Jerk," she muttered. She looked down at Ian who was smiling and stifling a laugh. "What?" she asked.

"Oh nothing." Even from where she sat at the top of the stairs she could see his eyes flash. She turned her attention back to her phone and asked Siri to call Margaret's home number. She waited until the answering machine picked up.

"Hey, Margaret, I'm sorry I missed you last night and today. There's no phone here at the house, so use my cell number. I hope you're feel better soon, and I'll talk to you later."

She ended the call and went back to her room, when she came back out, she had the phone and the new DC current charger. As she came down the stairs, she could hear Ian laughing. She plugged in her charger and laid the phone on the desk.

"What's so funny?" She turned toward Ian, who walked to the kitchen.

"Why do ye no' want ta see him?" He opened the cabinet and pulled down two mugs while she followed behind him.

"Who?" She watched him move around the kitchen.

"Yer boyfriend, of course." Madison gaped at him.

"I don't have a boyfriend, thank you. What are you doing?"

"Makin' tea, or wait, ye probably prefer coffee. Do ye take sugar? If ye dinna have a boyfriend, then who is Dean?" She said nothing, so he turned and looked at her. "Do ye take sugar?"

Madison shook her head no and sat down on the stool at the end of the island. This was the strangest day she had ever had to date. First she steps on a dead deer, and then she finds she is renting a house from an absolutely breathtakingly gorgeous actor, Dean wants to come and "visit" her, and now the actor is asking about her sex life. Ian set a mug in front of her and sat down on the stool on the other side of the island.

"What are ya thinkin' about?" he asked. She looked up from her coffee at him. *She's cute when she's confused,* he thought

"He's my boss." Now it was Ian's turn to look confused.

"Who?"

"Dean, the man you thought was my boyfriend. Although he wishes he were, he is not." She turned her attention back to her coffee mug and away from Ian's prying eyes.

"Oh." *Good,* he thought. "So ye're not with anyone, then?" The only response he got was her shaking her head no, h ne smiled and took a sip of his coffee.

"Are you?" Madison asked suddenly. Ian nearly choked on his coffee and looked at her in surprise.

"What?" she said. "You asked me. It's only fair that I should get to ask you."

"Nay," He coughed. "I'm no' wi anyone." *Good,* she thought. She got up and moved to the living room and placed her mug on the coffee table. She stood and looked at the framed tartan and asked him if it was the tartan of his family.

"Aye, it is." She had wrapped her arms around herself and gave a small shiver. "Are ye cold then?"

She jumped; she hadn't realized he was no longer in the kitchen, but standing next to her.

"A little. I can't seem to find the thermostat to turn up the heat."

"I'll show ye. In the meantime, how aboot a fire?" She watched him go outside to get wood and wondered why he was still here. Maybe because she had not paid him yet. She went to the desk and wrote a check for three months. There was a knock at the door, realized Ian must have his arms full of wood so she ran and opened the door for him. He went to the fireplace and dropped the wood on the hearth. She stood and watched him build the fire, and when he was done, she handed him the check. He looked at the check and smiled.

"This is quite a tip, ma'am." She looked at him and started to laugh. *Her laugh is like a song,* Ian thought.

"No, I thought I'd give you the first three months' rent." She was still laughing as she went and refilled her coffee mug. Ian went to the closet and put the check in his coat pocket. He knew that he *really* shouldn't hang around anymore, but he couldn't seem to leave. For some reason this woman was mesmerizing him, he looked at his watch and it was already five o'clock, it would be getting dark soon and he was getting hungry.

"Would ye like ta join me for dinner?" he asked, causing Madison to stop in midstride and stare at him.

"W-what?" she stammered

"Well, I'm askin' ye to have dinner wi me." She thought for a moment. *Madison, you dope,* she thought. *When are you ever going to get to have dinner with a celebrity?*

"Sure, where would you like to go?" She was mentally taking inventory of her clothes and trying to figure out a way to change and not take forever about it.

"Well, why canna we stay here and cook?" Ian arched his brow at her wince.

"There might be a slight problem with that."

"Why?"

"I can't cook." Madison stood by the island.

"That's okay. I'm a great cook." Ian smiled, walked over, opened the door to the walk-in pantry, and took out the apron. "Have a seat and I'll cook ye the best meal ye've ever had."

He was already at work by the time she sat at the island. Julie hopped up on the stool next to her and meowed; Madison gave her a pat and turned her attention back to the man in the kitchen. While he prepared, they talked about his life as an actor and how much he loved it and hated it. She told him about her business and why she was in Scotland. She couldn't remember the last time she had enjoyed herself more than she was in that moment. He opened a bottle of wine and used some of it in the mixture he was preparing. Then poured a glass for her and one for himself. The longer he was there, the more she thought of him as a person and not the actor she'd had the hots for ever since she saw his first movie. He was charming and sweet, and her cat loved him, which was a big plus in her book. She felt comfortable with him, which was something she didn't feel with most men. But with Ian, it was like she had known him for years. She only hoped it would last, and he wasn't just being nice until he had all her money, or trying to get her in the sack. She wasn't sure why, she doesn't know him, but that just didn't seem like his style. *Well*, she thought, *don't think about that now. Just have a good time and enjoy it while you can.* She watched him put two large pieces of meat on the grill.

"So, what are you making exactly?" she asked as she breathed in the succulent aroma that was wafting around the kitchen.

"Aberdeen Angus steak wi a mushroom and wine sauce. Served wi mashed potatoes and green beans." He looked up from the grill and had a horrible thought. "Do ye no' eat meat?"

Madison smiled. "Yes, I eat meat and I love mushrooms."

Instant relief flooded Ian's face and he went back to cooking. He prepared plated their meals, and they carried them into the living room. Madison placed her plate on the coffee table, and sat on the floor; Ian followed her example. They sat talked and got to know each other.

"Have you ever thought about being a chef?" She couldn't remember ever having a better dinner.

"That's rather a funny story. When I was growin' up, all I wanted ta be was a chef. So I went ta school and was top of my class. When I graduated, I got a job at one of the top four-star restaurants in town, and put under the instruction of the head chef. Aboot two weeks after finishing my training, I was fired." Madison stared at him with her mouth open and started to laugh.

"You were fired! Why?" it certainly wasn't for his cooking talents.

"Well, after I graduated from university, I had a summer ta work before I started at the restaurant, so I went ta work for a casting director friend who was doin' a play in town. She told me if I would help her cast the play, she would let me read for the lead. So I helped and not only read for the lead, I got it. It was the most fun I'd had in years. When I started at the restaurant, I was no' happy and it showed, so they fired me."

"What did you do?"

"Well, I went ta England and did a few odd jobs until I was lucky to score a role in another play. It took a few years, but I was able to get myself on my feet and eventually made it into films. None of which have done very well." He smiled. "But I'm startin' ta get exposure and more offers."

They sat for a few minutes in silence. Madison was watching the fire and Ian was watching her. She was leaning up against the love seat. She had her hair down and was absentmindedly twirling a lock around her finger. *She has such bonny hair*, he thought. After a time, she looked at him, her aqua-colored eyes were exquisite, while her smile seemed to brighten the room. When she still said nothing, Ian decided he needed to know what was on her mind.

"What are ye thinkin' aboot?" His deep brogue voice brought her back to the here and now. She loved the accent and hoped they wouldn't train it out of him like they have done with so many others like Pierce Brosnan, Gerald Butler, Sean Connery just to name a few. *When are film people going to realize women love accents?* she thought. He looked so handsome sitting there across from her, the light from the fire played on his features and making him more attractive than he already was. She wondered why he wasn't with a woman. How could he have gone this long without someone snatching him up?

"I was just wondering," she began, "may I ask you a personal question?"

Ian raised his left eyebrow and gave the sly smile that he was becoming famous for in his movies. It was a smile women would melt over. "Be me guest."

"I was just wondering why you don't have a woman in your life. And—" *No I can't ask him that!* she thought.

"And what?" Ian knew very well what she was goin' to ask, it wasn't the first time he'd been asked and because he was such a private person, she wouldn't be the last to ask it.

"If the rumors are true as to why there isn't a *woman* in your life?" Ian couldn't help but laugh, knowing the rumor.

"I dinna have a woman in me life simply because I dinna have the time. I'm always workin' and out of the country. It would no' be fair ta ask someone ta put up wi that. As to the rumor," he smiled knowingly, "I'm well aware of what they say, and the answer is no. I'm no' gay. I never felt it was worth contradicting the rumor because, me sexual preference, is me own business."

"I agree with you about your privacy." She should feel bad about asking and invading his privacy, but, nope, she didn't. "But I can't agree about your excuse not to have a woman in your life."

"How so?"

"I think a woman in love would be willing to put up with all the traveling and long hours. You just have to find the right one. Someone who's as busy as you; so when you aren't able to be with her, she has her own work to occupy her time. Someone who, when you were able to be together, you could come to this beautiful house and use it, instead of letting it go to waste."

"You like me house, then?" Oh he liked her, she was direct and disarming with a quick mind.

She looked at him in surprise. "Yes, I love it! Who wouldn't? The way it was built and the views from every room. Although, I have to admit, it would be nice not to have quite so many windows." She waved her hand to encompass the room at large. "But the care that went into building it shows." He was looking at her, eyes softening with appreciation, and it was at that moment she realized *he* was the one who built this house. "Well, sir, it would appear you have three wonderful talents. Acting, cooking, and the ability to build something with such beauty."

"How did ye know?" His smile made his eyes twinkle.

"That you built this house? It was the way you were looking at me just then." She couldn't help the heat that rose in her face while his eyes stayed fixed on hers. "Why would you never use this place?"

He looked back into the fire, and said nothing for a long while and when he did speak, Madison jumped.

"Ye're going to need a car while ye're here, are ye no?" The sudden change in topic was surprising, but since she didn't really know this man, she was not going to press the issue.

"Yes, I had not realized the house was so far from the village or I would have made arrangements before I left. Would you happen to know where I could rent or buy a car?"

Ian stood up and took both plates into the kitchen and started to wash them. Madison stood, followed him and began to help with the cleanup. They worked in silence. When they were done, Ian turned from the sink and looked at her, he wanted to kiss her for the warm words she'd spoken about the house. He decided then and there he wanted to get to know this woman better. She had a beautiful kindness and a warm heart. She was so close to him, he could just reach out and pull her to him, but thought better of it, cleared his throat and backed away.

"How aboot if I come by tomorrow and show ye the village of Lusta? And while we're out, we can get ye a car."

"Are you sure you wouldn't mind?" Her eyes light up. "Don't you have some picture to be working on?" He smiled and walked to the closet.

"It's no a bother at all." He told her while shrugging om his coat. "I find I like bein' wi ye." Adjusting his scarf, his smile became a wide grin at the blush rising in her face. "As for the movie I'm working on now, all my shots are finished, so I'm enjoyin' something of a mini vacation. What?" She had such a surprised look on her face.

"You like being with me? But you don't even know me." Ian moved closer to her, and when he was inches away, and since she was a good deal shorter than him, Ian stooped to look directly into her eyes.

"I would like ta get to know ye. That is, if ye dinna mind." She nodded her head and smiled. "What time would be good to come and get ye in the morn?"

"Oh, I guess about ten," she squeaked. Madison cleared her throat. "That will give me time to eat, shower, and get dressed."

"See ye at ten, then. Good night." He turned and walked out the door, when Madison realized she hadn't thanked him for dinner, she ran out the door to the porch.

"Ian." He turned and walked back to her so she would not come any farther out in the cold.

"Aye?" Hearing his name on her lips, it surprised him how much he liked. *Something to think about later.* He decided.

"Um, I just wanted to say thank you, for the house and for tonight." She should've put on a coat, than at least she'd have somewhere to shove her hands. "I had a good time and dinner was delicious." He took her hands in his and lifted them to his lips. When he kissed her knuckles, chills went through her whole body like a bolt of electricity. His emerald eyes devoured her face with such intensity, that she felt a little embarrassed. No one had ever looked at her like that before. She wasn't sure what it meant, but she knew she liked it. Ian saw the pink blush fill her cheeks and it felt like his heart warmed a little. It wasn't the blush of a fan seeing her heartthrob, no it was the blush of a woman who was genuinely attracted to the man standing in front of her. Yes, he wanted to get to know this woman better.

"Thank ye, my lady." Still holding her hand he ran his thumb over the tops of her knuckles sending warm shivers up her arm. "Ye had better get back inside before ye catch yer death of cold. I'll see ye in the morn." She turned and walked back into the house, before shutting the door, she turned giving him a quite smile.

"Good night Ian." Ian smiled as the door clicked closed. He had a joy in his step for the first time in years as he walked to his car. And he couldn't wait to see what tomorrow held.

Madison went upstairs to put on her pajamas and try to normalize what was left of her night after the afternoon and evening she was treated to. Afterwards she went downstairs to lay on the sofa and watch the fire Ian had built. Julie jumped up and settled herself next to her person. Madison took the blanket that was draped over the back and covered them both bringing a small meow from Julie.

"Don't worry. I just want to wait 'til the fire is either out or smoldering before we go to bed." Both cat and owner were asleep within a matter of minutes.

Chapter Four

Madison awoke the next morning from a sound sleep when she heard knocking on her front door. She sat up and yawned and looked out the windows and saw Ian. She then jolted fully awake and realized she had slept passed ten o'clock. She ran to the door and flung it open.

"Ian, I am *so* sorry. I overslept. After you left, I must have fallen asleep on the sofa watching the fire. Please come in." He stood in the doorway for a moment to drink in the sight of her. When he saw her last, she was wearing jeans and a baggy sweatshirt. Now she was wearing baggy flannel pajama bottoms and a tight-fitting tank top. Finally, he was able to see what kind of upper body went with the lower. She looked amazing with her ivory skin, beautiful full breasts, and a long swan-like neck with her chestnut hair was charmingly mussed from sleep. Ian walked in and shut the door behind him. She looked so alluring standing there in her pajamas, he wondered if he might be able to convince her to stay in them all day.

"Dinna worry yerself aboot it. I'll wait doon here while ye get ready." He continued to look at her with amusement and wonder.

"I'm sorry about this. I don't know what happened. I never oversleep." She turned and started to run up the stairs when Ian's voice halted her.

"Madison?" She turned, making her heart jump now that he was now standing at the bottom of the stairs.

"Yes?" Madison took in all the splendor that was simply Ian. *God, he looked so good in jeans, they showed off his muscular legs and fantastic, well,* she tried to sound less crass in her head, *ah screw it, ass.* He was still wearing his coat, but it was unzipped enough for her to see he was wearing sweater like the one he wore the night before. She still didn't know why he'd stopped her from going up to change. He appeared deep in thought as he looked up at her with a warmth in his eyes that took them several shades deeper in color. It was a look any woman, including herself, surprisingly, wanted from a man. Yet given her personal history as much as she liked his eyes on her, she also felt the need to cover up.

"Ian?" she finally asked.

"Huh?" He looked surprised by her voice, but it had snapped him out of whatever trance he was in.

"Did you want anything in particular?"

"Oh, aye! I'm sorry, make sure ye put on something warm. It's rather cold out."

Madison thanked him and made her way to her bedroom and shut the door. Once she was in the safety of her room she leaned against the door and closed her eyes. *God, he looks so good,* she thought. Madison gave herself a mental shake and stripped off her clothes. Downstairs Ian heard the shower kick on and he took off his coat and hung it in the closet, then made his way into the kitchen, retrieved a filter and ground beans for fresh coffee.

"If she is like most women," he told Julie, who had been following him around ever since he arrived, "she'll be up there for quite a while." The cat eyed him and offered a soft "*meow,*" as though hoping he might find something tasty for her, as long as he was fooling around in the kitchen. While Ian ground the beans and started the coffee maker, Julie continued to demand attention. After he finished his task, he bent down and scooped her up and smiled as her motor sounded instantly.

He noticed her food and water were a little low, so he deposited on the sofa, picked up the dishes and returned to the kitchen to refill them.

Madison stood in the shower letting the warm water pour over her body to wake her up before she started to wash. When she was finished, she wrapped herself in a large fluffy towel, stepped out of the shower and went to the closet. As per Ian's advice, she chose a pair of blue jeans, a black turtleneck shirt and red cashmere sweater. Madison went back to the bathroom and dried her hair. Hair finished and light makeup applied, after grabbing her boots, she sailed out the door. She scent stopped her in her tracks at the top of the stairs, the glorious scent of coffee brewing. Nothing matched that smell in Madison's mind.

"Mmm, fresh coffee," she sighed. "Was I up here that long?" she said quietly and looked at her watch. She'd remembered to set it for Scotland time the night before. It was only a quarter to eleven, forty-five minutes, that's not bad when you add in the shower, blow drying and light makeup. She shrugged her shoulders and continued downstairs where she found Ian in the kitchen adding cream to his mug. When he hadn't felt her presence, she cleared her throat. She'd never seen a man jump out of his own skin like he did, he spun around slopping even more of his coffee over the edge of the mug.

"I'm sorry, I didn't mean to scare you." She didn't laugh, but she could not hide her grin.

"Where did ye come from?" She looked at the spillage on the floor at his feet and behind him on the coffee covered counter where the initial mess was running all over the place.

"Upstairs," she quipped. "let me help you." Sailing passed the fridge she swiped the hand towel off the handle and started to clean up the spill. It took him a few seconds before he picked up a kitchen towel and began to help. After the coffee mess was clean, she gathered all the towels and started to walk away. In midstride she stopped and turned to him.

"Um, I just thought of something."

"What's that?" he asked as he picked up his mug to inspect what was left of his coffee.

"Is there a washer and dryer here and if so, where is it?"

Ian smiled, put down the empty mug, and took the towels from her. "Aye, follow me I'll show ye." They walked around to the desk in the living room, on the wall next to the desk was a sconce. Ian gave a little tug, a soft *pop,* and a section of the wall opened, revealing a descending staircase. He turned and laughed at her wide eyes and open mouth, he flipped on the light and down they went. At the bottom, the room with its hard damp dirt floor, was chilly and so small that when Ian reached up and pulled a chain from the ceiling, the room was lit completely by a single bulb. Ian watched her in amusement as Madison looked around at the small space and noticed the walls were rock. She'd obviously never seen a bare basement before, *Her idea of "unfinished" is probably cinder blocks and a concrete floor,* he thought to himself. As he watched her walk around, he realized she still hadn't put on her boots. *Well,* he thought, *these towels willna be the only thing I put in the wash.*

"Madison, the washer and dryer are over here." She walked over and watched him put the towels in the machine and turn the dial. He then switched his attention to her.

"What?" she asked, he was looking at her but still said nothing.

"Yer socks." They both looked down at her socked feet.

"Oh, oops." Shrugging her shoulders and chucking. "well don't worry, I'll put them in when I do a load for myself." With the washer open he stood staring. "I mean it. I don't want to take them off here. I'll get my feet dirty."

"Madison, give me yer socks, please." His brogue playful and deliciously smooth.

"No, I'll take them off upstairs when I'm no longer on the dirt floor and wash them later." She had flutters in her belly, and heat climbing up her neck to her face.

"Madison, I will give ye one more chance to give me yer socks. Otherwise I'm goin' ta take them from ye." His eyes were bright green and full of life and humor. Her own eyes glowed with equal humor as she started backing away.

"You will not have my socks, sir." She laughed and turned to run back up the stairs; however, Ian was too fast for her. His arm encircled her belly, and lifted. "Ian! Put me down!" her squeal and giggles were infectious as he pulled back off the stairs to him. He placed her on top of the dryer, casually rested his hands on either side of her and looked into her eyes, the brightness of her aqua eyes intensified with laughter.

"I will have yer socks, madam. Do ye yield?" eyes glimmering with playful determination.

"Never." She laughed. Ian then took that opportunity to move his hands to the sides of her waist. Madison still in the throughs of laughter placed her hands on top of his.

"What's the matter? Is the lady ticklish?" Flexing his fingers slightly.

"You will not tickle me, sir, and you will not have my socks either." Madison let out a squeal and shout of hysterical laughter. Ian, watched her face as he began to make good on his threat, was having more fun that he'd had in years. Finally, he stilled his tortuous fingers, while Madison tried to catch her breath.

"Do ye yield, me lady?" She shook her head no, and Ian placed his hands on her sides again.

"Alright!" she shouted. "You may have the damned socks." Ian grinned from ear to ear and removed her socks off one at a time and started the washer. He turned his attention back to the lovely woman next to him, to stop her from jumping off the dryer.

"Now what?" Madison threw her hands up in exasperation.

"I thought ye dinna want ta get yer feet dirty?"

"I don't, but you have taken away my only means of *not* getting my feet dirty." She crossed her arms over your chest.

"Well, ye canna walk on the floor in yer bare feet." Mirroring her stance with his arms crossed over his chest.

"And how," she asked, arching an eyebrow, "do you suggest I get up the stairs in my bare feet without touching the floor?" Madison yelped as Ian scooped her off the dryer. "What are you doing?" His face was so close to hers; she could feel his breath on her skin. For the first time, she caught his scent, which was a faint hint of cologne, but mostly, he smelled of clean, fresh air, it was intoxicating.

"Ye dinna want ta get yer feet dirty, right? So this is yer option." Before she could say another word he was walking up the stairs. When they reached the top, Madison reached over to shut the door so Julie wouldn't go down. Then, to her surprise, Ian didn't put her down but continued up to her bedroom. Once they entered the room, he placed her on the bed and backed away from her. She was so light in his arms and her scent of wildflowers was sending his scenes into overdrive. His need to kiss her and have his arms around her again, but he once again thought better of it and took another step away from her. He wanted to get to know this woman, not scare her away. He looked down at her feet and saw something was missing, but he could not figure out what it was.

"Where are yer socks?"

"They're in the closet in the far left-hand drawer." Rather than argue with him she told him. He opened the door and saw right away what was missing. She had taken up all the deerskins and put them in the closet. He laughed out loud picked out a pair of socks and went back to the woman who was sitting on the bed. Kneeling down, Ian took her left foot into his hands. He was about to put the sock on her when she pulled away. *Apparently she is ticklish all over,* he thought.

"Thank you, sir," she tucked her feet under her, "but I think I can manage that on my own." She held out her hand and he reluctantly gave over the socks. He stood and walked to the window, looking out, deep in thought. He couldn't remember the last time he'd had this much fun with a woman. It'd become apparent to Ian the night before, that she had begun thinking of him not as an actor, but as a man. It had been years since he'd allowed himself to be seen, really seen by anyone other than his family. And in the course of one night here was a woman who he wanted to be truly seen by. Not ready to unpack that revelation he focus on what was physical in front of him, the view out the window.

"Have ye been out here yet?" Madison looked up to Ian silhouetted against the window, looking toward the balcony.

"No. I think it's still too cold to go out there." She stood and joined him at the window. The view was magnificent, the land was untouched all the way to the mountains in the distance. With the bright sun and soft powder blue sky dotted with light fluffy clouds, she simply sighed, which drew Ian's attention back to her.

"What are ye thinking aboot?" She was a bleeden wonder to him.

"Oh nothing, it's just so beautiful and peaceful here. I wish I didn't have to start work on Monday." She had her head resting on the window frame as her eyes gazed over the masterpiece that was his homeland. He watched her watch the land that he loved so much. He's never met a woman who'd loved the land or the house the way she appeared to. He wanted to pull her to him, thank her and hold her. He'd only known her for one day, but it already seemed like an eternity. Madison lifted her head and turned to leave the room, at the door, she paused and looked back at him.

"Are you coming?" she asked. He tore his gaze from the landscape, smiling, and nodded.

Madison put on her boots then went to fill Julie's dishes, to her surprise they were already full. She stood there for a moment trying to remember if she'd filled them and forgotten. She shrugged her shoulders and went to the kitchen to make herself a travel mug of coffee. Ian stood next to her to fill one for himself as well. She glanced at him out of the corner of her eye, the dark green sweater he wore, cashmere maybe, was fitted and looked so damn good on him. She looked up at him, for he was a good deal taller than she, met his eyes and smiled. She felt the need to say something, anything.

"I like your sweater. It brings out your eyes." *You dope*, she thought. *Is that the best you could come up with?* She looked down at her coffee and walked back out of the kitchen. Ian stood by the counter and followed her with his eyes as she tried to escape his gaze. She was such a bonnie lass, and there was an innocence about her. He leaned against the counter and crossed his arms. He looked at the sweater he had on, it's not that he gets dressed in the dark, he just doesn't pay that much attention to his clothes. The only woman who ever complimented what he wore was his mother. This brought a smile to his face. As Ian moved away from the counter, he glanced down and noticed Julie at his feet looking up at him so he scooped her up and walked to the living room. Madison looked up from the love seat where she was sitting and smiled at him. She really liked the idea that Julie seemed taken with him, but she wished Julie didn't like him *that* much. She stood and walked to the closet.

"Shall we go?" she asked as she put on her coat. Ian put the kitty on the sofa and reached for his coat. Madison was ready to walk out the door when Ian's hand stopped her. He pulled her back in front of him and looked into her eyes.

"Ye need a scarf, tis Baltic out there." She watched as Ian retrieved the soft woolen scarf of the Mackay tartan she'd worn the other day. He gently placed it on her head, tied it under her chin and tucked the ends inside her coat. After zipping her coat the rest of the way up, he placed his hands on her shoulders. Her gaze stationed on the middle of his coat, he crooked his finger under her chin to raise her aqua eyes to meet his, where uncertainty could be read.

"Thank ye." His voice was soft and gentle.

"For what?" Butterflies fluttered in her belly while her voice was barely above a whisper.

Ian brushed his fingertips down her cheek reveling in her soft silky skin. She looked strangely alluring standing there in her coat bundled in his scarf. He wasn't sure how to put into words what he was thanking her for and until he was, he decided to keep silent. He smiled showing perfect white teeth, then leaned over her and kissed the top of her forehead.

"Just thank ye. Now we should be on our way." Ian led her to his car, held open her door then went around and climbed into the driver's seat.

Since Scotland is among those who drive on the left side of the road, Madison sat in the seat she was used to, but at the passenger not the driver, it was quite a mind trip. But as the passenger she was able to watch the beautiful awe-inspiring scenery go by, everything was green and gorgeous. Even though it was winter, like New Jersey nothing seemed to turn totally brown. The trees were, of course, bare, but the sheer size of them and their age made them majestic and spooky. As she took in all the scenery that passed her window Madison decided, in all her travels, she couldn't match the beauty that was currently in front of her. The landscape was virtually untouched, with a few houses were scattered here and there, but for the most part, it was vast and open. Back in the states there were large farms that had all kinds of land, but they always seemed planned and mapped. Here everything seemed old and new at the same time. After they had been driving for about forty-five minutes the small village of Lusta began to come into view. They crossed a small bridge and parked the car on the side of the road, while Ian explained they were going to have to explore on foot because the village roads were too small to accept cars.

Chapter Five

Madison wished she'd put some long johns on under her clothes to protect from the bone chilling air. But she would brace the cold for the opportunity to walk the village, it was as if she had stepped through time. Lusta was a small fishing village off the Bay of Loch, with a single unpaved road running through it, plenty of shops and all the modern conveniences. Yet, everything seemed to operate at a slower pace. As the village was bordered on two side by the bay, Madison looked out to the water to see all kinds of boats and fishing trawlers. Several of the boats were lined up at the dock unloading their catches of the day. Boats coming and going, it was such a sight. She also noticed, much to her dismay, none of the men were wearing kilts.

"I thought all Scottish men wore kilts." Taking her eyes off the water and glancing up to Ian. "Do they only wear them in the summer?" Her teeth were beginning to chatter from the cold. Ian decided, since she wasn't used to the kind of cold Scotland had to offer, it was time to get her into a warm building. He ushered her into the pub and sat in the back, thankfully for her, they were settled next to the fireplace. Ian ordered a pint for each of them. Once the waitress placed the ale on the table, Ian decided to answer Madison's question.

"Americans are fascinated by kilts, aren't they?" Chuckling. "The Scots wear them nowadays mostly for formal occasions, such as weddings or an annual ball, things like that. We find kilts are no' so weather friendly, and no' particularly comfortable." Madison drank some of her pint and thought for a moment.

"Have you ever worn a kilt?" she asked finally.

Ian smiled. "Aye, unfortunately. When me older sister got married we all wore kilts. As a matter of fact, she was married two years ago next week. It was bloody cold that day." He shivered at the memory at freezing his balls off at the wedding." I swore that if another person got married this time of year again, I would be conveniently out of town."

Madison laughed and took another drink of the dark creamy ale, finally beginning to warm up and could almost feel her toes again.

"Ye know I just thought of something." Madison drew her attention back to the man in front of her.

"What's that?"

"Well, ye really shouldna go out on yer own until ye know the layout of Skye."

"You're probably right, but I don't have a choice. I have to start working with the doctors and hospitals in the area. I only have six months to make a good pitch." Ian admired her dedication and ambition.

"I'll tell ye what. I will show ye around the Isle this week and show ye where all the hospitals and doctors are, and next week ye can start yer calls." When she said nothing, Ian spoke again. "What are ye thinking now?"

She had put down the glass and placed her chin in her hands and stared at him. She started to smile.

"You know, you really are a sweet man." When Ian laughed, she continued, "No! You really are. You don't have to do all that, you know. I have my phone and the convenience of Google Maps to help me bump along." She noticed a warm tingling feeling in her lips "What's in this stuff?" She lifted her glass and looked at it. "I'm not used to drinking beer and I'm afraid if I finish this I'll become drunk. So, here you take this, and I'll switch to water." She pushed her glass over to Ian and got the waitress's attention, "Miss, would it be okay if I could have some water or soda?"

"Aye, we're known fer our Caledonian carbonated spring water. What flavor would ye like?"

"Um, I'll tell you what, why don't you surprise me."

"Aye, back in a jiffy." The girl smiled and disappeared behind the bar.

"Ye're not much of a drinker are ye?" Ian laughed.

"No, I'm afraid I have a rather low tolerance. But that seems even more lethal than what is served in the States." she said, pointing to the glass of ale. Just then, the waitress came back with a bottle of fizzy water. She waited while Madison took a sip. "This is really good." She looked up at the waitress. "Thank you, what flavor is it?"

"Cherry and Watermelon."

"Well it's delicious. Thank you." She looked at Ian. "You know, I'm a little hungry, can we eat here?"

Ian was shocked, even though the pub had some of the best food on Skye, most tourist would consider a dive passing it without a second thought. She was not a woman who thought only of appearances, and the more time he spent with her the more he was beginning to like her.

"Aye, we can. By the way, it would be me pleasure to show ye around Skye. It'll be fun." They had lunch and spent most of the afternoon in the pub, next to the fire and talked. Around three o'clock Ian decided to show her the rest of the village. There were small grocery, butcher and bakery shops, everything was small, quaint and had an out-of-time feel to it all in all, the village was very picturesque. At the end of the docks were fish stands where the men sold their catches. People who were brave enough to come out in the cold were very friendly and stopped to chat. Of course they all knew Ian, but they were all interested in the woman he had with him.

Madison even got to meet Mrs. Stuart, a plump little lady with a welcoming smile. Her silver hair was pulled back severely to her head and worn in a coiled braid secured with what appeared to be a thousand hairpins at the nape of her neck. She had the look of a sweet old lady, whose kitchen was always be filled with cookies and pastries ready to be handed to anyone who had time to sit with her in the warm inviting room.

"Mrs. Stuart, this is Madison Danaher. She's the young American woman who is renting the house. Madison, Mrs. Stuart." Ian smiled graciously and then held his breath.

"This is Madison Danaher?" Her soft brown eyes looked Madison over, assessing. "Well, Ian Mackay, and how long will it be taken ye ta get this young lass into yer bed, then?"

Ian released the breath he'd been holding, and prepared himself for the shock he knew he would see on Madison's face.

"Excuse me?" was the only thing Madison could think to say. Ian smiled as he had known Agatha Stuart all his life and was accustomed to her silver tongue. He wanted to help Madison recover her embarrassment, but Madison beat him to it.

"Yes, Mrs. Stuart. That's an interesting question." She turned to Ian and flashed her brightest smile, "So Mr. Mackay, SIR, exactly how long will it take you?"

Mrs. Stuart enjoyed seeing Ian's ears turn deep pink from top to lobe for the first time since he was a small lad, and smiled.

"I like her, laddie. She's good."

Madison smiled at Mrs. Stuart. She had now seen firsthand how saucy and brazen the old lady could be, he was amazing. *This tiny little old woman is a hoot!* Maddy thought to herself. Madison thanked her for finding the house and stocking it so nicely.

"Ah, dinna worry yer pretty head o'er it, it was me pleasure, lassie. Ye know, of course, I was no' the one who brought in the fixins for yer cat."

"Yes, ma'am, Ian told me that he got the things for Julie." Madison smiled and looked at Ian.

"Julie?" Mrs. Stuart looked confused. "Was I mistaken? I thought ye came by yerself."

"On no," Madison laughed, "Julie is my cat."

With the sun was going down the cold temperature was only getting colder, so Ian and Madison said goodbye and started back to the car. On the way back to the house Madison spoke about how much she liked the village and couldn't wait to see more, while Ian happily listened. They'd been in the car for about twenty minutes when Madison began to shiver. Ian noticed it right away and told her to put her hands on the heater.

"I don't understand." Madison chattered. "I was fine before, now all the sudden I'm freezing." Ian reached across the console of the Wagoneer with his free hand and rubbed her knee.

"It's the air we have here. If yer're not used to it, it can freeze ye out. I'm sorry I should have paid more attention, and ne'er have kept ye out that long. We'll get ye back ta the house right quick." He continued to rub her knee as the first snowflakes began to hit the windshield.

By the time Ian parked in the driveway, she was shaking, and the snow was beginning to accumulate on the ground. Ian went around to help Madison out of the car, when her shaking made her knees wobble Ian scooped her up like she weighed nothing at all. Once inside, he placed her on the sofa and covered her with a handmade quilt he pulled from the cedar chest behind the loveseat. Ian set to work and made a fire, once it was a blaze he pulled off his coat and draped it over a chair. He went back to the sofa and pulled off Madison's coat and boots, she was so cold to the touch. Ian knew, there were times, the air in the Highlands just before a snowfall; if you weren't used to it, could give people symptoms of hypothermia. He knew he had to get her warm, but it needed to be a slow process.

"Where do ye have yer flannel pajama bottoms and top that go with them?"

"In the closet right-hand drawer." Julie laid as close to her as possible. Ian bounded up the stairs, it didn't take long to find the bottoms, but the top portion was more difficult. Finally he had a top, bottoms, and a fresh pair of socks. He went back downstairs, placed the pj's on the heart and found Madison still freezing. *Damn ye, Ian*, he thought to himself, *ye know better*. He sat down and pulled her to him covering them both with the quilt. As the fire blazed in the grate, the room began to warm. Ian looked toward the window to see snow collecting on the outside sill. He couldn't remember the last time he'd seen it snow this bad. After what seemed like an eternity Madison's shaking began to subside to a shiver.

"Madison?" His voice was low as he tried to hide his concern. "I have pj's and new socks for ye, they've been by the fire to get nice and warm. I need ye to put them on now, before ye start to get cold again." She looked up at him and he could read the question in her eyes. "No I canna help ye, but you need to stay by the fire. I'll go into the kitchen and make some coffee and soup while ye change." He smiled at her as he stood. "Dinna worry. I willna peek and I willna come in until ye give me the okay."

"I am so cold. I'm not sure I can get up. I'm shivering so much." She looked back at the fire and spoke.

Ian put his finger on the side of her jaw and turned her head toward him. Her eyes normally bright and lively were now dull and listless.

"If ye canna manage on yer own, I'll come back and help ye, but I need ye to try and do it yerself. Okay?" She nodded and stood up. Ian, true to his word, went to the kitchen to make coffee and soup, and kept his back turned. While he was busy, Madison stood by the fire for a moment to make sure he wouldn't turn around. She began to change out of her clothes and into her pj's, without losing the quilt. Not because she was afraid Ian would look—he told her he wouldn't, and she believed him—but because she was so cold. However, she had to remove the quilt when she changed tops. Finally dressed in the flannel pj's she started to warm up, putting the pj's in front of the fire was a good idea. Madison walked to the window, looked out to the front of the house to see the thick heavy snow piling up on the rails and floor of the porch. She wanted to turn on the TV and tune it to the Weather

Channel, then she remembered, no TV. She hear Ian in the kitchen and decided to join him.

Ian heard her moving around, he wanted to turn, but he wouldn't for fear of her not being dressed. He looked out the window over the sink and watched the snow. He knew just by looking at it that this was going to be a bad storm. He walked into the pantry and surveyed at the soup choices. Having no idea what she would like, he went back in the kitchen and saw Madison standing by the coffee maker. *Even in red plaid flannel pajamas she's bonnie,* he thought, with her thick wavy chestnut hair free and flowing over her shoulders. With the quilt still wrapped around her, he decided she must of still been cold.

He had only spent two full days with her, and couldn't explain the feelings he was having toward her. He had seen movies... hell, he had played roles where the hero fell in love with the heroine after twenty-four hours. However, he always thought it was bullshit. *"No one falls in love that fast"* he was known to say. Now, here he was standing in the pantry of his house staring at this woman and he was all mixed up. She was fascinating and fun, she was genuinely interested in him as a person and everything this land had to offer. She'd come to live there for six months, so she could bring a hospice to the Highlands. He knew very little of hospice, only that he had wished there was one around when his father was dying of cancer four years ago. Yet, with everything he knew about this woman, he still knew very little. He knew there was a man named Dean who wanted to be close to her, but for some reason she didn't appear to want his affections, actually, she seemed a little afraid of him. She certainly didn't want to talk to him, as was evident when she said she was losing her cell phone signal the other day. There was something she hiding something, he had no idea what it was, but hoped to find out soon.

"How are ye feelin?" He stood behind her and placed his hands on her upper arms. The scent of her hair made him think of Christmas morning just before a snowfall. All he wanted to do was bury his nose in it.

"Better I think, I'm still cold, but not as bad." He heard her sigh. "The snow's really coming down hard out there. I wonder what the weather report says." Feeling the warmth radiating from his body, all she wanted to do lean back against his chest. As if he could read her mind, he wrapped his arms around her and pulled her to his chest. She felt so good in his arms and he wondered if he could stand there forever, holding her.

"Is there a radio somewhere so we can get the weather?" Madison said sleepily.

"Aye, over on the desk. Here, take some coffee and go back to the sofa while I'll find a station." Ian handed her a mug and she returned to the sofa. Once she was seated, he turned on the radio. Unfortunately, the storm was blocking reception and getting a station was impossible.

"The storm must be blocking a signal from getting through." Ian joined her on the sofa where she sat all bundled up. Suddenly, Madison sprang to life, about ready to jump off the sofa.

"Wait a minute! What do ye want? I'll get it for ye." He put his hands on her shoulders keeping her from getting up, she hadn't realized how strong he was. Sure, he was built, but that didn't always equate to strength. It was kind of a turn-on.

"My laptop on the desk has wireless Internet. We might be able to get a weather report there." Ian retrieved the laptop and brought it back to the sofa. Since it was her machine, he gave it to her to look up the information. After a few minutes, they learned that the storm had reached blizzard proportions and those in the path of the storm were being urged to remain where they were and wait for updates. Madison looked over at Ian and was thankful he was safe indoors with her and not on the road.

"Well," she said, "there is a guest room and plenty of food. You'll stay here tonight."

Ian chuckled at her proclamation, Even if he had no intentions of leaving her alone until he was sure she was feeling better, he hadn't considered staying overnight. Madison put the laptop on the coffee table and leaned back into the sofa. When she started to shiver again, he pulled her to him, wrapped an arm around her and covered them both. She rested her head on his chest and curled up into the warmth of his body. It then he realized, this was why he had built the house in the first place. To curl in front of a warm fire with a woman, *this woman*, and for the first time in years he was at peace and truly happy. He looked down at her and saw she was awake and watching the fire crackle in the hearth. Ian couldn't help what he was doing, he knew he shouldn't but couldn't stop. He crooked his finger under her chin and drew her gaze to his, she was beautiful, and with flames reflecting in her eyes, it made her irresistible to him. He lowered and softly touched his lips to hers. When he was met with no response, he leaned back a fraction to search her face. He saw surprise not question, but what stopped him dead was the mix with fear. *Ian, ye idiot!* he berated himself, about to apologize for the misstep.

Madison smiled then, and to his surprise, reached up with her hand and touched the side of his face ever so slightly. His skin was warm and rough from the two-day growth of beard he always wore. Some women might be turned off by the scruffy look, but she found it sexy. His eyes were kind and she read he was worried, she to let him know with no words; she was not offended by his touch. Ian hovered to allow her time to stop him, and when she didn't, as he touched her lips, he was met with a sweet response. It wasn't a hot passionate meeting, but both of them knew what sparks were coming alive between them. They spent the rest of the night cuddled together watching the fire, sharing the occasional soft kiss. Julie at one point hopped up and curled into a ball next to Madison. Ian and Madison fell asleep in each other's arms on the sofa not knowing what the next days would bring.

Chapter Six

Ian woke, and for a split second didn't know where he was, a squeak drew his attention to Julie as she stretched and remembered he was with Madison on the sofa. At some point last night they must have stretched out on the sofa, the last thing he remembered, they were curled in the corner watching the fire. *Thank God for a very deep sofa*, he thought. Ian, lying on his back with Madison on her side, head pillowed on his shoulder, hand nestled under his on his chest. His eyes roamed over her delicate sleeping features; long lashes fanned over her ivory skin with a hint a rose underneath. *Face of an angel*, he thought. He carefully lifted his hand from hers and moved a lock of hair back behind her ear. She started to stir and opened her eyes.

The first thing she saw was Ian's incredible green eyes, she had actually been awake for a few minutes, but unsure on what to do. She didn't actually remember stretching out on the sofa with him last night. *Well, this is going to be awkward,* she thought, but she felt warm and safe lying next to him. Neither spoke; they just looked at each other. Julie, apparently, decided it was time they both got up. She had been perched on the arm of the sofa eyeing both of them, then began to walk softly up Ian's frame. When she reached her destination, she sat, Ian felt the light pressure of her weight between his legs. *This could be bad,* he thought. He looked down at her as she parked her fluffy bottom on top of his groin. He reached out and gave her a pat on the head. Just as Ian settled back into the sofa pillow, Julie leaped over the back of the sofa using him as a springboard. Whoever said cats were the dumb species never met this one. Ian grunted out in pain and immediately pulled himself into the fetal position, inadvertently throwing Madison to the floor. Once over the shock of her abrupt landing, she looked horrified at Ian's face, which was crimson and creased with pain. Madison realized instantly what had occurred.

"Nice going, Julie. Now go fix him an ice bag." *Does this house have an ice bag?* she wondered. She was a little unsure of the proper protocol in these circumstances. She remained on the floor, waited a few seconds, then asked if he was okay. Madison was so afraid he would be angry at Julie; he had every right to be she supposed. But to her surprise, when he was able to breathe again, he started to, *laugh.* She eyed him queerly and he laughed all the more.

"What is so funny?" She was still sprawled on the floor where she'd landed.

"I guess she wanted us up." His face, still red, eyes tearing, she wasn't sure if the tears were from the pain or from laughing so hard. He could see she was confused by his reaction while Madison assumed the new love affair between Ian and Julie had finally come to an abrupt end. She figured, most men would've been pissed as hell, yet, Ian stopped laughing and reached his hand out to stroke the side of her face, Madison leaned into his hand and smiled up at him. He took the opportunity and pulled her to him and kissed her softly on the lips. God, he wanted more, but he was *not* willing to risk her retreating from him. He leaned back into the sofa for a second, then sat up and stretched. As he stood he offered his hand out to help Madison up from the floor.

"I'm sorry boot throwin' ye ta the floor luv." Madison picked up the quilt to fold it.

"Don't worry, I'm sorry she... uh... you know." She gave a half smile.

"Oh, ye mean using me as a trampoline? Dinna worry I'm no' angry, had cats growin' up." That was all the explanation she needed.

Madison finished folding the quilt and went to the front window and gaped. Snow covered everything and she guessed the depth at maybe a foot, moreover it was still coming down. She asked Ian to open her laptop for a weather update while she made coffee and something to eat. She was starving then remembered they'd missed dinner. Thankfully after watching Ian cook the other night she knew where most of the pots and pans were. As she placed the frying pan on the burner she noticed, like the countertops, all the pots and pans were copper with stainless steel, *fancy*. From the fridge Madison snagged the eggs, ham, cheese, onion, mushrooms, and tomatoes, she selected a broad blade kitchen knife and began to dice.

Ian was still on the computer when she finished and went back to the living room to see what was keeping him. As she got closer she could see the weather map of the Highlands. As a general rule she never paid much attention to the weather. South Jersey winters were so mild that weather wasn't a serious issue, but she could see from the map that they were good and buggered.

"Well, what's the verdict?" She stopped behind the sofa and leaned on the back. Ian leaned back resting his head between her hands and looked up at her.

"Are ye ready for this? We're in the middle of a blizzard that is expected ta last for three days. The prediction is for an estimated three to four feet of snow. The local authorities are warnin' everyone to no' leave their homes until further notice."

"You're kidding?" Madison smiled and then gave a small chuckle. "You mean you and I are stuck here for the next couple of days?" Ian saw her smile and his heart leaped; he was afraid she would be upset about being stuck with him.

"'Fraid so. Fortunately, I have clothes packed up in plastic tubs in the cellar. I can grab those and move them to the guestroom." He leaned forward and closed the laptop and stood to his full height. She decided, unlike most people, he looked good in the morning. *Who am I kidding?*

she thought. *He would look good in a garbage bag.* He walked around the sofa and the two of them went to the kitchen.

"So, what would you like in your omelet?" Madison asked and Ian looked at all the fixings she had out and laughed.

"Well, ye're certainly prepared for any response." He told her what he wanted and sat at the end of the island and watched her cook. He heard Julie playing in the living room and turned to see what had her attention.

"Um, Julie has one of those things ye put in yer hair. Do ye want me to get it from her?" Madison looked up and snickered.

"No, she would've found it sooner or later, and I have hundreds of them. She loves them, you see, and no matter where I put them, she always finds them. So rather than getting mad and taking them from her, I just let her have it and buy more. I've had that one for over a week now, I thinks that's a record." Madison finished and handed his omelet to him, and then started on her own.

"I thought ye said ye couldna cook?" Ian laughed.

"I can't, but I'm a whiz when it comes to breakfast." She smiled and told him to eat while it was warm.

"I'll wait," he said.

"Start. Good manners spoil good food." She finished with hers and sat on the stool across from him, noticing he had not started to eat, but waited for her. They ate in silence with a few chuckles at Julie while she played. After they finished eating Madison replaced the empty juice glasses with full cups of coffee.

"Lord, I hope we have enough coffee to last till the snow subsides." She frowned. "I hadn't realized how much we were drinking." Madison started to clean up when Ian stopped her.

"Stop. Ye cooked; I'll clean the mess." He looked around. "And what a mess ye've made," he teased.

"Ooh." She shoved him weakly and sat back down on the stool to watch as he cleaned. It wasn't in her nature to sit and watch while others worked, but she liked the sharing of responsibilities.

Madison glanced out the window and sighed, snow was coming down with a vengeance. She had never seen snow like this before, and wondered if it would be too deep to move around in. *South Jersey and Philly have an occasional snow, but nothing like this,* she mused. She stood up, went to the sink where Ian was and looked out the window. She could see his car, but the snow was clear up to the bottom of the doors on the Jeep Wagoneer. A chuckle rising up when she noticed he drove the same thing she did and wondered what else they had in common. She looked over at him and smiled.

Turning her attention to the fireplace, she saw the coals smoldering and decided they'd better build the fire up again. Without saying a word, she walked to the living room and surveyed the wood. There wasn't much left, but they could always go out to get more, she hoped. It was true she had never built a fire before; she had gas logs at home, but how hard could it be? She had watched him build the last two and figured it wouldn't be too difficult. Along with the cut wood there was kindling and paper. She took several wads of newspaper and threw it into the stone opening. She then took some scrap wood and tossed that on top of the wadded paper. She looked at the wood. She wasn't sure how much of anything to put into the fire box, so she piled in enough to make the paper, kindling and logs equal in amounts. Which was about four times as much as what was needed.

Unbeknownst to her, having finished with the breakfast dishes, Ian was watching her from behind the sofa. He was stifling a laugh, it was obvious she had no earthly idea what she was doing. He was going to have to stop her before she blew up the house and the two of them with it. He didn't want to make her feel like a simpleton who couldn't do anything. However, if she put any starter-fluid on that mess she had stuffed into the fireplace, she would surely blow them both up. As he saw her reach for the bottle of fluid, he spoke up.

"Madison?" She turned and stared at him. "I think with the amount of paper and kindling ye have there, fluid might no' be necessary." Under other circumstances, Madison's back would've gone up if anyone, especially a *man*, had tried to correct something she was doing. After all, *she* was the one who told people what to do and how. However, with Ian, the instinct to prove herself capable never rose, she wanted to help, but was actually relieved that he spoke up since she really didn't know what the hell her was doing. She put the fluid down and stuck a match to the paper and within a matter of moments the fireplace was ablaze. Madison jumped back.

"Holy... shit!" she exclaimed.

The fire was so big; it was the first time the screen was placed in front of it. Madison looked over at Ian and grinned with pride.

"This is the first fire I've ever built."

No shite, Ian thought.

"I think we're going to need more wood, though. We have more, don't we?"

Ian couldn't explain it, but he was so happy just to be in the same room with her and the prospect of being marooned with her for several days was delightful. "Aye there is plenty of wood, but some should be brought in so it can dry out. Tell ye what, while ye shower and change, I'll get the wood and bring it in."

Madison moved away from the fire and walked over to stand before him. Ian visualized her wearing pajamas made of the Mackay tartan. *Interesting,* he thought.

"I want to help you, and besides, I want to go out in the snow. So why don't we *both* shower and change. Then once we're dressed, we can *both* get the wood." Ian smiled at her. She had the look of a kid who just learned school was canceled due to snow and wanted to play. He doubted very much that she wanted to play the same way he did, he wanted so much to kiss her, but decided to wait. *Don't rush it,* he warned himself. He backed away from her to avoid temptation. Madison noticed the retreat and was surprised and a little confused.

"Well," Ian said and cleared his throat, "sounds good to me." He turned and started up the stairs. Halfway up he stopped and looked back down at Madison standing where he left her by the sofa, lost in her thoughts. "Madison?"

She looked up. "Huh?" She was sure she had read him correctly, she was sure he wanted to kiss her. Why the retreat?

"Are ye comin up?"

"Yeah." She still made no attempt to move, so Ian retraced his steps and stood in front of her. Madison was studying the wall over his shoulder with her brows drawn together not meeting his eyes. He puzzled over the question of why she seemed to have difficulty meeting his gaze unless he forced the issue. This time, though, she was going to have to look up on her own, he decided.

"What's wrong?" Her focus snapped to his as if she was brought out of some self-induced trance. Her eyes looked bright like she was, on the verge of what, Ian had no idea and he stepped back.

"Nothing, I was just trying to figure out an enigma that's all." She slapped an overbright smile on her face, gave him a friendly pat on his shoulder, moved around him, and jogged up the stairs.

"What the bloody hell just happened?" He looked down at Julie as she made her way up the stairs after her person. However, she was block from entering when Madison had shut the door. Ian climbed the stairs and went into the guest room. Before shutting the door, he allowed Julie access. It had been a long time since he'd been in this room. It was the smaller of the two. The bed was queen size and had a handmade log frame similar to the one in the master suite. The room lacked a closet but had a large oak armoire, which he opened and found it void of his clothes. Ian had asked Mrs. Stuart to move his things out of the master, tub them up and he would move them to the cellar. "Shite."

Ian huffed, then went to retrieve the tubs and hang his clothes in the armoire.

Ian heard Madison's shower turn on and knew from experience that if he turned on his, both showers would lose hot water. He glanced about the room and sighed, there were two windows, one next to the bathroom door that, like the one in the kitchen, overlooked the front drive. The other window was more of a large picture window-size opening that overlooked the kitchen. Because of the open floor plan of the downstairs, if you stuck your head out far enough you could see the entire first floor. It seemed strange now that there was not a pane of glass in the opening, but when he built the place the room was intended to be used as an office. Later Ian never felt the need to add the window since he never use the place.

Ian sat on the edge of the bed. As he took off his socks and shirt Julie hopped on the bed and walked over to stand on his lap, he smiled and began to pet her. After some time he heard Madison's shower shut off, he sighed, picked up Julie, placed her on the bed while he stood, walked to the bathroom and turned on the shower. It was small and compact, but was equipped with everything needed. He stood in front of the sink and peered at his reflection in the mirror, a shave was needed, but it was something he always hated doing. As a matter of fact the only times he shaved on a daily basis, was when he was filming, and the role required a clean face. Otherwise he was always adorned with a two or three day growth. He had occasionally grown a beard, but it never lasted long. The mirror fogged over from the heat of the shower, Ian stripped the rest of his clothes off and stepped beneath the hot running water. As he washed his hair, his thoughts went to Madison. He wondered why she had changed her demeanor so abruptly. Maybe he'd ask her once they were back downstairs, *aye, I will.*

Madison heard the guest room shower come to life. Standing in front of the mirror with a towel wrapped around her, she began to blow-dry her hair. She couldn't understand Ian's backing away from her. Had she misunderstood what was happening between them? She puzzled over the last few days. In the beginning, she thought, sure he was attractive, *Hell, girl he's a Greek God in the flesh.* "calm down Maddy." Giving herself a stern look in the mirror. Aside from his looks she smiled at how thoughtful it was of him to offer to show her around. But when he took care of her, she realized just how truly kind he really was. Her mind went to the kiss the night before. She was so surprised by it and hadn't known how to act, but when he kissed her again she felt alive. The way he held and cared for her, she almost wished she was still cold just so he would continue to hold her.

"Oh knock it off, Maddy. Just get dressed. He's not interested in you; he was just being a nice guy," she said aloud.

She finished drying her hair and went to the closet to pick out her clothes. She pulled out her jeans, but instead of a baggy sweatshirt or baggy sweater; she took out a navy blue fitted chenille sweater. She got dressed and surveyed herself in the full-length mirror. She'd always liked this sweater, It used to be loose on her, but she washed it before reading the dry clean only tag and it shrank. It wasn't skintight or overly revealing, but it was snug to her figure and showed her body wonderfully. She smiled at her reflection. In her estimation she looked damn good, but she hoped she didn't look like a floozy or like she was trying to be a lure.

She left the confines of her room and just as her foot touched the top step, the guest room door opened. Ian and Julie stepped over the threshold. *What the hell was Julie doing in there?* she thought to herself. *This is getting out of hand.* She gazed at Ian. *Does that man own anything other than fitted sweaters that show off his build?* She mentally panted. Madison's heart leaped and began to beat very fast. His sweater and jeans were both midnight black, his bright eyes looked questioningly at her.

Ian took one look at her and wanted to run back to the safety of the guest room. She was sexy as hell in the snug-fitting sweater and jeans.

Her hair was pulled up in a clip, which showed off her wonderfully sculpted shoulders and swan-like neck. *If this is what she plans ta be wearin' over the next days,* he thought, *I'm goin' ta be takin' a lot of cold showers.* She looked like a goddess. But there was something different about her. When she ran up the stairs, she seemed upset and maybe a little deflated, but now she looked radiant and determined. Madison smiled and walked down the stairs without saying a word.

Once in the living room, she slipped on her boots. As Ian came down the stairs, they never took their eyes off of each other. He decided he was going to have to figure this woman out. She finished with her boots and walked to the closet and put on her coat and the scarf. Ian was right behind her watching her every move. Madison was fully aware he never took his eyes off her, she zipped up her coat and turned and their eyes connected.

"Well, shall we get some wood?" *Oh my god! What the hell did I just say?* Horrified at her choice of words. They hadn't spoken since they went upstairs and now Madison's cheeks burned.

"Aye." Brow arched he smiled. *At some point today,* he thought, *I would like ye ta tell me what made ye act strange with me earlier.* Ian opened the door for her and ushered her outside.

Even though there was a roof over the whole of the front porch, thank to the winds, there was still quite a bit of snow piled up. Thankfully, the wood was kept around the corner of the wraparound porch, otherwise they would never be able to get to it. The snow was coming down even harder than it had been earlier that morning, even the fence lining the cliff edge was hidden by a wall of white. Madison decided this must have been what was referred to as a white out. As they trudged through the snow on the porch Madison slipped and fell. Ian tried to help her, but nearly slipped himself.

"Are ye okay?" he said, holding out his hand to help her up.

"Yes, thank you." Madison laughed. "The snow is deeper than I thought it would be on the porch." They reached the snow-covered wood, they made several trips back and forth between the fireplace and the wood pile. After they were finished, Ian decided to shovel a walkway to the woodpile.

"That's a good idea, is there another shovel so I can help?" Madison watched him ponder her question, there were two, the other one needed a new handle the following winter. "With the way this is coming down we're going to have to come out several times to keep on top of it.

"Good point. I think there might be on in the basement, provided the handle was mended. If ye dinna mind checkin' the cellar, I'll begin ta shovel out there." Ian watched Madison pull on the sconce and disappear into the stairwell. He then went back outside and walked to the small shed that was by the woodpile and retrieved the snow shovel. He surveyed the wood and was concerned they didn't have enough to last through the storm. If the snow continued at the current rate they would be stuck here for quite a while. "Although I canna classify this as being stuck," he said to himself, grinning.

By the time he was finished, he realized Madison hadn't returned. Ian went in search, leaving the shovel by the door. There was no sign of Madison, but he saw Julie sitting by the closed basement door. Figuring the door must have blown shut behind her when she went down. He pulled on the sconce and sure enough she was sitting on the stairs. Madison looked up at him and gave a small smile.

"I didn't know there wasn't a way to get out if you shut the door," she said.

"Oh, lass I'm sorry, I should've told ye how ta get out of the cellar." He held out his hand and helped her to her feet. "Ye see, I never lived here after the house was built, so I never got a chance ta finish off the cellar way." Ian pointed to the sconce just inside the stairwell and gave it a small tug. "Here, ye just give this a little tug and the door will open." Madison smiled and handed Ian the extra shovel, that had not been repaired, she did have some salt. "Not sure what help this will be with the snow fallin' like it is, but what the hell." She followed him outside to help with the application on the porch. After they were finished, they came back inside and hung up their coats.

"I think I should tell ye that there may no' be enough wood if this storm lasts more than a few days." When she said nothing, he continued. "It might be a good idea ta no' have any more fires unless the power goes out. If we lose power, we may be needin' the wood for heat."

"Okay." Madison picked up the laptop to put it back on the desk. Ian was amused by her trying to avoid him and went to the kitchen. He looked at the pot and decided he was sick of coffee, he stepped into the pantry and found some tea. Madison heard the kettle whistling from the kitchen and wondered what he was doing.

"What are you doing?" she asked as she walked into the kitchen.

"Oh she speaks," Ian said with a smile. "I'm makin' tea."

"Tea? Why?" Madison hopped up and sat on the counter by the sink to watch Ian pour boiling water over loose tea leaves in a round china teapot.

"Because I like tea, and it's better for ye than coffee." He looked at her from across the counter. She was sitting with her arms and legs crossed. Ian wasn't sure if it was the sweater she was wearing or the way she had her hair, but something was making it harder for him to keep his distance like he should.

"Do you not like coffee?" she asked to break the silence and to hopefully stop the way Ian was looking at her, she regretted wearing this sweater.

"Well, it's no' me favorite, but I'll drink it if it's around. Or if I'm tired and need a little pick me up. What, ye no' like tea?"

"To be honest, no." She laughed at the dumbfounded expression on Ian's face.

"How can ye no' like tea?"

"You're cute." She chuckled. "I've never tasted any that I liked. So, I don't drink it." Ian smiled as he filled his mug with his freshly steeped tea. He moved around the counter and stood in front of her.

"Ye couldna have tasted verra many teas then. Try this." He handed her his mug and watched her face as she tasted. He knew by her expression she liked it and wanted more. "Well, what do ye think?"

Madison smiled. "I don't like it." *Lier,* he thought, laughing. "What's so funny?" She handed him back the mug and was about to jump off the counter when his hand rested on her thigh stopping her. She instinctively recrossed her arms, the movement seemed out of character and strange to Ian, but he decided to ignore the body language. Since she was sitting on the counter, she was only mere inches shorter than Ian instead of the usual foot. He put his mug down on the island counter behind him, and turned his attention back to her. He looked into her eyes, and for the first time since he had met her, she looked anxious. He couldn't understand it, she showed nerves when they'd first met, but in the short time they've gotten to know each other the nerves and trepidation had all but vanished. He placed his hand gently on her cheek and softly traced her lips with his thumb. Ian moved closer to her and noticed her breathing quickened.

"Ian?" Okay, now she was really confused, his behavior toward her was so back and forth. As soon as she wrapped her head around what she thought he wanted, he seemed to change direction. "What are you doing?" A nugget of fear crept into her mind, like someone else she knew. He could hear fear in her voice and stopped immediately. He didn't move away from her, but he did drop his hands and rested them on the counter on either side of her.

"What's wrong?" His deep voice was low and rumbled luxuriously through her. "Did I misunderstand? Do ye no' want me touch?" Madison lifted her eyes to meet his and Ian saw it. Full blown fear. There was no mistaking it.

"Oh God no. It isn't that. Trust me." Maddy was starting to feel trapped, she knew her reaction was misplaced. There was nothing to fear from Ian, but the past was breaking open from the box where she had locked it away. She looked back down at her hands and once again tried to jump down off the counter. However, Ian was determined to keep her where she was until he knew what was causing the fear he had seen.

"Why are ye afraid of me?" The question should have shocked her, but she knew she had given him no reason to think differently. "I can see fear in yer eyes, and since I'm the only one here, I can only assume that I'm the one who put it there."

"I'm not afraid of *you*. It's just that...." Ian needed to see her eyes and since she kept them on her hands, he drew her chin up with his finger until hers met his.

"Just what?" he prodded when she said nothing. "Madison? Just what?" She lowered her head, she was so angry with herself. For a multitude of reasons, but at that moment, she couldn't seem to rein in her now-flooded emotions. Ian saw the small dark blue circle form on her jeans when a tear dropped onto her leg. He placed both hands on either side of her face and brought her eyes back to his. Madison's aqua eyes were bright with swelling tears. He could feel her start to tremble. He immediately drew her off the counter into his arms and carried her to the sofa. As Ian sat keeping her in his arms, she placed her hands and forehead on his chest and allowed a few tears to slip past her resolve.

"What happened to ye?" He drew her in tighter, felt her tense, then relax seconds later. He had a feeling she was trying to keep her emotions close to the chest as they say. He didn't want to pry. *The hell, I bloody well do!* he corrected himself. After such a short time, he was already emotionally invested in this woman and that meant wheedling out her woes and helping where he could. *And if this is over some mistreatment from a former bloke, it meant beating the shite out of the bloody bastard.*

"Madison?" She said nothing, but he knew she was listening. "I want ye to tell me what's wrong. Something has obviously frightened ye, please tell me what it is." The normal strength in his tone had softened like he was dealing with a cornered skittish wild animal. When Madison spoke, her voice was small and tiny, Ian had to strain to hear it.

"I can't tell you. I can't tell anybody." She was mortified at her behavior. She hadn't had this kind of, not quite a meltdown, but panic in years. She could only chalk it up to Dean's advances and the dream that ensued after them.

"Ye *can* tell me, I want ta know and if I can, I would like ta help ye." He looked down at her and wiped the tears away from her eyes with his thumb. "Please." The pleading emanating from his eyes nearly broke her. She couldn't tell him, *but God, I wish I could tell someone,* she thought. She started to stand, but once again Ian had a secure hold on her.

"I'll tell ye what, how aboot if we start slow."

"What do you mean?" Madison was beginning to get her voice back.

"Why dinna ye tell me what was bothering ye earlier today and we can take it from there." She looked at him in question. "What?"

"I thought you were the one who was upset." When he looked at her in question she explained. "I thought I was reading your signals wrong, and that's why you backed away from me this morning." Now Ian understood her new behavior.

"Oh, luv," he said, resting his forehead on hers and chuckled. "Ye were no' readin' me wrong, but the reason I backed away was because I wanted to kiss ye this morn." He smiled. "I'm no' talkin' a little peck on the lips here. I wanted to devour ye this morn. I decided last night ta try and take this slow, so I wanted to keep me distance." Madison's face was a picture of surprise, and Ian smiled. "Has it no' occurred ta ye that I have had a hard time keepin' me hands off ye?"

"No," she whispered and Ian smiled and nodded his head.

"Well, I have, and that sweater is no' helpin'. For that matter neither were the plaid flannel pajamas." She looked down at her sweater and absentmindedly crossed her arms in an attempt to cover herself. She really wished she hadn't worn this sweater. Ian saw the movement and put his hand on her arms to halt her so she wouldn't cover what he was enjoying so much.

"Dinna cover up." He ran his fingertips down the side of her cheek. Now that they were on the same page so to speak, she could read the hunger for her in his eyes and felt heat rise in her cheeks. Ian arched his left brow and smiled. "Are you hungry?" Madison straightened her back and Ian laughed. "For dinner, ye goofball." The tension left her immediately.

"Yes, I would love some dinner." Relief evident in release of tension in her whole body. "The day has gone by so fast; I hadn't realized what time it was. Ian?"

"Aye."

"Thank you for not pressing the issue. Please be patient with me." Ian cupped his hand softly on her cheek.

"Ye're welcome. I canna promise that I willna still try to make advances, but I will go no further then ye're comfortable wi'. I'm perfectly willin' and happy ta go at *yer* pace." Madison had never had such kind words spoken to her by a man she had just shut down. She couldn't help what she was doing. She leaned into him and placed her lips on his. It was brief, but when she broke away, she didn't back away. Their eyes locked. Ian wrapped his arms around her, rested his hand on the middle of her back and ran his other hand up to cradle her neck. He pulled her to him. He was inches from her mouth.

"May I kiss ye, luv?" His voice was hoarse and full of desire. She couldn't speak, so she just nodded her head to give him the permission he sought. Ian drew her into his embrace until her soft warm lips met his, he knew he should keep it light, but he wanted more. Ian drew her tighter to him making causing her to gasp, giving him the access he craved to better taste her. Madison's ran her hands up his chest as their kiss was deepened. God he tasted fabulous; he had such a talented mouth. As his tongue explored hers and their lips moved in unison. The butterflies in her belly were doing the conga in the best possible way. *Could you have an orgasm just from kissing?* she wondered. She didn't know, but she would gladly bet that if it were possible, he would make it so. *Make it so, Number One!* she thought. He heard her small moan and knew he better pull away before he frightened her again.

Ian reluctantly withdrew from her warm mouth and stared at her. His breathing was deep and heavy as was hers. Neither said a word, then a single tear fell down Madison's cheek. Ian brushed it away with his finger.

"Was that the wrong thing ta do?" His voice was still hoarse. Madison shook her head no. "Then why are ye cryin'?"

"Beauty does that to me." Ian drew her back to his lips and kissed her again. There was no mistaking her reaction this time; her arms went around his neck, and she opened herself to him completely. Madison felt safe for the first time in years. Ian's strong hands running up her back felt so good, however, once again he pulled away from her.

"Maddy luv, if we continue wi' this I will no' be able to control meself." He looked into her eyes. There were no more tears, only trust. "Ye have no idea how much I want ye right now. And as much as pains me ta say it, I think we should stop and calm down before something happens that ye are no' ready for." When she still said nothing, he kissed her again, only this time the kiss was soft, and quick. "Besides, I think we need to have some conversations first."

She looked at his eyes and then down to his lips. She didn't want to talk about it, she wanted to go on kissing him. But deep down, she knew he was right, they couldn't continue this way. She scooted off his lap and stood by the fire. After a while she turned back to the sofa where Ian still sat. She couldn't believe it. She actually wanted to tell him what she was afraid of and why. The only problem was, what would he think of her afterward? *Will he no longer want to be with me? Hold me? Or kiss me?* she thought. Once again it was as though Ian was reading her mind. He stood and went to her. He took her face in his hands and raised her gaze to his.

"I dinna want ye to feel pressured or threatened. Ye can tell me at yer own pace. Just remember I will think no less of ye, no matter what yer secret is." He kissed the top of her forehead. "Tell ye what, why do we no' eat something and see where that leads, then. Okay?"

Madison smiled and he drew her into his embrace. They stood for a moment with him holding her and then finally they walked to the kitchen arm and arm to find something to eat.

Chapter Seven

Ian lay in bed looking at the ceiling, thinking about Madison and their evening together. They found pizzas in the freezer, doctored them with extra toppings they devised from the fridge and took them to the living room to eat, where they shared a bottle of cabernet. They sat together on the sofa but decided against a fire because they were conserving wood in case of a power outage. After they finished eating, Madison remembered the DVDs that she had in the desk drawer.

"How about a movie?" she asked as she moved to the desk.

"No TV. Remember?" Ian reminded her with a smile, then walked to the kitchen with the uneaten food.

"I've got my laptop. It won't be the same as a TV, but the picture will fill the screen." She went to the desk and opened the drawer where she put the DVDs she brought. Ian looked up when he heard the draw slam shut.

"What?" Ian's voice called from the kitchen as he slid the leftover pizza in the fridge.

"Nothing. You know, I am actually kind of tired. How about we call it a night and go to bed." She scurried away from the desk and was halfway to the stairs when Ian stopped her. He looked over her shoulder toward the desk.

"What's the matter with ye?" He moved around her and started toward the desk. Madison turned and rushed to block his path.

"Would you like to play cards?" she stammered. "I know some really good card games."

"Maddy girl, what are ye hidin' in the drawer?" Ian found humor in her twitching hands and guilty posture. She was behaving like a child who was about to be busted by her mother for smoking in her room.

"Nothing, and anyway it's my drawer." Ian arched his eyebrow and crossed his arms in front of his chest. "Well, for the next six months anyway." She smiled.

Ian reached behind her and tried to open the drawer, but this time *she* was too fast for *him*. As he leaned down to open the drawer she reached out and placed her hands on his sides. She had no idea if he was ticklish or not, but he quickly jumped away from her hands. He looked at her in surprise and gave a devilish grin, and advanced. Madison smiled and backed closer to the desk.

"Ian, what are you doing?" She started to laugh.

"Exactly what ye thought ye were goin' ta do ta me. By the way, me lady—" His movement was so quick Madison didn't have a prayer of getting away. He scooped her up and hoisted her over his shoulder. "—I am no' ticklish."

"Oh, Ian, put me down." She laughed while she began to kick her feet trying to wiggle down, but Ian's hold was too strong.

"Now what's in this drawer that ye dinna want me to see?" he asked, laughing.

"Nothing. Put me down. This is so unfair! PUT ME DOWN!" she yelled in laughter. Ian bent down and opened the desk drawer she was protecting. Inside he found the DVDs and he recognized all but three of the titles. He smiled because the titles he recognized were his. She had quite a collection of his work.

"Ian, put me down," she demanded. He shut the drawer and swung her around until she was cradled in his arms. Bending his head, he took her mouth with his. She hadn't thought the contents would provoke this attention, but she decided to go with the flow. She wrapped her arms around his neck and allowed him to deepen the kiss. Never in his life had he wanted a woman like he wanted Madison at this moment, and he had only laid eyes on her a few days ago. Remembering that he wanted to take things slower with her, he reluctantly broke away from delicious mouth and looked into her eyes. They were a deep blue and full of the heat and need he was feeling. But he saw something else, a thread of apprehension that told him she wasn't ready. Take it easy, his common sense told him, the lass was afraid of something. He could guess, but better to hear it from her. He lowered her to her feet and stepped back. She had confusion in her eyes.

"I dinna think it is a good idea if we do any more of *that* tonight. I already have ta take a cold shower. I dinna want ta have to take an ice bath too." His small joke made her laugh and he knew she wasn't hurt. "So, why don't we watch a movie and then go to bed."

"Sure. Since you've had a look at what I brought, you can choose." Her cheeks glowed pink and Ian moved toward her again. Only this time she was the one who backed away. "How much ice does the fridge hold?" She laughed.

Ian nodded, but couldn't contain the grin that spread across his face. He picked from the three other titles that were not his. Unfortunately, he wasn't the least bit interested in any of the films she's brought. So he picked one that looked the longest. Madison set up her laptop and waited for him on the sofa. He handed her the disc and sat down next to her, the title bowled her over.

"*Pride and Prejudice*! I had no idea you would be interested in a Jane Austin film." She loaded the disc and sat back in the cushions. She was banking on Ian pulling her to him, and she wasn't about to discourage the act. She cuddled up next to him and they watched the black and white movie in its entirety. Once the film was over, Ian walked her to her bedroom door, made a theatrical display of kissing her hand, clicked his heels together and bid her "Good night, me lady." Then he went to the other bedroom and closed the door.

Ian stood at the window looking out at the snowy landscape. He had no idea the movie was going to be so as long or so boring. "What the hell kind of word is 'Prodigious' anyway?" he muttered. Yet, the chance to being able to hold her and have her so near during the two hours was worth the torment of watching the horrid film. She was so relaxed and content. When the movie was over, he wanted to pop in another so he might hold her that much longer, but as the film drew to a close, he noticed she was falling asleep. Ian had a sudden, or not so sudden, urge to steal into her room and make love to her.

"Ian what is the matter wi ye?" he asked himself. He had no idea how to handle this level of attraction, so intense, so quickly; he didn't expect this to happen. One thing was for sure, he was going to have to get ahold of this before he went out of his mind. He wondered if Madison was sleeping or if she was staring out the window as he was. "Go ta sleep!" he scolded himself. He stripped down to his boxers and slid into bed, hoping to sleep, but knowing Maddy was on the other side of the wall, wearing very little clothes, "Oh aye, ye daft idiot, tha's a sure way ta get ta sleep." He went to the bathroom, splashed some cold water on his face and went back to bed. After Ian closed his eyes, he started to think about anything he could that would make him go to sleep. Anything at all, things like scooping the litter box.

The sound of Madison's cries and whimpering roused Ian from his sleep. He lay in bed for a few seconds to make sure of what he was actually hearing. When the whimpering became more dramatic, he realized she must have been having a nightmare. *Should I go to her?* he deliberated. *Nay,* he thought, *stay where ye are. If she wakes up and finds ye in her room, she's libel to be more frightened.* He sat up in bed and listened to her trying to decide what was the best course of action. She sounded so sad and helpless. He wondered what she was dreaming about. Ian leaned back against the headboard, drew his arms up and laced his fingers behind his head and closed his eyes. When was the last time *he* had been tormented by a nightmare? After a moment, he remembered.

It was just before his father died, two days before the premiere of his first major film. He dreamed his father stood up at the end of the movie and began to boo Ian's performance. The gold velvet curtains had closed at the end of the credits. Ian and the cast were standing on the stage at the front of the theater by the screen taking their bows when the booing started. The cast walked off stage, leaving Ian to endure this horror and degradation alone. Then the cast booed him from the wings. By the time Ian could struggle from the dream to waking, the entire theater was booing him and him only.

Of course, by the time the premiere was upon him, Ian was a nervous wreck, sick to his stomach and wet with perspiration under his tuxedo. The evening, however, was a triumph, and his father loved his performance, as did the rest of the audience. Ian swore he' never forget the dream and he supposed he never did. Shaken from his memories, by a small scream coming from Madison's room. Ian threw back the covers and raced through his door to hers. When he reached for the doorknob to Madison's room, he paused to listen before entering. Slowly he opened the door; thankfully Madison had left the bathroom light on. Whether she had done it by accident or design, Ian didn't care. As he walked to her bed he saw her legs thrashing under the blankets. *Whatever she's dreaming aboot is scaring the hell out of her,* Ian thought. He sat on the edge of the bed and looked down at her. She was lying on her back with her arms thrust above her head as if someone were holding her down by her wrists. She was breathing heavily and shaking her head back and forth. Ian gently moved the hair off her face and softly called her by name.

"Madison, wake up. Ye're havin' a nightmare." Ian heard Julie meow and watched her jump onto the bed and sit down next to Madison. The cat eyed her distressed owner and then licked Madison on the forehead.

All of a sudden Madison let out a blood curdling scream. She began to kick her legs and punch the air with her fists. Ian ducked from the assaults after her left fist connected with his chin. He took hold of her shoulders and gently shook her awake. Once her eyes flew open he let go of her and straightened his back.

"Are ye alright luv,?" he asked her. Madison brought her hands up to her forehead and began to shudder. She lowered her hands and looked at him.

"What are you doing here?" Her voice wasn't angry, but she didn't seem real happy to see him either. *Why is he sitting on my bed? And where the hell were his clothes?!* she wondered as she noticed Ian was clad in only a pair of red boxer shorts.

"Ye were havin' a nightmare. I heard ye screamin' and came in to make sure ye were okay." He looked down at her and noticed she wasn't wearing anything. *Oh shit!* was all he thought. *Where the hell are her pajamas?* Thankfully, she was completely covered up with the exception of her arms. "Are ye okay?"

"I'm fine. The dream is not new to me. I'm used to it. I'm sorry I woke you," she explained, tugging the sheet up to her chin, embarrassed.

"Do ye want to talk aboot it?" When she said nothing, he spoke again. "If it would make ye more comfortable, I can sit on the bench by the window."

Now that she was fully awake, she really looked at him and saw true concern in his eyes. She decided it was time to tell him about her fears where they came from. After all, they were each highly attracted to the other and made any bones about wanting to, without putting too fine a point it, jump each other's bones. There was not question either, that the emotional connection went beyond physical, he should know what he's getting into. Besides, Madison realized for the second time that night, she wanted to tell her story, at least she wanted to tell Ian her story.

She moved to sit up and remembered she wasn't wearing any nightclothes. Her complexion went white and her eyes widened. Ian rightfully assumed she had just remembered her sleeping attire, or lack of it and went to the closest to retrieve a T-shirt for her. After she put it on, she turned her attention back to Ian and asked him to sit down. When he began to move to the bench Madison stopped him.

"Would you mind sitting here?" She indicated the edge of the bed where he was sitting before. Ian asked no questions, but just sat back down.

"Okay." Madison took a deep breath and began. "First, thank you for being patient with me and not pushing. You've been considerate, caring and I can't tell you how much I appreciate that. It has been a long time since anyone has shown me the kindness you have over the last days and you deserve an explanation. I think I should give you some of my background first." Madison took another deep therapeutic breath before she spoke again.

"I'm an only child. My father died of a sudden massive coronary, before I was born. My mother met Michael Danaher at a support group for widowed spouses. Two months after my father died, my mother realized she was pregnant. This was a huge concern for her as my father's family apparently never approved of her marriage to their son. She lived in fear that my father's family would take her baby to raise themselves. Michael's wife died in childbirth as did their baby. He was devastated that not only did he lose his wife, but the child as well. My mother needed help and Michael wanted a family to care for. They became close friends, and saw each other fairly often away from the group. They talked about their losses and her situation and decided to marry before my father's family learned about my mother's pregnancy. Michael's name is on my birth certificate. Unfortunately my mother had a very hard time with the birth and died in the hospital two weeks after I was born. Michael raised me alone.

"He was a wonderful man. I couldn't have asked for a more loving dad. I always called him Poppy, because that's how he always referred to himself. I asked him why once and he said, 'You had a daddy, and he would have loved you as much as I do if he had lived. I don't want his memory lost to you.' When I graduated from high school he gave me a gift. He handed me an envelope and inside was a photo of my mother and my father with a letter she had written while she was carrying me."

Her eyes teared up slightly when talking about the man who raised her and loved her like his own blood.

"While I was in college, I met Adam Gilmore. I worked for Tender Care Hospice as a part-time receptionist from eight in the morning until two in the afternoon and then went to classes in the afternoons and evenings. Free time wasn't plentiful, but what I had, I spent with Adam.

"He was such a charmer, and good-looking. Poppy didn't truly trust him, but I was in love, so he wasn't as vocal about his objections as he wanted to be. Which was something he regretted until the day he died. Adam and I were married a year after I graduated. I was only nineteen years old."

"Wait, how did you manage to graduate from college at nineteen?" Ian interrupted.

"Oh, well I wanted to get it over with as fast as I could, so instead of taking the summers off, I did the summer sessions. That way I was able to graduate much faster than my peers." She smiled "That and I was always somewhat of an overachiever."

"Ah." Ian smiled. "Good for you, lass."

She paused to take a breath. She took the glass of water off the nightstand to take a much-needed drink before she went on.

"The first month we were married was wonderful, but slowly, things started to change. His sweet demeanor became hard and harsh. He never used to yell and suddenly he was yelling at me all the time. Like I said, I was only nineteen and I thought I was doing something wrong. Poppy never remarried after my mother died, so I had no real example of how a marriage was supposed to work. I didn't have a mother to talk to and I didn't want to tell Poppy, because I knew he didn't like Adam, so I tried harder to make things work.

"Then one evening six months after we were married, he didn't come home. When he still hadn't come home by the time I had to get ready for work the next morning, I was nearly out of my mind with worry. I imagined all kinds of things that could have happened to him. I called the office and told them I would not be in and started calling hospitals and people we knew. Finally in the middle of the afternoon Adam came home and he was drunk as a skunk and angry as hell."

Adam walked through the front door of his and Madison's house slamming it shut in his wake. "MADISON! Get your ass down here NOW!" Adam stood in the middle of the foyer and waited for his wife to come into view. Nineteen-year-old Madison stood at the top of the stairs and looked down at her husband. He was drunk, but she was so relieved he was safe and unharmed. She swallowed her initial anger at his behavior and thoughtlessness for putting her through the night of worry. She ran down the stairs and nearly launched herself into his arms.

"Oh, Adam, thank God you're okay. I was so worried about you." She backed away and looked at him. She could smell the booze on him *and* perfume that was not hers. "Where the hell have you been? I had to call out of work and all over town to try and find you." Without any warning the back of Adam's hand flew out and struck her across her face. It was a sharp unexpected blow and she crumpled to the floor. When she was down, Adam drew back his foot and kicked her as hard as he could in the abdomen. She nearly lost consciousness.

"Don't you ever lecture me! Do you hear?" Adam bent over, grabbed hold of her arms, harshly picked her up and slammed her against the wall. Tears were coursing down her face, which enraged him, and he hit her again and again until she was knocked out cold. He watched her slide down the wall and come to rest on the floor. He walked to the kitchen and grabbed a glass and filled it with water. Returning to stand over the battered form of his wife, he dumped the contents of the glass on her beaten and bloody face. She woke and looked up at her husband.

"Go upstairs and clean yourself up. You're a mess, and not very appealing, I might add. I will be there in a moment." Madison eased herself off the floor and limped to the stairs. "Oh and Madison, don't you *dare* leave that room until I get up there."

She made her way upstairs, stepped in her shower and began to wash the blood off her face. She stood under the hot water for a long time crying and wondering what she had done wrong to provoke such an attack. Little did she know that the attack was far from over. When she was finished in the shower, she put on her robe and walked into the bedroom. Madison wasn't surprised to see Adam in the doorway. He told her he would be up, however, she wasn't prepared for his quick advance on her person. He grabbed her upper arms and threw her down on the bed. When she tried to get up, he swung out and hit the side of her face with the back of his hand. Adam climbed on the bed and straddled his wife and tore apart her robe exposing her naked body.

"Adam! What are you doing?" she screamed. She tried to cover herself and get away but Adam hit her again nearly knocking her nearly unconscious a second time. He seized her breasts in his mouth and began to bite at her nipples. It was so painful, she pleaded with him to stop. When he was finished with his assault on her breasts, he raised his head and leveled his eyes with hers.

"Don't you move," he demanded. He rolled off the bed and jerked off his pants. She realized his plan and turned her head toward the telephone. *I need help*, she thought. When she looked away, he grabbed her jaw roughly with his fingers and forced her gaze back to him.

"Dare to take your eyes off me again, you'll live to regret it. Do you hear me?" She nodded her head, tears were streaming down her face. *This is not my husband. What has happened to my husband?* she asked herself.

Adam hurriedly stripped off the rest of his clothes and stood glaring at his wife. He slowly walked back to her and stood by the bed. Then suddenly Madison was yanked off the bed and thrown to the floor on her back. Adam knelt down between her legs and looked into her eyes. They were full of fear and bright with tears. He loved the fear, and the fact that he put it there was even better. He felt a power he had never felt in his life.

"Adam, please, don't do this," she begged. That was all he needed. Without any warning he put one hand under the small of her back raising her hips from the floor and drove himself deeply into her with a force even he didn't realize he had. Madison cried out in agony as her sensitive flesh ripped and tore. She tried desperately to get away, but Adam grabbed ahold of her hair and pulled for emphasis to each of his repeated and painful thrusts. The more she begged him to stop, the more brutal his drives became. Once he was spent, he collapsed on top of her. Madison lay there crying, bloody, and in pain. Her face swelling and her body aching from the blows. *I have to get away. I have to get away* was the only thing going through her mind, but as she tried to move he tightened his hold on her.

"Where do you think you're going, cunt?" her eyes bulged as his large hand wrapped around her throat and squeezed cutting off her air supply. "You can't possibly think we're finished." Adam watched her struggle to get air, "You want to know where I am every minute?" finally he released his grip enough to allow her to draw breath. "You don't have to worry. I'm here, and I'm going to make love to you, my devoted wife." He smash is mouth on hers, while with his free hand he rammed several fingers into her already abused vagina. Her strangled screams fueled his desire to have her again. "You don't have to worry about me or where I am." He arched his body over hers and looked down at himself, throbbing, rock hard and growing larger by the second. He flipped her over onto her front, lifted her hips and began to brutally sodomize her. Her screams of in pain and begging him to stop only intensified his desire to deal her more harm. He slammed into her again with each word. "We're … going … to … do … this … all … night … long!"

Chapter Eight

"That night he raped me a total of six times, it was only when I didn't have any fight left that he finally stopped. I was so sore and beaten I couldn't go to work for a week. When I was finally able to go back to work, people would ask, but I always told them that I had fallen down the stairs or something equally cliche. I don't know what made his behavior change. Or maybe he was always that angry and I refused to see it. I don't know. The attacks happened again. Not every night, and sometimes not for weeks. Just about the time I thought he had worked through whatever his problem was, the brutality would begin again. This went on for six months. Until one day I found out I was pregnant. When I told him about the baby, he beat me so badly I miscarried right there in the front hall. When I started to hemorrhage, he stepped over me and went out the door. I crawled to the phone and dialed 9-1-1. While I was in the hospital I was told I would never be able to have children. Because I was beaten so badly the doctors called the police and Adam was arrested.

"Poppy took me back to his house when I was released from the hospital, and I lived there until after Adam was sentenced. It took about a year, but he was convicted and sentenced to three years in the state penitentiary. I filed and was granted a divorce and then I took back my maiden name. I was married to him for a total of two years. Poppy found out about the beatings, the doctors told him when they called him to come to the hospital, but I never told him of the rapes.

"The people at work were never told anything, but I guess they knew what was going on. Poppy died two years ago. I haven't had a relationship since. Adam had been the only man I'd ever been with, and to be honest, we had only made love once before the beatings began. I was a virgin when we were married and on the wedding night we made love for the first time. But because of the pain then, I guess I wasn't very good at it and Adam wasn't willing to try it again. So I guess you could say, I have never had a good experience with sex."

She stopped speaking and looked into Ian's eyes, she couldn't read them, they seemed expressionless and his face, blank. Finally, he stood and walked to the picture window and looked out. As she told her story, Ian became more enraged with every word. *I knew there was some type of abuse involved,* he thought to himself, *but nothing compared to what she just described.* Suddenly it occurred to him—she said he was sentenced to three years, so he would be out now. He turned toward her.

"Where is he now?" Ian did not trust himself to say any more than that. He was afraid his anger would show, and she would misunderstand.

"He's still in prison. I'm to be notified when and if he's granted parole. In the first year of his sentence he came up for parole, but was denied for behavioral reasons. A few months later, he attacked a nurse in the infirmary. He was put in solitary confinement and given six more years for the crime. By then the prison shrinks were involved and he was transferred to the prison infirmary wing. His attorney have apparently requested parole hearings since then, but so far, the doctors at the prison have judged him mentally unfit for society at large." When Ian still said nothing, she was about to continue when he moved from the window and sat back down on the bed.

"Ye know, no' all men are the same." He looked into her eyes and brushed his hand gently down her cheek. "No all men hurt and humiliate women."

"I know that," her smile was small and it didn't reach her eyes. "it's just that since Adam, whenever I'd begin to get close to a man, the nightmares would begin again. Only instead of Adam's face, I'd see the face of the man I was becoming involved with, and he'd come at me the same way Adam did." She shivered at the memories of Adam and the nightmare still fresh in her mind. "After the dreams started, I couldn't continue the relationship, and I certainly couldn't tell them why. I mean what was I supposed to say, 'Sorry I can't see you anymore. I'm afraid you'll rape me down the road'? I mean, come on." She looked at Ian and became concerned. He looked awful. "Ian?"

He felt like his heart had been pulled out of his chest. *She had dreamed that I raped her, and that's why she was backin' away from me. Was that what she was dreaming aboot tonight?* He wondered. He looked at her and saw the concern. *She ha been honest with me,* he thought. *I at least owe her the same courtesy.*

"Is tha why ye had been backin' away from me before? Was tha what ye were dreamin' aboot tonight? Me, rapin' ye?" The words were like acid on his tongue, and he couldn't hide the hurt from her.

Madison guessed she really shouldn't be surprised by his question. She had just told him that she had nightmares about every man she had tried to date seriously since Adam.

"Ian, look at me." He raised his gaze to hers. "You are the first man, the first person, for that matter that I have ever told any of this. I've never had a nightmare about you, and I think that's the reason I was able to tell you." She reached for his hand and squeezed. "I was having a nightmare tonight, but you weren't the man. You... you asked me once why I didn't want Dean here. Well, I had a nightmare about him the night he tried to take our friendship to the next level."

"Was he who was here tonight?"

"Yeah, and I can't seem to shake it. There've never been so many before," She ran her hands over her face and up through her hair.

"usually, I have one and that's it. But this one keep repeating several times since that night, like it's on some kind of loop."

Ian stood and went to the bathroom and splashed water on his face. Madison threw back the covers, turned on the bedside table lamp and grabbed her pajama bottoms from the floor by the bed and pulled them on. She had no idea telling him her secret would be so easy or that finally being able to tell it would have such a therapeutic effect. She felt as though a huge weight had been lifted from her shoulders, but her concern was now for Ian. She still didn't know what he was thinking. She stood by the door to her room and watched as he dried his face and turned out the light to her bathroom.

He paused in the doorway to gaze at the remarkable woman across the room from him. He couldn't explain the gambit of feelings running through him, he wanted to kill the man who had caused her so much pain, but he was in jail. He wanted to hold her and protect her, but he knew she would not want pity. Mostly he wanted to vanquish her fears and prove to her that making love to someone you cared about could and *should* be beautiful. She had never known a true lover or felt the sensual closeness a man and a woman can reach while making love. She had trusted him with something she had never shared with anyone before, and he had no idea how to react to this new information. However, he knew he better do something and fast or she was likely to think her past had destroyed, for him, what seemed to be growing between them over the last couple of days. He moved closer to her, never taking his eyes from hers.

"Should I not have told you?" For once she wasn't trying to hide her face or lower her eyes from his gaze. He stopped in front of her and cupped her face in his hands. He bent down and softly brushed his lips over hers.

"Nay, luv. Ye should have told me, and I thank ye for doing so," he said against her lips and kissed her again. "I'm sorry for all ye went through. I wish ye had never learned the worst of some men. Why don't we go down to the kitchen and have some coffee or tea." He dropped his hands and went out the door when Madison's voice stopped him on the first step.

"Ian?"

He turned on the stairs, facing her. She placed her hands on top of his still bare shoulders and ran them up his neck. His skin was warm and soft. She pulled him closer to her and placed her lips on his. "Ian, kiss me." She pleaded. Ian leaned into her mouth and kissed her passionately, still holding onto the railing, he wrapped his free arm around her waist, pulling her toward him. He heard her moan as she ran her hands up into his hair. Her soft sensual touch set his blood a blaze with a hot burning craving to devour her. He wanted her so much his head was beginning to swim. His arousal became painfully hard, he knew if he didn't break this up they were going to go too far.

Ian reluctantly broke his mouth away from hers. "Maddy, I want ye so much I canna stand it, but if we don't stop this here and now," resting his forehead on hers he took a deep steadying breath. "I'm not sure I'll be able to control meself."

"I don't want this to stop. Please don't stop," she whispered, Madison never took her eyes off his while she spoke. "Please, make love to me."

"Are ye sure?" His voice was hoarse, and he didn't trust it not to break. "Because I can wait until ye're ready."

"No, I don't want to wait, I'm sure."

It was all Ian needed to hear, he captured her mouth with his and backed her up until he was off the stairs. Once on solid footing, Ian scooped her up, never breaking from the kiss and carried her to the master suite. He placed her feet on the floor, finally taking his mouth from hers. He cupped her face and looked into her eyes, the aqua color now a deep blue and what he could see heat, want, need and utter and complete trust. This was a woman who'd endured unimaginable traumas to the point where she'd been unable to allow herself to trust or become intimate with a man because of it. Now she was in his arms and asking him to make love to her. Ian felt humbled by her faith in him.

"Maddy, are ye sure you want to do this? I want ye to know ye can tell me to stop whenever ye need me to and I will." she smiled, wrapped her arms around his waist and put her head on his chest. Ian followed her lead and drew her into his embrace. He placed his chin on top of her head and breathed in the scent of her hair.

"I'm not going to lie, I *am* nervous. But I've never been so sure in my life. I want to be close to you." She looked up into his eyes. "I *want* to make love with you," she whispered, "and I can't imagine anyone I'd rather be here with than you." When Ian heard her sweet words, he closed his eyes, and his heart gave an enormous leap of joy. He leaned back away from her a little and with the use of his fingers he drew her spectacular aqua eyes to his. He pressed his lips to hers. She opened her mouth to his wondrously delicious kiss. Madison stood on her tiptoes and wrapped her arms around his neck and surrendered herself.

Ian backed her to the bed until she had to sit on the edge, while he knelt down before her. She finally allowed her eyes to greedily soak up the sight of his gorgeous body. She'd seen him before in his films wearing nothing but a towel, but that was nothing compared to the real thing. She ran her hand over his hair and wondered why he had it so short. *Must be for the film role he just finished,* she thought. Her gaze moved over his handsome face and burning emerald, green eyes, down to his bronze sculptured chest. Broad shoulders, muscular arms and chest made him look powerful and a little intimidating, but Madison knew better. Ian placed his hands on the back of her hips and pulled her forward until her thighs were on either side of his narrow waist and she was pressed up against him. Ian looked into her eyes and saw the trust and admiration reflected there. He asked her again if she was sure this was what she wanted and when she nodded her head, he gently slid his hands from her hips up under her shirt. When she jumped slightly, he froze.

"That tickles," she whispered. Madison leaned over to turn out the lights and Ian kidnapped her hand in his.

"I want to be able to see ye, luv. Please leave the lights on." His husky voice caressed the rough edges of her spirit.

"I have scars." Her voice was small, almost confessional. "I don't want you to see them." Ian raised up on his knees and kissed her forehead.

"I want to see all of ye, including yer scars." He lifted her arms over her head and pulled her T-shirt free from her body. *She's wondrous,* he thought. First he saw how beautiful she was, her full breasts, creamy skin was almost iridescent. Then he saw why she wanted to hide in the darkness. Her breasts particularly around the nipples were covered in scared-over bite marks, her flat belly was also marked by several scars. *Apparently the bastard used more on her than his fists,* Ian thought. He placed his hands on her smooth naked ivory breasts and using his fingers began to play with her nipples until they became erect. Ian slowly lowered his head gently pressed his lips to her breast before taking her nipple into his mouth.

Madison's breath froze in her lungs when Ian placed his mouth on her, remembering the pain when Adam had done the same thing, but the pain never came. Instead, she was filled with a pleasure she wasn't prepared for. The more Ian suckled, the more sensuality she experienced. He pressed her back and lowered her to the mattress. He heard her moan and dragged his mouth from her breast and brought his mouth back to hers. Ian gently moved them to the middle of the bed and being careful not to crush her, he positioned himself over her. She felt so natural under him. Her perfect breasts pressed against his chest, which made him want her more than he already did. Ian wanted to worship every part of her and savor every pleasure-filled moan she released. He moved his hot kisses from her mouth to her eyes and ears. Then he moved on to her neck finding a sensitive spot below her ear, down her throat until he stopped once more on her breasts where he lingered, then he trailed kisses to her stomach. Which she was not expecting, and she started to giggle until he placed his hands on the tops of her pajama bottoms and began to slowly pull them down while trailing hot kisses in their wake. Giggles forgotten as he found another noteworthy spot behind her knee. Cataloguing all the areas that give her pleasure Ian moved further up her legs until he was at her apex.

Madison eyes flew open when he place his mouth on her most sensitive area and began to explore. Not sure what she was supposed to do, she was about to object until her body over road her mind over and she began to feel.

"Oh...god," eyes closed head thrown back Madison was drowning in a new kind of pleasure. Her body had a mind of its own, arching off the mattress, hands clutching the sheets, while a feeling she'd never experienced started to curl her toes. She felt Ian's hand covered her breast while his tongue performed magic on her.

Ian watched her start to come undone, but he wanted her to fall over the edge she was holding on to. He gently moved his fingers slowly in and out of her. He felt her tightness and knew he would have to go slowly. The last thing he wanted to do was hurt her. He wanted to give her pleasure and let her know the beauty not the pain. Ian could feel her tense up even more, she was close, but holding herself at bay back.

"Don't hold back luv, let go." Finally, she cried and arched her back to match the rhythm of his fingers as her orgasm consumed her. It was his, her first and it was his, she was exquisite in the throws and all he wanted was to give her more. Ian quickly stripped off his boxers and kissed his way back up her body. He settled himself on top of her, hips resting between her her legs and kissed her deeply, exploring the aftershocks and pants from her spent orgasm. When her soft moan escaped her he positioned himself and slowly, exquisitely began to slide into her. He realized quickly in order to enter her completely she was going to have to experience some discomfort.

"Maddy, luv, I'm sorry, but this is going to hurt a little. I will try to make it swift." She nodded her head and Ian quickly thrust himself into her tight space. She winced in pain and Ian quickly lowered his mouth to cover hers. He was still for a moment to allow her body time to relax after the initial shock of his entrance. As he kissed her, he could feel wetness on her face. He leaned up and saw a single tear descending from her eye. Ian's heart broke, he hadn't wanted to hurt her, and he knew he had.

"I promise there will never be pain again, luv, trust me." She nodded and kissed him with trust and something she wasn't ready for yet, Ian could see the emotional coaster on her face and waited. When her hips rocked slightly couldn't wait any longer. He began to move his hips slowly and gingerly until she was used to it. He'd always buried his face in the neck area while in bed with a woman, but now he wanted to see everything that played across Madison's face, he wanted so much to please her, bring her joy, passion. Madison ran her hands up his arms and laced her finger around his neck. As he saw her features relax, he quickened his movements, she felt so good, like she was made for him. Madison arched her back and moaned in triumph. Her eyes flew open and looked up at Ian's.

"Do ye want me to stop?" Ian's voice cracked, *God please donna say yes,* he thought.

"No...don't stop!" she cried. "Ian," she whispered. She was glorious, eyes locked on his, skin glistening, "Ian." His name was like a talesman on her lips. She began to match the rhythm of his movements.

Ian lowered himself and kissed her sweet mouth. She broke away and cried out again. Finally, Ian felt her tighten around him, just before she exploded under him. His name on her lips in that moment was enough to have him follow her with his own. He collapsed on her for a moment to catch his breath, then rolled to his back so he wouldn't crush her. Both breathing heavily as Ian pulled her to him and wrapped his arms around her. Madison's head on his shoulder with her hand on his chest, she could feel the hammering of his heart, and realized it was matched hers.

"I'm sorry I hurt ye, luv. I promise it will never hurt again." His deep voice rumbled in his chest, drawing Madison's sleepily eyes to his.

"You couldn't hurt me Ian, and you made it perfect." She smiled wistfully. She closed her eyes, rested her head back on his shoulder. After a moment she spoke again. "I'm so blissfully relaxed." She sighed happily. Seconds later her eyes popped open, and she giggled. "And *hungry.*" She looked up at him, eyes bright. "Can we sleep for a while and then go and get something to eat?" Ian smiled as he leaned down and gently kissed her lips and told her that was fine. He re-covered them with the comforter and watched her sleep for a while, then turned out the light and transferred his attention to the window. The snow was beginning to lighten up. Madison curled closer to him and sighed as she slept. Suddenly a small voice came from her sleeping lips.

"Ian."

His heart warmed and a contented smile came to his face. He felt a sense of joy he had never known. He relaxed his body back into the pillows, closed his eyes, and slept.

Chapter Nine

The sound of a phone ringing roused both of them from their sleep. Since the house didn't have a landline phone they both knew it had to be one of the cell phones. Ian looked over at the clock on the side table.

"It's three o'clock in the morning, who would be callin' now?" he asked sleepily. "Is that yers or mine?"

"Maybe it's mine." Madison started to sit up and then fell back into the mattress and Ian's arms. "Oh, let it ring. I'm too tired to get up." She snuggled back into Ian's embrace and listened as the phone gave way to silence. Just as they were settling back to sleep, the phone sprang to live again, and this time Madison recognized the ring. *Symphony Fantastique* by *Berlioz*

"What the hell?" She sat straight up and took the chenille throw from the foot of the bed, wrapped it around her and sailed out of the room.

"Do ye want me to come with ye?" Ian asked.

"No, there's no reason we should *both* get annoyed." He listened as she went down the stairs and answered her phone.

"Hello."

"Hello, Madison? How are you, it's Dean."

"I know who you are. What do you want?"

"You don't sound particularly pleased to hear from me."

"Well, to be honest I'm not. Do you have any idea what time it is?"

"Yeah, it's ten o'clock."

"In New Jersey, it's ten o'clock, you moron! In Scotland it's three in the morning! And what the hell makes you think you can call me at ten o'clock at night. anyway?" *Can't this guy take a hint?* She was seething.

"I knew you would be lonely there with no one around, and I saw on the news you've had some bad weather and would be stuck for days. I thought I'd call and keep you company since you wouldn't have anyone with you, and besides, I thought you might be missing me by now."

Now she was really mad "Dean, do *not* call me again unless it's business related, and then, only during business hours. If I have any information for you I will call in. Otherwise, see you in six months!" She ended the call and wanted to slam the phone down on the desk, *but these damned phones are too expensive to break, and frankly Dean isn't worth the effort or the cost of a new phone.* She thought. Even so, she still used some force when putting the cell down on the desk where it had been charging. She wanted to scream with frustration at the gall of this infuriatingly moronic imbecile who was unfortunately her boss. God, she wished she could block off communication with him, but she knew it wasn't possible. "Damn it!" she muttered.

"Ye know ye shouldn't do that, ye could break the phone. And remember, there are no land lines in the house." Madison spun around to see Ian lounging against the newel post at the bottom of the stairs without a stitch on. She felt the warmth coming into her cheeks and knew she was blushing, he seemed so casual about his nudity. She reached for the Merino wool Mackay tartan draped over the back of the loveseat and tossed it to him with a smile. Ian took the blanket and arched his eyebrow at her as she walked to the kitchen.

"Wrap it around you. I don't want you to get, um... sick." Madison turned on the lights and looked at Ian out of the corner of her eye and saw he had indeed wrapped his torso in the tartan. It hung low on his hips. *Now that's a turn-on,* she smiled to herself, and gave him her full attention. She opened the fridge looking for something to eat when Ian's hands came around her waist and pulled her back against him. He felt so good with his body next to hers, making her never want to leave his side. Ian's hands started to roam upwards over her breasts and to her throat. He bent his head down and began a sweet seductive kisses on her neck that made her knees go weak. She turned in his arms and looked into his eyes. She could see from the deep emerald color, that he was in the mood for more, but as much as she wanted him too, she was just afraid she was still too tender yet to indulge him at this moment.

"Ian, I can't do anything right now I'm ..."

"I know, I just like touching and kissing ye." He murmured as he bent down and kissed her again. Madison wrapped her arms around his neck and deepened the kiss.

She said against his lips "I am beginning to have second thoughts about waiting."

Ian chuckled and gently ran his fingers down her cheek, "No luv, we should wait awhile, and beside I don't know bout ye, but I'm hungry."

They turned to the fridge and brought out the eggs, cheese, ham, onion and mushrooms for omelets. Ian sat on the stool at the end of the island and watched as Madison mixed up the eggs and cut up the ingredients. She looked like sex on a stick in the blanket toga she was wearing. He wanted to know what the phone call was about. He knew it was the man named Dean and he was jealous. *This is a new feeling,* he thought, *I've never been territorial.*

"So, who was on the phone?" Ian asked casually.

"Dean," she sighed. "I don't know why he won't just leave me alone. I told him before I left I wasn't interested and then again when I spoke to him after I arrived here, I told him the same thing. For some reason he won't take the hint." She handed him his plate and started to make her own.

Ian took a bite of his omelet and decided to keep the conversation going.

"Why was he calling so late?" *and can I throttle him for it?,* he wondered.

"Well it's only ten o'clock there." She said sarcastically and continued. " He called to keep me *company* since I would be alone. He wanted to comfort me because he knew I might be missing him by now. Auuggh! OOH! He is just the most infuriating man I have ever met in my life! What?" She looked up at Ian who was staring at her with amusement. He motioned toward her omelet that she had just transformed into scrambled eggs because of her agitated state.

"I see ye preferred to have highly over cooked scrambled eggs instead." She looked down at her pan and surveyed the mess she had made of the eggs and slumped her shoulders. Ian laughed and walked over to her. "Here luv, have my plate, and I'll make something for meself." He led her back to the stool and sat her down. He picked up the frying pan and realized she'd scorched the eggs badly enough he was going to have to throw the eggs away and soak the pan in hot soapy water.

After Ian pulled out a new frying pan he started to prepare an omelet for himself and continued the conversation.

"So he thought he would call ye because ye were going to be here all alone huh? When ye think about it, it's kinda funny." He said and Madison looked up from her plate.

"You're not angry?" she sounded so surprised

"Hell no, why the hell should I be angry? Ye're with me." He smiled and turned off the stove and slid the flat egg onto a plate and sat across from her. "Did ye think I was angry?"

"Well, I was concerned you might be. It doesn't matter, how's your egg?" Ian reached across the counter and took her chin between his thumb and forefinger and held her there for a moment while he looked into her eyes. She was the most sincere creature he had ever beheld. *God help me*, he thought, *for I am falling in love with ye.* He lowered his hand and looked down at his eggs, interestingly enough he was no longer hungry, but not wanting to waste the ingredients, he worked his way through the egg. Madison stood and went to the window that overlooked the front of the house. The snow was much lighter then it was when she and Ian went up for bed after the movie. She suddenly had a dreadful thought. *Will he leave as soon as he can and never come back?* She started to shiver, yet when Ian smoothed his arms around her and pulled her to his chest, the thought went instantly from her mind.

"How bout a fire, lass?" Madison relaxed back into his chest and leaned her head up to look at him. He was so handsome and for now at least he was hers and hers alone. For the first time since her graduation day when Poppy had given her the letter from her mother, she was truly happy and never wanted to lose the feeling.

"A fire, sir, sounds wonderful." Ian kissed her on her forehead and went to the stone opening to build the blaze. Madison sat in the corner of the sofa and drew her knees to her chest to watch him. She felt a pull at her hair and noticed Julie had jumped to the back of the sofa and wanted attention. Madison leaned her head back and she and the cat nuzzled heads before Madison picked her up and placed Julie in the small space between her belly and knees. This was one of Julie's favorite ways to cuddle. Madison couldn't see how; it looked awfully uncomfortable to her. Ian turned his attention to Madison after his fire was burning, she looked comfy and relaxed all curled up and Ian couldn't wait until he was sitting next to her. As he walked closer, he noticed she wasn't alone, Julie was sitting... well, actually he couldn't really make out where she was sitting or how. He sat on the sofa next to his lady and gave the small ball of white fur a pat on the head.

"How in the hell is that comfortable? She is completely smushed." Ian laughed.

Madison looked up from her furry friend and smiled.

"I have no idea, but whenever I sit like this, she curls up and falls asleep. It's kind of cute actually. You know if we are going to be up for a while, we should probably put on some sort of clothes, so we don't get sick."

Ian, dismissing the curled-up kitty, pulled Madison into his arms and embraced her tightly. He knew she was right, if they continued to wear nothing but blankets they would likely get sick. He considered returning with her to the bedroom and making love to her again, then he remembered she was still a bit tender, and he had just built a fire. *Damn it*, he thought. He told Madison to stay put and he disappeared upstairs. Madison took the time Ian was away to look out the window and realize the blizzard had turned into a light flurry with the moon trying to peek through the clouds. She scooted a disgruntled Julie off her lap, and walked to the window to look toward the cliff, and for the first time in two days, she was able to see the fence at the top of the cliff. Although the snow on the ground didn't look to be melting by any means, she knew that with the end of the blizzard, it wouldn't be long before snowplows would be in motion. She hoped that she and Ian would have a couple more days of private time together.

"What might ye be lookin' at?" came Ian's wonderfully smooth masculine Scottish brogue from the stairs. She turned and saw he had put on flannel pajama bottoms, but was still bare up top. Madison didn't mind that he wore no shirt, she liked looking at his beautiful body. Draped over his arm were a robe and nightgown, Madison didn't own anything like those and looked queerly at the nightgown and robe. Ian handed her the items and noticed the suspicious look in her eyes.

"It's a long story," Ian said, knowing she was wondering about the gown.

Madison took the floor-length cream-colored satin gown from his arm and ran her fingers over the delicate embroidery on the bodice. She noticed the gown had never been worn for the tag was still on it. She then took the robe made of the same satin material also still tagged. Even though her own tastes didn't run to such delicate things she had to admit these were beautiful. She looked up into his eyes and saw a twinge of what might have been sorrow. She raised her hand and touched his cheek.

"Ian, I would like very much to know."

"Ye might not want to wear them if I tell ye," he warned.

"I might not want to wear them anyway, but I would like to know why they would put that look in your eyes." He looked at her beautiful face and saw only tenderness and affection.

"Okay," he sighed. "Put those on so ye don't get sick and I will tell ye where they came from." Madison made a move to go around him when he stopped her. "Where are ye goin'?"

"I was going to go upstairs and put these on."

Ian crooked his head to one side. "Why? When ye can change down here?"

"Because I have privacy up there." Ian understood instantly and cupped her face in his hands and placed a tender kiss on her lips.

"Maddy luv, I love the way ye look, please don't be ashamed of yer body. Believe me when I say it's perfect, every single inch of it." He loosened the blanket and let it fall to the floor and puddle around her ankles. He took in the beauty of her soft ivory-colored body and gently ran his hands down the sides of her arms. He knew why she was ashamed. That bastard she was married to had beaten her so badly, her body was covered with vicious scars. Ian could feel hatred swelling for what that man had done to her. Because of what had happened to her in the past, she was left with not only the physical scars, but mental scars as well. Ian vowed if he had to, he would spend the rest of his life making her feel as beautiful as a queen and filling her life with all the love and tenderness a man and a woman could share. He bent and kissed her neck ever so softly and drew her into his embrace. Her silky, naked body and breasts pressed up against him and he felt such a need to protect her from the world. She wrapped her arms around his waist, which brought a smile to his face. He knew then that his heart belonged to this wonderful woman in his arms and hoped that soon her heart would his.

Ian raised his head and took a small step back from her. He took the gown from her arms, pulled off the tag and began to place it over her head. Madison put her arms up to help him with his sweet task, as he pulled the gown over her body, he ran his large warm hands down her long frame. Ian stood, looking at her; the gown seemed made for her form. The cream-colored satin gown was fitted in all the right places and flowed everywhere else. She looked absolutely gorgeous standing there with her long, thick, wavy chestnut hair falling over her shoulder and her aqua eyes brighter than ever.

"God, ye're beautiful," he whispered. He tore off the tag in the robe and slipped it over her shoulders. Once she was covered, Ian could relax his muscles. He wasn't sure if he would be able to wait long before he made love to her again. Although he knew he would have to. He took her hands in his and pressed his lips to her open palms. His touch was so soft Madison could feel her knees get weak and threaten to give way. Ian led her to the sofa and sat down next to her and gazed into the fire.

"Ian?"

"Um."

"Will you tell me about the house, why you built it and the gown?" She drew back from his arms and put her hand on top of his.

"Aye. Five years ago, I was engaged ta be married ta my school sweetheart Alexandra, and we were going ta make our home in Scotland. She was in nursing school, and I was just getting into films." He stopped to take a breath and got up and went to the kitchen. When he returned he had two glasses and a bottle of red wine. He popped the cork and handed her a full glass and poured one for himself. "We wanted ta have a house no one had ever lived in, so me father sold me the land ta build one. I had always enjoyed working with my hands and me father was an excellent carpenter. I took a year off from working and me father and I drew up the plans for the house, and with the help of me family, we worked night and day. Finally, after six months, it was finished. Since the wedding was only a month away I decided to give her the house as a wedding gift.

"Wait, you mean Alexandra didn't know you were building the house?" Madison asked in astonishment.

"No, I wanted it to be a surprise. So that weekend I called her at school and told her I had a surprise for her, and I wanted ta know if I could come and get her. She told me she was busy and couldn't, but after I begged, she finally consented. I was excited ta show her what I'd accomplished and the home where she and I were going ta live and fill with children. So I drove ta the school and picked her up and brought her here."

As Ian parked the car he jumped out and ran to the other side and helped the blindfolded Alexandra out of the vehicle. He led her up the stone walk to the front door. Once they were inside, he took the blindfold off his companion.

"Surprise!" he bellowed. He clasped his hands together and looked at his fiancée for a clue as to what she was thinking.

"What is this!" Her voice turned harsh and angry.

Ian was baffled by her reaction. "What do ye mean? It's the house we're going ta live in and fill with children."

Alexandra put her slim hands on her nonexistent hips and walked to the center of the living room and surveyed the house. Her expression nasty and disapproving. "I can see it's a house, you dumb olf. Were the hell did it come from?"

Ian couldn't understand what was happening, she'd never spoken to him like this, and he was unsure how to handle it.

"I built it for us, for ye as a wedding gift. Do ye no' like it?"

"*This* is what ye took a year off work ta do? Ta build this... this... SHACK!" She stomped her feet as she sailed out the front door and past him. Finally, he recovered himself and ran after her. He caught her by the wrist before she got to the car.

"Wait! I don't understand. Why are ye so angry? Ye said ye wanted to remain in Scotland and that ye wanted a house no one had ever lived in."

She yanked her wrist from his grasp and backed away.

"Take me back to school!" She stormed back to the car and waited by the door for him to open it. They drove back in silence. He couldn't understand what was happening. She was normally so sweet and considerate of his feelings, *maybe she'd had a hard day*, he thought. *Maybe she was just overtired from work.* These thoughts rattled through his mind all the way back to her school. Once he pulled the car to a halt in front of her dorm, she got out and slammed the door shut without even so much as a goodbye. He sat there in the car and watched as his fiancée canter into her dorm and slam the door behind her. He decided to give her a few hours to cool down and then he'd go to her dorm and find out what was really wrong.

After Ian had eaten dinner at the local pub, he drove back to Alexandra's dorm and parked the car. Because it was coed school, and he was known by attendant, he could walk in without any problems. He had been here several times over the last four years, so he knew his way around. He walked down the hall until he came to her door. Normally, he would have just walked in like he had done for four years, but given the way she reacted at the house, he decided to knock. He stood for a moment, and when there was no answer, he knocked again. Still no answer. He assumed she must have gone to a late class and decided to go in and wait for her. When Ian opened the door, he couldn't believe his eyes. There in bed were Alexandra and another guy. Ian didn't know what to do, so he entered the room and quietly shut the door.

"IAN! What are ye doing here!" she screamed and scrambled out from under her bed partner.

"I think I am the only one who is entitled to the screaming here Alex." Ian's voice was dangerously calm and low. "Who is this?" he asked, pointing to the young man trying to gather all his clothes and get dressed.

"Ian, calm down, let me explain," she begged.

"Oh, I think under the circumstances I'm very calm. So this is why ye didn't like the house. I was keeping ye from yer lover." Ian looked at the young man and moved away from the door so he could leave.

"Ye told me that you broke it off with him!" the nameless boy yelled as he ran from the room.

"So," Ian sighed as he shut the door and leaned against it. "Ye broke it off, huh? Funny, I don't remember ye telling me that. When was it? How long have we been *separated?*" he sneered.

Alexandra was still sitting on the bed holding a sheet to cover her naked body leaning against the wall looking at Ian with contempt. Her short blond hair was messed from the act she was engaged in when he arrived.

"Six months." Was all she would say.

"SIX MONTHS!" he shouted. "Ye have been shacking up with another man for six months! Damn ye, woman! Why didn't you just tell me ye wanted out? Why did ye have ta lie and make me think that we were going ta have a future?" He was enraged and hurt.

"I can't marry ye, I never could. Yer never around. Yer always on some movie set or out of the country. I need someone who is going to be here. Not a man who gallivants all over the world bedding every women he meets."

He'd never laid a hands on a woman in anger, but she was trying his patience, he clenched his fists together and placed them behind his back.

"I have never been unfaithful to ye, never." He couldn't say any more. He turned and left the room leaving the door open.

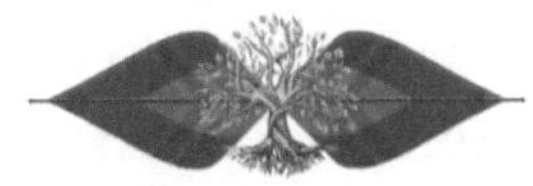

"And you never came back to the house?" Madison asked after a while.

"No, I never did. Not in any real capacity. I came here and there to maintain, but I never moved in. I've also no had a serious relationship since. Oh, I've had dates and some fun, but I've no had another partner. Come to think of it, until ye I hadn't made love to a woman in four years." Ian knew the difference to making love and some fun in the sheets.

Hoping to lighten the mood, Madison said, "Well I got you beat; 'til you it had been eleven years."

Ian knew she was trying to be funny.

"No, luv. Until me, ye were a virgin to making love, untouched to the pleasure." He reached his hand out and traced her jaw line with his fingers. She looked down at the gown.

"You bought this for her to wear on your wedding night. didn't you?" she asked quietly

"No, actually, ey mother did." Her gaze shot up and locked on his in shock.

"Your mother?" she breathed.

"Aye, she wanted grandbabies more than I wanted children and I guess she figured that would do the trick." Madison looked down at the gown and shot him a look that made him laugh. "Donna worry, that's not why I gave it to ye. I thought it was pretty and would look nice on ye. Course I had no idea how nice it would look."

"That's why you think the way you do about not having a woman in your life, because of how your relationship with Alexandra ended? Don't you think it's kinda unfair to judge all women because of what one did?"

Ian wanted to ask the same question to her about men, but he knew that would be unfair, for what he went through was nothing compared to her. He knew she was trying to understand him better. He didn't really want to answer the question because the truth was; that *was* why he had never entered a relationship and now he guessed it was kind of a childish reason.

"Aye, I supposed it was unfair, but I was hurt beyond repair, and then later I was working so much I really didn't have the time. I guess I decided I wouldn't allow my heart to be touched for fear of it being broken again. That is of course until I met the right woman." Ian looked at Madison as she brought her gaze from the fire back to his and he got butterflies in his stomach. When she still said nothing Ian took her in his arms and held her close. She looked up at him and smiled. Ian bent his head down and kissed her. As he was bringing his head back Madison ran her hand up his chest and around his neck, trapping him inches from her face. She raised up a bit and kissed him on his forehead, cheek, nose, chin, and then his mouth. Her kiss was warm and sensuous.

"Ian?" she whispered against his mouth.

"Aye?"

"Make love to me." She gasped as he took her mouth with his and kissed her with all the desire and heat burning through him for her. He wrapped his arm around her and placed his hand on the base of her back. With his hand on her back, he pulled her toward him while he laid them both down on the sofa. Even though the sofa was extremely deep, Ian still threw the back pillows off to give them all the more room.

He looked down at the beauty that was with him and saw only trust and a powerful need for him. Once again he wanted to make sure she was pleased and not hurt so he would go very slow. He lowered himself on top of her using his elbow as a brace so as not to crush her.

Madison looked into the eyes of the man over her and felt safe and warm. He was so caring, and could she dare say loving? She raised her hand to his face and traced his lips with her fingertips. He took her hand in his and kissed the tip of each finger before he kissed her. As she placed her hands on his sides, he jumped.

"Yer hands are cold, luv," he chuckled. As she drew her hands away, he told her she could put them back. "Even though they're cold, I love the feel of ye touching me." Ian brought his mouth back down on hers as she ran her hands from his side up his muscular back to his broad shoulders. His kisses began to trail down her neck, to her throat and on her chest above her breasts. Ian sat back on his hunches and placed his hands on the satin gown around her ankles and began to push the soft silky fabric upwards. Careful to caress every inch in her body as he did so. Once she was free of the gown, she raised up off her back and wrapped her arms around his neck for a long embrace. Ian buried his face in her neck and took long deep breaths of her scent. He gently removed her arms from around his neck enabling him to stand and take his flannel bottoms off.

When he was naked, Madison looked at his glorious form silhouetted before the fire and held out her hand to him, beckoning his return to her. He took her hand, but instead of coming to her, he pulled her to her feet and had her join him in front of the fire. Ian ran his hands through her soft silky hair and admired the way the fire played pleasingly on her body. He scooped her up into his arms and knelt down on the floor. Placing her gently on the rug and lowering himself onto her. Using his fingers he slowly brought her to peek, watching her come undone while the firelight played over her wanton features was the sexiest thing he'd beheld. When she came back down to earth, Ian withdrew his fingers and slowly entered her, causing her to catch her breath.

As they made love, the darkness outside gave way to dawn. For the first time in three days, the sun shone over the Highlands,. The warm light from the sun that seemed to be sent from the Gods to rid the Highlands of the hard times. It was as if the sunshine was symbolizing the dawning of a new day and a new life for all, washing away old wounds and sorrows.

Chapter Ten

For the next few days, Madison and Ian played together in the snow during the day, and when they became too cold, they would retreat inside to cuddle in front of the fire. Sometimes they talked, sometimes they laughed, and sometimes they just sat quietly together and enjoyed each other's presence. They shared the cooking. Madison made breakfast and Ian prepared dinner. Nights were spent making love and laying in each other arms. Neither Ian nor Madison could remember a time when they had been happier. After four days their glorious solitude ended when Ian looked out the kitchen window, and saw a plow truck slowly making its way up the drive. He had a sudden attack of sorrow because the "honeymoon" was now over, and he knew they would be returning to reality. He looked back to the breakfast dishes he was cleaning and heard Madison's shower shut off.

"What do ye think me chances would be of convincing her ta pretend we're still snowbound for a couple of lifetimes?" he asked Julie, who was perched on the counter watching him work. Dishes finished he headed for the stairs when he heard a cell phone come to life. He recognized the ring and knew it was his agent. He considered ignoring the call and then thought better of it. He backed off the bottom step and took his phone out of his coat pocket.

"Aye?"

"Ian Mackay, where the hell have you been?" an Englishwoman's voice screeched over the line. "I have been trying to ring you for almost a week."

Ian held the phone away from his ear; he was fond of the woman, however, her voice sounded something like a squirrel in pain and when she was angry, listening to her was nearly unbearable.

"Victoria, if ye would pay attention to the news ye would've noticed that we've had a blizzard here."

"Yes, I saw that you'd some snow, but that doesn't mean you should have shut off your cell phone. Where are you anyway?"

"I'm at the house on Skye and I turned off the phone so the battery wouldna die since I've no land line phone here."

"Skye?" she questioned. "I thought you never used that house? Oh well, the reason I rang was to let you know that Spielberg and Universal Pictures are doing a new film, and Steven wants you to play the lead. It's a love story and they've already signed Alexandra Daddario to play opposite you. What do you think about that?"

He was quiet and thought for a moment. This would be a real coup for his career, but he always hated it when Victoria would expect an answer from him about a part before he had even reviewed the script. Moreover, for the first time, he realized, he had no burning interest in doing a film now. He knew if he took the role, he would be required to leave Scotland, which meant leaving Madison and *that* was something he had no desire to do.

The ensuing silence wasn't the response Victoria Townsend had anticipated. "Ian, did you hear what I said?"

"Aye. I heard ye."

"What's the matter with you? Don't tell me you're thinking it over." She chuckled. "You're to be in LA on the first of the month. I can overnight the contracts to you along with the script, but you don't have a lot of time. By the by, this film takes place in the United States. You're brogue is becoming a bit pronounced." Her voice was becoming impatient. "You have never taken this long to answer me before. You're not ill are you?"

Ian winced at the criticism.

"No, I'm not ill and nothing's wrong. You know, Victoria, I've been working nonstop and taken every film that has crossed my path. I've done eight films in four years. I think I could use a wee break. So why don't you tell Mr. Spielberg 'thank you but no' and he can give the script to someone else."

"WHAT!" she screamed. "Are you daft? This is Steven Spielberg we're talking about, and no I won't tell him you turned him down. That would be utter insanity. No! Look, I know you're tired, and of course you could use some time off, but now is not the time. If you are ever going to break into the American audience this is the film that will do it for you. You can*not* let this one go. You just can't. And *I* can't allow you to pass on this one."

Ian knew she was right. This is what he had been working toward. Being accepted by the American audience was important to his career, but he just couldn't bring himself to be taken away from Madison for three months or more. "I'm sorry, Victoria, but I just—" He felt Madison's hand on his elbow and turned to look at her. "Let me call you back, Victoria." And without another word to his manager, he ended the call and gave Madison his full attention.

"Victoria is your manager and she has a film for you?" Her voice was soft and had a calming effect. He could smell her bath soap and shampoo. She smelled like wildflowers and Ian wanted to gather her in his arms and breathe in her scent.

"Yes, Spielberg wants me for the romantic lead with Alexandra Daddario, but I told her no."

"A love story," Madison breathed; then her eyes widened to the size of dinner plates. "You what? But why?" She couldn't believe it.

"Because I would much rather be here with you. I told her I needed a bit of a break." He turned toward his jacket pocket and was about to put the phone back when Madison blocked his path.

"You can't turn this down, Ian. You really can't. Do you realize that of all the movies you have been in, not one has been a love story? And besides, Steven Spielberg! Ian, you can't let this one go by. Ian, do the film."

"But what about you?"

"What about me? I have my own work to do. I have a board of directors to answer to. Once I start setting up appointments, I'll be seeing doctors and hospitals. That will keep me pretty busy. If I am what's stopping you from taking the project, please don't let that happen. I assume you'll have to be away for the filming?" Ian nodded. "Well," she continued, "believe me when I say I don't want you to go away, but it's your job and I respect that. I'll be here when you get back. I promise." She smiled and raised up on her tiptoes and kissed him quickly on the lips. "Now, call her back and tell her you'll take the film."

"I haven't even seen a script yet," he protested meekly.

"Don't worry." She smiled. "No matter what it is, it will be great because you'll be in it." Ian bent down and pressed his lips to hers, lingering there for a time. Her confidence and unconditional faith in his ability made his heart swell with pride. When he broke away Ian noticed a slight blue tinge under her eyes. *She looks tired,* he thought. *I guess she should be.* He had kept her up most nights with their bedroom acrobatics. She stepped away and went to the kitchen while he called Victoria to give her the okay on the film and get all the information he would need to prepare.

Afterward, he told Madison that he had two months to get his lines memorized and put on some muscle mass.

"I haven't noticed there's any need for improvement." She grinned.

Ian chuckled. "Thank you, my lady. That's my decision. The character is a construction worker who spends a lot of time without a shirt on and I want to put on some mass, that's all. At least while I'm gone, you'll get a little more rest." He chuckled and Madison raised her eyebrow at him and then laughed.

"How long will you be... what's it called... on location?" she asked as she picked up Julie, sat on the arm of the love seat and smiled up at him as he put the cell back in his coat pocket.

"Three months," he said regrettably as he leaned against the closest door frame and crossed his arms over his broad chest.

"Three months!" she gasped, but recovered quickly. "Three months isn't so bad." She squeaked unconvincingly. "It will go by fast. I have so much work to do and you'll be so busy that you won't have time to even think of me." She looked down at the purring white fluff resting comfortably in her arms.

"Yes," Ian said. "It could even be longer depending on how scheduling goes. You never know when you start. Sometimes all goes without a hitch and then other times, there are small delays, or nothing seems to go as it should and the time drags on. You just never know. In the past, I've used lulls on one project to fly out and work on another." Ian walked to the love seat and reached out to rub the cat Madison held. She looked up at Ian's face as he spoke of the possibility of pitfalls in his work.

"What happened?" she queried.

"Oh, I don't remember exactly. It had something to do with weather or costuming or—"

"No, I don't mean that. What happened to your accent?" His speech pattern had almost become perfect Hyde Park London.

"Oh," Ian said, grimacing. "I'm sorry, my brogue becomes a 'bit pronounced' when I spend much time at home. I'm working on it, but I'm afraid it's too easy to backslide when I'm here. Have to keep on top of that."

"Don't," Madison said. Ian looked rather confused by the emotion in her voice. "Please don't let them do that to you." This was an issue Madison felt strongly about ever since she was old enough to notice individual actors. "They did the same thing to Pierce Brosnan and Rod Taylor and Gabriel Byrne. They weren't quite as successful with

Connery, but I think that had more to do with his own stubborn streak than anything else," she muttered. "But for God's sake, don't let them do it to you."

"Madison, I'm sorry, but I have no idea what you're talking about." Ian sank down onto the love seat and looked up at her.

"Your brogue. Don't let them train that out of you. It's charming! Hell, it's sexy!" She sounded so serious, Ian began to laugh. He reached for her and pulled her from the arm of the love seat to the cushion next to him.

"I mean it," she said. "I don't know why the powers that be always want to make actors all sound alike. They take a guy or woman for that matter, and train away their natural accent. I'm not sure why, but by the time *the moguls* are through, these people who all spoke differently and with individuality, all sound alike and as though they all came from the same little closeted hoity-toity neighborhood in London!" She looked up at Ian and he was grinning at her like she was an errant child.

"Well, it's true." She laughed. "Take a survey of one hundred American moviegoing women. Ninety-nine percent of them will tell you they would much rather hear Pierce Brosnan speak with an Irish lilt than to listen to him be James Bond in every film."

"And what about Connery?" Ian began to nuzzle her neck and Madison started to giggle.

"I'm trying to make a point here." She struggled to keep her mind focused.

"Mmm, aye, but ye're a real turn-on when you get causey." His lips traveled from her neck, up her throat to her mouth until he captured her lips with his. She gave in and became quite interested in this newest cause when there was a knock at the door. They both moaned at the interruption. Ian lifted his head and drank in the intensity of Madison's eyes, then reluctantly dragged himself from the love seat and went to the door.

With one last look back at Madison resting against the cushions, Ian opened the door. Standing in the doorway was a well-dressed man in his early forties holding a suitcase.

"Can I help ye?" asked Ian.

"Yes, you can start by taking my bags to the guest room. Is the lady of the house home?" The unnamed man shoved his bags at Ian and stepped over the threshold.

"DEAN!" Thunderstruck, Madison sat upright on the love seat to see Dean Michaels standing just inside the doorway. And a rather annoyed Ian holding a suitcase. Madison stood as Dean briskly strode across the expanse of the room toward her. When he reached her, he put his arms about her waist and lifted her off the floor. Ian dropped the suitcase and it landed with a loud thud by the open door. Thankfully for Dean, Madison recovered first.

"Dean, put me down!" she ordered and shoved away from him. "What are you doing here!"

"Well," he laughed, "I said I would come here and visit you on my vacation, didn't I?" Dean took off his coat and scarf and tossed them to Ian. "Here put those away, would you?"

"And I distinctly remember telling you *NOT* to come here. I've already made my feelings *very* clear on this issue." She walked over to Ian took Dean's coat, grasped the handle of the suitcase from where it had landed on the floor and brought them back to Dean. "Our relationship is professional only, Dean. I haven't asked you to come here. And I feel I should tell you, I resent your intrusion into my personal life. Please leave."

Dean took the items from Madison and put them down and looked back at her. "Shh, please, baby, let's not argue in front of the help." He turned his attention back to Ian. "Thank you, you may leave us now."

"I think the lady asked ye to leave." Ian ground out through his teeth. Fists clenched and blood boiling he manages to keep his voice low, but even to Madison's ears, there was a barely contained threatening tone.

"Ian, this, as you've probably already guessed, is Dean Michaels, the CEO of my company. Dean, this is Ian Mackay, and he is not a servant. He owns the house!" Dean looked at the man standing by the door and finally noticed he was wear sleep pants and t-shirt, then slid his eyes back to Madison and looked her up and down. His eyes widened then shifted to searing glares it finally registered she too, was sporting her pajamas.

"What the hell has been going on here!" His attitude changed from happy visitor to suspicious lover, as he screamed at her. "Have you been shacking up with someone behind my back?!" That was Ian's cue. In two strides he had stepped between Madison and Dean.

"Either ye walk out of here on yer own two feet, or I escort ye out." The look he shot Dean was filled with such animosity and loathing, but Ian was impressed with his own self-restraint, when what he wanted to do was plant his fist squarely in the middle of Dean's face.

"I beg your pardon? What right have you to interfere with a man and his lady?" The bravado of alpha male was rather counterproductive due to how intimidated by Ian he was. As Ian straightened his stance projecting, "Come any closer and you'll be sorry" air, Dean began to back away. They were both the same height, but Ian was more powerfully built, which made him seem more intimidating without moving a single muscle. Madison had seen actors portray this in movies. Hell, she had seen Ian do this in his films, but to see it in person, it was spectacularly sexy as hell.

"I have every right to interfere. First, the lady is in my house, and therefore, my responsibility." By now Ian was slowly on the move. With every forward step Ian took, Dean moved backwards. "Second, she asked ye ta leave, and ye haven't, and in Scotland that means yer'er trespassin'." Madison watched as Ian was, for lack of a better word, herded Dean around the room to the front door. "Third, and most importantly, the lady yer'er referrin' ta is *my* lady and I haven't done this much explaining in years. Don't push me, *Mister* Michaels." Dean found he was backed up to the door with retreat no longer an option he flicked his eyes to Madison as if to ask if she approved of the lout's behavior toward her guest. She was once again seated on the arm of the love seat beaming with pride before she stood, picked up Dean's things, walked to the door, and placed the suitcase at his feet and draped his coat over the expensive piece of leather luggage.

Normally Madison might have been more sensitive to his feelings and used slightly more tact in a situation of this type, but Ian had more than defended her and she felt it was her responsibility to back his actions with her own. *Besides, Dean is being a presumptuous ass,* she thought to herself.

"Dean, I am only going to say this one more time. I don't now nor have I ever wanted your affections. I made a huge mistake allowing you to kiss me in my office that day. It will never happen again. You're my boss, and I respect your position, but I, too, am an officer in the company and you are not affording *me* the respect that I deserve. This," she added, waving her arm to indicate their surroundings, "this behavior, *your* behavior is harassment, whether you realize it or not, and I have a witness. I will contact you when I have some information concerning our business interests here. Otherwise, I have no reason to talk to you at all. Don't call me outside of business hours and *never* come here again." Ian reached behind Dean, and opened the door. Dean glared at the tall man with his arm affectionately around Madison.

"Madison," Dean's highbrow, elitist air made even less appealing as he spoke. "I'm confident that you'll soon reconsider your rash decision and want me to return here.

"You daft, prick." Ian muttered.

"So," Dean said, glaring at Ian, before turning his attention back to Madison, "I will bide my time until you have this *gutter rat* out of your system. I'm a little surprised, mind you, that you would give yourself away so cheaply. After all, why would you prefer hamburger to prime rib." He smirked at yourself up before returning to me."

Dean didn't have a prayer; the next thing he knew a large fist crashed into his nose. Ian hit him with such force that Dean fell out the door, landing squarely on his ass on the front porch floorboards bleeding profusely. As Ian turned to pick up the bag and coat he noticed that Madison's hand was covering her mouth and her eyes were as wide open as they could get. Ian tossed the bag and coat out the door beside the injured man.

"If you ever come around here or bother Madison in any way other than what's required for business purposes," Ian smiled satisfactorily. "I'm afraid I'll surely kick ye're ass from here to Inverness." Ian watched as a white towel was thrown out to the bleeding man. He looked back at Madison.

"We can't have him bleeding all over the lovely snowy porch, can we?" She shrugged her shoulders and turned her attention back to Dean as he stood.

"I will have you arrested for this. I don't care what country we're in; this was assault!" Dean had the towel under his bleeding nose while making his threat.

"Ye're welcome ta call the police," Ian smiled, "if ye can find one I'm not related ta. I doubt ye'd get much sympathy. We donna talk ta our lasses like that in Scotland." He shut the door and turned back to Madison. "Ye kissed that guy, did ya?" he asked laughingly. Madison wrapped her arms around his waist, and they stood lingering in their embrace.

"Call it a momentary lapse of reason," she said finally "He caught me completely off guard. It was at the end of the workday, I was in my office gathering files and some paperwork to take home with me. He came in unexpectedly, and I'd just fixed myself a drink and when he showed up, I offered him one. I don't know if he assumed I wanted to get cozy or what he thought, but the kiss was really different. We've hugged or shared a peck on the cheek, more the friendly gesture, not what he seemed to be interested in that night in my office. Frankly, I didn't know how to react. He kissed me and I shouldn't have allowed it, but I was more stunned than anything else. When I could gain control of the situation, I managed to put a stop to what I fully believe he intended, but now he won't leave me alone." She rose up on her toes and laid her lips on his. "Thank you for what you did."

"I'm only sorry I didna act sooner. I should've kicked him out as soon as I found out who he was." Ian walked to the kitchen. "Change of subject, did ye notice the plow was here?" He turned to see Madison staring out the window overlooking the front yard. "What's wrong?" He walked to her and saw her reason for discomfort. Dean was leaning up against one of the roof supports on the porch. Ian felt the heat of anger and went to open the front door.

"Hey! I've already broken yer nose, man. What exactly do I have ta break next ta get rid of ya. The lady wants ye to leave, and so do I!" he bellowed.

Dean casually turned to face the extremely irate Ian. "Yes, you did, but as you can plainly see I have no car and my cell phone for some reason won't work." He smiled smugly.

Ian heard Madison's voice from inside "He's right, mine won't either. Ian try yours." Ian dug his phone out of his coat pocket and turned it on. He waited but a signal never came.

"I don't understand it," Ian said. "I was just on the phone with Victoria not more than an hour ago."

"Victoria? You're shacked up with my girlfriend while schmoozing on the phone with another woman. Madison, you do realize you can do much better, with me." Madison spun around and saw Dean was now standing in the doorway leaning against the doorjamb, much like he was in her office.

"I am not your girlfriend, and I never will be your girlfriend. Besides, Victoria is his agent." She walked over to Ian's side. "What are we going to do? He *can't* stay here."

"If ye don't have a car, how did ye get here?" Ian asked suspiciously.

"Limo. I saw no reason to ask the driver to wait, since I knew I would be staying with Maddy." Dean reached out to touch her face when Ian locked his hand around Dean's wrist with an iron grip.

"If ye try ta touch her again, so help me God, I will beat the bloody hell out of ye." He warned and looked down at Madison. "I'll get dressed and drive him to town. He can hire a car or get on a bus, or," he directed a smile toward Dean "ski back to Inverness."

Madison scooped up Julie as she tried to run out the open door. "Shut the door, you fool, you almost let my cat out in the snow."

Ian reached out with one hand and slammed the door, ignoring the fact that Dean was still standing in the doorway. He looked back at a smiling Madison.

Chapter Eleven

"Oh, Ian," she laughed, "I meant Dean." She reopened the door, the force of which hitting Dean in the face nearly knocked him unconscious. He was holding the bloody towel to his already damaged nose with one hand and had braced himself against the side of the building with the other. He didn't appear to be too steady on his feet from the second blow. The unpleasant scene was rapidly becoming a disaster. "Come in here and shut the door." She went to the kitchen, filled a plastic bag with ice and wrapped it in a towel for Dean's nose that was now swollen to twice its normal size.

"He can't stay here." Ian met her as she walked back to the living room. "He's likely ta be all over you once I leave the room to dress."

Madison looked toward Dean, who was seated on the sofa. Julie was sitting on the floor at his feet. As he bent down to pet her, the cat let out a vicious growl. Dean ignored the warning and reached out to pet Julie's head. In one swift movement, Julie sank her needle teeth into Dean's hand while her claws raked across his exposed wrist. Dean groaned and jerked his hand back to safety. Julie then leaped to the arm of the sofa, and perched there, never taking her glaring eyes from the man she had just attacked. Ian was the first to react with choked laughter. Madison looked up at Ian. "I think I'll be fine." She smiled. "She seems to have taken on the role of bodyguard easily enough." Ian planted a kiss on the top of Madison's head and headed toward the stairs.

"Aye, she seems to be a verra goood judge of character." He chuckled.

"Might I have a towel for this?" Dean asked looking down at his bleeding hand.

"Sorry, but ye already have a towel for your nose." Ian yelled from the top of the stairs. "Only one to a customer."

Madison handed Dean the ice pack on her way up the stairs. She found Ian in the master suite they had been sharing. Ian took off his flannel bottoms and slipped on his jeans. He was sitting on the edge of the bed putting on his socks when Madison came into view. He looked up as she walked into the bedroom and knelt down at his feet.

"I am so sorry about all of this," she said. Ian looked into her worried eyes, he gently ran his fingertips down her face, and drew her in for a small kiss.

"This isna something ye could've foreseen, luv. It's no' yer fault. I have to admit, though. If I dinna get him out of here soon, I'll likely bloody the walls with him. I think ye should be verra careful. He seems to be obsessed with ye." He stood and went to the closet and pulled on a sweatshirt, which brought a smile to her face. "What?" he asked

"That's my sweatshirt, Ian." He looked down and laughed, even though it fit him, the picture of Winnie the Pooh and Eeyore across his broad chest wasn't very masculine. "Do ye think I won't be able to intimidate Mr. Michael's in this, then?"

Madison sat on the edge of the bed. "You couldn't intimidate my cat with that thing on." Ian striped off the shirt and found one of his sweaters and pulled it on. He turned his attention back to Madison and walked to her. He placed his hands on her shoulders and looked deep into her eyes.

"I meant what I said. Please be careful. I dinna think I could handle it if anything happened to ye, luv." He pulled her from the edge of the bed and into his embrace and held her close. "I dinna think ye realize that ye hold my heart in yer hands." She looked up at him in surprise. "Aye, luv, ye do, and do ye want to know something else?"

"What?" she whispered

"I've fallen in love with ye." Her eyes became bright with tears. Ian's heart melted as single teardrops fell to her cheeks.

"You have?" she asked in a very small voice.

"Aye, luv, I have." He wiped the tears from her eyes and bent to kiss her lips.

"Oh, Ian—" He stopped her by placing his fingertips on her lips.

"Shh, don't say anything now, ye'll tell me of yer feelings when ye've sorted them in yer mind. There's no rush. We have a lifetime." He bent to kiss her again when they heard a male voice scream out in pain. "Bloody hell!" Ian bellowed and they ran from the room and down the stairs. They both stopped short as they reached the bottom step to take in the scene in the room. Dean had flattened himself against the wall in a corner with Julie standing guard in front of him. Her back was arched, her ears were flat against her head and her tail was a puffed mass pointed toward the ceiling. Even Madison had never heard such evil noises come from her fluffy friend's throat before.

"Where the hell did you find an attack cat!" Dean yelled at Madison as she bent to pick up the agitated kitty. Ian once again stepped between Dean and Madison.

"Ye're trying my patience, raise yer voice to her again and I will break more than yer nose." He warned. Ian put on his coat and gloves. "Here." he thrust the snow shovel at Dean. "Ye can dig out the car while I warm it up." Ian smiled and added, "It hasn't moved in almost a week." He opened the door and followed Dean out before winking at Madison.

Madison walked to the window to watch as Dean shoveled out the Wagoneer and Ian climbed in to start it. Unfortunately, for Dean the snowplow had done its job well. The access drive was clear, but the snow had been pushed from the drive to the back and sides of the SUV. Madison couldn't help but laugh as she watched Ian sitting in the warm cab of his vehicle while Dean struggled with the heavy wet snow trying to unbury it.

"Serves you right," she muttered. She glanced down at her fierce protector who was now purring and content. "You are a good girl, Julie." Julie meowed her agreement.

After what seemed like an hour, Dean still wasn't done and an annoyed Ian hopped out of the cab and took a shovel from the back and began to help. Within a matter of minutes, the snow was cleared away and Ian and Dean were on their way to the house. Madison opened the door and Ian walked in and kissed her as he moved passed which brought a glare from Dean. Ian picked up Dean's suitcase and tossed it to him, then turned to Madison.

"I'll be back as soon as I can." She placed her hand on his cheek.

"Please be careful. I couldn't bear it if anything happen to you." Ian's heart swelled with warmth and joy as he bent and kissed her. She wrapped her arms around his neck and deepened the kiss, Ian laced his arms around her waist and lifted her off the floor. As Dean watched the display of obviously sincere affection, he saw red seething with anger. *Why is she making a spectacle of herself?* he wondered. *I'll have to remind her not to embarrass me like this again.*

Finally, Ian placed her feet back on solid ground and backed away from her. *God I wish I could take ye upstairs,* he thought. He turned his attention back to the man behind him and smiled as he extended his arm toward the open door.

"After you."

Dean glared at Ian and walked through the door without a word. Ian followed and closed the door securely behind him. Madison watched from kitchen the window as they drove away. She went upstairs, gathered up all the clothes she could to make a load of wash and took them to the washer. After she was finished, she took her cell phone and tried to call Margaret, still no signal. *Damn,* she thought.

Madison went to the large fireplace and started a fire. Once the snow had stopped falling, Ian said they could make more use of the wood. He'd taught her how to safely build a fire so when he wasn't around she'd be able to enjoy a friendly blaze without burning the house down with her in it. Once the logs were flickering, she took her laptop and sat on the floor, to begin to make outlines of how she wanted to market the hospitals and doctors in the area. She couldn't use her cell, but thankfully she was able to pop online and find some places to start. Hours later the stiffening in her muscles told her it was time to take a break, She leaned back and stretched to work out the kinks, then decided a hot shower might be just the thing. Shower finished, Madison dressed in jeans and one of Ian's sweaters, with his scent lingering in the fabric wrapped around her like a warm cocoon. She slid her feet into her slippers and went down to the washer and put the clothes in the dryer. As Madison closed the door to the basement, she looked at the clock.

"Three o'clock… they've been gone for so long," she glanced out the window. "The roads must still be bad. Come on, Julie, let's make some lunch." She looked down at the kitty and walked to the kitchen. Julie jumped on the counter and watched as Madison made two egg sandwiches. From the pantry she took a can of tuna, scooped it out onto a plate, and set it on the counter for Julie.

"That's for being such a loyal friend and capable bodyguard," she told the kitty as Julie began to devour the smelly mess, while Madison sat on the stool and ate her sandwiches. After the two were finished, Madison did the dishes and went back to her laptop to continue working.

She didn't look at the clock again until it was dark, and she had to turn on a light so she could see her screen without squinting. It was almost seven o'clock, *Where is he?* she thought. Madison started to really worry and began pacing, she flipped open her cell phone, but, still no signal. Outside snow was beginning to fall again, and she knew it would make driving more difficult. She heard the dryer's buzzer and wondered how long that had been buzzing.

"Come on, Julie. Maybe folding the clothes will help take my mind off Ian not being home yet," she said. Julie headed toward the cellar door meowing. "Yeah," sighing, "I don't think so either." Madison retrieved the laundry and took it up to the bedroom. Julie followed in her wake, and when the basket was set on the bed, Julie hopped into the collection of warm clothes. Madison watched as Julie made herself a cozy nest among the warm clothing and laughed.

"Come on, you silly goose. Get out of there I have to fold them and put them away." As she picked up the purring ball of fur, it squeaked in disapproval. Madison didn't pay her any mind and began to fold and hang the clothes. When she was finished, she looked at the clock again and saw that it was past seven thirty and still no Ian. *God I feel so helpless*, she thought. *I can't even go out and look for him because I don't have a car.*

"Oh God what if something has happened to him, Julie?" she asked her purring friend. "God please," she prayed, "please keep him safe and bring him home." She left the room and started toward the stairs with purpose. *To do what?* she thought. She dropped to the first step and sat there trying to decide her next move.

The longer Madison sat, the more she worried, and the more frantic she became. She looked at her watch. Eight o'clock. Ian had been gone nine hours. Madison wasn't familiar with the roads, she'd slept most of the way from the airport when she arrived. She really had no idea how long it might take to get from one place to another, but she was fairly certain it didn't take nine hours to get to Lusta and back. Something must've happened, she knew it. She dreamed up the worst possible scenarios, Ian lying bleeding in a snowdrift somewhere was top of the list and she could feel the panic rising. Madison had her head buried in her hands, rocking to keep the panic at bay when the door opened. She looked up and saw Ian standing in the doorway.

"Ian!" She bolted down the stairs and raced into his outstretched arms. "Oh God, I thought something had happened to you!"

"Shh," he soothed, "it's okay; I'm here now, and I'm fine. I tried to call all day, but I could never get a signal. I'm sorry I worried ye." He lifted her chin with his forefinger and saw she'd been terrified something had happened. Her face was streaked with tears.

When Madison looked up at his face, she sucked in her breath. "Ian, what happened?" The cut over his right eye look angry and swollen. "I knew it! You had an accident!" He took her hands in his and brought them to his lips.

"Don't worry about that, it was no an accident, now," he said. "I'm bloody great, luv! And Mr. Michaels is on a plane back to the States never to return." He pulled her to him again and held her for a long time before he let go.

He lowered his arm to her waist, and as they walked to the kitchen together, Ian noticed she was wearing his sweater. He didn't mind, *in fact it kind of looks sexy on her,* he thought. He opened the fridge and took out a bottle of wine, popped the cork and poured them each a glass and met Madison's gaze.

"Ian," she said softly, "please tell me what happened. And what do you mean Dean is on a plane headed back to the States. I thought you just took him to town so he could hire a car." She took the wine that he offered and followed him upstairs to the bedroom and the bathroom beyond. As he started the water running in the tub, Madison put down her glass and went to him.

"Stop, stop," she said softly. She placed her hands on either side of his face and looked into his eyes. Something different was there, but she couldn't figure out what. "Oh, Ian, what happened?" He pulled her to him and buried his face in the nape of her neck.

"I love ye Maddy." He seized her lips with an ache with need and desire, when he broke from her, his eyes were a deep emerald green. The water in the tub was nearing the top, so Madison leaned over and turned off the faucet, then helped Ian pull off his sweater. Rather than ask again, Madison watched as he unbuttoned his jeans and stepped into the tub. He eased himself down into the hot, soothing water, stretched out, and closed his eyes. Madison sat on the edge of the tub and looked at the cut over Ian's eye and the bruising on his ribs. *Dean did this to him,* she thought. *I'd like to take a club to his head. Better yet to hit Dean Michaels where it hurts, the money. Maybe I can have him fired?* she thought, then promptly dismissed the idea.

"Maddy, luv?" came Ian's sleepy voice.

"Hmmm?"

"Will ye come in here wi me?"

"Wouldn't you rather sit in the warm water and relax your muscles?"

"I can relax better if ye're next to me." He opened his eyes and gazed into hers. "Please."

Madison stood and took off her clothes. Since they had become lovers Madison was becoming more comfortable with her body, she stepped into the tub and Ian sat up and placed his hands on her thighs. While his hands guiding her, Madison lowered herself into the water straddling his legs just above his sensitive area. Ian wrapped his arms around her and began a trail of seductive kisses down her neck, to her collarbone, coming to rest on her breast. As Ian suckled, Madison let her head lean backward and closed her eyes. She marveled at these wondrous pleasures Ian had introduced into her life. When she realized what he was planning to do, Madison spoke and drew Ian's gaze to her.

"Ian, are you sure you should do this? Shouldn't you be relaxing your body?" Her eyes were dark blue, she wanted more than anything to make love to him, but was concerned about his bruising and sore muscles.

"Aye, luv, I'm sure." She looked down at the gash above his eye, "I'll tell ye bout that, but now all I want is to lose meself in ye, I want ta lose meself in the woman I love." She lowered her lips to his as Ian cupped her face with his hands and deepened the kiss. Madison knew that Ian had always made sure that she was given an immense amount of pleasure when they made love, but this time she wanted him to feel the way she had the first time they had made love to each other. She brought her lips to the gash over his eye and spread her own trail of kisses along the side of his face and down to his chin. She was sure Dean was responsible for this damage to Ian's handsome face, and she felt, too, she was inadvertently responsible for Dean showing up in the first place. She trailed her hands down his chest, over his belly until she found him. As he fingers explored him, Ian closed his eyes and moaned as she worked him over.

When she was ready, she raised up on her knees. So in tune with her, Ian placed his hands on her hips and guided her gingerly until he sheathed inside her. It was a new position for her and wasn't sure what of the mechanics, but Ian's guidance, it wasn't long before Madison began to rock her hips back and forth and up and down. Ian adjusted his position and took her breast in his mouth. Madison threw her head back and let out a cry of ecstasy. Ian brought her mouth to his. As she became more accustomed to the position and the rhythm, reveling in the knowledge that she knew she was giving him pleasure. She marveled at her own ability to please him. Finally she understood why Ian loved to watch her come undone, there was a thrill in her as she watched Ian, the way his hands flexed on her hips, he head leaning on the back of the tub. His own moans escaping his lips, and knowing she alone had given him that pleasure. For the first time, he was unable to contain himself and released a bellowing cry as his orgasm consumed him. Ian wrapped his arms around Madison and placed his head on her chest. With him still inside her Ian took her breast in his mouth, placed his hands back on her hips and began to move them again. Madison ran her hands up his arms to the back of his head. Both moaned in gratification as they reached their peek together. Madison slowly slid off of him and lay in the warm water snuggled next to him. Ian rolled over and kissed her deeply as his hands trailed down her stomach. Before he reached his destination Madison caught his hand.

"Ian I can't go again, I'll drown if I don't get my breath. Give me a minute," she said and giggled.

"I can't help it, ye just look so good and I can't seem to keep my hands off ye." He kissed her again, running his hands down her side.

"Ian," she said against his lips, "I'm hungry and unless I'm mistaken you haven't eaten since this morning."

"Womon! Do ye always think of food at the most inopportune times, then?" he teased, just before a grumbling sound came from his stomach, and they both laughed.

"AYE," she said, "and we both win!"

Ian stepped out of the tub and held his hand out to Madison for assistance. They dried each other with fluffy white towels and might have missed the whole purpose of leaving the tub, had Ian's empty belly not reminded them once again. After they had dressed in their pajamas, they went down to the kitchen. Ian boiled pasta and served it with Alfredo sauce. Madison took their plates to the living room and sat on the floor in front of the dwindling fire. Ian followed with glasses and a bottle of wine.

After they had finished eating, they cleaned up the dinner dishes, banked the fire and put the screen in front of the glowing embers, before going upstairs to bed. Snuggled together beneath the covers, Madison tried to hide her yawn, but Ian knew how tired she must be. It had been a hell of a day for both of them.

"Close yer eyes, luv, and sleep," he murmured bringing a smile to her lips as she cuddled closer.

"Ian, I love your accent."

his own analogy. "Just so you know, It wasn't necessary for you to practice before coming to me? Be that as it may, you needn't be concerned that I won't take you back. However, if you choose to prostitute yourself with this local, please have the courtesy when you're done whoring, to clean

Chapter Twelve

Two days after Dean was ushered out of Scotland, Ian received a package containing his script for his upcoming movie. He spent the days working on his lines, while Madison was marketing to the doctors and hospitals in the area, while the evenings were for dinners, talking about their days, and making love. They saved the weekends to enjoy each other, and Ian took her on day trips around the Isle of Skye. The couple began to make regular visits to the village of Lusta and spend time with Mrs. Stuart. The two ladies were becoming fast friends and decided when Ian went away to film, they would continue their regular visits.

Three days before Ian was to leave for filming, Madison invited Mrs. Stuart for dinner at the house. The evening was filled with mouthwatering smells and flavors thanks to Ian's expertise in the kitchen. Stories told by Mrs. Stuart about Ian and his younger days when he'd get his butt waked with a wooden spoon for swiping a scone from her bakery kitchens. The story brought a lyrical laugh from Madison and a phantom twinge for Ian. When the sun started to sink it was time to call it a night and Ian walked Mrs. Stuart to the car.

"Mrs. Stuart, I should like to ask a very important favor of ye."

"Ye do know me given name do ye no'? Tis Agatha." Mrs. Stuart had her hands on her plump hips as she scolded him. "Come now boy, how many times have I been askin' ye ta call me by me given name? Must I ask it of ye again?"

"At least one more time, Mrs. Stuart." He smiled.

"Ah yer a hopeless case, Ian Mackay. Go on now, what might yer favor be?" When Ian still said nothing, she prompted, "Well ask the damn thing, boy, I havena all night. I want ta get home before the night comes."

"I want to know if ye'll keep an eye on Maddy while I'm away."

"Why? She has already said she would be callin' on me from time ta time. Why should a grown wooman need lookin' after? She seems taken with ye well enough. Do ye no' trust her then, laddie?"

"Ye canna tell her I've asked ya. Her pride is involved, there's a man, I believe is obsessed wi her and it's possible he may try ta make things difficult for her."

"Do ye think she might be in some sort o danger, then?" She was instantly alarmed. She hadn't known Madison very long, but in the short time she had gotten to know her, Mrs. Stuart had already begun to feel protective toward the girl.

"No, no I donna think so, but all the same I dinna want her ta be left alone too much. Will ye do it?"

"Ah sure, laddie. It would be me pleasure. She is such a nice lass and ye seem ta be quite taken wi her as well. That's good." She patted his cheek. "Well, goodbye, young man, and thank her again fer the invitation." Ian closed the door to the car he had called for her. As the taillights fell out of view, Ian made his way back into the house where Madison was in the kitchen finishing with the dinner dishes.

"Yer a sexy lass me darlin."

"You two were out there for a long time. What's the big secret?"

Ian stood behind her and kissed the back of her neck. "Donna try and change the subject."

She giggled. "You obviously wanted to talk to her about something you felt the need to exclude me from, so out with it."

Ian sighed and sat at the end of the island. "Well, me lady, since ye came ta the conclusion that I didn't want ta talk in here, why should I tell ye what was discussed?" he teased.

"Fine, don't tell me. I'll just ask Mrs. Stuart when I see her next." She finished drying the last dish and put it away when Ian scooped her up into his arms.

"No ye willna." He smiled. "And if ye do, she willna tell ye."

Just then Madison's phone rang. "If that's Dean, I'll chuck that phone right out the window."

"Oh no you willna!"

"Here, put me down. That's Margaret." Ian placed her feet on the floor and gave her a love tap on the rear as she walked to the desk to answer the phone. "Hello," she laughed.

"Hey, Madison, I haven't talked to you in a while, how are you?."

"I know and I'm sorry. I've been really busy here. What's up?"

"I wanted to let you know I'm going to be sending you a package with your bills and some statements. Also, Mr. Goldblum wants to have a meeting with you sometime over the next couple of months to go over your progress."

"Good Lord," she sighed. "I've only been here for two months and he's already pestering me." She laughed.

"I know, I just thought I would give you a heads-up. So, how's it going?"

"Good, I've made some really good contacts and so far they seem to be interested."

"Cool, say doesn't that Scottish actor Ian Mackay live there in Scotland somewhere?"

"Oh, I think so." She looked at Ian and smiled.

"If you see him, can you get me an autograph?"

"Well, we'll see. I better go now I have an early day tomorrow."

Madison hung up the phone and started to laugh hysterically.

"What's so funny?" Ian questioned from the love seat, Madison leaned against the desk.

"My administrative Assistant wants to know if I can get an autograph from Ian Mackay. Also my boss wants me to go to Philly sometime in the next couple of months to go over my progress."

Ian stood and began to walk toward her. "Dean?"

"No." She smiled. "Samuel Goldblum, the owner and president of the company." Ian stopped in front of her and placed his hands on her shoulders and looked in her eyes.

"Ye aren't planning to invite anymore people to dinner before I leave are ye?"

"No, why?" Ian dipped his lips to her neck hitting the pot that melts her knees every time.

"Because I donna plan on letting ye leave, and no one will be allowed in for the next two days and three nights." Without another word, Ian scooped her up in his arms and carried her to the bedroom. Where they lived for the next three nights and two days, leaving their nest only to eat and stretch their legs.

On Monday morning Madison awoke to Ian tripping over the cat in the dark.

"Bloody hell." He laughed as he landed on his rear. Madison flipped on the light and saw Ian sitting on the floor and Julie perched on his knee.

"What's going on?" she asked sleepily.

"I was tryin' ta get dressed and ready ta leave before the car came ta take me ta the airport." Ian stood up and took off his flannel bottoms and traded them for a pair of black denim jeans.

"Wait, what do you mean 'the car'?" She sat up and pulled the sheet to cover her naked breasts.

"I've ordered a limo to take me ta the airport." He pulled on a white button-down dress shirt and tucked it into the waist of his jeans. He took his boots from the closet and sat on the edge of the bed.

"I thought I was taking you to the airport." He looked at her and saw hurt in her eyes by his decision to hire a car.

"I'm sorry, luv. I meant ta tell ye about tha'. I dinna want ye drivin' on the roads that far yet. Yer no' that used ta them as yet. I also dinna want ye drivin' back upset."

"Oh." She looked down at her hands folded on top of her lap. "Can I ride with you to the airport?"

"Nay, luv," he sighed and traced his fingers down her cheek bringing her gaze to his. "It's hard for me ta leave ye," his voice in a low whisper, "and I donna want ta make it any harder for either of us." He leaned to her and placed a small kiss on her lips.

Ian finished lacing up his boots and gathered all his bags and dropped them downstairs by the door. As he started to retrace his steps to the bedroom, he saw Madison standing on the bottom step. She had put on one of his button-down dress shirts, *God ye look sexy*, he thought. Her hair was pulled up in one of her clips, eyes bright, almost iridescent. Ian walked over to her and gathered her up in his arms and held her tightly.

"Ye have no idea how much I want ta stay here wi ye, instead of going ta do some damned movie." Madison buried her face in his chest and took in as much of his scent as she could.

"No you have to go. It's your job." She pulled back and looked into his eyes. "Anyway this is a love story and from what you would let me see of the script, it's bound to be a good one. You'll be absolutely wonderful in it." Ian pulled her back to him and kissed her warm lips. They were interrupted by a knock at the door, and Ian knew it was the driver to take him away from his Maddy for several months. Ian felt an instant and unreasonable hatred for the poor man. He reluctantly pulled away from her and opened the door, indicated the luggage and told the driver he would be out shortly.

"Sure, Mr. Mackay, but ye best hurry so ye dinna miss yer plane."

"Aye, thank ye." Ian shut the door behind the driver as he left with the bags. Ian turned back to Madison. He felt as though his heart was being ripped from his chest as he looked at her, arms wrapped around herself. Her Caribbean blue eyes were shockingly bright with the tears she was desperately trying to keep from shedding. Ian opened his arms to her as she ran to his embrace. He could feel her trembling and his eyes began to mist up as well.

"Ian," she sniffled, "I have been wanting to say this to you ever since you told me you loved me. Ian I—" Once again he stopped what she was about to say by placing his fingertips on her lips, like he'd done every time she tried to tell him. He wanted her to wait until he wasn't a daily fixture in her life so she could truly work out how she felt.

"Nay, luv, dinna tell me now. For if ye tell me now I will no' be able ta leave." He kissed her delicious lips and drew her in for yet another embrace. He never wanted to let her go, but he knew he didn't have a choice. "Come now, luv, I have ta go."

"Ian, you're the one holding me hostage, not the other way around." She smiled. He looked down at her face and wiped the tears from her eyes and kissed her forehead.

"I'll call ye when I get settled in LA."

"Okay." They kissed once more. As Ian was on his way out the door Madison stopped him. "Ian, remember, most women, including myself, love accents. Especially the Scottish brogue." Ian grinned at her and kissed the tip of her nose. Then as fast as he had entered her life, he was gone from it. She watched as the car drove away and looked toward the bay. The sun was coming up. The glow was warm on her face and she knew that soon the land would give way to life and warmth. Madison walked back inside and shut the door. As though signifying the return of reality, her phone rang.

"Hello ... yes, Dr. Connors, I would love to come and speak to your staff. Today would be fine. I can be there by ten o'clock. Wonderful, I'll see you then." Madison hung up the phone and looked down at Julie, who was at her feet.

"Well, it's just you and me now kid." She bent over and picked up the purring kitty. "Come on, let's get dressed and go to work." Julie gave a small meow and nuzzled Madison's cheek.

About eight thirty Madison came downstairs wearing her navy blue silk pantsuit with her hair pulled back in a French twist. She went to the kitchen and started a pot of coffee brewing. While the pot was brewing she gathered everything she'd need for her talk to the hospital staff. As she went through her supplies Madison noticed her handouts were starting to get low.

"I have enough for today," she told Julie. "But I'm definitely going to need more before I do any more in-services. Remind me to call Margaret tonight and have her send more."

Madison burst out laughing as she just realized what she had asked of her cat. Rather than wait till later, she shot her assistant a quick email to replenish her in-service materials. She grabbed her long black cashmere overcoat from the closet before starting the task of loading Ian's Wagoneer with all her supplies for the in-service. With the last of the supplies pack away she returned to the house once more to fill her travel mug with coffee then pull the plug on the pot. She leaned against the counter facing the living room, it felt so strange to have no one but Julie in the house. Almost as soon as she arrived, she had been there with Ian, and now he was gone for several months. She was alone and for some reason it frightened her, she gave herself a mental shake and reached for her purse and keys her phone rang.

"Oh shit," she groaned. It was *Symphony Fantastique* by Berlioz. "What does he want now? Hello."

"Hi, Madison, how are you?" Dean's voice slithered over the airwaves and made her shiver.

"Dean," she sighed, "what do you want, and why are you calling me at four in the morning?"

"Because it's nine in the morning there. Say, I wanted to talk to you about the man you are shacked up with. You know—"

"Dean, damn it. You're my *boss* not my boyfriend and I would appreciate it if you would stay out of my personal life." *What do I have to do to get through to this guy?* she thought.

"Madison, baby, I am your personal life." He cooed.

"AAAGGGGHHHH!" She punched the End button so hard she nearly broke a nail. She was on her way out the door when her phone came to life again. Not waiting for the ring to persist Madison dug her phone out of her purse and answered, "WHAT!" she screamed.

"Maddy? Are ye alright, luv?" Ian's voice spilled over the line.

Madison stopped in midstride. "Ian?" she breathed.

"Aye, what's the matter?"

"Oh, I'm sorry, Dean called a minute ago and I guess I'm just angry. Where are you calling me from?" She hopped in the cab of the Wagoneer and leaned back to listen to Ian's wonderful voice.

"No' ta worry, me lady. I'm callin' from the tarmac, we're waitin'. So, ye heard from Mr. Michaels again have ye? If he starts ta be a real problem for ye call me and let me deal wi him."

Madison could tell by his voice he was worried and meant what he said about dealing with Dean. "No, don't worry, I can handle him. So how long is your flight?" She started the car and turned it around so she could drive out to the road.

"Fourteen hours with the time difference, but I'll be on board for at least six hours. Give or take. Donna ferget to let the phone connect to the car, luv." Madison smiled and waited for the telltale noise of the cell and car becoming one.

"Will you call me when you get to the hotel?"

"Aye, lassie, I will. Where ye off ta?"

"Dr. Connors wants me to talk to his staff at the hospital about hospice. So I'm on my way there now."

"That's good. He's a big doctor fer ye. Good luck, Maddy me darlin."

"Thank you, sir. Oh I'm here at the hospital. Ian before you hang up...."

"Aye?"

She took a deep breath. "I love you." Before she let him say anything she ended the call and smiled. There were butterflies in her stomach and joy swelling in her heart. Yes, she loved him and now she was able to tell him so. She pulled into a parking space closest to the door and turned off the engine. As Madison unbuckled her seat belt, her phone rang again. Knowing it was Ian calling her back, she answered it charmingly.

"Hello?"

"Madison, why the hell did you hang up on me!" Dean's voice bellowed over the line.

Madison fell back into the seat of the Wagoneer exasperated.

"Dean! Don't call me anymore!" Once again she pushed the End button, flipped the silent switch, and jammed the cell in her purse. She opened the door and noticed a young man standing a mere few feet away wearing a doctor's smock.

"Would ye be Madison Danaher, then?" asked the young man. He was the same height as Madison, maybe a little taller. He was extremely well built for a man of his age. Madison guessed he was twenty-two maybe twenty-five. *He's a good-looking kid,* she thought. Light blond hair and hazel eyes, cleft in his chin like Cary Grant and a face like a young Marlin Brando and built like the Henry Cavill's Superman. *Is this guy a doctor or a bodyguard?* she wondered.

"Yes, I'm Madison, and you are?"

The young man smiled and extended his hand to her. "My name is Patrick O'Connell."

"Nice to meet you, Patrick." Noting the different speech pattern. "You're not Scottish are you?"

"No, ma'am, I'm Irish. Why don't I give ya a hand with all yer stuff here, yeah?" He followed her to the back of the Wagoneer.

"Yes, thank you. You seem awfully young to be a doctor."

Patrick smiled, "Ya know tha's what the woman I operated on this morn' said before she went under." They both laughed as they pulled everything out of the back of the SUV. "Nay, ta be honest, I'm alo' older than people think."

"Yeah? How old are you?" With everything unloaded and piled on the cart she carried with her, Madison pushed the button for the back door then locked the vehicle.

"Thirty-five,"

Madison stopped and looked at him. "No you're not, you can't be, that makes you older than me."

"Really, how old are *you*, then?" he teased.

Madison laughed and started toward the hospital entrance where Patrick led her to the amphitheater and helped her set up before the rest of the staff arrived. Almost as soon as she was finished organizing her display, the nurses, social workers, and doctors started to fill the seats. Madison waited until everyone was seated and quiet then she began her presentation.

"Hello, everyone, My name is Madison Danaher from Tender Care Hospice based in Philadelphia, Pennsylvania, in the United States. I'm here to talk to you about the benefits of having hospice care available for your terminal patients in this area. Now, can I have a show of hands for those of you here that are familiar with hospice in general?" She waited and only four hands went up out of a possible fifty. "Only four of you, good, I like dealing with a fresh meat." Laughter rang out in the room and Madison relaxed.

"Alright, first I'm going to tell you what my company does, and how we can be of service to you and your terminal patients. And please, in the interest of keeping the flow of explanation, please hold your questions until I've finished." She took a sip from her travel coffee and set to work.

"Hospice is an organization that goes into the private home of the patient who is in the final days of life. It's a way of allowing the patient to remain in their own home or with family, as opposed to spending the sterile hospital atmosphere. In most cases, the patient is more comfortable, and their passing is more restful. We will go in nursing homes or assisted living facilities where the patient, their families, or the facility has asked for our services.

"Patients' families aren't billed for the services extended by hospice. We're supported by Medicare, Medicaid, or private insurance. In most instances we provide all the equipment needed to make the patient as comfortable as possible, such as hospital beds, wheelchairs, oxygen, etc. We supply medications such as morphine and other meds for pain depending on how advanced the disease along with meds for anxiety such as Ativan. We provide "comfort pack," which includes pain and anxiety meds, laxatives, some of which come in both liquid and pill form. We also supply, depending on the disease, such as brain cancer, an emergency pack, which includes meds for seizure. Any meds previously taken by the patient are studied by the visiting nurse and evaluated to decide what is needed and what can be eliminated. Any meds the patient needs that we aren't already providing must be approved by the attending.

"Although it's asked and recommended, patients aren't required to sign a DNR before being admitted onto our care. Anyone may recommend a patient to Hospice, but before we can take a patient onto our service, the attending physician will need to sign off on the order.

"We send certified home health aides to the patient anywhere from two, in some cases, as often as seven times a week, depending on what is needed by the patient and the family. The CHHA are there to service the patient as far as keeping the patient clean and comfortable. They change sheets and bathe the patient, basically they do whatever needs to be done for the comfort of the patient. They will also just sit and talk or read to the patient while the family member runs errands. If the patient is alone and doesn't have a caregiver, the CHHA can also prepare meals for the patient, do laundry, and wash up dishes.

However, a home health aide is never to be considered a maid, by either the patient or the family.

"The nurses will visit as often as is needed by the patient and the family, but generally they visit twice a week depending on how busy the caseload.

"We also have on staff, the hospice social worker who is required to visit the patient and family at least once, but will go back as often as the family or patient requests. They provide support for the patient but also for the caregiver. We have chaplains who will also visit if the family or patient requests. Usually our chaplain will call to ask if the patient would like for him or her to visit. We will also provide volunteers who will visit patients for however long is needed for the caregiver to run errands or make scheduled appointments. Once the patient has passed, we stay with the family or caregiver for up to one year to offer support and grief counseling."

"Terminal disease is a difficult ordeal for the patient, of course, but also for the family. Having the patient in his or her own home or the home of a family member can do a great deal in the way of comfort for all concerned. It makes the passing easier for everyone. What I'm asking of you today is to consider referring terminal patients to our hospice organization."

A young doctor at the top of the theater spoke up when Madison finished her initial explanation.

"Miss Danaher? Who will ask the patient if they want to sign the 'do not resuscitate' order?"

"The admitting nurse," Madison replied. And another hand shot into the air.

"What if the patient can't sign or isn't capable of speaking for him or herself?"

"In that case, we need the signature of the power of attorney. And before you ask, if the patient has no designated power of attorney, and there is no available spouse. Then, unfortunately, we can't accept the patient to our service."

A nurse in the front row raised her hand.

"How long can a patient remain on your service?"

"The general rule is six months. However, that depends on the patient and the particular disease, as long as there is a steady decline they can remain on our services."

A young woman standing quietly along the side wall shyly spoke up. "Where do ye find the aides and nurses ta staff your hospice?"

Madison smiled at the shy girl. "Some of our nurses come to us from doctors' offices, hospitals or are retired, but feel the need to keep their skills up to date. As for the CHHA they come to us in much the same manner."

On the table Madison laid out her business cards with her cell number, pamphlets, and other handouts for the staff to take on their way out. She handed out cards with the address of the storefront location next to Agatha Stewart's bakery in Lusta.

"I'm not completely settled in the office yet, and I'm waiting for a shipment of materials from the home office, but you're welcome to stop by anytime during the day from nine to five o'clock. I'll be happy to answer any questions you might think of later."

Madison spent a full workday at the hospital. Some of the staff needed to return to their shift, but those that could, stayed to ask questions about the hospice she planned to open.

Dr. Connors was the last to approach while Madison packed what was left of her materials.

"I'm sorry; I could only catch the last part of your presentation, rounds." He explained. "From what I heard, you were well received." He reached out to take her hand in his and give it a friendly squeeze.

"Yes, went very well. I'd like express my thanks for allowing me to talk to your staff." She smiled.

"It was a hell of a presentation, Danaher!" Patrick O'Connell came bounding down the steps of the amphitheater. "I've been listening to the feedback and looks like there are several docs who might have patients. As a matter of fact, I have two patients I'd like to refer as soon as you're set up and have staff."

"That's great, I'll be ready to work soon. But right now I'm putting you to work." She said, smiling at the handsome young Irishman and handing him a carton. "You can help me carry what's left of my supplies to my car."

She shook hands with Dr. Connors, loaded the cart and Patrick's arms with the rest of her materials and followed him out the door.

Chapter Thirteen

With the Wagoneer loaded with the last of her marketing supplies, Madison drove to the storefront she'd rented from Mrs. Stuart. As it turns out, Mrs. Stuart owned the property next to her bakery. She was now Madison's landlady. This was the temporary site for the Lusta branch of Tender Care Hospice. It wasn't a massive room, but it was bright, centrally located, and available now, which was the most important qualification. Beside Mrs. Stuart pointed out the space was clean, well-tended and perfect as Madison's first office space, of course she was right. Thankfully there was a rear entrance, and she was able to drive Ian's SUV around back to unload.

Madison parked in the back and walked in through the back door. With the lights off and the space empty the windows threw long shadows over the bare walls and floors. Barren walls aside, Agatha had been correct when she said the room was clean, she'd been using it as a storage for all of her baking needs, since the last tenant vacated. Madison looked about the empty space and wondered where Mrs. Stuart's things had gone to. She found the light switch and flipped it, as the room became illuminated, the space was definitely large enough to accommodate her needs for the time being, but the bare walls and concrete floors needed to be brought to life.

"Ye'll be needin' ta have some workers come and liven the place up a wee bit." Madison was startled by the voice and spun around to see Mrs. Stuart standing in the connecting doorway to the bakery.

"Agatha." Hand to her chest Madison felt her heart skip several beats. "Hi." She chuckled, "I'm afraid you're right." She glanced around the room and sighed. "I hope I'll can find someone who can do the work and fast."

"Oh?" Agatha questioned.

"I gave a presentation for Dr. Connors and staff at the hospital this morning, and it went over very well. I'm hoping to have some staff applicants soon, and one of the doctors already told me; he has a couple of patients to refer as soon as we're set up and operating."

"Dr. Connors, huh? Well, he's a big-time doctor in these parts. Doctors." She sniffed. "Ne'er been much use ta me. If ye'll be askin' me, they should all go back to the devil where they belong." Madison arched her brow by Agatha's declaration, and then laughed out loud.

"Come now, Agatha" came an Irish brogue, Madison turned to see Patrick O'Connell standing in the back doorway. "Ya don' really feel tha' way bout doctors." He smiled as he walked in.

"You know each other?" Madison questioned.

"Aye, I'm her doctor." He walked over to Agatha and put his arm around her much like a son would do his mother.

"I'm fit as a fiddle," Agatha scolded. "I dinna need a doctor. Much less a doctor who I coulda birthed."

Madison smiled at the friendly banter. There was no doubt Agatha was very fond of Patrick, or Madison was sure the older woman would've told him otherwise. *In some pretty colorful way no doubt,* she mused. Patrick walked around the room examining every corner, then turned back to Madison.

"This place will need alo' o work, ya know." He shoved his hands in the pockets of his coat. "If ya be needin' any help, I can lend ya a hand."

"That would be wonderful, thank you!" The tension she wasn't aware she was holding in her shoulders melted in relief at the offer. "I'll definitely take you up on the offer. I'm determined to make it shine like a bright new penny before people start coming to inquire about jobs and the services we offer."

"That's not gonna be possible," he sighed.

"Why not?"

"Because," he said, smiling, "ya already have someone a' the door." Madison turned to see a young woman peering in through the front windows. Madison opened the door and invited in the same shy woman who was at the in-service that morning.

"Hello, may I help you?" Madison asked while she quietly assessed the young woman. Like before when she spoke up at the hospital, her voice was quiet and shy. She was a pretty with fair skin and blue eyes set on the floor

"Aye, ma'am. I was wonderin' if ye might be hirin' home health aides." She spoke softly as she tucked stands of jet-black hair that had fallen from the tight twist behind her ear.

"Well, I will be, but right now I can't give you any work. Mainly because we don't have any patients."

"Oh," the unnamed girl said meekly. "I'm sorry ta have bothered ye." She turned to walk away when Madison stopped her.

"Wait, I just thought of something. Can you answer phones, and possibly help get the office set up and running?"

Finally, the downcast eyes flashed up and looked straight at Madison.

"Do ye mean it? I've never worked in an office. I'm no' sure I'm exactly qualified for tha' kind of a position."

"Well," Madison said, "you answer your own phone when it rings. Don't you?"

"Aye, I can answer a telephone."

"Then you're hired. I'll need you to be here every day to help set up the office and place the desks and cabinets. You're to answer the phone and take messages while I'm working in the field. How does fifteen pound an hour sound?" Knowing the conversion rate was roughly twenty dollars, Madison hoped she wasn't undercutting the girl.

The blue eyes widened in awe. "Fifteen pounds an hour? I do'na make that at the hospital as an aide."

"Oh," *I don't know if that's a good thing or not.* Madison laughed. "What's your name?"

"Elizabeth Campbell, ma'am."

"Well, Elizabeth Campbell, come on in and meet everyone." Madison ushered the young woman to the middle of the room where Patrick and Agatha still stood. "Everyone, this is Miss Elizabeth Campbell and my first employee, Elizabeth this is Agatha Stuart." Madison motioned to the older woman and watched as Elizabeth tentatively extended her hand to Agatha.

"It's a pleasure ta be meetin' ye, lass. Yer name is Campbell, is it? Good strong name ta be havin'."

"Aye, Mrs. Stuart, thank ye." Elizabeth's voice was small and tentative, but Madison and the rest of her newfound friends would soon draw her out.

"And this is Dr. Patrick O'Connell, but you must've met at the hospital already."

"Nay, not likely. Aides dinna generally mix wi the big nubs at the hospital."

"I'm sorry ta say she's right. But it is a problem that I hope to rectify from now on. It's a pleasure ta meet ya. Should we call ya Elizabeth or Mrs. Campbell, then?"

"I'm unmarried, sir," Elizabeth said, looking to the floor again. *Good,* Patrick thought. "I like to be called Elizabeth," she continued.

"Ah, well, then I'll call ya Lizzy." Patrick's captivating smile held Elizabeth's gaze long enough to bring a pink tinge to her cheeks. *She's a pretty lass, I like the blushin on her,* his smiled widened.

"Well," Madison said, "Patrick, it's getting late. Don't you need to get back home to your wife?"

"Nope, not married." He grinned as he kept his gaze trained on Lizzy.

Madison and Agatha had been watching the sparks fly as the two clapped eyes. Madison looked at Agatha, smiled, and raised her eyebrows. Agatha nodded her head in agreement of their unspoken plan to play matchmaker. As much fun as she was having, it was getting late and since Madison wasn't familiar with the roads, especially at night, she suggested that they call it a day. She decided she would be back in the morning to start making plans for the renovation, looking Patrick with the unspoken question if he wanted to join she was met with excitement and enthusiasm.

"Sounds good ta me," Patrick smiled while rubbing his hands together. "I've a couple of patients I need ta check on, but other than tha', ye've got me for the day." He looked down at Elizabeth. "How bout ye, Lizzy. Can ye help tomorrow?"

Lizzy smiled at the warm friendly group before her, she decided she'd be very happy here. "Aye, I can help all ye need."

"Done and good fer it, lass!" Agatha exclaimed. "And while ye're all workin' yer tails ta the bone," she said, "I'll bake." Earning a chuckle from the group.

Patrick and Lizzy helped Madison unload the Wagoneer, soon after it was agreed to meet in the following morning around eight o'clock. As Madison drove back to the house she had a sudden pang of loneliness. She realized then, she was going back to an empty house, no Ian to greet her, talk about their day while she sat with him in the kitchen where he was king. *You can handle this,* she thought. *After all, you were the one who told Ian that the right woman would be able to deal with his schedule.*

"And I will," she said aloud. "dammit."

Arriving back to a dark house was never the plan. In the past she'd always made sure to be home well before the sun sunk, for two reasons. One so she didn't have to drive in the dark on roads she wasn't quite used to yet and two, she want to ensure that she and Ian would have plenty of time with each other before they went to bed. Yet here she was, drop dead tired, dark house, cold hearth, and no Ian. *Yup, this sucks.*

After Madison turned on some lights, put her things away, she changed into pajamas. For dinner, it was egg sandwiches, and she and Julie ate together at the island. Meal finished Madison cleaned her plate and put Julie on the floor, and pulled out her iPad, sat at her desk and created a list of the renovations for the office space. She wanted a warm and inviting space, a pleasant environment for office staff to work, but also, a kind of refuge for nurses and aides to relax in, between visits to patients. *Maybe we could even have an office cat,* she thought. Animals helped ease stress, and she knew how stressful this work could be for the staff, all staff not just the ones out in the trenches.

She decided reclaimed, wide-plank hardwoods for the floors and thought about color tones. No point in thinking about the finish until she found the flooring. The building was older, and the walls were aged plaster with cracks and patches. She could fix the plaster, or drywall over them and then paint. She wasn't all that knowledgeable when it came to that kinda of thing, so she'd have to find someone who was. *On the list it goes.* Furniture was next, she needed to source some office furniture. *Maybe Agatha knows someone who sells furniture,* she thought. It'd be less expensive to get the supplies she'd need in Scotland, besides, she was determined to see to it that, not only were the renovations cost effective, but she also wanted the local people to benefit financially from the project.

Madison stayed at the desk for several more hours, making notes before finally heading to bed. With her iPad connected to the printer; it made printing her lists a breeze. As she crawled into the large, cold bed, she missed Ian all the more, and ideally wondered why he hadn't called yet. Just as the thought popped into her head, her cell phone came to life downstairs. She flung the covers back, ran out of the room, raced down the stairs and snatched the phone to answer it.

"Hello?" she said out of breath.

"Hello, luv?" Ian's sexy brogue warmed her insides.

"Ian." She sank down into the love seat and smiled. "I can't tell you how wonderful it is to hear your voice."

"Same here, luv, are ye okay? Ye sound out of breath?"

"Oh, I'm fine, now. I was in bed when the phone rang, and I ran down here to answer it. Are you in LA?"

"Aye, I got in aboot two hours ago, but me brain was so fogged, I figured I better take a wee sleep or I'd make no sense when I called ye."

"Where are you staying?"

"The Beverly Wilshire Hotel. How was yer day?"

"Good! The in-service at the hospital was a success. As a matter of fact I've hired my first employee and made a new friend."

"Oh?"

"Mm, Dr. Patrick O'Connell. Nice guy, and he's going to help Elizabeth and I to set up the office."

"Dr. O'Connell? Isna he Mrs. Stuart's doctor?"

"Yeah, as it turns out, do you know him?"

"Aye, and ye've the tight of it there luv, nice guy. Who's Elizabeth?"

"The girl I hired to answer the phones. She's an aide at the hospital and sat in on the presentation. When she came to the office afterwards, I hired her to answer the phone, she also agreed to help set up the office too. After I have everything settled and some patients, she'll go out in the field as an aide. Nice girl and I think Agatha and I are going to play matchmaker for her and Patrick." She smiled at his chuckle.

"I'm glad you and Mrs. Stuart are becoming friends."

"When do you start filming?"

"Tomorrow, the bulk of the film will take place in New York." He couldn't stifle the yawn that came with the jetlag.

"Then why go to LA if the film is taking place in New York?"

"Because, most of the sound stages are here, but a fair few outside shots will be filmed later in New York."

"Oh okay. Well, I assume when filming starts, you don't have free time to yourself?"

"Aye, I won't, luv, but donna worry. I'll make time ta call ye." There was a short pause. "I miss ye, Maddy."

Madison smiled "I miss you too. The house seems so empty without you." The loneliness she felt when she same home came the forefront of her mind making her sigh quietly. "But we're both going to be so busy and have much to occupy ourselves while we're apart. The time will go quickly." *Liar!*

"Aye, well, but ye can still take a wee minute during the busy day ta miss me, lass." He laughed. "I ha better let ye go back to bed, I know ye have a busy day tomorrow. I wish I could be there wi ye snuggled up in yer flannel bottoms. I love ye, Maddy me darlin."

Madison giggled at the mental picture painted by Ian.

"And I love 'ye' too." she smiled as she ended the call.

Madison stayed on the love seat for a moment before putting the phone on the charger and heading up for the night. Before she settled herself back in bed, she set the alarm for six o'clock. She scooted under the covers and sighed as Julie jumped up and curled next to Madison's chest and began to purr.

The next morning, dressed in blue jeans, red flannel button down shirt, she made her way downstairs and grabbed her boots from the closet to put on. A quick glance at her watch told her she still had over an hour before she needed to be at the office. In the kitchen she put the tea kettle on, and made a pot of coffee. After the water had boiled and the coffee was finished brewing, she filled her travel mug with coffee and three more with hot water. Madison took the tea that Ian had made for her and some others and put them in a thermos bag. She collected her lists and notes from the printer, snagged up her purse and keys on the way out the door.

Madison arrived at the rear entrance of the office, and saw Patrick had already arrived. But there was only one car. *Where is Lizzy?* she thought. Madison parked the Wagoneer, hopped out of the cab and went to the back door to unlock it. Once inside she saw the lights were already blazing and the door that connected Agatha's bakery to the office was open.

Closing the door behind her, she heard laughter coming from the bakery kitchen. When she entered the kitchen, she found not only Agatha and Patrick, but also Lizzy sitting around the large butcher-block table.

"Well, good morning, everyone," she smiled brightly, as Patrick rose from his seat and took the thermos bag from her and put it on the table. "I brought some hot water and tea for everyone. I wasn't sure what you'd all liked, so I brought everything I had." Chuckling as the plethora a tea was pulled form the bag.

"Ye're such a good lass," Agatha said. "I ha made pastries for everyone to eat before ye all start yer day."

Madison sat down on one of the stools, handed out the travel mugs filled with hot water and motioned toward the collection of teas. She winked at Agatha as Patrick returned to his seat, next to Lizzy.

"Well," she said, smiling, "after I got home last night, I made lists of everything we'll need to make this place simply shine." She spread the lists out in the center of the table for everyone to look at and they began to go over them together.

"There's an old bugger in the village here tha' makes furniture fer a livin'," Agatha offered.

"Really, do you think he could make the office furniture?"

"I dinna see why no'. Wha' else has the old codger go' ta take oop his time? But would ye rather ha the things brought in from America?"

"Why the hell would I want to do that?" Madison scoffed, "When there are people here who can profit from this build?"

"Good on ye, lass!" Agatha praised.

"Now, we'll need to hire someone to come in and decide what's best for the walls," Madison said.

"We dinna have ta do tha' Miss Danaher," Lizzy interjected. "I know how ta do tha' meself. All we need is someone ta bring the materials ta us."

"Lizzy," Patrick said, beaming, "you know how ta do tha'?"

"Aye, I do, Dr. O'Connell." She smiled.

"Lizzy, you're a wonder!" Madison said. "But we're going to be very informal here. My name is Madison or Maddy. In this office we will all be on a first-name basis."

"Oh, Miss. Danaher!" Lizzy's eyes grew very large and round. "Ye're gonna ta be me official employer. I dinna think it'd be proper ta be callin' ye by yer Christian name," she breathed.

"New job, new rules, kiddo." Madison reached out and patted Lizzy's hand.

As they finished going over the plans for the office, Agatha began to get customers in the shop. After Lizzy looked over the walls, the decision for drywall was made and Patrick was elected to go for the supplies needed, while Madison and Lizzy prepared the room. With Patrick off on his mission, Madison and Lizzy got to know each other.

Madison learned Lizzy was twenty-six years old and from a small family. Her mother was the cook and her father, the butler for a wealthy family in Inverness. Because her parents lived in one of the cottages own by the family they worked for Lizzy basically lived alone in the family home in Lusta. Her parents sent her money to help maintain the family home and with Lizzy's small income or the hospital she was relatively comfortable. Since the village was so small Lizzy didn't see the need for a car and like most, walked everywhere.

"So how far away do you live from here?" Madison said after a while.

"No' far, no more than a mile or two. Tis a far cry from the five-mile trek I would make ta the hospital every day," she said.

Before the conversation could go any further, Patrick came back with an envelope full of receipts for Madison, along with her company credit card. Trailing behind him was a long string of men and workers.

"These men are ta load in all the supplies, we brought drywall, lumber, nails, screws, and joint compound and paint. They're all able-bodied buckos and can help get the walls up before the day is spent," Patrick finished with a smile.

"Terrific!" Madison exclaimed.

The rough hand-drawn blueprints were examined, and with Lizzy basically in charge of the work crew, Madison and Agatha went off together in search of flooring and furniture. Their first stop was to the local Iron Monger.

Chapter Fourteen

"**I**ron Monger," Madison read the sign over the shop door. "Andrew Douglas Proprietor." *Iron Monger,* she thought as they walked into the shop. *It's a hardware store.* She smiled to herself. But oh boy, she was quick to learn that Mr. Douglas's establishment was more than a hardware store. He carried everything from harnesses for horses to nails in his shop. You could buy almost anything except coffee, and even that wouldn't be necessary as he offered them a steaming mug of tea as soon as he spied Agatha.

"Andrew, we've no time ta be chattin' wi ye, this morn. We've business ta do and our time is limited." Agatha scolded in a huff. "Meet Miss Madison Danaher. I've let her me empty shop and she's settin' oop an office to do good works fer the sick. So away wi yer weak tea and act the expert ye pretend ta be!"

Andrew Douglas never blinked at Agatha's less-than-gracious attitude. He set his mug on the counter and they got down to business, the smiling greeting never left his weathered face. Maddy asked about the wood floors and he told her she'd find no better than Angus Jamison when it came to all things wooden. One corner of the shop was devoted to lighting fixtures, and she spied several that would be lovely in the office if they were dusted and cleaned. The price was agreed upon for the light fixtures, and everything promised for delivery on Thursday midday.

When Madison and Agatha were back out on the sidewalk, Madison asked about Andrew Douglas.

"He seems like a nice man," she ventured.

"Aye. Andrew's a good sort, bu' a pestier bugger, ye'll never hope ta meet," Agatha grumbled despite the smile tugging at her mouth. "He's been after me ta wed since me own dear sweet Jamie passed on, bless his tortured heart."

Madison stopped dead in her tracks. A little history was what she had hoped for, but this brief narrative took her by surprise.

"He wants you to marry him?"

"Aye. I've told him I dinna want ta wed another, but he willna leave it be. Where I a young lass, I might consider his offer. But I'm no' a young anymore, I spent thirty years learnin' to dream of one man. I've no mind to start over learnin' ta dream of another. Besides, dirty messy buggers they are." She looked over at Madison. "Men," she clarified. "Trackin' in their mud and cow dung like some good fairy was gonna come ta mop up after 'em. I mopped and cleaned aplenty, I can tell ye, low those many years. Then as is the curse of woomen want, they want ta bed ya and their dung covered boots still reekin' under the bed. All the while expectin' ye ta worry yer head tha' they might be dippin' their wick in some other poor daft female. No thank ye ta tha', again."

Madison burst out laughing at Agatha's last words, although Agatha didn't see the humor. She felt she had spoken the God's truth and that was all there was to it. And when she stopped walking, she pointed to the building by the side of the road.

"Ah. Here we are. This is Old Man Jamison's place." Madison turned and looked behind her. Lusta had disappeared in the distance. *And we have to walk back,* she thought to herself.

Angus Jamison, a small bent man with a bushy mustache to match his bushy eyebrows and friendly bright blue eyes. He was pleased to see Agatha and invited them both into his shop, a lean-to behind the compact square house.

"Tis good ta see ye, Missus. How long ha it been since I crafted the counters and stools fer yer shop?" he asked.

"A good deal longer than I care ta discuss wi ye, Angus. I'm here to introduce ye ta Madison Danaher. She's opening a business in the village. She'll be needin' office furniture. Desks, chairs, shelving, and the like. Also flooring. It came ta me mind tha' ye might be the one ta help her wi tha'."

"Danaher, is it?" Angus squinted his eyes at Madison. He rubbed his chin and leaned against a worktable strewn with hammers, chisels, all kinds of pegs and screws. "I canna say tha' I know any Danaher's in the village. Ye'd be Irish, then, might ye?"

Madison was prepared to give a brief history of Poppy's family to the interesting older man, but Agatha wasn't so inclined.

"We're no' here ta discuss the lass's heritage, ye bloody fool. Are ye interested in her business or are ye no'?'

"Acourse I'm interested in doing business wi the lass, Agatha, but there's no a reason that we canna ha a moment o' friendly talk first, is there?" Angus squared off with Agatha and it looked like a full-scale argument was going to ensue.

"Ye're wastin' the lady's precious time, old man. Do ye wanna talk or are ye no' interested in the increase o' a few pounds in yer coffers?"

"Agatha Stuart, yer're the most uncommon stubborn cantankerous woomon I've ever ha the misfortune ta know! And I do know ye, Missus, dinna forget tha'! It willna hurt ta sit a spell and get ta know the lass. How else can I learn a whit what she might be wantin'?"

"Dinna talk ta me aboot how ye think ye *know* me, Angus Jamison! I willna ha it!" Agatha Stuart was turning red.

Madison could tell the two were warming for a battle of last words, and felt she'd better jump into the fray before it became a full-blown war. Then she'd never get her furniture problem settled.

"Mr. Jamison, I'm very interested in your skills as a furniture craftsman. Agatha tells me you make lovely things, and I want my new office to be very inviting." Madison interjected, raising her voice slightly to be heard over din, bringing both Scots to silence. She continued in the same vein, telling Angus what she needed in the way of desks chairs and comfortable benches for visitors. She asked about a picnic table and a few chairs or benches that might be set up outside the office. Thinking it would be nice to give the staff a place to sit for lunch and enjoy the view of the bay where the fishing boats dock.

Angus was able to accommodate all her building needs, but suggested for her to take a look at the items he'd already built and had yet to sell. The three made their way to the barn at the back of the property to have a look. When Angus opened the door, the main floor of the building flooded with light nearly taking Madison's breath away. The huge warehouse-like room was filled with hand crafted furniture, making it difficult to navigate the maze of tables and chairs, of all sizes shapes and styles.

He led her to the back of the barn where she saw a wonderful array of desks, that made her mouth nearly dropped open. *My God,* she thought, *he could furnish ten offices just from this one room. The workmanship was exquisite.* Agatha could read Madison's mind from the expression on her face and was pleased.

"Me da built some of these pieces." Angus added after a few moments. "I learned me trade from him, the work in here is a mixture."

"You have some magnificent pieces here, Mr. Jamison." She ran her hand over the top of one of the desks and could feel the warmth of the oak under her palm. "You're much more than a craftsman. You're an artist," she said with sincere awe.

Angus's chest swelled with pride in his father's skills and in his own. And he smiled at Agatha as Madison took out her cell phone and called Patrick at the office.

"Patrick, is Lizzy free to answer the phone?"

Patrick passed his cell phone to Elizabeth, who looked up at him in question.

"Madison would like ta talk wi ye."

Young Elizabeth Campbell was not accustomed to getting calls on cell phones from anyone; much less a new employer put the phone to her ear with hesitancy.

"Aye, Miss Danaher?"

"Lizzy I'm here with Mr. Jamison in his warehouse and he has a variety of furniture to choose from. What type of desk are you interested in?"

"Oh, Miss, I dinna need a fancy desk. Just a wee table will do me nicely," she said.

"Okey-dokey. I'll choose something."

From then on Madison was like a kid in a candy store. She chose a desk for Lizzy. A table to hold a coffee maker and refreshment supplies. She picked a medium-sized cabinet with storage space underneath to display pamphlets and handouts. She chose a second desk for whoever was to be the next employee she expected to hire soon. She chose a coffee table to sit with the two guest chairs she hoped to find upstairs on the next level of the barn. She asked about shelving, and he showed her a variety of bookcases in another corner of the first floor. She finally chose a lovely Queen Anne table of soft gleaming cherrywood to use as her own desk, and an armchair to match. She thanked him for allowing her to purchase his work and also for letting her see what true artistry can be. He took her to yet another part of the massive barn to look over some wide chestnut planking that had been reclaimed from a 200-year-old church some years ago and wondered if that would suit. Maddy ran her hands over the wide boards.

"Oh God, yeah, I think they will suit beautifully. Will they need to be sealed so they won't get damaged?" She looked over at Angus's furrowed brow. "Don't misunderstand. I have no interest in staining or changing the color in any way. I just want to protect what's there."

"Do'na worry, lass, we'll be protectin' them alright." He smiled.

"Perfect." She handed him the room dimensions and square footage.

They agreed that the flooring would be delivered and installed when the painting finished on Friday. After the floor was finished, the furniture would come on Monday. The two women had begun their return walk to Lusta when Madison turned to Agatha.

"If you had said how far out of town Mr. Jamison's shop was, we could have driven my car. Are you up for the walk back?" *Am I?* she thought to herself.

"Ack, lass, and how old do ye think I am? Tis only a mile or two. A good stretch of the legs. Besides, Angus is a backward bugger. If we'd come up in yer fancy car, he woulda taken ye for a city lass and no' shown ye a stick. But walkin' ta his door put ye wi the local folk. I know Angus Jamison like the back of me hand. He may be thinkin' he's a wise duff, but he's just a man and dumb as the rest of 'em," Agatha huffed.

"Have you known him long?"

"Aye. We were promised back when the dew was new on me cheeks."

Madison stared at the plump woman walking beside her. She had quite a spring in her step and Madison had to shuffle to keep up. *You're full of surprises, Agatha Stuart,* Madison thought.

"You were engaged to be married?"

"Aye." Agatha smiled and looked out over the hills in the distance. She made no other comment and Madison was more than curious to hear the rest of the story.

"But you didn't marry," she pressed.

"Nay. We dinna."

And that's all, Maddy thought. *You were pleased as punch to tell me what a "bugger" old Andrew Douglas was.* Madison couldn't contain herself.

"May I ask why not? It's none of my business, really, and I don't mean to pry." *Like hell,* she heard a little voice say in her head.

"Nay, I dinna mind telling ye the tale. We were promised and ta be wed come end of the sheerin' season. Me family ha a wee farm no far beyond the Jamison place. We ha chickens and a few cows. But our main cash crop was wool. Me da was a sheepman at heart. Never cared a whit for growin' anything but wool. I was a looker, if ye can buy tha one, back then and all the folk said we were the great pair, Angus and me. He was quite a buck himself. Didna stoop like ye see now. One evening me da was finishin' turning the land before the first snow o' the season, and the nag threw a shoe. He sent me ta town ta have her shod, and I stopped ta see if Angus wouldna care ta share the ride wi me. His mam said he'd done with his chores and ha gone to the pub himself fer a pint before supper. I left the horse wi smithy and walked ta the pub. I figured ta have a pint wi me Angus." She glanced up at Madison to make sure she had her full attention. "I strolled inta the pub and had a look see fer Angus."

The narrative stopped and Madison waited for Agatha to continue. When nothing more was said, Madison began to worry that telling this story had upset her new friend, and Madison felt the pang of guilt. Agatha heaved a sigh and straightened her shoulders.

"Tha black-hearted Angus Jamison dinna have his wick out, but he was primin' it! There he sat canoodlin' the town whore. The wench on his lap fer the whole village to see or be hearin' aboot wi in the hour."

Oh shit, thought Madison. "What did you do?"

"Me first thought was ta jerk the slimy bitch off his lap by her hair and plant me size six boot direct in the middle of his balls!" She took a deep breath. "But me mam and me da taught me ta always be a lady. So I walked over ta the two of 'em and smiled. I told the fast Lucy if there was anything left o that little pecker after she heaved her fat ass off it, she was welcome ta it and wi me blessins."

Madison burst out laughing. "You didn't?"

"Aye, lass, I did. And the pub was full to spillin' over wi the lads. They all heard and laughed the same as ye did yerself just now. Then I turned me back on the bastard and walked oot the door."

The rest of the walk back to the village was passed in relative silence. Madison wasn't sure how she wanted to react to Agatha's story. She had obviously loved Angus when she was a girl, and what she found in the pub that late fall afternoon, had to have shattered the girls heart. Yet, Agatha didn't seem to be carrying a torch for the older Angus, and Madison had to admit, it was a whopping good story.

When they reached the office, Madison was overjoyed. The drywall was up, and joints seams were taped and mudded. It was fairly obvious to anyone who looked, that Patrick and Lizzy had had some kind of good-natured battle with the joint compound. They were both covered with the gray stuff. And it seemed their relationship had progressed, Lizzy was grinning from ear to ear and she looked at Patrick with wide blue eyes filled with laughter. Patrick seemed to be looking at Lizzy a lot and his eyes held a kind of wonder. Madison and Agatha both took in the scene and appreciated the same observation. They looked at each other and smiled knowingly.

"You've been busy around here, I see. This is marvelous! I never expected things to have progressed this quickly." Agatha laughed out loud, and this time it was Madison's turn to receive the elbow in the midsection.

Madison told Lizzy and Patrick about the flooring and furniture she had picked out at Mr. Jamison's shop. She purposely failed to mention the desk that she had purchased for Lizzy, wanting it to be a surprise for Lizzy when it arrived on Monday.

They all agreed it had been a long day and was time to call it quits and have some dinner at the pub down the street. Madison also invited the workers that Patrick had hired and bought dinner for everyone. Pleased with all the progress the mood was celebratory mood, and the meal lasted longer than Madison had anticipated. It had been a successful day, but she was beat, and shortly after everyone had finished eating, she thanked everyone again for all their hard work. She told Lizzy to take the morning off and not bother to come to the office until noon.

"Oh mum...Miss Madison, I'll have to be there in the morning to put the second coat of joint compound on the wall seams. Me uncle would be verra disappointed if I dinna do me job oop tight, like he taught me.

But I'll start early so as to let the mud dry in time to sand for the paint." She looked as bright as if she had just had a full day's rest. *Ah, youth,* Madison thought.

"Well, I won't be in until later," she said. "I have to order the phone service and the paint won't be delivered until one anyway." Madison said her goodbyes and Patrick walked her to her car.

"Patrick, thanks for all your help today."

"No' ta worry, I had alo' of fun. Unfortunately, I willna be much help ta ya fer a while. I'm booked solid wi patients fer the next few days." He smiled.

Madison thanked him once more, got into the Wagoneer and drove home. She walked into the empty house and missed Ian terribly, but she was exhausted, and once she stripped off her clothes and climbed into bed, she fell asleep immediately.

Chapter Fifteen

As the week moved along, Madison, Lizzy, and Agatha sanded, primed, and painted the walls a soft ivory yellow. On Friday, as promised, the flooring was delivered and laid. The men who laid the flooring told Madison that since it was glued, it needed to lay undisturbed for twenty-four hours. So Madison told Lizzy to take the rest of the day off and come back on Monday at eight thirty. Madison spent the rest of the morning on her cell phone ordering phone service and supplies for the office. In the afternoon Madison called Margaret and asked her to order cell phones and beepers for new employees.

"I'm also going to need some printers and computers," she said.

"Sure, how many are we talking about here?" asked Margaret.

"Oh, I think three for now. But Margaret, I want good ones. Not any like that piece of shit you have there. I also want a color laser printer."

"Well, okay, but you know Mr. Goldblum will have a fit if I don't clear all this with him first."

"Aye, I know," Madison sighed

"Hey, do you realize you're beginning to pick up an accent?" Margaret laughed.

"Am I really?" Madison beamed. "Cool. I have to go, I'll call you later and see how everything is coming."

As Margaret hung up the phone, she noticed a man coming toward her. He was moderately attractive, but Ian Mackay or Henry Cavill, he wasn't. He was dark complexioned, and as he came closer, she realized he was tanned from the sun. He wasn't very tall, maybe about five nine. When he reached her desk he stopped and looked down at her.

"May I help you?" she asked. His eyes were a dark brown almost inky black in color.

"Yes, I'm looking for Madison Danaher. Is she around?" His voice was gruff and deep.

"May I have your name?" She wasn't sure who he was, but he seemed familiar somehow. She wasn't sure why but he was setting off warning bells.

"Yes, my name is Jason Danaher, and I am working on my family history and would like to ask her some questions about her father Michael."

"Did you say you were looking for Madison Danaher?" came Dean's voice from down the hall.

Adam Gilmore spun around to face the man who had just spoken up. "Yes, I did. As I was telling the young lady here, I am a relative of the Danaher line and I wanted to ask her some questions about her father."

"Well, why don't you come to my office and we can talk."

Adam followed Dean to his office and sat down in one of the chairs in front of his desk.

"So," Adam said, "is Madison here?"

"No, I'm sorry, she's gone out of the country on business."

"Too bad, I was really hoping to talk with her. You see, my daughter was diagnosed with diabetes. My wife's family has no history of that disease, and after the doctors finally got Jennifer's blood levels under control, I decided to do a search into my own family blood line. In my research, I came across Michael Danaher, and as I was going to be in town on business for a couple of days, that I would look him up."

"Oh, well, I am sorry, but Michael Danaher died some time ago."

"Yes, I learned of his death yesterday, but in doing so, I also discovered he had a daughter and I thought she might have passed along any family history to her."

Dean, not knowing the true origin of Madison's family was buying the simple story hook line and sinker.

"I see, well I'm sorry to say, but she is in Scotland for six months and won't be returning any time soon."

Adam put on a grieving face and Dean spoke again, "But I'll be speaking with her tonight. I'll mention that you came by and if you will leave me your number, I'm sure she'll want to get in touch with you."

"Oh thank you." Adam took the paper and pen Dean offered and wrote down a phony number and handed it back to him. Just then Dean was called out of his office, and asked if the man called Jason Danaher would wait for him to return.

Once the CEO left the room, Adam noticed Dean's cell phone sitting on the desk and picked it up. He scrolled through the cellular phone book and saw that Madison's number was listed. He slipped the phone into his pocket and sat back in the chair just as Dean came into the room.

"Well, I don't want to take up any more of your time," Adam said. "Thank you for listening." They shook hands and Adam left Dean's office.

An hour later Dean was looking for his phone. "I could have sworn I had it with me. I can't believe I left it at home."

As Adam entered his hotel room he marveled at how easy it was to find out so much about his little wife, and in such a short period of time. Not only where she was but that she had been whoring with the boss.

"It'll probably take a couple of days for that moron to figure out that his phone was stolen," Adam chuckled out loud. "I'll have to get all the information I can and fast so I can dump the phone."

Adam took out his freshly stolen laptop and started to look up hotels in Scotland. After several hours of calling, he found that Madison wasn't staying in any hotel he could find.

"She must be renting a house somewhere," he said aloud. "But where?"

He remembered that Dean had said she was there on business. He looked at a map of Scotland pinpointing his interest on larger cities, and realized that finding her was going to take a long time.

"Well, I have all the time in the world," he said and decided to start his search in the morning with a fresh mind.

On Monday Madison arrived at the office at seven in the morning. As she walked in and turned on the lights, she looked around at the room. Although the space still lacked furniture, it was a pleasant happy room, and she was pleased by the way it looked. As she stood, she could smell fresh pastries and knew Agatha had been in the bakery for several hours. She went through the door that adjoined the bakery and the office and entered the kitchen. Sure enough there was Agatha baking up a storm. Madison stood for a while and watched her new friend in awe as she moved around the kitchen. She was quick as a young girl and every bit as fussy. Madison watched as she saw Agatha separate the pastries to different trays. When she didn't look up, Madison cleared her throat.

"No need to do tha', lassie. I knew ye were here when ye walked in ta yer own office," Agatha grumbled.

Madison laughed and sat down on one of the stools around the butcher-block table. A small plate with Danish and a cup of tea appeared in front of Madison. As Madison sat and sipped her tea she heard Lizzy come in the back door of the office.

"We're in the kitchen," Madison sang out. Lizzy appeared in the connecting doorway and smiled. Madison motioned for her to grab a seat and Agatha set out tea and a Danish for Lizzy. Lizzy and Madison ate their breakfast and heard a knock on the front door of the office. Madison looked at her watch and figured it was the furniture and left to answer the door.

Sure enough, there was Angus Jamison peering in the front window

"Good morning!" Madison said as she opened the door to allow him entrance.

"And a good monrin' ta ye as well, lass!" Angus smiled. "If ye dinna mind, I'll be usin' the back door if ye ha one, ta haul in yer pieces.

"Angus ye old bugger ye know perfectly well there is a back door," came Agatha's voice from the doorway to the bakery.

Madison, not wanting to allow another war of words, spoke up. "I'll move my car so you can park your truck and unload." She left the room and, not knowing how big Angus's truck was, moved her car several shops down. As she hopped out of the cab, she saw a large flatbed covered with tarps pulling up behind the building. It was then that Madison noticed Angus hadn't brought any men to help unload the full truck, and with only she and Lizzy to help, she knew they would need assistance. She pulled out her cell phone and called Patrick. She told him of her dilemma and asked if he knew of someone who might want to earn some extra money.

"No need for that. I can help, Danny. Will be there right away. And fer God sakes, don't let Angus move any o those pieces till I get there."

Madison smiled at her new nickname.

While they waited for Patrick to arrive, Madison persuaded Agatha to give Angus some tea and Danish. The four of them sat around the butcher-block table and Madison chuckled at pairs banter. Since Agatha and Angus's shared history, Madison wondered if she'd had been secretly carrying a torch for Angus all her days.

As they sat, Madison's mind wandered to thoughts of Ian and realized how much she missed him. *I hope the filming is going well*, she thought to herself. Her daydreams of Ian were interrupted by a male Irish brogue.

"Hello, everyone!" Patrick stood in the doorway of the kitchen wearing his doctor's scrubs and coat.

"Oh, Patrick," Madison sighed. "Were you on your way to the hospital?"

Patrick came into the kitchen and stood next to Lizzy and spoke. "I don't have ta be there fer several hours, but I figured since this is on the way ta the hospital, I would just leave from here." Patrick looked over at Angus and smiled. "Well, Angus, let's have a look at the fine pieces ye have brought ta fill this wonderful office, eh." He then looked down at Lizzy. "Would ye give me the honor o helping me ta bring them in?"

Lizzy beamed. "I would be happy ta, sir."

Madison smiled and followed the three of them out the door and watched as Patrick climbed onto the bed of the truck, pulled back the tarp, and revealed the gorgeous pieces she'd chosen. The sun reflected off the glistening hand rubbed finish of the desks and other pieces. Lizzy and Madison went to the back of the truck and both grabbed the end of the first desk and guided it down as Patrick slid it from the truck. Once they had all the pieces on solid ground the three of them began to carry them into the building. Angus kept asking if they needed assistance, and as much as a fourth person would have been a help;

they all knew his back would not be able to handle the load. As they carried the last desk in, Madison had to ask.

"Angus," she breathed, "how on earth did you get all this on the truck in the first place?"

"Me sons came over and loaded them," he explained.

Your sons, she thought to herself, *he married.* She wanted to ask about his history, but now wasn't the time. After the office set up and they were a little better acquainted she might ask. *Or,* she thought, *I can ask Agatha when we're alone.*

As Madison, Lizzy, and Patrick were placing the furniture the phone company arrived to install the phones lines. When the final desk was set, one of the workers asked Madison if those would be the final resting place for the desks.

"Yes, I believe so." Madison thought for a moment. "But it might be a good idea to put in some extra jacks, so we can expand and allow for computer access."

"Aye, will do," he said and continued his task.

The furniture was placed, the phone lines installed, and the workers had left, Madison took the opportunity to stand back to admire the office, and she couldn't have been happier. It was absolutely beautiful. The mixture of wood grains and color tones in the furniture were warm and inviting, and the wall color and old chestnut flooring seemed to have a calming, almost comforting effect. It was the ambiance she'd been striving for, knowing that the people coming in would likely have no prior experience with hospice. Madison wanted the office to have the feeling of sanctuary, and she felt they had accomplished the goal. Madison decided to show Lizzy her new desk and asked the girl to join her at the front of the room.

"What do you think of this desk, Lizzy?" she asked as she smiled.

"Oh, miss, tis a wonder, ta be sure. I dinna think I ha ever seen such beauty in me life." Madison watched as Lizzy ran her slim fingers delicately over the top of the oak desk and looked at the piece in awe.

"I'm glad you like it, because it's yours." Madison laughed at the shocked expression on Lizzy face.

"Oh no, I couldna ever work on anything as fine as this." Madison smiled and wrapped her arm lovingly around Lizzy's shoulder.

"Oh, yes you can, and you will." Madison gave her a small squeeze. "Like I said before, you're in the big times now, kiddo." Madison's cell phone came to life and she recognized Dean's ring instantly and begrudgingly answered the call.

"Yes?" she answered and waited for a response that didn't come. "What?" she bellowed in the phone. Not being accustomed to such a sharp tone the group in the looked at her in surprise. Madison, however, paid them no mind as she continued with her phone call. "Dean, I've told you before not to call me unless it was business related. What do you want?" There was still no answer, but Madison knew that he was on the line for she could hear him breathing.

"Madison." A soft male voice came over the line.

"Don't call me again!" she demanded and hung up the phone with anger.

Agatha spoke first. "Well, lassie, what was that aboot?" She knew, of course, and decided that it was the man who was harassing Madison and making life stressful for her.

"Oh nothing, just a nuisance." She shoved her phone into her pocket, left the room, and heading to the kitchen for a cup of tea. As she sat down to drink the tea, her phone rang again.

"Hello?"

"Maddy, me darling, how are ye?" Ian's lovey voice soothed over the line.

Madison smiled, it wasn't the first time Dean had called to instigate inappropriate conversation, that Ian seemed to follow immediately behind to cheer her up. *It's like he knows when I need to hear his voice,* she thought.

"Ian, I so happy you called."

He could hear the need in her voice and knew that something was wrong. "Madison, what happened?"

"Oh nothing really, Dean just called, don't worry. How are you?"

"Fine, filming is going verra well and we'll be leaving for New York soon."

"Cool, do you have any idea of how long the filming will last?"

"No' yet, but I'll able to take a break and come home for a couple of days."

"You will?" Madison voice was bright and full of anticipation.

"Aye, me lady."

"How soon?"

"Maybe within the next two weeks." He smiled as her frustration had vanished.

"Oh, Ian, that would be wonderful!" she breathed.

"Aye, it would, I canna wait ta see ye and feel ye in me arms."

"Ian?" she said quietly.

"Aye."

"Agatha is here with Patrick and Lizzy. The office renovations were completed this morning. We were just admiring our handy work."

"This is yer way of telling me ye're no alone then, and canna express yer affections."

"Aye." She grinned.

"But if ye could, ye'd tell me o yer vast and great love fer me," Ian prompted.

"Aye." Her grin broadened.

"And ye'd tell me of the lovely things we'll do together *and* ta each other when I can be wi ye again."

"Aye."

"Are ye turnin' a lovely shade of pink, then, darlin?"

"Aye!" Madison laughed out loud. "*Are ye satisfied, then?*" she mimicked.

"Well, I willna say I'm exactly satisfied, but I can hear tha' yer mood is brighter. So I've accomplished something."

"You have indeed, kind sir. And I thank you."

"I love ye lassie."

"And I, you," she breathed.

As Madison hung up the phone, she turned and her cheeks flamed as she saw Patrick standing in the doorway. *How much did he hear?* she wondered. Just as she was about to ask, her phone gave way again, looking at the read out told her it was her office calling.

"Hello?"

"Madison?"

"Hello, Samuel, how are you?" she asked the owner and president of Tender Care Hospice.

"Good. Can you come back to Philadelphia tomorrow? I would like to meet with you and go over your progress."

"Tomorrow?" She began mentally listing the items still to be accomplished before she felt comfortably leaving the new office. "No, but I can get a flight on Wednesday. Would that be alright?"

"Absolutely. See you then."

Madison hung up and went into her office to make the announcement.

"Well, guys, it looks like I'm going back to Philadelphia for a meeting with my boss on Wednesday." Madison looked at Lizzy and continued. "While I am gone can you keep an eye on things here, and answer the phones?"

"O course. How long will ye be gone?"

"I'm not sure, hopefully, no more than a few days. Oh, and Lizzy, why don't you come over for dinner tonight at the house. In fact, why don't you all come?"

"Ah sure we would be delighted ta come and join ye fer diner," Agatha accepted.

"How about you, Patrick?" Madison asked. "Would you be able to come also?"

"O course. What time?" Patrick smiled.

"How does six o'clock sound to everyone?" she asked.

"Sounds perfect," Patrick exclaimed. "I'll pick Agatha up on me way from the hospital, and if Lizzy would allow me ta," His hazel eyes settled on Lizzy. "I could pick ya up as well."

Lizzy looked up from her desk and directly into his eyes. "I would love ta ha ye take me ta dinner." She smiled.

"Great! Then it's all settled." Madison clapped. "I'm going to go home and make the flight arrangements and start to prepare dinner. See you all at six." She waved and sailed out.

Once in the door, Maddison realized she had no idea what to make for dinner or how to make it.

"God, I wish Ian was here." She told Julie who was demanding attention as Madison opened her laptop to look up some recipes. After some searching, she found one that appeared to be simple and easy enough and printed it out.

Now that she knew what was for dinner, she called British Airways and made the reservation to leave Scotland on Wednesday and booked her return flight for Saturday. A glance at her watch told her she had three hours before dinner needed to be prepared, so she went upstairs to pack a few things for the trip. Julie sensed something was going on and was constantly under foot. Madison nearly tripped over her several times before finally making the kitty sit on the bed. After Madison had been upstairs for a while, there was a knock at the door.

"Bloody Hell it's six-thirty!" She bellowed and ran downstairs to open the door. "I am so sorry! I lost track of time and haven't started to make dinner." Embarrassment washed over her.

"Donna fret yer head over it, lassie," Agatha soothed. "We'll help ye cook." A sigh of relief flooded over Madison, and she led them to the kitchen.

After the meal was finished Madison asked if Lizzy wouldn't mind staying at the house and watching over Julie while she was gone.

"No, I wouldna mind in the least. I luv cats and she seems a friendly sort."

Madison showed her where the guest room and where the spare key was kept. She took her to the cellar so she would know where the laundry facilities were in case she needed them while Madison was away. Then told her to use whatever was in the house in the way of foods or appliances or firewood to make her stay comfortable.

When they finished their tour of the house, Lizzy joined Agatha in the living room while Madison went to the kitchen to prepare a tray for coffee and tea. Patrick joined her in the kitchen and asked if she would mind if he came over and looked in on Lizzy while she was away.

Madison smiled. "No, I wouldn't mind at all." She looked over at Lizzy and Agatha who were sitting in the living room and then back to Patrick, "I think she would enjoy your company," she said, grinning, for she knew what was on Patrick's mind, even if he didn't know himself yet.

When the coffee tray was ready, Madison carried it to the living room, and the four of them sat and talked for a while in front of the fire Patrick built. Even though spring was turning the days warmer, the nights were still chilly, and a glowing fire was welcome. After a while Agatha began to doze and Patrick decided it was time to get her back home and they took their leave.

Madison climbed into bed and thoughts of Ian filled her mind. She missed him terribly, especially at night. She didn't go to the office the next day, but decided instead to stay in the quiet house and organize the report for her meeting with Samuel Goldblum.

On Wednesday she stood in her kitchen at four in the morning, having a cup of coffee and waiting for the car to arrive to take her to the airport. Suddenly there was a knock on the door and since the car wouldn't be there until five, she figured it was Lizzy to stay with Julie. And sure enough, there was Lizzy *and* Patrick with her bags in his hand.

"Well, good morning," Madison said, smiling, "to you *both*. Please, come in." As Lizzy and Patrick entered the house, Lizzy took her bag from Patrick and went to the guest room.

"Patrick," Madison chuckled, "why are you up this early?"

"When I was droppin Lizzy home the other night, she mentioned she was to be here before you left this morning. Since, I had ta be at the hospital early, I offered ta drive her here." He smiled.

Lizzy came back down and thanked Patrick for the ride and he took his leave. Madison gave a nod of approval to Lizzy and went back to the kitchen to pour her a cup of coffee. They sat at the island and chatted until it was time for Madison to leave, but not before she picked up Julie and gave her a hug and kiss goodbye.

"I love you, Julie girl," she told her cat, "and Lizzy here will take good care of you while I'm away." She looked at Lizzy. "Won't you?"

"Oh, aye, I will," Lizzy said. "Ye dinna need to worra aboot a thing."

Madison put down the kitty and walked to the door without a look back, and off she went to Philly.

Chapter Sixteen

Madison arrived in Philly at noon on Wednesday. She was on Scotland time so her body was telling her it was five o'clock and her workday should be nearly over, but decided to go straight to the office. Thanks to Margaret, Madison's Wagoneer was in the airport garage, and she didn't have to call a cab or a limo. *Although, I wouldn't mind having the limo right now,* she thought.

As she began her half hour trek from Philadelphia International to her office she'd already begun to miss Scotland. She couldn't wait to go home to the wonderful house she shared with Ian and the fantastic new friends she had made. Or to get back to the wide-open spaces, the friendly people, and the much slower pace of the Highlands. The "City of Brotherly Love" didn't seem to be as loving as it had before she left it. Everyone was in a big hurry to get wherever they were going, and nobody was going fast enough to suit the guy behind. Madison began to feel claustrophobic and had to roll down the windows, took in a deep breath, and got a nose full of the car exhausted air Philadelphia had to offer. As she sat at a traffic light just before the office, she wondered if Ian was in New York yet. *If he is, he's only two hours away,* she thought. *Nope, you're here on business and nothing else.* When she pulled into the parking garage of her building, she decided to call Lizzy and to confirm her safe arrival. She parked her car in her designated spot and called the office in Scotland, but there was no answer, smiling Madison called Agatha's bakery and waited.

"Aye" came Agatha's voice

"Hey, Agatha, it's Madison."

"Ah how are ye, lass?" Agatha smiled. "Does tha mean ye've landed, then?"

"Aye," Madison sighed. "I tried to call Lizzy at the office, but she must have left already."

"Aye, she did that." Agatha's voice became quiet. "And she dinna leave alone."

"She didn't?" Madison breathed.

"Tha' Dr. O'Connell came and took her home."

"Agatha," Madison scolded, "when are you going to start to call him Patrick? He calls you Agatha for heaven sakes and everyone knows that you approve of him, otherwise you would have sent him packing by now."

"Is it? Well," she chuckled, "Are ye done with yer work for the day, then, lass? Because I am and I'll be wantin' ta get ta me own hearth before another bumblefuck rings me doorbell fer a pastry. So I'll leave a note fer Lizzy ta let her know ye've called this day." And with that, Agatha ended the conversation, and a laughing Madison had no choice but to go to work. *Dammit,* she thought to herself.

Madison leaned back into the seat and sighed. *This didn't seem like work when I was in Scotland,* she thought. *Oh, well.* She climbed out of the Wagoneer, collected her briefcase, laptop, and overnight bag and headed for the elevator.

The doors slid open, and Madison walked out of the elevator through the glass doors of Tender Care Hospice on the tenth floor. The receptionist looked up from behind her circular mahogany desk and smiled at Madison.

"Well, hello stranger! Welcome back," she said.

"Hi, Susie, how are you?" She waved as she breezed by the desk and continued on down the hall to her own office door.

Margaret's desk was vacant, but Madison could smell fresh coffee brewing, and something else she couldn't quite identify. When she went through her private office door, she spied Margaret leaning over the gleaming glass and chrome desk, a cloth in one hand and a bottle of Windex in the other.

"Good afternoon!" Madison said.

Margaret jumped and as she turned, she accidentally sprayed Windex about the room. Madison laughed.

"I hadn't realized that cleaning was part of your job description." She grinned.

Margaret laughed too and reached out and the two hugged their hello.

"I just wanted your space to be tidy when you got back, and I don't approve of the way your desk has been cleaned. It always looks kind of streaky to me. How was the flight?"

"Long. You know if you don't like the way maintenance does their job, you should mention it to them." She chuckled and shook her head. The desk always looked fine to her and decided it was her own fault for choosing a desk with a glass top anyhow. "What time am I supposed to meet with Samuel?"

"He left a memo that he'll be in at two. There's no notation for what time he's to meet with you."

"Good. That gives me time to freshen up a little. It was a long flight and I feel like I've been in these clothes for a week. If Samuel buzzes, tell him I'll be there in twenty minutes."

"Okey-dokey. Your gray suit is hanging in the bathroom closet," Margaret said as she returned to her own office, closing the door behind her, while Madison walked into the bathroom.

"Thank you, Samuel, for this bathroom," she said aloud as she slipped under the warm spray of shower. When Samuel Goldblum promoted her to chief operating officer of the company, he'd made quite a show of presenting her with the office. He'd almost apologized because it wasn't a corner office with wraparound windows, but had been very excited to show her the connecting bathroom, dramatically enhanced with a full shower. Madison had been somewhat embarrassed with the opulence. But Samuel assured her that in her new position; she would often be attending business meetings and dinners directly after working hours and would need a comfortable place to change.

Madison was changed and freshly groomed twenty minutes later. She walked out of the bathroom and reentered her office to find Dean lounging on her sofa.

Jesus! she thought to herself. *What the hell is he doing in here?*

"Madison, my love, it's nice to see you." Dean rose from the sofa and oozed across the floor. "Come here, honey, so I can give you the welcome home you must have been waiting for since you got off the plane."

Madison closed her eyes and sighed. *If I close my eyes maybe he will go away.* She thought and pinched the bridge of her nose and opened her eyes, *nope still here.* "Dean, what exactly do I have to say, to make you understand that I have not, nor will I ever be interested in you romantically. This is a business office, for God's sake. We have a business relationship, and that's it." She deliberately circled behind the chairs to reach her desk in an attempt to avoid him. He, however, was too swift and cut her off before she could reach her desk.

Taking Madison's arm, he pulled her to him and pressed his lips to hers. Madison raised her fists to his chest and tried to push him away. As she struggled from his embrace, she drew back her double fist and jammed it into his chin. Taking him completely off guard, he drew back and momentarily let go of her.

"What the——?" he exclaimed.

Just as he reached out for her again, a male voice boomed his name.

"Dean!" Samuel Goldblum stood in the doorway. One hand on the brass knob and the other clutched against the doorframe. For the first time since Madison had known him, he looked truly angry. His normally blue eyes were a hard steel gray. His thick graying eyebrows slanted downward in an angry crease. Before entering the room, he turned to Margaret and said, "You may go to lunch." He stepped into the room and closed the door firmly behind him.

"What is going on in here?" he demanded. He looked at Dean. "Leave us," he ordered.

Madison let out her breath and glared at Dean as he smiled and strode from the room. *Shit,* she thought, *now what am I going to do?* When the door closed behind Dean, Samuel's expression changed from anger to concern.

"Samuel, I'm truly sorry about this. I never meant—" But he stopped her as he raised his palm to ward off her apology.

"Don't apologize. Just tell me what happened." He walked to the sofa and sat down, indicating for her to take a seat also. "Take a deep breath and start at the beginning. I'm gathering from the right hook, that you didn't invite Dean's attention."

"No. I didn't. And I feel that I must apologize for being unable to somehow to convince him of that."

"Have you had problems like this with him before today?" When Madison hesitated, Samuel continued. "Talk to me," he said.

"Actually, yes, since the day last January when you gave me the okay to go to Scotland," she said as she sat in one of the two wing chairs across from the sofa.

Samuel's eyes flashed and his brows shot upward. "This has been going on for four months?" Madison nodded. "Have his actions ever become more forceful than what I just witnessed?"

"If you're asking if he has ever been more *physical* forceful, the answer is no. However, he did show up uninvited in Scotland a few months ago." When Samuel remained quiet, Madison continued. "The day you gave me the okay to go to Scotland, Dean came to my office. It was late and I was trying to get my desk cleared and work caught up before I left. For some reason he'd apparently decided it was time that our relationship moved on to a new and more personal level. I will admit that when he kissed me, I was so taken aback that I didn't stop it right away. However, once I broke away, I did tell him that I was not interested." Madison took a breath and went on. "I don't know why he thought we had anything beyond a professional relationship, but since that night I have not been able to convince him otherwise."

Samuel leaned back into the sofa and pressed his elbow into the armrest and took his chin in between his forefinger and thumb. "Tell me about his appearance in Scotland."

Madison pushed herself out of her chair and began to pace about the room. *I don't believe this is happening,* she thought. With visible effort, she relaxed her shoulders, looked at Samuel and began to speak. "This is so awkward. It's like trying to explain to my dad what happened when I refused to go under the bleachers with the captain of the football team."

Samuel smiled and perked up a bit and said, "Yeah? What did happen?" He chuckled.

Madison laughed and felt almost cleansed. She sat back down in her chair with ease.

"Maddy I have known you since you were seventeen years old, and I have come to think of you as the daughter I never had." Madison looked into his wonderfully kind eyes and knew that she could tell him anything.

"As you know I am renting a house from Ian Mackay. One morning in February Dean showed up on my doorstep, and as I said he was uninvited. I asked him what he was doing there, and he said he had come to spend his vacation with me and intended to stay at the house. He acted as though we were lovers who had been parted for a month and in need of some kind of fulfilling reunion. I reminded him that we had only a professional relationship and I did not want anything more form him. I asked him to leave, but he refused. He continued to refer to this fantasy love affair that he insists we're having."

"If he refused to leave, how did you get him to go?" Samuel asked.

"Well, Ian who owns the house was there at the time. When it became obvious that my efforts to get Dean to leave were having no effect, Ian stepped in." She took a breath. "But had Ian not been there, I might never have gotten rid of him."

"Ian?" He arched his eyebrow and smiled as Madison's cheeks began to color. "Now, how would you like for the situation to be handled?"

"I don't know. I've tried everything I can think of, and he won't listen to me. Or leave me alone. He continues to call me at ridiculous hours and tries to have conversations that have nothing to do with business. To be honest, I don't even know how this whole thing got started. He talks about dates he says we've had and we have only had business dinners. I have tried everything I can think of, and I confess; I'm at a loss. And I hate bringing a problem like this into the office."

"You didn't bring this into the office, Maddy. He did with his inexcusable conduct." Samuel let out a breath. "It appears that this situation calls for a more forceful resolution. Would you mind if I handled it from this point on?"

"Yes, frankly. I should be able to take care of this on my own," she said with frustration.

"Maddy, you've been trying to handle it on your own for four months. Unsuccessfully I might add. Why don't you let me have a whack at him—it?" he corrected with a wink.

Samuel rose from the sofa and walked toward the door. He smiled down at Madison and patted her hand as he passed her. Just then there was a knock at the door.

"Come in," Madison said.

Margaret opened the door and stuck her head into the room. "Mr. Goldblum, the reporters are here for the press conference. They're waiting in the conference room."

"Thank you, Margaret. Tell them Madison and I will be there in a moment." Samuel, knowing what her reaction would be, turned and looked sheepishly at Madison.

"Press conference?" Madison asked.

"Yes, I've invited the press core to cover our announcement of opening an office in Europe."

"Is that why you brought me back here?" she asked, brow arched.

"Well, we could have covered your progress report over the phone, but I felt that since you were in charge of the new office, you were the one that should talk to the press about it." Samuel put his hands behind his back and hunched his shoulders. "And I knew that if I told you there was going to be a press conference, I would never get you out of Scotland. Besides," he straighten and grinned at her. "I missed seeing your smiling face." He recovered his professional composure. "Now, I'm even doubly glad you're here. We can take care of one situation and eliminate the more unpleasant one." He opened the door to leave her office and then turned toward her.

"Put on your professional COO smile and I'll meet you in the conference room in ten minutes." He closed the door behind him and walked purposely to Dean's office and went through the door without knocking.

Dean looked up from a half-reclining position in the heavy leather swivel chair behind his desk and smiled. Samuel looked at Dean and thought, *It's a good thing I don't have my father's walking stick, or I would surely put lumps all over this schmuck's swelled head.*

"We'll be meeting with the local press corps in the conference room in five minutes. Be there. Immediately following the press conference, kindly meet me in my office," he stated, and without further comment, Samuel turned on his heel and left the doorway.

"Absolutely," Dean answered, but Samuel was gone before the word was completed.

Madison walked confidently into the office conference room with a smile on her face, and a short typed speech in her hand that Margaret had given to her. Samuel glanced over at her and indicated that she was to stand by his side. Flashbulbs went off and microphones with Network logos clipped to the front were held forward. Samuel spoke first.

"Ladies and gentlemen, I'd like to introduce our Chief Operating Officer, Madison Danaher. Our new European office was Madison's brainchild and since she is in charge of this expansion, I'll let her tell you of our progress." He smiled to Madison and invited her to speak. Madison smiled back and turned to face the room.

"Good afternoon. As Mr. Goldblum has already mentioned, Tender Care Hospice has expanded outside the boundaries of the United States and opened an office in the Highlands of Scotland."

Madison read the prepared statement Margaret typed for her, then fielded questions from the local press for the next twenty minutes. When the questions became repetitious, she closed the conference by thanking the press for their interest and excused herself from the room.

After the reporters filed out of the office, Samuel went to Madison's office.

"Maddy, it's been a long day for you. Why don't you go home and rest for a few hours. I'll send a car for you about eight o'clock. We'll have dinner together and go over your progress report in a more relaxed atmosphere, enjoy a nice meal, and catch up. And maybe, you could tell me about Ian.'" He smiled. Madison could feel her cheeks turn rosy. Samuel chuckled and closed the door as he left her office.

"Okay, Mr. Michaels, let's dance!" he mumbled as he reached for the knob on his own office door.

Samuel walked into his office and closed the door firmly behind him. Dean stood before the window gazing out at the Philadelphia skyline. He turned when he heard Samuel enter.

"That went very well, I thought," Dean said, referring to the press conference.

"You did, huh?" Samuel said quietly as he walked behind his desk, sat, and leaned back into his executive chair and eyed Dean with contempt.

"Yes." Dean wasn't sure what the point was of this meeting. *Maybe he wants me to go to Scotland and watch over Madison for a while,* he thought to himself with a grin.

"Dean, are you aware why I have asked you to meet with me?" Samuel wanted to see just how delusional the guy was.

"Well, I assume you wanted me to look after Madison and the Scotland office." Dean strolled to one of the guest chairs in front of Samuel's desk and seated himself comfortably in it.

"Hmmm. That's interesting. Would you please explain to me the relationship between you and Miss Danaher?"

"Maddy and I have been enjoying a rather intimate relationship for some time now, although I'm sure you'll agree that our personal lives are our own." Dean smiled and leaned back, resting himself on the chair back.

"I see. Yes, normally I would agree that employee's personal lives are their own, however, when one employee is harassing another, it automatically becomes my job to step in." He paused and Dean looked shocked.

"Harassing? Who is she harassing?"

Samuel smiled. "No, Dean. *She* is not harassing, *you* are."

"I'm not harassing anyone. That's a ludicrous accusation. Who said I was guilty of harassment?" Dean rose from the chair and turned for the door.

Samuel stopped him with his next words.

"Your job and your future depend on you putting your ass back in that chair. Now," Samuel said. His voice was quiet, but the force it wielded was obvious.

Dean returned to the chair and sat quietly, and before Samuel continued, he buzzed his secretary. "Louise, please ask Samantha Mathews to step into my office at once?"

Dean began to be visibly rattled. This was not turning out exactly as he had pictured.

"What is this about, Samuel?"

"You can wait." Samuel leaned forward in his chair and rested his laced fingers on the top of the desk. "What's the matter, Dean, are you beginning to get nervous?"

The two men sat staring at each other until the door opened and Samantha Mathews walked in with her tape recorder.

"Samantha, I'd like for you to record this conference." The Human Resources manager pushed the button on her recorder and Samuel continued. "Today's date is April 10, 2025. This meeting is concerning harassment charges against Dean Michaels, Chief Executive Officer of Tender Care Hospice. These charges against Mr. Michaels are brought by Samuel Goldblum, President, and Chairman of the Board." Samuel looked over to Dean when he finished speaking. Samantha kept her eyes focused on the recorder.

"You're bringing harassment charges against me? When have I ever harassed you?" Dean was stunned. Samuel looked toward Samantha again and continued.

"These charges of sexual harassment against Dean Michaels, I am bringing on behalf of Madison Danaher Chief Operating Officer of said company."

"WHAT!" Dean surged out of his seat.

Finally, Samuel turned and focused his full attention on Dean.

"It has come to my attention, as a firsthand witness, that you have taken it upon yourself to create, to put it mildly, an imaginary romantic relationship between yourself and Madison Danaher COO of this company."

"IMAGINARY? Samuel, that's ludicrous! Maddy and I—"

Samuel spoke quietly. "Dean, I am not by nature a violent man. And I abhor rudeness in people, but shut and sit back down!" Samuel leaned forward in his chair. "Don't talk to me about you and Maddy. There is no you and Maddy. Is it true that you did indeed go to Scotland uninvited and intrude on her private life?"

"Of course, it's not true. We made plans before she left for me to join her in Scotland for my vacation. Jesus, then when I got there, I found her whoring with some other guy."

Samantha looked up in time to see Samuel's complexion change from slightly flushed to crimson. She had never witnessed Samuel truly angry, and was almost shocked to see his expression at that moment. She also witnessed his obviously difficult struggle to maintain an outwardly calm demeanor.

"What Madison does and with whom in her free time is her business. Not yours, and I am offended by the use of that word in reference to Madison. Curb your language or you'll find yourself unemployed and out on the street." He waited a beat, then continued. "There were no plans made between yourself and Madison." He stated. "You may have announced that you intended to visit her on your vacation, but you were not invited. In fact Madison specifically asked you not to go to Scotland. She had made her position quite clear to you before she left, that she wanted nothing more and would never want anything more from you than a professional relationship." Samule chuckled without humor. "I don't know if you are too stupid, or just too conceited to grasp that concept. Which is it?"

Dean was struggling with his own anger. His eyes blazed with fury, but he remained seated although he wanted to bolt from the chair and defend his actions with vehemence.

"The woman does not want your attentions." Samuel stood up and moved from behind his desk to stand in front of Dean looking down at him. "Right now, I am having some major concerns about your judgment. Not to mention your mental competence. In addition, I might have to question my own judgment. You are chief executive officer of this company. I would hate to think that I hired an unstable man to run this place. Someone who thinks he can abuse the power and the position he has been given."

This meeting was not turning out the way Dean had anticipated. He was more than angry, he was embarrassed. Nobody spoke to him in this manner. His qualifications as CEO appeared to be in question now, and all because Madison chose to deny their personal relationship, which was frankly none of Samuel's business. With great effort Dean straightened his body in the chair, trying to assume a dignified composure.

"Samuel, I don't know what Madison has told you, but she and I have had a meaningful relationship for a while now, and I'm trying not to be offended—" Samuel cut him off.

"You're 'trying not to be offended,' Dean?" Samuel warned, "Let me assure you that I can fire you right now, just based on what I saw in Madison's office this morning. Don't make it worse by saying something stupid. I assume you are aware of company policy. To form a liaison with someone of rank in this company is in itself, grounds for termination."

Dean stood up and moved away from Samuel. He spoke defiantly. "There is no such policy," he proclaimed.

Samuel smiled and leaned back on the desk and looked at Dean with triumph. "There is now."

"Samuel, I know what you think you saw in Maddy's office, but let me assure you, it was nothing more than a lovers' spat."

"Did you hear what I just said to you?" Samuel's steely eyes drilled into Dean's. "If not, I'll rephrase. If you continue to sexually harass Miss Danaher, I will terminate your association with this company. Without reference. Good God, Man, Madison has the right to sue you in a court of law. Successfully, I might add. And as far as I can tell, she has two witnesses to speak for her."

"Who?"

"Well, the man in Scotland named Ian...." Samuel smiled. "And me. Let me make something perfectly clear. If the CEO and the COO can't work together because the COO has to have a restraining order, one of the company officers will be replaced." Samuel leaned forward. "And Dean it will not be the chief operating officer."

Dean straightened to his full height cloaking himself with presumed importance. "You can't fire me, Samuel."

"Dean," Samuel sighed, "you are not a priceless asset to this company. And even though it would not be pleasant, if you continue to harass Madison I *will* fire you. Replacing you won't be easy, I admit. Up until now, you've been a credit to the company, and you've had an excellent grasp of your duties and responsibilities within the company. However, if this unacceptable behavior of yours continues, I'll be forced to find someone who will not abuse the power as you have done. The name *Tender Care Hospice* refers to the patients. Not the staff."

"Samuel, are you giving me an ultimatum?" Dean was shocked.

"No. I am making you a promise. Either you cease to contact Madison Danaher other than for business purposes or I promise, you will be fired."

Dean looked up at the ceiling and shook his head. "After all these years, I can't believe we've come to this. You would take her word over mine?"

"I have known Madison since she was seventeen years old, Dean." Samuel smiled with his memories. "I've watched her grow from a young inexperienced girl to a competent knowledgeable, principled woman. I know her, and I recognized what I witnessed in her office this morning."

Dean turned on his heal and left Samuel's office. Samuel looked back to Samantha Mathews and thanked her for attending.

"I'm confident there's no need to remind you that this meeting was confidential, and that what was discussed will remain within the parameters of your capacity as Human Resources manager." Without waiting for her to respond, he continued. "Please transcribe what was recorded. Three copies for signatures. I'll want them on my desk before you leave this afternoon. Ask Louise to come in here as you leave."

"Yes, sir, right away." Samantha smiled, collected her steno pad and recorder, and left the private office. Samuel heard muffled voices in the outer office. and a few seconds later, Louise Clayborne entered.

"Louise, I want a company policy written forbidding interoffice dating. Do it now please and bring in a copy for my signature." The older woman gave a crisp nod and left, closing the door behind her.

Samuel sat down behind his desk. He felt tired. He leaned back in his chair and thought about Dean and the meeting that had just ended. *Bastard*, he thought.

Forty minutes later Samantha brought the papers she had prepared for Samuel's signature. He slid them into his briefcase, and left the office.

"When you finish with the policy memo, sign my name and file it," he said on his way past Louise's desk. "Send a car for Madison at eight o'clock. She's going to the Trove for dinner."

Louise Clayborne had worked for Samuel for over thirty years. She knew him like nobody else in the office with the exception of his brother Andrew. She knew when he was pleased and when he wasn't. Right now, he wasn't. She recognized it. She also figured out what the closed meeting was about. She wasn't surprised. She'd never really cared much for Dean Michaels. Just a little too slick, and too sure of himself for her money. And her guess was, his extracurricular activities had finally caught up with him.

"And about time too," she mumbled aloud.

Chapter Seventeen

Madison pulled into the driveway at her townhouse, turned off the ignition, and as she walked to the front door, a feeling of exhaustion washed over her. After the day she'd had, all she wanted was to go home and crawl into bed. As she slid the key into the dead bolt and opened the door, depression joined exhaustion. This wasn't where she wanted to be, this wasn't the small cozy house she wanted. *Hell, I'm not even in the right country anymore,* she thought. Even though the townhouse was hers, bought and paid for, it was no longer *home.* Madison walked inside and wrinkled her nose at the dry stale air that filled the interior. She set her briefcase and overnight bag on the floor and flipped the switch by the door. Lamps on either side of her sofa came to life to brighten the room, but that didn't seem to brighten her mood. She crossed the living room and opened the sliders, then turned to survey the cold dismal stuffy room. *This isn't home anymore,* she thought.

"I don't even have Julie here to cheer me up," Madison said aloud and sank down into the cushy gray suede sofa and rested her head on the back. "I want to go home," she said, and felt as though she was going to cry. She closed her eyes in an effort to ebb the flow of tears and could almost feel herself drifting off to sleep. Just before she was completely gone, she heard her phone ringing in the distance and opened her eyes. Reluctantly, she rose from the sofa and went to retrieve the noisy intruder from her purse.

"Hello," she sighed.

"Maddy, me darlin'!" Ian's voice danced over the line.

"Ian?" she breathed. "Is that you?"

"Aye, luv, hope I'm not disturbin' yer sleep."

"My sleep? How did you kn—" Madison questioned and then remembered that Ian had no idea she was in the States and not more than two hours away from him. "Oh! No, I had to come back to Philly for a meeting."

"Ye're in Philadelphia now?" Ian's joyful voice filled with an anticipation that brought a smile to Madison's face. "Fer how long?"

"I leave to fly back home on Saturday."

Ian's heart missed a beat when Madison referred to Scotland as *home*. A smiled spread across his mouth and his chest seemed to swell with warmth and pride. "I suppose ye'll be workin' the whole time ye're there, then?"

"Nope," Madison said with a smile. "I finished all my work today. I am going to dinner with my boss tonight though, we need to go over the Scotland progress. Other than that, I'll have nothing to bide my time until I leave."

Ian was silent for a moment and then spoke. "Ye know, I was thinkin...."

"What were ye thinkin'?" Madison mimicked.

"Well, filming on Thursday and Friday does no' involve yers truly."

"It doesn't?" Madison asked quietly.

"No." Ian's stomach filled with butterflies. "I was thinking that if ye wouldna mind, maybe we could spend those days together. Tha' is if you would like ta."

"Would I?!" Madison cheered. "Oh, Ian, how can you ask? Can you come here to the house? More importantly, how long will it take you to get here?" When Ian laughed, Madison's smile broadened.

"Aye, luv, I can." Madison gave Ian the directions and told him where the spare key was hidden. "Will ye no' be there, then?"

"Yes and no. I don't know." She laughed out loud from sheer joy and excitement. Suddenly she was no longer exhausted or depressed. "I haven't been here for three months, we're going to need groceries, wine, and other supplies. I'll make a list and shop. This way, if I'm out when you arrive, you can let yourself in and get comfortable." Madison took a breath. "I should warn you, though; I never quite finished unpacking after I moved in, and some of the rooms are still filled with boxes."

"Is the important room free o boxes?" he asked, voice smooth as silk.

"And what room would that be, good sir?" Madison's cheeks grew rosy.

"Why, the bedroom, me darlin! O course."

"Aye, it's 'free of boxes.'" Madison laughed.

"Good, then we can make up on all the lost time." Ian paused and chuckled. "Are ye blushin' then, luv?"

"Ian?"

"Aye?"

"I love you."

"And I you, me darlin."

"You have no idea how much I needed to hear your voice tonight."

"I canna deny the same need, luv, but I ha better leave ye go, so ye can rest and dress for dinner with yer boss." Ian took a breath and then had a horrible thought. "Madison?"

"Mmm?"

"This dinner meetin', it's no' wi Dean Michaels, is it?"

"No, with Samuel Goldblum."

"Oh good. I luv ye, Maddy, and I'll be wi ye tomorrow."

"Till tomorrow, then, I love you too, Ian."

As she disconnected she hugged it to her chest. She took a deep breath and then looked at her watch. It was five o'clock, which meant she would be able to sleep for an hour before she had to get ready for dinner. *Like I could sleep now,* she thought and grinned. She climbed the stairs and was met with the same cold empty stale air. Madison walked into her bedroom and opened the slider to allow fresh air to flow through the room. She turned and surveyed the room and once again came to the same realization she had when she first entered the townhouse. *This really is no longer home,* she thought.

Madison turned on the lamp on the bedside table and drew back the bed covers. Using her phone she set an alarm. Rather than putting on her nightgown, she stripped down to her panties and bra and crawled between the sheets. She had been revived by Ian's phone call and the anticipation of his arrival tomorrow. As she was removing her clothes, she laughed at the idea of being able to sleep, but it had been a long flight and a stressful day. Almost as soon as her head hit the pillow she was out. As she slept, thoughts of Ian filled her head. She dreamed of him and the deep green of Scotland and how happy they'd been together in the house Ian had built. She saw them walking along the cliff watching the waves roll into shore as he took her in his arms. It was a romantic tender scene. Madison and Ian wrapped in each other's arms at the edge of the cliff, with the waves gently lapping in the background. Then the waves became smaller but louder. Instead of gently breaking on the sand and rocks, they began to vibrate toward the beach. The sound of lapping changed to an annoying drone. Madison turned to look at the water and wondered, *what is wrong with this picture?* She looked back at Ian, and he smiled and cast his eyes toward the sky. "Timin' is everything" he muttered.

Madison opened her eyes, rolled over, and slammed off the alarm on her phone. She turned onto her back and pulled the covers to her chin. She wasn't ready to rise from her slumber or let go of the dream; however, she knew if she lay there any longer, she'd fall back to sleep and be late for dinner with Samuel.

"Yeah," she grumbled, "timing is everything." She threw back the covers and padded to the bathroom. She turned on the shower, and while she waited for the water to get warm, she went to the closet to choose something appropriate for dinner with Samuel. She hadn't taken her entire wardrobe to Scotland, of course, but the selection of business dinner clothes was limited. She chose a black pantsuit and a red silk blouse to go with it. She laid the clothes on the bed and returned to the shower. She allowed the steam and hot running water to wash away her grogginess before she picked up the bottle of shampoo and began to lather her hair. After she was finished showering, she dried herself with a towel and slipped into her robe.

Madison sat down at her vanity to blow-dry her hair and apply her makeup. She styled her hair into a French twist and put on what little makeup she wore. She chose her mother's black pearl necklace and matching teardrop earrings to wear with her suit. When she was dressed, she surveyed herself in the mirror, and liked what she saw. As she left the room, she grabbed the matching purse off the bed and went downstairs. In the dining room she switched purses and glanced at her watch.

"Seven thirty, I have time to make a small list of things needed at the store," she said aloud and sat down at the table with a pen and notepad. Just as she was completing her shopping list, the doorbell chimed, and after checking to make sure it was the driver, she grabbed her purse and went out the door.

As Madison rode to the restaurant, she mentally went over the progress she'd made in Scotland and how she was going to present it to Samuel. As they neared the Trove, she remembered that Samuel wanted to know about Ian. *God,* she thought. She and Ian had never talked about this possibility. She wasn't sure how he would want her to handle questions about their relationship if it came up.

"Well, you'll just have to wait and see," she said to herself as she walked through the doors of the lavish Trove restaurant.

The maître-d met Madison before she got to his podium.

"Good evening, Miss Danaher." He smiled graciously. "Mr. Goldblum arrived only moments ago and is already seated. If you'll allow me, I'll show you to your table."

"Good evening, Jeremiah. Thank you." She followed the maître-d through the restaurant toward the back where the noise level was almost nonexistent. Samuel saw Madison when she entered the dining room. He also recognized the appreciative glances she received from other diners as she passed their tables. He was proud of her. *She is an attractive woman,* Samuel thought. *Intelligent, creative, intuitive, competent, the list goes on and on. She is a credit to her sex. She has definitely earned her position in the company.* Just before Madison reached the table, Samuel stood.

"Good evening Samuel. I hope you haven't been waiting long," she said.

"Not at all, I only just arrived myself." Samuel motioned to a chair. "Please," he said, and Jeremiah seated her.

Once they were both seated, Jeremiah gave a slight bow.

"Enjoy your dinner," he said and returned to greet his next guests. A waiter had appeared at Jeremiah's elbow and asked if they would like to start with a cocktail.

"Aye, I would a glass of cabernet," Madison said as she picked up the dinner menu.

"Yes, madame, and you sir?"

"Sounds good to me, I'll have the same," Samuel said as he smiled at Madison in awe.

"I shall return with your drinks directly and take your dinner order." The waiter disappeared and Madison felt Samuel staring at her and she looked up at him.

"What?" she asked with laughter in her voice.

"Aye?" he said with a smile and a twinkle in his eyes.

Madison's jaw dropped, and she lay the menu aside. "Is that what I said?" She drew her hand up to her mouth and began to laugh.

"Yes. It was." He grinned. "You're becoming a Scot, young lady." Samuel smiled. Before Madison could respond, the waiter arrived with their drinks and took their dinner order. When it was the two of them Madison picked up her glass of wine to take a sip as Samuel spoke. "So, tell me about this Ian fellow."

Madison nearly spit her wine all over the table and Samuel. She'd half expected him to ask about Ian, but she assumed he would use some sort of ruse or lead up to it gradually. She looked at him in shock to find him stifling a laugh at her expense.

"What would you like to know?" Madison choked.

"Well, I don't want to pry," *the hell I don't,* he corrected if only to himself, "and if I have overstepped my bounds, feel free to tell me so. I can't help being concerned since you haven't had a relationship since your marriage to Adam." Although Samuel didn't know the particulars, he was aware that she was married to a man who treated her very badly. He knew the marriage ended in a rather messy divorce. Only Ian knew what really happened. "Your father is gone, and, to my knowledge, you have no other family. I hope you won't mind if I feel a certain amount of responsibility for you and for your welfare. As a result, I'm interested to know about the man you have let into your heart."

"What makes you think I've let him into my heart?" she asked coyly and smiled. It was nice to think that someone felt a responsibility for her and truly wanted her happiness.

Samuel said nothing but just looked at her in a fatherly fashion. The same way Poppy had looked at her many times.

"Oh, all right." She smiled and took a taste of wine she had wanted earlier. This taste, however, was more of a gulp than a sip, which made Samuel smile. "As you know the house I've rented outside of Lusta belongs to Ian Mackay. I met him the day after I arrived, and we've become friends. He has been very kind and helpful to me since we met."

"Are you in love with him?" Samuel asked softly. Madison looked into Samuel's eyes and saw his concern. She also saw the same *"you can't fool me"* look that she had seen on Poppy's face when she was a youngster and debating whether the truth was better than trying to fudge it.

"Yes. I am," she sighed.

"And is he in love with you?"

"Yes. He is," Madison said with a smile that radiated happiness and pride. She was glad to be able to share the news of her happiness with Samuel.

"Have you talked together about the future?" he asked. He was pleased to see her happy and he could tell she was, in fact, very happy. It was written all over her face.

"Yes, and no," Madison replied. "Have you ever heard the name Ian Mackay before?"

"I'm not sure. It does sound familiar, but I'm not sure in what context. He isn't *wanted by the law* for anything, is he?" Samuel looked at her with widened twinkling eyes, and Madison laughed out loud.

"Ian is an actor. He's done very well in Europe, and is trying to crack the American audience. That's where he is now, filming a movie that is to be released first in the US. He still lives in Scotland and as far as I know, he has no plans to change that."

Just then the waiter came and placed Madison's Black Angus steak and Samuel's pasta on the table before them.

"So," Madison said after the waiter retreated, "what would you like to know about the progress in Scotland?"

Samuel dropped his eyes to his plate and smiled at the abrupt change in subject, but he decided not to press the issue as Madison seemed to be becoming embarrassed.

"How soon do you think you will be able to take in patients?"

"That's one thing I'll need to have handled here. We'll have to list the office in Scotland up on the license in Pennsylvania as well as with the Healthcare Improvement Scotland. When that is accomplished and I can hire a start-up staff, we can actually begin taking patients onto the service."

"How many employees are you planning on?" Samuel asked as he took a bite of his pasta.

"Well, I have one now. Actually she's almost a jack-of-all-trades." Madison smiled as she told Samuel about Lizzy. "Elizabeth Campbell is a certified home health aide who attended the presentation at the hospital, and applied for a job with us the same day. She showed up at the office, before it was really an office and helped set up the place. She's a home health aide/carpenter/drywaller/painter/decorator! She's also manning the office while I'm here. When I get someone to take her place, and have patients, I'll put her in the field. She's a wonderful kid, and I think she's got a good career ahead of her. And once I know we can take on patients, I'll hire two nurses to case-manage, one more home health aide and someone to run the office."

"Good, but you know you will also need a social worker and a chaplain," he pointed out.

"That's right," she sighed. "See? I told you I haven't done this in a long time." Madison took a bite of her steak. It was good, but nothing like Ian's. They continued talking about the office in Scotland throughout the remainder of their meal. Samuel approved of the central location of the office and Madison's logic for construction, decorating, and furnishing using local craftsmen and merchants.

"You've done well, Madison. But I'm not surprised. It's no less than I expected." Samuel smiled.

"Thank you."

"So, when do you fly back to Scotland?"

"I go back Saturday."

"Oh, then you will be in the office tomorrow and Friday." Samuel took a sip of his wine and looked back up at Madison's face and burst out laughing. She looked absolutely mortified. "What? Do you have something planned?"

"Um, well no," she hedged, "but I was hoping to have a couple of days to rest and take it easy before returning to work."

"I see." He was still laughing. "Well—" He stopped as the waiter came to collect their empty plates and to ask if either of them cared for dessert. "Not for me. Thanks."

"No. Thank you." Madison smiled. Samuel placed his credit card in the guest-check folder, which the waiter picked up and disappeared. Madison picked up her water goblet and drained it in almost two gulps which made Samuel laugh. She looked at him. "Why do I get the feeling you're having a grand old time watching me squirm?" she asked.

"Because I am." When Madison looked stunned, Samuel took the time to explain. "You see, I have not seen you this happy in years. Now, don't get me wrong." He held up his hand in a gesture that asked for patience while he completed his reasoning. "I've seen your enjoyment when you're involved in a big project. I've appreciated your satisfaction when the completion of a project brings big profit to the company. I know you're fulfilled by your competence and success at the office. But that's work related, not your *personal* life. It gives me a great deal of pleasure to see you experiencing joy in something other than business. It's been a long time coming for you, and it makes me happy to see. So forgive me if I can't help teasing you a bit."

"Thank you, Samuel." She chuckled "And thank you for not insisting that I come in for the rest of the week. I really appreciate it."

The waiter returned with the receipt for Samuel to sign and thanked them both and disappeared again. Both Madison and Samuel rose from the table and walked to the front of the restaurant saying goodbye to Jeremiah on the way out the door. The limo Samuel had ordered for Madison was waiting for her. Samuel opened the rear door for her and waited for her to sit down.

"Good night, Samuel. It was a lovely dinner. I enjoyed talking with you." Madison slid into the car and then looked up at him. "And thank you for sending me to Scotland."

"You're very welcome, girlie. Oh and by the way—" Samuel rested his hand on the top of the open door as he peered into the limo and smiled knowingly at Madison. "—when you see Mr. Ian Mackay tomorrow, give him *my* thanks." And with that Samuel shut the car door, leaving an astonished Madison all alone in the back seat.

Samuel smiled as he stood and watched the car drive away from the curb.

"Isn't it remarkable how someone else's happiness can make other's feel so good?" he said to the valet as he handed the uniformed man the ticket for his car. And he did feel good. He felt like laughing. He was going to be forever grateful to the man named Ian, whom he hadn't even met yet. He was proud of Madison. She had gone through some bad times over the last few years. A difficult divorce and the death of her father had been tough pills for her to swallow, but she hadn't allowed those difficulties to destroy her. Nor make her bitter. She was successful in business, and it was time for her to find happiness in her personal life. He looked down at his watch. It was past ten o'clock. *I hope Angie hasn't gone to bed already,* he thought as the valet brought his car to the curb. He wanted to tell his wife the news regarding the Scotland project, but he also wanted to tell her about Madison. Angie had grown quite fond of Madison over the years. *She'll be pleased to hear about this new development,* he thought as he slid behind the wheel and pulled out into traffic.

On the way home, Madison reflected on how dinner had gone and the abrupt subject changes. It filled Madison's heart with how much Samuel had come to care for her. He was concerned about her health, her happiness, and her welfare in general. She looked down at her watch. It was ten thirty, and she was so tired. Madison rested her head on the back of the seat and closed her eyes. She was asleep instantly and dozed the rest of the way home. She didn't open her eyes again until the driver stopped the car in her driveway. Madison straightened up and waited for him to come round and open her door. She thanked the driver as she got out of the car, and then walked to her front door. She slid the key into the dead bolt and opened the door and once again experienced the sense of loneliness she'd felt that afternoon when she walked in the townhous.

"But Ian will be here tomorrow," she said aloud and went to the dining room laying her purse on the table. She made a tour of the downstairs turning out all the lights and checking the sliders and front door. Satisfied that they were securely locked, she climbed the stairs to her bedroom.

Upon entering her room, she felt a breeze coming from the screen porch and noticed the slider was open. "Can't believe I forgot to close that before I left. Not smart, Maddy," she said, but it had been a sunny warm day and the night air smelled sweet, so she continued to her closet to undress. She hung her suit on a padded hanger and reached for a nightshirt from the shelf. When she came out of the closet, she removed her mother's pearls and laid them on the vanity. As she stood by the vanity, she noticed a familiar scent. She turned toward the balcony and there standing in the doorway was Ian.

"Ian!" she cried and ran to his outstretched arms.

"Maddy, luv," he breathed. He wrapped her in his strong arms and held her close. They stood in silence thankful to touch after a two-month separation. Ian felt dampness penetrate his shirt and pulled back to look down at her. She lifted up her aqua eyes to his and they were bright with tears. Ian had dreamed of her sparkling eyes ever since he left Scotland. Now they were intensified with tears. "Maddy, darlin' please donna cry." He gently brushed his fingertips across her cheeks and rested his hand on the side of her jaw.

"Ian." Madison raised her hands to the sides of his face and marveled at the fact that he was there with her. His emerald green eyes were beginning to mist over. "I love you so much—" She wasn't able to say more as Ian brought his lips to hers and kissed her with all the heat and desire he had stored in his heart. Maddy ran her hands up his now very muscular arms until they rested on his shoulders. She could feel Ian's hands caressing her back and traveling to her buttocks. She gave a small, but very promising moan and Ian barely lifted his lips from hers as he spoke.

"I canna tell ye how much I've missed ye, luv." He captured her lips again, and she felt warmth flood her body. Finally, he released her mouth and held her away from him. "Let me have a look at ye." He smiled and Madison stepped back. Holding her arms slightly away from herself, she slowly turned in a circle. She was wearing a short cotton nightgown with spaghetti straps. When she came to a stop before him, she looked up at Ian and smiled.

"Now you." She giggled. Ian stood perfectly erect. He tightened his abs and copied her slow circle turn. He wore a T-shirt and jeans, which hung low on his hips. He was tan and had increased his muscle mass considerably for the role he was filming. Although Madison appreciated what she saw, she had liked the way he looked before, and wondered if he was going to keep this new look after the film was over. The extra bulk was almost intimidating. His hair was longer, which she liked very much, and hoped that would remain after the film. When he stopped in front of her, he gathered her hands in his. "Thank you for coming tonight instead of waiting until morning," she said. "What a fantastic surprise." They remained still for seconds drinking in the sight of each other.

"Are you hungry?" she asked. "I'm not sure what I have in the cupboards, but can I fix you something?"

"Nay, lass. I've eaten. I picked up a sandwich before I got on the plane." She looked tired. He could see a bluish tint beginning to shadow under her eyes. As much as Ian wanted to have her right that second, he knew she needed to sleep. For if he had his way, she would not see much sleep over the next two days. "Why don't we go to bed and in the morning we can go to the market together."

Madison was pleased he wanted to sleep. She was exhausted and could think of nothing better than to close her eyes nestled in Ian's arms. "Sounds wonderful!" She smiled and followed him to her bed. While Ian stripped off his jeans and shirt, she turned down the bed, got under the covers and waited for him to join her. Ian climbed into bed and turned out the lamp on the bedside table. When he lay back onto the bed, Madison snuggled in as he wrapped his arm around her, pulled her closer and rested his chin on the top of her head.

"Ye feel so good in me arms, darlin'." He kissed her hair and took in the wonderful scent of her.

"Mmm." She sighed. "This is nice." By the time she finished speaking, she was asleep. Ian lay awake for a long time. This was where he wanted to be, with his "Maddy Girl." Wherever she happened to be, if he could be with her, he was home. If he didn't know it before, he knew it now, that this was the only woman he would ever want for the rest of his life. Ian closed his eyes and allowed himself to drift off to sleep.

Chapter Eighteen

The next morning Madison awoke to find herself alone in the bed. She bolted to a sitting position and the blanket fell to her lap. Sitting straight up in the bed, she looked about the room in confusion and disappointment. *Had it been a dream?* she asked herself. Or had she missed him so much she had only imagined Ian was there last night? Madison fell back into the mattress and closed her eyes trying to force the dream to return when she heard a familiar voice from her bathroom. Her eyes flew open, she sat back up, and turned her attention toward the bathroom door. Ian was standing in the doorway with a thick fluffy white towel wrapped around his midriff just above his hips. *God he looks good,* she thought.

"Good mornin' luv." He grinned and padded to the bedside where he sat down next to her and brushed his lips across hers. Madison drew the covers to her waist, and leaned back into the pillows.

"I thought I'd dreamed you last night." She sighed.

Ian reached out his hand and traced the side of her cheek. "No Luv, ye didna dream me."

"How long have you been awake?" she yawned.

"Oh, boot two hours," he said.

"Two hours!" she moaned. "Why didn't you wake me?"

"Because, luv, I knew ye needed yer sleep and ye looked sa peaceful in yer slumber." He stood and let the towel drop to the floor. Stepping toward the chaise lounge where he had left his clothes the night before, he slipped on fresh pair boxers, pulled on his jeans, and tugged a white

T-shirt over his head. "How about ye scoot yer luvly backside oot o bed and when ye're dressed, we can get the supplies ye wanted. Then we can come back here and make up for the days and nights we've been parted."

Madison slid from under the covers and walked very slowly until she stood in front of him. "Why don't we start to catch up now and go out later?" she asked softly. Ian looked into her eyes and saw the dark blue color he had known so well. He glided his hand under her hair to the back of her neck and pulled her against him. Just before their lips met, their stomachs growled simultaneously. He chuckled.

"Maddy, I donna know about ye, boot something tells me if we donna nourish these bodies of ours, they'll be tay weak fer making much o anything." He leaned down placing a small tender kiss upon the tip of her upturned nose and gazed into her deep azure eyes again. "We've got time, luv."

Madison was about to protest when she heard her stomach again and decided she was indeed hungry. "Okay, let me get dressed and we can go to the store." She turned toward the closet, and stopped suddenly. "Ian, are you sure you should go with me?"

"O course. Why?" He sat on the bed to put on his shoes

"What if you're recognized?" she said from inside her closet. Ian set his shoe back on the floor, rose from the bed, and walked slowly to the closet.

"And wha' if I am?" he asked, standing in the closet doorway. He watched as Madison finished dressing. "Do ye nay wish ta be seen wi me?"

Madison was reaching for a pair of sneakers from the shelf, she'd just made contact with the shoes when she turned toward him.

"Look out!" The shoes tumbled off the shelf, Ian was quick enough to catch one shoe before it clunked her on the head, but the second shoe hit its mark.

"Ouch!" She frowned. "What did you say?"

"I said, 'look out.'"

"No. Not that." She grimaced, rubbing the top of her head.

"I asked if ye—"

"I heard what you asked, but—"

"Then why did ye want me ta repeat it?" A deep groove was starting to form between Ian's eyes and Madison could see the beginnings of anger. "Are ye hurt?"

"No. I'm not hurt. Ian, why wouldn't I want to be seen with you?" She took the shoe he was holding and picked up the other one from the floor.

Ian backed out of the closet and walked to the bed where he sat and picked up his own shoes again.

"Ian?"

He sat staring at his shoes before turning his gaze to her.

"This is fair new territory fer me, Maddy. It's been a long time since I've put my feelings out there and maybe I'm a wee bit insecure." He gave a halfhearted laugh when her eyebrows bounced into her bangs. "Aye, it fair surprises me too."

Madison sat on the bed beside him and laid her fingertips on his leg. "Maybe we're both a little insecure. I asked because you're a film personality. I don't know anything about your world, Ian, and I was concerned about you being recognized out and about."

"I doubt I would be anyway. I'm no' tha' well known in the United States and I donna look the way my handful o devoted fans are accustomed ta seein' me."

"All the same, what if you are recognized?" Madison stood to slip on her black jeans and blue chenille sweater, then sat on the floor, much like a child would, to put on her shoes.

"Then I get recognized, wha's the big deal? Did ye think all twelve of my fans might trample ye tryin to get me autograph at the market?" He chuckled.

"The 'big deal' is that you won't be with some glamorous movie star." She finished with her shoes and stood looking down at him. "You'll be with me." Ian was stunned. Madison turned, heading back into the closet. She grabbed a jacket from one of the hangers on the rod and tried to exit her closet, but by then Ian had recovered and was standing in the doorway. She attempted to go around him, but he had no intention of letting her pass.

"Wha' is tha supposed ta mean?" he asked as he crossed his arms over his broad, muscular chest.

"Nothing, I guess." He seemed formidable blocking the closet door. She smiled. He was so dear to her. "It just occurred to me, that if you're recognized in the public eye, maybe it should be with some glamorous babe that would fit the right image or... something." Her voice trailed off as the expression on his face began to change.

"Oh, Maddy darlin," Ian was finally beginning to understand, and he laughed out loud. "come here, luv." He took her hand and led her to the bed where they sat down together. He took her face in his hands and pressed his lips to her forehead and then her nose and finally her lips. "Luv, if I am goin' ta be seen in public wi a wooman, it willna be wi some 'glamorous babe' ta keep up appearances. If I'm recognized and I've go' a wooman on me arm, I want it ta be the wooman I am in luv wi and no' some 'babe' as you put it, or side piece."

"Ian, I think now is a good time to talk about what we want to say to people when it comes to our relationship."

"Ye mean, do I think we should be open and aboveboard?" Ian drew in his chin and took on a serious tone. Then laughed out loud again.

"Yes. And I don't think this is a laughing matter. It could become a serious issue when you consider your career in the States, and your audience." She was embarrassed and a little exasperated. Ian sobered somewhat in deference to her frustration, but the smile didn't disappear from his face.

"I think we should be honest about it, darlin'. I'm an actor, no a rock star. What we ha is no shameful. We're in love, and I donna wan ta hide it in the dark. However, if ye feel uncomfortable that it might get inta the papers or tabloids, I would be willin' ta make no comment on the subject and try ta keep it as private as possible."

Madison was silent for a moment before speaking. "I don't want to hide our relationship either, but I also don't want to hurt your career. I know that when an actor gets a new girlfriend or boyfriend, privacy seems to end and *nothing* is sacred." She took a deep breath. "Let's face it, if our relationship becomes public knowledge, the paparazzi will start digging around in my past. Do you want my history with Adam on the front page of the *National Monitor*? 'Ian Mackay's Mistress and Her Jailbird Ex'. Film at eleven," she mumbled. "Something like that could be very damaging for you." Madison took a shaky breath and continued. "I don't think we need to hide from our friends and family, believe me. I do love you. I didn't think I could ever love again. You've made me whole. You've made me feel warm and cherished and adored. I want to share this miracle with my friends. I have no family and I wish I could share this with Poppy." She smiled and cupped his cheeks in her hands. "He would love you too." She kissed him gently and dropped her hands back to her lap. "I'm not suggesting that we are never seen in public together either. But I think it would be better for you if we just stick to 'no comment'. Or just say we are very good friends."

Ian looked at the woman beside him and smiled. She wasn't worried about herself. She was concerned about him and his screen image. And deep down he knew it would not be easy for him if their relationship was to become public. *Unless we were married,* he thought.

Suddenly Ian blinked from the mental jolt. This was the first time since Alexandra that the idea of marriage had become a complete thought in his mind.

"Ian, are you mad at me for bringing this up?" Madison asked. He had not said anything or interrupted her while she spoke.

"Wha?" He blinked again, and then refocused on her worried face. Leaning over, he placed a gentle kiss on her lips. "Mad at ye? Nay, I'm no angry. I was just thinking, 'just very good friends' never works. The next day the *National Monitor* headline would read, 'Ian Mackay Hides Pregnant Mistress Behind Melons in Produce Aisle o Local Market'!" He ducked his chin into his chest and lowered his voice. "Film at eleven." Madison laughed and the worry evaporated from her eyes, which is the effect Ian had hoped for. "I dinna wan ta hide our relationship either, but ye're right about privacy. Once it hits the papers, there's no' much sacred. We'll go for 'no comment.' If I'm recognized, the tabs willna let it go, but if ye'de feel more comfortable, we'll try to keep our relationship as private as possible fer now, anyway." He stood and offered her his hand. "So, lass, are ye no goin' ta get some food fer yer starvin' secret lover? Because if ye willna feed me soon, I canna promise ta perform later wi' me usual noteworthy stamina."

Madison burst out laughing. "You're incorrigible."

"I've never needed much encouragement where ye're concerned, darlin', but I do need sustenance from time ta time, fer ye fair wear me out." He wrapped his arm around her waist, and the two of them went downstairs together.

Madison grabbed her purse from the dining room table on the way out the front door. As she was locking the door her phone came to life and she dug in her bag to answer it.

"Hi, Madison," Margaret's voice flowed over the line. "I won't keep you. I just wanted to let you know; I've sent a package with your latest mail to Scotland. So it should be there when you return." Margaret also went on to tell Madison about the man who came to speak with her claiming to be a distant relative.

"Really? Hmm. I wasn't aware Poppy had any family other than me. Oh well, must be a popular name."

"Maybe, but I don't trust him. There was something about him that seemed so familiar, but I can't put my finger on it."

"Well, I wouldn't worry about it. He probably has one of those faces, familiar and untrustworthy. He didn't have a big fat magazine subscription book under his arm did he?" she asked, giggling at her own weak humor. "I better go; I have to go to the market. Thanks, Margaret, for calling."

"You're welcome and if I don't see or talk to you before you go back to Scotland, have a safe trip."

"Thanks, I will." Madison flipped her phone shut and turned her attention back to Ian. "Well, shall we go?" Madison smiled.

"Aye. What was tha aboot?" Ian asked as he slid onto the soft leather passenger seat of Madison's Wagoneer.

Madison started the engine, threw the SUV into gear and backed out of the driveway. "That was Margaret letting me know she had sent my bills and things to Scotland." Madison pulled up to the traffic light and flipped on her turn signal.

"That was it?" Ian asked as he looked out the window at the shops in the area. He had never been in New Jersey before, so everything was new.

"Yeah pretty much," Madison took a sharp turn to get into the Wegmans parking lot before the light turned red again.

The swift movement caught Ian off guard, "Woo! Are ye daft wooman?" He half smiled.

"What? I didn't want to get hit so I had to make the turn in a hurry." She looked at his face and began to laugh as she parked the car. "I'm sorry if I scared you." She was laughing so hard her stomach was beginning to hurt.

"Wha's so bloody funny?' he asked as he unbuckled the seat belt.

"You should see your face," she choked.

"What aboot my face?"

"It's ghost white." She got a hold on her laughter and wiped at her eyes.

"Are ye always this mad behind the wheel, then?" he asked.

"No, have you ever driven in the States before? Or have you always had drivers?" She chuckled as they walked toward the entrance of the store.

"Drivers. Why?" Ian said after a while.

"Well, driving in the States is not the same as driving in Scotland. Everyone here is in a big fat hurry to get wherever it is they're going." She took a cart from the cart carrel outside the door and started inside the building.

As they made their way around the store picking out items, Ian was never far from her. He had his hands on her as much as he could without looking indecent. Rubbing her shoulders or her arms, reaching for her hand or just brushing her fingers when she picked up an orange to smell the aroma.

"I never realized how erotic the produce section could be," she whispered as they selected bright orange citrus and filled a plastic bag. Ian grinned and kissed her neck when he thought no one was looking.

It was true he had been in the States many times, but he had never been to an American grocery before. It was fascinating how they were similar and drastically different from what he was used to. They walked up and down the aisles and as they came across things they wanted or something neither of them had ever tried, Madison would throw it in the cart, being careful to choose things that wouldn't spoil if they weren't eaten before Madison returned from Scotland. *If she returns at all,* Ian thought to himself.

As they walked out to the car, Ian's mind began to wander. He thought of different ways he could convince Madison to stay in Scotland after the office there was running on its own, and once again the idea of marriage became part of his thought processes. A smile came to his handsome face. They reached the car and Madison opened the way-back-door. She looked at the cart full of bags and then at Ian. He was smiling and he seemed to be out in his own little world.

"Ian?" she said.

"Um?" He looked back at her.

"Can you help me here?" Ian looked first at her and then down at the cart full of groceries realizing they had reached the car.

"Oh, aye, sorry I was wool-gathering." He bent down and took the bags from the cart, placing them in the back of the Wagoneer while Madison put the cart back in one of the carrels in the parking lot.

"So what were you thinking about?" Madison asked as they strapped on their seat belts, and started the engine.

"Nothing in particular," he fudged. "Just how happy I am ta be near ye." He reached for her hand and kissed her fingers.

"That's so sweet," she cooed. Her smile was bright and full of joy as she pulled out of the parking lot and headed back to the townhouse.

When they had unloaded and put all the groceries away in the kitchen, Madison shook her head in awe. *Why did I buy all this?* She wondered. She was only going to be there for two days and they had enough food for a week. *It's not safe for me to be in the grocery with this man,* she thought. *I lose all track of the basic plan.*

As Madison put the last of the grocery bags by the door for the next trip, she felt Ian's arms encircle her and pull her body into him. He felt so good next to her. *There is no other place or time in the world I would rather be,* she thought. Ian dipped his head and lovingly placed kisses on her neck and earlobes.

"Aye, lass. Me either."

"Hmmm?" she sighed.

His hands moved from the sides of her waist over her stomach and up to her breasts.

"There's no place on this earth I'd rather be than here in this moment with ye," he breathed. "Make love with me, lass."

Madison let out a small moan and turned in his arms. Ian took her mouth with his and drew her in tighter. He never wanted to let her go again. Madison laced her arms around his neck and deepened their kiss while threading her hands through his hair. Ian's hands roamed over her body. Finally, he scooped her up in his arms, and she let out a small squeak of surprise. Ian lifted his lips from hers and looked into her deep blue eyes. Madison ran her fingertips down the side of his face and traced his lips. Without a word Ian began to walk up the stairs to her bedroom.

Upon entering the master suite, Ian placed her on her feet and before Ian could stop her Madison was out of his grasp and walking toward the sliders on the other end of the room.

"What are ye up ta?" he asked with amusement as she pulled the blinds closed.

"This isn't the Highlands," she said, "with no one around for miles. Here, people will haul out their binoculars to look in your windows if you leave the blinds open." When she was confident their privacy was achieved she turned and saw Ian holding back a laugh. "Don't you dare laugh at me." She smiled. "Unlike you, I'm not interested in the world's view of my body."

"And it's such a bonnie body ta view." He smiled. "Especially by sunlight," he said as he slowly began to advance toward her. When he reached her side at the sliders, he drew back the blinds and her face was bathed by the buttery glow from the late afternoon sun. "But I donna wish ta share it wi the world either." He let the blinds drop back over the glass and gathered her into his arms. "Now, I'll repeat me request o a moment ago. Make luv wi me, lass."

Chapter Nineteen

Four hours later, Ian lay on his back with his arms over his head. Madison's head lay on his shoulder and he heard her sigh with satisfaction. He looked down at the lovely woman lying in his arms and smiled.

"Now, I'm *verra* hungry," Ian sighed and laughed when Madison poked him in the ribs with her fingers.

Madison sat up in bed, pulled the top sheet over her breasts and looked down at Ian.

"You were the one who wanted to continue over and over again."

Ian reached up with his hand and laced his fingers on the back of her neck so he could pull her back down to him. "I didna hear ye complainin'," he said against her lips before capturing her mouth with his. Before his hands could work their magic on her again, she pushed gently on his chest.

"Ian," she laughed "You just got done telling me how hungry you were."

"Aye, I di tha', but I dinna specify fer wha'." He chuckled. Madison kissed him on his forehead quickly and slipped off the bed and out of his reach. She dashed to her closet and retrieved a pair of cut-offs and a tank top to pull on. When she was dressed, she emerged from her closet to find Ian *still* in bed sporting a glower on his handsome face. She burst out laughing.

"Wha's so funny?" he asked from the nest of pillows.

"You are," she giggled. Ian leapt from the bed and made a dash for her but anticipating his reaction, she was too quick and was out of the bedroom and down the stairs before she spoke. She laughed from the bottom of the steps. "I am going to make something to eat," she called to him. "If you're interested get dressed and come down." She smiled and sailed into her kitchen.

"She's goin' ta cook?" Ian said aloud. "Now there's a fair threat." He chuckled.

Madison stood in the middle of the kitchen and surveyed the room. She had never cared for this area of the townhouse. Nor had she spent any significant time making use of it. She scanned the white vinyl covered cabinets, the cinnamon granite countertops, the white matte finish refrigerator and stove top. It was a very attractive and functional food prep space.

"Now what?" she murmured. "Basically, I just promised that I would cook. Something...." She tentatively opened the pantry door, and had picked up a blue box of Macaroni and Cheese when her phone rang. It was not a ring she recognized, but it would delay her other option at the moment. *Saved by the bell,* came to her mind. As she reached for her phone, Ian's hand came softly down on hers.

"No interruptions please, luv. Can we be a wee bit selfish wi our time? Let the calls go fer now," he said quietly. Madison put her phone back down on the counter and looked into Ian's eyes while the ringing gave way to silence. She smiled and brought his hand to her heart and held it there for a moment.

"Yes," she breathed and was rewarded with a smile that threatened to make her knees weak. "How can love grow so deep in such a short time?" she murmured as it ran through her mind.

"Because if we're verra lucky, it's right and true," he answered as he brought his lips down to hers and lingered there. "And lasting," he said after a time.

Madison lifted her arm to encircle his neck but in doing so, she bonked him in the head with the box of mac and cheese. Ian blinked and brought her hand down into view.

"And wha might this be?" he asked. She blanched a bit and her complexion began to turn crimson.

"Dinner?" she offered.

"Mm-hmm." Ian looked grave as he took the box from her hand and examined the label. "Did ye ne're hear o the time honored path ta the heart o a man, lass?"

Madison giggled, and her eyes flashed brightly into his. "I've decided to let you love me for my body, rather than my culinary skills."

"Ye've a great deal more ta offer a man, other than yer sweet body, luv. However, yer culinary skills willna top the list. I think ye've made the wisest decision." He chuckled and tapped her nose with his finger. "Why donna ye let me handle the cookin', luv?" It was more of a statement than a question.

Madison sighed with relief and moved out of the way. That was when she realized that the old adage about the kitchen being the heart of the home was true. Ian's kitchen in the Highlands was the heart of the home. This room was pretty and seemed efficient enough, but it was rather blank and empty. There was no place to sit and watch the chef work. There was no conversation area. This room was utilitarian, but had no warmth. Madison decided then and there, she really hated her kitchen. If she wanted to sit down, she had to move to the dining room or the living room. That would take her away from Ian, and that was unacceptable. She made a mental note of looking for some kind of kitchen furniture on her return from Scotland. *Now why does that seem so depressing?* she thought. After pouring them each a glass of chilled chardonnay, she went to the empty wall and sat cross-legged on the floor.

Ian was slicing carrots when he noticed her on the floor against the wall. He wiped his hands on a paper towel, walked over, and reached down for her. She stood and he slipped his hands around her waist lifting her to the countertop.

"Ye dress up the kitchen better up here near me, luv," he said when he resumed his slicing.

"I guess when I get back here, I'll have to see about getting a table and chairs or stools or something to sit on in this room," she said, and again the idea seemed a depressing one. Ian looked over at her, his eyes holding hers for a long moment.

She watched as he made his way around the kitchen with ease. It was amazing. It was as though this room was his own, and he had been preparing food here his whole life. He knew right where everything was, without asking. Apparently her preparation utensils were in their proper place in the grand kitchen scheme. She could thank Margaret for that. She was the one who set up the kitchen when Madison moved in. She began to smile for she had no idea where anything was in the place and she lived there.

She enjoyed watching Ian cook and he seemed to enjoy himself too. There was closeness there in the kitchen together; talking companionably while Ian worked his miracles with her cookware and the groceries they had bought together.

Thirty-five minutes later, Ian picked up two dinner plates of pan-brazed chicken with mushroom sauce, glazed carrots, and new potatoes with parsley butter, and started for the dining room. Madison was in awe of his talents. She hopped off the counter and collected the wine bottle and their glasses and followed him.

They ate in silence for a few minutes. Both enjoying the tender flavorful meat, and glistening sweet carrots. As they ate, Madison was reminded of their meals together in Scotland, about her return to Ian's house near the cliff, and how happy she would be to be going home.

"How much longer is your filming going to last?" she asked after a while.

"No much. Maybe a couple o weeks, three at the most." He smiled.

"Then you'll be coming back to Skye?"

"Aye, luv, I will." His eyes twinkled.

"Good." Madison finished her meal and took her plate to the kitchen to start on the dishes. Ian brought his plate in and began to help her. "Oh, no you don't. You cooked, so I will do the dishes." She smiled. "Why don't you take the rest of the wine and glasses and have a seat in the living room. It'll just take me a couple of minutes to clean up out here."

"Are ye sure ye'll be able ta find where everything goes?" He mocked jokingly as he made his way to the sofa and sat down, chuckling when a hand towel was chucked at his head. He could hear the dishes clinking and wanted to go back and help, or just be in the same room with her, but he knew she would only shoo him away again. He turned on the TV and began flipping through the channels.

After a while Ian didn't hear any sounds coming from the kitchen. He looked over the back of the sofa, but Madison was no longer in view. He rose from the sofa, walked toward the doorway and peered in to see that she wasn't in the kitchen at all. Ian scanned the downstairs to find her and decided she must've gone upstairs and followed what he assumed was her example. The master bedroom was empty, as was the bath and closet. He then made the round of the other rooms upstairs. He opened what he figured was the guest room and found that it was still loaded down with boxes begging to be unpacked, but no Madison. He went on to the next room and found that this room was completely empty of boxes and Madison. Ian was beginning to get a little worried, so he retraced his steps to the master bedroom and looked out on the balcony but still no sign of her anywhere. He was about to recheck her closet when he heard a loud thud downstairs. He raced out of the room and down the steps. When he reached the bottom, he still saw no sign of her.

"Maddy?" he bellowed.

"Yeah?" came a faint answer.

"Where in the hell are ye?" His heart was pounding and he was beginning to sweat.

"Basement. In the laundry room." He spun around and spotted a door ajar under the stairs. He yanked open the door and took the steps two at a time. When he reached the bottom he came to an abrupt stop. There was his precious Maddy sitting on the floor, clothes strewn about her, an upturned basket and a step stool toppled over next to her. She wore a scowl on her face but one look at him and she began to laugh. Ian's breath whooshed out of his lungs as his heart began to slow, and return to beating at a normal rate.

"Wha' the bloody hell happened?" he asked as he helped her to stand.

"I was trying to get down the soap and the basket fell off the dryer and I dropped the soap on the dryer trying to stop the basket from falling. This," she said, indicating her current position, "is the result." She smiled and looked up at him and saw he looked distressed. "What happened to you?"

"The kitchen got quiet, and I looked out there, but ye were gone. So I began to search fer ye. I looked all over the house and couldna find ye. Then I heard a crash, and I had no idea where ye were. I was worried." He bent and picked up the basket and placed it on the dryer. "Hey, I saw the bag ye brought wi ye, where did all these come from?"

"Oh, well. I was in such a hurry to leave here last time that I apparently forgot some clothes in the dryer. So I thought I would rewash them and take them back with me when I go back home."

Ian helped her scoop the clothing from the floor and she loaded it into the washing machine. They returned to the living room and sat cuddled on the sofa together. Ian picked up the remote and began to flip through the channels again. He stopped on the news when he saw Madison's face looking back at him from the screen.

"Hey ye'er on TV!" he said and gave her a loving squeeze. He adjusted the sound and turned his attention back to the news. As they both watched the press conference she had given on Friday, Madison heard her cell phone ring.

"My public," she said and got up to answer it. "Hello?"

"Hello, Madison" She froze as the gruff male voice crawled over the phone.

"Who is this?" she asked quietly, she knew who it was, but hoped she was wrong.

"Oh I think you know who I am," Adam sneered.

"What do you want? How did you get this number?" The trembling in her body made her voice wobble.

"Why, I want my lovely wife, of course. What else would I want?"

"I am *not* your wife anymore, thank God! And don't call me again or I'll let the warden deal with you."

"Oh, dear sweet *stupid* Madison." His voice was like pure evil sliding over the airwaves into her ear. "You'll be pleased to know; I don't have a warden anymore. We can finally be together again, and you'll *always* be my wife, baby." Madison could hear him laughing as she hung up on him, slamming the phone down as if it had bitten her.

"Maddy?" came Ian's voice from behind her. She spun around and wrapped her arms around his waist while taking in deep gulps of air. "What's the matter? Let me guess. Ye're a hit in the new industry and the networks are fighting fer the exclusive rights to yer next press conference." He chuckled as he circled his arms around her small frame and laid his cheek on the top of her head. "Ye're trembling, luv! I know ye hated doing it, but tha news isn't as disturbing as my phone call earlier." He had wanted to put off telling her about his call as long as he could, but time was running out, and he held her closer.

"What was your call about?" she said in his chest.

"It was Sean-Patrick, the assistant director. He wants to re-shoot one of my scenes first thing in the morning."

"So what does that mean?"

"It means, luv, that I have to leave tonight instead of tomorrow morn'."

Madison gave a large jolt and her eyes flew up to Ian's in fear. "Tonight? No you can't! You can't leave tonight. You have to stay tonight."

"I can't, luv. As much as I'd like ta stay, I ha ta be on the set at 5:00 a.m. fer filming. If I stayed, I would ha ta leave here at one thirty anyway, so tha' I could be there in time fer wardrobe and makeup." Madison's tremble had increased to a near uncontrollable shaking. "Maddy, darlin', wha's the matter; I can hear yer teeth rattlin'." When she gave no response but continued to shake, he smiled softly as he drew himself back slightly holding her away from him. "Madison, this canna be—" But the expression in her eyes stopped him cold. He saw desperate fear and it nearly terrified him. "Wha'? Wha' is it?"

Maddy searched Ian's face. She saw concern and love and worry. *I should tell him,* she thought to herself. Her mind was racing with jumbled thoughts. *He would want to know. I don't want to be here by myself. I'll never be free of Adam and the past. If Ian stays here, he'll be exhausted on the set. This is the kind of scandal that could ruin him. Adam will ruin Ian and me. I should be able to deal with it on my own. Oh for heaven sakes just tell him and let him make his own decision.*

The longer Madison was silent, the more fearful Ian became. He could tell as her eyes looked into his that she was trying to decide what to tell him. How much to tell, how she was going to tell him, whatever it was, and this hesitation was beginning to unnerve him. His hold on her arms tightened.

"Just take a deep breath, luv, and tell me." When she still didn't speak, he led her around to the sofa and down while he took the coffee table facing her. Holding her hands in his. "Relax, darlin', and tell me wha's troublin' ye. Whaever it is, we can fix it together."

"I think Adam was released from prison." The words rushed out of her mouth with such force, she had to take another breath. Ian seemed stunned for a moment. *This will make trouble for him,* she thought and pulled away from him. She rose and walked quickly to the other side of the room wrapping her arms around herself. When she turned and looked at Ian again, his face showed the almost animalistic anger. He stood where he was but stretched out his arm and offered her his hand.

"Come and sit wi' me, luv." She walked to the sofa and Ian gently unlocking her arms and took both of her hands in his, guiding her back to sit next to him. "Why do ye think he's out?"

"My phone call. The one from my adoring news fans." She tried to lighten her mood with humor, but her forced laugh more resembled a choke. "It was Adam. When I threatened him with the warden if he called me again, he said he no longer had a warden. I don't even know how he got my number."

Ian placed his arm around her shoulders drawing her into his broad chest and leaned back into the sofa. "Come to New York wi me," he said.

"What?"

"Come back and stay with me in New York. I'll be finished there in two or three weeks. Maybe less. Then we'll return ta Scotland together."

Now, it was Madison's turn to be stunned. She turned and looked up at him.

"I can't do that!" Ian started to speak, but Maddy pressed her fingers to his lips. "I can't do that, Ian." She seemed to have calmed a little and she took a cleansing breath. "For a number of reasons. In the first place, bringing a woman back to New York with you will cause you no end of questions. Secondly, I can't hole up in a hotel hiding from Adam. I can't allow him to do that to me. I'll just go back to Lusta. He doesn't know anything about my life really. He'll have no idea where I am."

"I've already told ye, I donna care a whit aboot questions." Ian placed his hands on either side of her face hoping to make her see reason.

"Well, I care. And I won't allow Adam Gilmore to taint your career with scandal. My life with him. His time in the slammer. It could be devastating for you. We've already talked about this. Besides, I can't be away for two or three weeks. I have a job and an office to get running in Lusta. I'm good at my job. I've spent years working to achieve the confidence Samuel has in me. I can't—no, I won't let him down. I'll go back and do my job. I'll be fine." She drew in another breath and smiled at him. Drawing his hands from her face, she dropped kisses in his palms before pulling them against her heart. "I'm okay now, really. I'm sorry I scared you. I guess I just wasn't ready to hear Adam's voice. It brought back uncomfortable feelings that I wasn't prepared for. I'm fine. Really!"

Ian watched her straighten her back and pull herself together as she spoke. It was a magnificent effort and she accomplished it with willpower and an inner strength he admired. *She's a bonnie lass,* he thought, but his smile was forced.

"Wha' time does yer flight leave on Saturday morn'?" He was strained, but he knew better than to force her into anything. She had a man who once did that, and he refused to force anything on her. Even if it was for his own peace of mind.

"At six thirty, but I have to be there at four thirty, why?"

"Ye werena goin' ta tell me aboot this, were ye? Tha's wha' ye were doin' a few minutes ago. Goin' over it in yer mind, no' tellin' me."

Maddy opened her mouth to protest, but Ian quirked his eyebrow and looked squarely at her. She closed her mouth and dropped her eyes to her hands in her lap.

"I'm either part o yer life now, or I'm no' a part o it. Yer happiness, worries, and woes are important ta me just as I hoped mine were ta ye," he said. Again Maddy started to speak, but thought better of it. "I'm in luv wi ye, Maddy. Ye're no bein' fair ta me if ye keep me oot o the loop. We're no' on our own any longer. We're together and wha' concerns one o us concerns the other. I donna want ye ta ever keep things from me. Especially when tha' something is this important."

"I was going to tell you." Ian's arched his brow at this. "I was, but I did consider that this might not be the best time to do it. I didn't want to be here alone, but I didn't want you to be too tired to work tomorrow either. And I didn't want to worry you, and I can see now that you are. It's okay. I'm okay now. I panicked, but I'm fine now. Really. I'll go to a hotel at the airport tonight and pay in cash. I'll be fine. Tomorrow I'll get a flight out and go home a day early."

Ian drew her back into his arms. "We will both go to a hotel at the airport tonight and we will both be fine."

"Ian, you have to be in New York at 5:00 a.m. tomorrow. You can't screw up the shooting schedule just to babysit me. I'm fine now," Maddy protested, but Ian wasn't having any of it.

"Ye're right, lass. I am worried, because o the deep luv I ha fer ye. I'll no' let ye stay by yerself as long as Adam knows ye're in this country. They can wait for me or film around me fer a couple o hours. I'm no' hard ta deal wi' on set and Sean-Patrick knows it. If I tell him I canna be there until a wee bit later, he'll know it's for a damned good reason. Are ye packed and ready to leave?"

Madison nodded. "Mostly," she said.

Ian grinned at her and tapped her nose with his forefinger. "Off wi ye and get it all done. I'll make some calls, and we'll go."

She returned her tapped nose with a brief kiss and went upstairs to finished packing. While she was gone, Ian called his assistant director to say he had a family emergency and would be unable to get to the set before seven in the morning. He was firm and gave no details other than he would be back on the set as close to seven as he possibly could. He was right about Sean-Patrick Doherty's opinion of him. He knew Ian wasn't temperamental or a drama king. If Ian said it was an emergency, that was all Sean-Patrick needed to hear.

"Don't sweat it. Do what you have to. We can work around you."

Ian made a reservation in his father's name at the airport Marriott hotel, then went about straightening up before going upstairs to gather his own things.

They spent the rest of the evening in their suite at the Marriott. They ordered a late light supper and a bottle of chardonnay from room service and picnicked on the floor in front of the gas fireplace. It was peaceful and reminded Madison of the roaring fires they shared at Ian's house in the Highlands. The next morning, she felt rested and more of the confidence she had assured Ian she had the night before. He wasn't fooled by her bravado, he knew she was rattled by Adam's phone call. More than rattled, he knew she was terrified. She needed this time to gather her control and she needed him. He liked that, being needed. And he felt a sense of pride too that she felt safe with him. After what she had been through with Adam, allowing herself to feel safe with a man was quite an accomplishment. He was glad he was the one to give her that.

After the morning routine was finished, Madison and Ian took the shuttle to her terminal. He walked his girl to her gate and sat with her until it was time for her flight to board. Before she walked into the boarding ramp he put his arms around her and kissed her soundly. *Right here in front of God and everybody,* she thought. She was tempted to check to make sure they went unnoticed, but decided it was a waste of time that could be better spent. So when Ian finally ended the kiss, she leaned into him and kissed him again. Then gave him her most winning smile and walked onto the boarding ramp.

Madison found her seat and fastened her seat belt. She leaned her head back on the headrest and closed her eyes savoring Ian's kiss. *Right there in front of God and everyone,* she thought again. *I so love that man and I'm going home to Scotland.*

Her eyes remained closed while she thought of the last twenty-four-plus hours she had spent with Ian. Soon she was sleeping peacefully with a smile on her lips. She dreamed of Ian and the house on the cliff. It was a lovely dream and she was enjoying the images she saw, until Adam's voice intruded in her mind and she awoke with a start. It was the phone call and hearing Adam's voice threatening again after eleven years. *Don't think about him,* she told herself. *He's not going to ruin your life again.* She turned toward the window and concentrated on the clouds, allowing her mind to wander. Then she remembered Margaret telling about a man who came to the office asking questions about her, claiming to be a relative. Her eyes were wide open now. As the plane was still boarding, Madison dug out her phone to make a quick call, *dear God I hope I'm wrong.*

"Madison Danaher's office," Margaret's voice sang out.

"Hi, Margaret, I just wanted to call and let you know I'm on my way back to Scotland and was wondering if there was anything else I needed to know."

"No not really."

"Well, okay, then. Oh hey, just a thought. The guy who came asking questions, did he give you a name?"

"Yeah, let me think. Jason Danaher, why?"

"You said that you didn't trust him, and you thought he looked familiar. Why was that?"

"I don't know. Just the way he looked. I can't quite put my finger on it, but it was really creepy."

"Did he talk to anybody other than you?"

"Yes, as a matter of fact. Dean came out of his office, probably because he heard your name mentioned, introduced himself, and took the guy back to his office and shut the door. I don't know what they talked about, but they were in there for a long time." Margaret was quiet and finally spoke again. "Is everything alright?"

Madison was beginning to tremble. *It was Adam,* she thought to herself. *He was the one who talked to Dean for quite a while. How much information did Dean share with him?* "Yes, everything is fine. Is Dean in yet?"

"Yes."

"Connect me." Madison waited while Margaret transferred the call, keeping any eye on the flight attendants as they helped an older gentleman to his seat.

"Madison. How are you?"

"Dean, I don't really have a whole lot of time to talk. The man who came to the office by the name of Jason Danaher, what did you tell him?" she was getting frantic.

"Oh yes, I remember him. He was some kind of relative of your father's. He was looking for information about the Danaher family."

"I know what he said. I want to know what you said to him." *You asinine toadstool!*

"Just that you were out of the country on business, and would not be able to talk to him."

"Did you say where I was?" *Oh God please say no.* But as much as she hoped no would be the answer, she knew it wouldn't.

"I don't remember, why?"

Madison disconnected the call as the sound of the outer door closed and started putting all the pieces together. *Adam came to the office claiming to be a relative and Dean bought the story. Told the guy that I was out of the country on business. The damn fool probably told him where and for how long too,* she thought to herself. *Adam called the cell phone not the house phone. Which means, he was expecting me to be in Scotland. OH shit! He thought I was out of the country when he called.*

Raw fear was taking hold of her again. She was racing back a day ahead of schedule to the one place that should be safe and no longer was. She felt the plane jerk as it began to taxi down the runway. She was flying into the lion's den, wide eyed and couldn't do a damn thing about it.

Chapter Twenty

Madison had been too preoccupied to think about ordering a limo for the drive from Inverness International to Lusta. She sighed and decided she would have to look into a cab or rental car or even the local bus as she made her way out of the first-class cabin. But when she stepped out of the boarding ramp, there stood old Shawn Conner holding a sign bearing her name. Madison smiled her relief at the sight of his dear craggy face, and greeted him warmly. She enjoyed the ride through the Scottish Highlands.

"Home," she whispered, as images of Ian, and the mountains flashed through her mind. Followed by brief pictures of the cozy house on the cliff, dinners by the fire and everything surrounded by laughter and warmth. She could feel the tension drain away as her body began to relax.

Madison could hardly wait to see Julie, and called out to her as soon as she stepped through the front door, but the furry feline friend wouldn't have anything to do with her. Maddy called to her again when she spied Julie curled on the back of the sofa. Julie opened one eye, stretched to a standing position, then turned her back on Madison and repositioned her recline with her tail gently swishing the air behind the sofa. Lizzy came hurrying from the kitchen with her arms outstretched to Madison.

"Jesus Mary and Joseph! Ye're back a day early! It's say gud ta see ye. Ye've been missed!" Lizzy beamed as she enveloped Madison in a huge welcoming hug. Maddy wasn't surprised when she spotted

Patrick coming out of the guest room upstairs just as Lizzy was backing away from her. Patrick on the other hand was dumbfounded to see her standing at the bottom of the steps. *He should be embarrassed,* she chuckled to herself, as Patrick stood gaping down at her while sporting nothing but a pair of colorful briefs and his argyle socks. Madison lowered her head in an effort to hide her growing smile. She wanted to give Lizzy another hug and say *"that-a- girl!"* but figured she better not.

"I'm so happy to see you guys!" she said. "It's good to be back." Lizzy's eyes followed Madison's to the second floor, and her face began to flush. She squeezed Lizzy's hand, and then followed Julie to the kitchen to give the couple a moment of privacy.

Madison set her purse down on the counter and bent to pick up her furry friend. Julie protested for a moment and then nuzzled into owners chest and began to vibrate a most affectionate purr. Madison smiled then hugged her friend.

"I guess we must go through this ritual each time I leave you for a few days, huh, Julie? I don't know why you get so bent out of shape. You know I'll always come back to you, goose." She spoke softly to Julie and felt the rough feline tongue on her neck.

When she felt she had given the new young couple more than enough privacy, she returned to the main room to see what kind of mail she had received in the packet from Margaret. Madison flipped through all the usual bills and junk mail until she came to an envelope from her attorney. With rather shaky hands, she opened the envelope. This was the letter she had been dreading since the day her husband was sentenced. She was hoping it would tell her that Adam was being kept for three more years on the advice of the penitentiary psychiatrists. However, it wasn't to be. He had in fact been released on parole. Unfortunately, her attorney didn't mention the stipulations of Adam's parole. Madison read the entire missive, and then skimmed back to the date of his release. Adam had been a free man for over a month. The letter was dated three weeks after Adam was set free. Madison heard Lizzy and Patrick coming downstairs and jammed the letter back into the envelope and shoved it in the top drawer of her desk. Until she knew exactly what her situation was, Madison felt the need to keep this quiet.

"Well, I think I had better be on my way." Patrick smiled. "I took your bag up to your room."

"Thank you, but you don't have to leave on my account." She reached out and took his hand in hers. "I realize I'm a day early, but something came up. Please don't rush off." She spoke as calmly as she could. She really didn't want to be there by herself just yet.

"Ah ye're sweet lass, Danny." Patrick smiled and squeezed her hand. "But I'm not after leavin' just because you've returned. I have ta be at the hospital this morn fer rounds. I admit, though, I was plannin' ta come back once I had finished at the hospital, but—"

"But nothing, you are more than welcome to come back." Madison beamed, relieved at the prospect of having people around her. "Unless of course, you two would rather be alone." She winked at Lizzy.

"I am say embarrassed," Lizzy said in a meek voice, her face starting to crimson. Patrick held out his arm to her and Lizzy nestled herself against him as his arm encircled her waist.

"As ye can see, our relationship has undergone somewhat of a wee change since you left." He chuckled.

"Yes, I'm happy for you both! But I wouldn't exactly say it's a surprise." She smiled and looked at Lizzy. "And why in the hell should you be embarrassed?" she asked. "If anyone should be, it's me. I was in such a rush to get back. I should have called to let you know I'd be back early. It was thoughtless of me, and I apologize." Just then Madison's cell phone came to life and she nearly jumped out of her skin.

"Hello," she said in the most confident voice she could muster.

"How ye holden up, luv?"

"Ian! You have such a knack of calling me when I need it most." Madison turned away from Lizzy and Patrick and walked farther into the living room. "I'm okay, I guess."

"Any more calls?" His voice was full of concern and worry.

"No, but I did get a letter from my attorney informing me Adam was released. And get this! He's been out for over a month." She lowered her voice and spoke urgently into the phone. "Ian, what if he knows where I am? It's so isolated out here and I'm here alone." Then she let out her breath and chuckled. "I guess I'm 'no holdin' up' so great after all," she mimicked with a sad chuckle.

"Ye're doin' just fine, darlin'. I finish up here in a week. Then I'll be flyin' back to ye and ye'll no' be alone anymore."

"Good! I miss you." She laughed. "And I'm fine, really. Maybe a little jumpy, but intact and unharmed. And I'm not really alone. I have a wealth of friends close by. I love you. See you soon."

"Aye and I you, darlin'."

Madison disconnected and took a deep cleansing breath. She straightened her back, and when she turned around it was to find Lizzy and Patrick wrapped in each other's arms, grinning at her. Now it was Madison's turn be embarrassed and feel her face flusg. Lizzy smiled and turned back to Patrick kissing him goodbye just before she shooed him out the door. A firm knock nearly rattled the door, just as Patrick reached for the knob. Madison went rigid with fear as Patrick swung the door wide, and there standing in the doorway was Agatha Stuart.

"Agatha!" Madison shouted with glee and ran to Agatha's open arms. "I am so happy to see you." Madison smiled as she held her dear old friend close.

"I'm glad ta see ye too, lass, but ye're crushin' me." Madison let her go and allowed Agatha access to the house. Patrick took this moment to slip out the door and leave the three friends to the business of whatever it was that women talked about for hours on end.

"Well, Lizzy girl, had the sheets had time to cool before yer landlord walked through the front door?" Agatha smiled smugly as she elbowed Lizzy in the ribs hard enough to make the breath whoosh from Lizzy's mouth. "And how was the trip?" Agatha asked as she ushered Madison to one of the sofas and sat down.

"It went well. I met with my boss, gave him my report and he was pleased with our progress so far. And gave approval to hire a full staff and begin marketing more heavily. He'd set up a press conference, which I didn't know about until the day I arrived." She grimaced. "I don't care for public speaking, but our Lusta branch is official and public knowledge now, so the world knows what we're doing here."

Agatha sensed a multitude of fleeting emotions racing through Madison. *Something's no' just right here,* she thought.

"Well, I'm glad ta hear ye made the big man in your business happy. Now, what about the young bucko in yer life?" Agatha smiled slyly and winked at Lizzy. "Did ye see any of Ian while ye were in town?"

Madison looked at her and realized that she had been foolish to think Agatha Stuart wasn't aware of what was blooming between she and Ian. "Yes, I saw some of him."

"No wonder ye look say much better than ye did for the two months before ye went across the water." Agatha eased into the back of the sofa and harrumphed with disgust, shaking her head. "I've nay ever understood why men think it's only them tha' feels the need fer a roll between the sheets! Tha thing danglin' between their legs doesna give them some kind of exclusive radar, ye know. As though we woomen donna ever have the same urges." Madison and Lizzy gaped at the older gray-haired curmudgeon as she compared the sexual drives and responses of men and women. "So why are ye back a day early?"

Thankful for a change in subject matter, Madison hadn't realized she had been holding her breath during Agatha's educational disclosures. She, too, leaned back into the sofa.

"Well, I had finished everything I needed to and decided there was no reason to stay longer."

Agatha had been watching Maddy closely, examining her reactions and demeanor. *Well, it's no' the lad, then.* She mused. *Something else is burrowin' into the lass.*

Madison began to fidget under Agatha's scrutiny. She realized it was foolish of her to think she could hide anything from the dear older woman. "Besides, I wanted to come home and get back to work. Now that Samuel has given me the go-ahead, I'm anxious to hire more staff and begin bringing in patients. This project is my baby. I guess I couldn't wait to see it walk."

"Uh-huh," Agatha said. Holding Madison's eyes locked with her own, she patted Lizzy's knee. "I've brought scones warm from me oven, lass. Do ye have a bit o tea ta go wi them? Madison's ramblin' is provin' ta be quite amusin', but I dinna think all this hot air will keep the scones warm fer long."

Lizzy sat for a moment watching the two other women. Her boss was certainty hiding something, and the dear older woman was determined to wheedle it out of her. Madison's cell phone broke the moment of silence and she nearly leaped off the sofa at the intrusion. She recovered quickly picked up the cell but waited before speaking into it.

"Madison?" Adam's voice slithered over the airwaves. Color drained from her face, and she could feel cold creeping up her spine.

"What do you want?" Controlling her voice, she tried to sound as calm as possible so as not to alert Lizzy and Agatha, she failed miserably. The two women were up and next to her within a second.

"Oh, Madison," he slimed, "I have already told you what I want."

"We have nothing to say to each other, Adam. Don't call me again." She was beginning to lose the tenuous grip on her composure.

"You know," Adam went on conversationally as if she hadn't spoken, "I understand you left the States yesterday. Are you glad to be back in Scotland?"

The question, along with the knowledge that he knew where she was, robbed Madison of the last vestiges of composure. She wanted to ask how he knew about Scotland, but Adam beat her to the punch.

"You have a very forthcoming, and I might add, stupid boss. He said you were in Scotland. I was having a rather difficult time locating you exactly, but then one day as I was sitting in the rat hole of a room I had, I saw that Madison Danaher was going to be giving a press conference about her work in Scotland. You looked so good on the screen that day. You've matured, darling, and ripened considerably."

"The press conference," she breathed. "You saw the press conference?"

"Saw it? Honey, I was there." Madison's heart was beating so hard it felt like it was about to shoot out her chest. Adam knew she was getting scared, and he could feel himself growing hard by the sensation. "Now, did you really think I would miss your big TV debut? Of course not, only bars could have prevented me from being with you for such an event, and by the way, baby, the bars are gone. I love you."

"No you don't, and I don't love you. I'm fully aware of your recent release. My attorney has informed me of your parole. I assume your parole officer has informed you; you can't leave the country or come anywhere near me. Not anymore. Adam, leave me alone." She had her hand on the back of the sofa giving her the physical support she needed. Agatha and Lizzy were looking at each other worried, not knowing what was going on but wanting desperately to help. Agatha reached out offering her hand to Maddy who grabbed it and held tight.

"Now, Madison, do you really think a little thing like some silly piece of paper or an ocean, for that matter can keep me from you?" As Adam began to laugh, Lizzy took the phone from Madison and hung up. Madison had the sensation of blood draining from her brain and her knees going numb before she collapsed on the floor at Agatha and Lizzy's feet.

When Madison regained consciousness, she was disoriented and frightened. She lay very still and let her eyes roam the room. She was in her bedroom in Scotland. That's when it all came rushing back to her. Adam's release from prison, the phone calls, and he knew where she was, at least he knew she was in Scotland. She sat up and saw Agatha dosing in the chair and Patrick and Lizzy asleep in the window seat. Madison heard a familiar cry and watched her loving furry Julie walk up from the foot of the bed to her open arms.

"Oh, hey there, Julie," she whispered, "did you miss me? I missed you." Madison propped herself against the headboard while Julie curled up in a ball on her lap, and purred as Madison stroked her soft silky fur. The house was quiet and peaceful while she thought about that last few days. Eventually, her belly began to rumble at the lack of food. She lifted the mildly protesting sleepy kitty off her lap, and quietly crept from the room trying not to wake anyone.

Halfway down the staircase, she stopped and surveyed the inside of the house. *I've behaved like a schoolgirl,* she thought to herself. *This is Ian's house. I'm perfectly safe here, and I've allowed Adam to throw me into a panic. I just can't let him to do that to me.*

She went to the kitchen and made some very strong coffee for herself, filled the tea kettle with water for the others, and turned the burner on under it. Sitting down on a stool while she waited for the coffee and the water to finish, she thought about the two phone calls from Adam. Madison gave herself a mental shake as she retrieved four mugs from the cabinet. She poured boiling water into one of the mugs and filled hers with coffee. When she took a sip of her coffee, her eyes flew open, and she nearly choked.

"I guess I made it a little too strong," she coughed to Julie who was watching her intently.

Madison set the mug down and went back upstairs to her bedroom. All of her guests were still asleep. She walked to Patrick first and gave him a small shake. When his eyes came open, Madison raised her finger to her lips to let him know she didn't want the other two to wake just yet, and motioned for him to follow her downstairs.

When they reached the kitchen, Madison handed him the mug of hot water and the basket of tea bags.

"What are you doing here?" she asked after he selected the tea he wanted.

"Lizzy called me at the hospital and told me you collapsed, so I came right over. How are you feeling now?" he asked as he reached for her wrist and began to check her pulse.

"Silly. Scared. Embarrassed." She pressed her fingers to her temples. "Terrified. Did they tell you what happened?"

"Only tha' you had an upsettin' phone call."

"Boy is that an understatement." She blew out breath.

"Are ye plannin' on callin' Ian, then?" Madison and Patrick looked up to see both Lizzy and Agatha standing on the stairs. Agatha had asked the question and they all looked at Madison waiting for an answer. Madison glanced quickly at Patrick. *Does he know?* She wondered.

"What makes you think I would call Mr. Mackay?" Madison asked.

"Oh stop playin' coy, me girl!" Agatha shouted. "Do ye think me and Lizzy are the only ones ta notice the two of ye? Every breathin' body on the Isle knows the way o it between the two o ye!" Madison looked at Lizzy and Patrick as they both nodded their heads confirming Agatha's statement. She moved from the kitchen stool and sat down on the bottom step of the stairs, looking back to her friends.

Patrick held up both hands in defensive move. "We never said a word!" he assured her. "It wasn't necessary." He chuckled.

"Well?!" Agatha said, her fists stationed on her hips.

"I don't feel… I don't think… no, I'm not going to call Ian." Madison held up her hand to halt the disapproval of her decision. "Since you all seem to be aware of Ian's and my relationship, I can understand why you feel you or I should phone him. However, he is already aware of the situation. Filming will be done in a week, and he will be back then. I'm not going to try to force or guilt him into coming all the way back home before he's completed his project."

"Do ye mean he knows aboot this call ye had here, then?" Lizzy asked as she picked out a tea packet from the basket.

"Well, no. He doesn't know about the call yesterday or this morning or… is this the same day? How long did I sleep." Madison stood and looked at all of them. "And no one is going to tell him either!" she warned.

"It's Sunday," Lizzy offered. "Ye slept the rest o the day and the night through." She frowned displaying the concern of all three.

"Danny," Patrick said, coming toward her slowly, and sat beside her on the step. He was taking the place of the brother she never had. "Of course we willna be tellin Ian, but ya have ta. He has a right ta know about it."

"No, I won't tell him, not yet. He needs to finish the film. Once that is done, and he's back home I'll tell him. He's concerned enough as it is. I won't worry him further, and you mustn't either, please." She was already feeling the guilt of keeping this from him. After all, they had spoken of this after Adam declared himself. '*Yer happiness and worries and woes are me happiness worries and woes,*' he had told her. *Maybe I will tell him,* she thought. "In the meantime, I think I WILL go to the police and let them know about all of this. That way if it happens again, the authorities will at least have some sort of record of it."

"You should also call yer big boss," Agatha said as she sat down on one of the sofas. Madison looked up at her in question.

"Samuel? Why in heaven's name would I want to do that?"

"To let him know this man is botherin' ye again."

"What does Samuel have to do with this?" Madison asked.

"Doesna the man work wi ye?"

Now Madison understood. None of them knew, other than Ian, that Madison was married and divorced. They all thought Dean was the man on the phone. *This is all getting too complicated,* she thought to herself.

"No, he doesn't work with me. Let's all sit down where we can be more comfortable." She got up from the step and walked to the sofa sitting beside Agatha. "You've all kind of become my family, so I guess I should explain some things to you." She waited until they were all seated and began. "There's really no need to go into all the gory details, but to understand what is going on now, you need know some things that led you to the present situation. The man on the phone is Adam Gilmore, and I don't work with him. The simple fact is, he's my ex-husband." The more Madison explained the more tightly she clasped her hands together in an effort to keep them from shaking. "I was very young when I married him. Too young. Six months into the marriage the abuse began. As I said, the details aren't that important now. The crux of the situation is that I was granted a divorce and Adam convicted of second-degree murder." Lizzy opened her mouth to speak, but Madison held up her hand to stave the question and continued. "There were other charges against him, but the most important and most damning against him was the murder charge. He was sentenced to seven to ten years. Later another six years was tacked on to his sentence."

"Why six more?" Patrick asked in controlled anger and outrage. He would never understand why some men got their rocks off on abusing women and children.

"When he came up for parole he was denied. He was angry and attacked a nurse in the infirmary. That's when the prison shrinks took over. They recommended he remain in prison for psychiatric treatment because he was still a danger to others, as well as himself." Madison stopped and took a sip of her coffee, shivered, and continued. "Anyway, he must have been a model prisoner for the last few years, because when he came up for parole this time, it was granted. Adam was released a month ago and now he's apparently on the hunt. For me. He knows I'm in Scotland, and to make matters worse, because he saw the press conference, he knows where in Scotland as well."

"If he knows ye're here on the Isle, why in the hell are ya here?" Patrick asked.

"Because I didn't realize he had seen the press conference until I was back. He not only saw it, he attended it as well." When the other three faces looked startled, she went on. "There must have been a news ad on TV during the day. 'Local Hospice group goes international! Story at noon.'"

"This is why ye're here early, isn't it?" Agatha asked quietly.

"Aye, it is. He called my cell phone and I assumed he thought I was in Jersey. Or at least Philly. The press conference never occurred to me. Didn't know that either until he called yesterday. It didn't matter, though. Apparently. Adam showed up at my office right after he was released, claiming to be some long-lost relative. So Dean took it open himself to give out more information than he ever should have. So he already knew I was in Scotland, but until the conference, he didn't know where exactly."

"Ye're sayin', tha' Dean bucko tha' Ian tossed oot the door on his arse a few months back gave your ex-husband information concernin' yer whereboots?" Agatha asked and Madison nodded confirmation. "Well," Agatha harrumphed, "there's reason enough ta phone yer big boss. That bastard ha nay business ta be givin' oot information aboot an employee ta a total stranger. And dinna be rollin' yer eyes at me, lassie. I'm a business wooman meself and livin' in a small town, but I ha enough brains in me head ta know ye donna give oot personal information aboot yer help ta someone ye donna know. Ye need ta inform yer big boss o the dumb arse he's got workin' in his business! The man should be tossed out in the gutter where he belongs! If he worked fer me, he'd be looking fer a job ten minutes ago."

"Yes, well, you're probably right about that. Dean is a jerk, and a dumb one at that, but I have other issues now. Most importantly concerning Ian, and why I don't want anyone to phone him about this latest call from Adam. Ian has worked very hard to get this break into American films. It's a huge jump in his career. He has a top-flight director on this picture. One of, if not *the* best. I don't want anything to ruin his chances there." She paused to look sternly into the eyes of each of her friends individually for emphasis. "I'll go to the police in Lusta and make them aware of my situation. Other than that, all I can do is keep busy and try not to be alone as much as I can, until Ian gets home. I'll also call my lawyer to learn the conditions of Adam's parole. I'm pretty sure he would be in violation, whatever the conditions, if he left the country."

"Well, that settles it." Patrick stood and moved to sit beside Madison. "We will all be stayin' here 'til Ian comes back to ye. Agatha, Lizzy, give me keys and I will pick up some things for all of us after I'm finished at the hospital this evening."

"Oh no," Madison protested. "That isn't necessary. I don't need babysitters and I don't need an army of watchdogs. But thank you!" She smiled. "Besides, I don't have enough rooms for all of you to sleep."

"Don't even think aboot sayin' no," Lizzy scolded. "Agatha and I can bunk together in the second bedroom and Patrick can sleep doon here on one o the sofas. Here's my key, and I'll give you a list of what ta get." She handed Patrick the key to her house.

"And mine," Agatha said as she passed hers to him as well.

Just then Madison's phone rang and she reached for it, but before she could pick it up, Patrick had the phone in his hand.

"Hello."

"Hello, who is this?" came a male voice over the phone.

"This is Dr. O'Connell. Who's calling?"

"Doctor! Why are ye there? Is Madison okay!" Ian's voice was frantic.

"Who is this?" Patrick insisted.

"Ian, Ian Mackay. What's wrong wi' her?"

"Ian! Hello! This is Patrick. I'm a friend of Madison's and she's fine. Here." Patrick handed Madison the phone and backed away.

"Ian?" Madison asked.

"Maddy are ye alright? Why is there a doctor there?"

"Don't worry, Ian, I'm fine. Patrick and Lizzy were watching the house and Julie while I was away, that's all. Believe me, everything's fine."

"Thank God!" He let out a lengthy breath. "I was callin' to make sure ye were alright. I had some time between scenes, and I just thought I'd check in wi ye."

"I'm fine. Truly. But thanks for calling. It's nice to hear your voice. As long as I do have you on the phone, Ian, I've been mulling over an idea."

"Aye?"

"Do you think it might be a good idea to go to the police and let them know about Adam. You know, to give them a heads-up that he's out of prison, and that he's been harassing me by phone." She held her breath to wait for his reply.

"Darlin?"

"Yes."

"Have ye had another call?"

Shit, she thought, *a simple "yes" or "no" would do. If I lie to him, will he find out? If I lie to him and he finds out, will he be angry? If I tell him, will he screw up his film and come running here?*

"Madison?" Ian was getting more insistent.

"Ian, please don't overreact. Yes, I have received another call; however, Patrick, Lizzy, and Agatha have all agreed to stay with me until you are free to return. I'm not alone here, and I think Adam may just be trying to get to me verbally. It occurred to me this afternoon, he can't come here without breaking his parole, and if he does that, back to the slammer he goes." She laughed nervously.

"Thomas Mackay." was all Ian said.

"Huh?"

"My brother, Tommy Mackay. He's Chief Inspector. Go and ask for him. I'll call and let him know ye're comin'. He'll know wha's best, and take care o ye 'til I can get ta ye. I'll see ye in a few days, luv."

"Ian please don't be angry with me," Madison pleaded.

"Mad at ye? Are ye daft wooman? I'm worried aboot ye. And I donna want anything ta happen ta ye. I'm in love wi ye, Maddy darlin'. Keep safe."

"I will and I love you too."

Agatha chuckled and slammed her elbow backwards into Patrick's belt buckle. "At least tha' much is settled!"

Madison hung up the phone and turned to her audience. "Rather than leaving us here," she told Patrick. "Why don't we go with. You can drop me at the police station while Agatha and Lizzy are collecting what they'll need for the next few days."

"Sounds good ta me," Patrick exclaimed. "We have a workable plan."

"Me too," said Lizzy and Agatha in unison.

Chapter Twenty-One

After Madison showered and changed they drove to Lusta and parked the car behind Madison's office.

"Since I'm here, I might as well stop in here and check on a few things. When I'm done, I'll walk over to the police station and talk to Chief Mackay." As Madison opened her bag to search out her door keys, Patrick gently seized her arm.

"Will ye listen ta the foolishness?" Agatha sputtered. "Never in all me days ha I—"

Capturing Agatha's arm with his free hand, Patrick essentially silenced her pending tirade.

"We've come ta see the chief o police. Not ta work." Patrick put on his best brotherly smile. "Now come along, Danny." And he marched both ladies down the alley to the police station. Lizzy shook her head in awe. *He has the way aboot him. That he does,* she thought. *He can command the commanding Madison and hush the irascible Agatha without so much as a raised eyebrow.* She sighed and smiled as she followed the three down the alley.

The alley was lined with a series of doors leading to small privately run shops. Madison used to picture young American towns looking just like Lusta did now, Although Lusta probably hadn't changed one iota in all its hundreds of years in existence.

When the group reached the correct door, Patrick opened it and all three of the ladies filed in one after another. The room was small much like the new hospice office, with a large storefront window facing the main street and worn plank floors that squeaked in various spots. There were three desks placed about the room with no particular pattern. None of them occupied at the moment. The walls were dark aged wood paneling and the light in the room was limited to what daylight came through the large window at the front of the room. There was one inadequate overhead light in the center of the ceiling that might have had a glass globe covering it at one time, but each desk had a lamp to aide in doing paperwork. Extension cords in varying colors wound around the baseboard and over the doorframes ending in the two outlets on either side of the room. The space would never be classified as inviting. It seemed cold and damp, but it was serviceable. Maddy shivered as she looked at her surroundings. *I guess as a jail, it's not so bad, but I wouldn't want to spend the day working in here,* she thought.

Finally, after what seemed like ages, the front door opened and in walked a man who was the spitting image of Ian except for the mustache he wore. He was a few years older, with hair silver at the temples, green eyes just a shade paler than Ian's, but the body type was identical to mass Ian had acquired for his currant role. Tommy's very presence filled, if not overpowered the room.

"Agatha, ye darlin' auld girl. Wha' in the devil are ye doin' here?" His brogue was so thick Madison was wondering if she would be able to understand him. "Ah now which one o ye young lassies has caught the eye of me baby brother, then?"

"Thomas," Agatha warned. "ye're ta keep a civil tongue. We're here in an official capacity." She took Maddy's hand and placed her other hand on Maddy's shoulder. "This is Madison Danaher. She's a successful businesswoman and she's just opened the hospice service down the street next ta me bakery. She's an American come ta work and live in the green o the Highlands, and she's had trouble follow her, bless her poor soul, and ye're ta treat her respectful, de ye hear wha' I'm sayin' ta ye?"

"Thank you, Agatha, for that wonderful introduction." Madison rolled her eyes skyward before she outstretched her hand to Thomas. "I take it Ian has already been in touch with you and explained some of what has been happening."

When Thomas took her hand in his, Madison realized she was mistaken about his size compared to Ian. This man was *huge*. His hand made Madison's look like a child's.

"Aye, he did that, but he dinna tell me tha ye were such a beauty." He took her elbow and led her to one of the empty desks. "Now, I understand ye were wed ta the bugger some years back."

"Yes." Madison began to fidget in her seat.

"There's nay need ta be nervous, lass, nay harm will come ta ye here." For such a large man, his voice was reassuring and surprisingly soft. Madison felt herself relax.

"It's not that," she said. "It's just that I feel a bit strange talking to a member of Ian's family about something like this."

"I see. So tha's the way the wind blows? Well, if it'll make ye feel any better aboot it, I'll tell ye; I feel a wee bit strange lookin' after the woman me brother's been pumpin'." Madison's eyes popped open wide, and her mouth dropped open.

"Thomas Michael Mackay!" bellowed Lizzy. Everyone in the room turned their gazes toward her. Lizzy was always such a quiet little thing, never raise her voice to anyone. "Ye're speakin' ta a born lady, ye are! And shame on ye! Ye'll apologize right this instant!" she ordered.

Tommy Mackay's laughter boomed out of his massive chest and made the walls rattle.

"I'm sorry, lass. I do apologize ta ye and ta ye too, Lizzy girl." He chuckled a little more and then patted Madison's knee. "Donna pay me nay mind. Tha' was just me way of breakin' the ice, ye might say." He looked up at Agatha. "Ye willna tell me own Sara aboot me embarrassin' the young lasses, will ye, Aggie auld girl?" Agatha's raised eyebrow was her only response.

"Willna ye all sit or de ye have business ta take care o aboot town?" Patrick and Agatha looked at each other, but Lizzy folded her arms across her chest and sat down firmly in one of the empty chairs.

"Now, lass, aboot yer problem. As ye can see we are no a large force here, so protectin' ye might be difficult. But if ye can give me an idea wha' the fella looks like, I can have me men be after lookin' out fer him."

"Well, therein lies the one of the problems. I haven't seen him since the day he was sentenced. He has apparently changed a great deal. I mean, he said he was at a press conference I held in Philadelphia, and I didn't notice him. Of course I wasn't exactly looking for him either, but he said he was there in the same room with me and I had no idea. The only thing I can tell you is that he has a large scar down the right side of his face. It's a relatively wide scar and runs the full length of his face, but for all I know he has a beard now which cover most of it.

"He's out on parole, and although I don't know the details of his parole, I can't imagine he is allowed to leave the United States, or even the state of New Jersey without permission from his parole officer. I may be worried for nothing, but I confess, I am concerned. I've received three disturbing phone calls from him in the last few days." She rubbed her damp hands on her jean covered thighs. "He implied that he was coming to find me. He's not mentally stable, and to be honest, I don't know how he managed to convince a parole board that he should be allowed to be free. I don't know if it will do any good or even if you have the manpower, but is it possible to have someone around the office and the house when I am there? Just for a short time, of course. Until I have some idea—"

"I can do tha, lass." He smiled, and began to ask her about Adam and her past relationship with him and what led up to Adam's incarceration. It was difficult for Madison to talk about she and Adam in front of her friends, not to mention Ian's brother, but as she told her story, she received positive responses from all around her. She began to feel more relaxed and less ashamed for her predicament. She had always felt somewhat foolish for being so duped by Adam in the beginning, and she was afraid she would see the same opinion written on the faces of those who listened, but that wasn't the case. There was no other expression on any of their faces except caring concern and full support. After the interview was finished, Madison asked Thomas if he and his wife would like to come to the house for dinner. He accepted the invitation and they agreed on a time.

Patrick, Agatha, Lizzy, and Madison stopped at Agatha's and Lizzy's houses to collect enough clothing and personal items for their stay with Maddy and then drove back to Ian's. Once back at the house Lizzy and Agatha kicked Madison out of the kitchen and began to prepare a meal for six people.

"Ye would only be in me way. Ye're a nice tidy lass, Maddy girl, but ye donna know how to boil yerself out of a paper bag," Agatha told her. "Go read a book or take a nap or play wi yer business papers. Or ye could be callin' yer big boss and have that fool Dean booted oot o yer group."

Madison grimaced at the laughed rebuke. However true it was, it didn't sound so good when stated aloud and with such authority. She wanted to retort that she was a whiz at breakfast, but since she assumed nobody was interested in eggs, she just left the kitchen willingly.

"It might be true that Maddy isna in top form in the kitchen, Agatha, but how de ye expect her ta learn if ye just push her oot. Ye might think aboot showin' her how ta prepare a few things." Lizzy spoke softly after Madison had left the area.

"Maddy is a business wooman and a mighty high-up one a tha'. She makes a pretty penny and so does the lad. They'll eat a the pub or hire a cook. Ian is a good cook. He can teach her. It can be one o those cozy things young folks do tagether," Agatha said without looking up from the salad vegetables she was chopping.

Chapter Twenty-Two

While Lizzy and Agatha were busy in the kitchen Madison looked around and realized there was one thing missing from this fabulous house, a table. It had never occurred to her before. She and Ian always ate in front of the fire or on the island in the kitchen, which was fine, but now she was having six people to dinner and had no table for them to lay their plates. She couldn't very well ask six people to sit of the floor with their food in their laps. She wondered if Ian had any sawhorses and boards in the shed that might be put together on short notice to serve as a table. She went in search of a solution and stepped into air that smelled fresh and sweet.

She stopped and stood for a moment breathing deeply. She could smell the sea and it reminded her of a dream she had had about she and Ian standing on the cliff by the fence. She walked to the fence above the cliff, recalling the dream. Then just as fast as the memory came into her mind it was gone again. Madison was beginning to get the feeling someone was watching her. It was an awful feeling and she turned around to face whoever it was that was spying on her. To her surprise it was Patrick standing on the front porch. He began to walk toward her as she leaned against the fence rail.

"Ye know ye shouldn't come out here alone," he said as he got closer.

"Maybe, but it occurred to me; I have six guests coming to dinner and no table to serve them from. I was going to check the shed for a couple of sawhorses and boards, but the air smelled so good." She smiled up at him. "I guess I got sidetracked. It's so lovely here." Madison dropped her gaze to the ground, the grass was so lush and green. She kicked off her shoes and raised her face to the sky. The sun popped out from behind a cloud, and brightened up the land, casting a warm glow on her face. Patrick looked at the woman next to him and felt privileged to know her.

"And what are ye thinkin' aboot now?" he finally asked.

Madison opened her eyes at the sound of Patrick's voice, and focused her attention back on him. "Well, how to seat my six dinner guests for one thing." Then as if by magic, she spotted what appeared to be an old wooden picnic table leaning against the side of the house and her eyes brighten. "Do you suppose we could all fit around that?" she pointed to the table and Patrick followed her to the side of the house to inspect the old table.

The closer they got to the table, the bigger it appeared to be. Upon close inspection, there was no question, it had definitely seen better days, but it was a table and it meant her guests wouldn't have to sit on the floor. They decided they could make use of the oversized relic. Patrick took one end while Madison the other and the two of them half dragged, half carried the mammoth table near the fence overlooking the sea.

Maddy stood back with her hand outstretched. "I offer for your inspection my newly discovered antique outdoor dining table for small casually intimate dinner parties." She beamed.

"And not a moment too soon!" Patrick smiled back as he nodded toward a red truck pulling to a stop next to Ian's Wagoneer.

Thomas Mackay hopped out of the driver's side and ran to the passenger door offering his hand to help his *very* pregnant wife climbing down from her seat. As the two of them walked toward Madison and Patrick, she noted that Thomas Mackay's wife was a tiny little thing despite her immense belly. She looked to be no more than nineteen years old, but knew that his wife was closer to his age that the nineteen she appeared to be. She had long poker straight blonde hair and deep green eyes. She looked almost like a child next to Ian's brother who towered above her. Madison held out her hand to Thomas as soon as they came closer.

"How nice to see you again, Mr. Mackay. I'm so glad you could come." She smiled. She felt a little awkward now welcoming Thomas to his own brother's house.

"Ah, there's no a need ta be say formal, call me Tommy. Nobody ere calls me 'Thomas' unless I've done somethin wrong and I'm in fer a tongue lashin'. And this is me wife and the luv o me life Sara. Sara, me darlin, this is Madison Danaher and acourse ye already know the doc."

"Yes, I'm happy to see you, Patrick, on a nonprofessional level. And I can't tell you how delightful it is to meet you Madison Danaher."

Madison chuckled. "You're not Scottish."

Sara laughed. "No, I'm English." Sara looked at her husband and smiled. "So tell me, how did you meet our Ian?" Tommy took her arm and led her farther into the yard toward the table.

"I hope you don't mind sitting out here for dinner. The house is wonderful; however, there isn't a table in the place." Madison began to fidget.

"I don't mind in the least; this is a perfectly lovely spot to eat. I've always thought this was the most glorious view. But are you sure this the safest place for you to be?" Sara's question caught everyone by surprise, including her husband.

"Safe?" Madison questioned "What would make you ask?"

"Oh dear. It seems I've spoken out of turn. I do apologize, but you see, when Tommy is talking on the telephone, he thinks unless he's screaming, the person on the other end can't hear him, and I think he might be stone deaf. I wasn't trying to eavesdrop, I assure you, but I could hear the entire conversation between Ian and Tommy from the kitchen where I was doing the luncheon dishes."

"Dishes!" Patrick bellowed "Ye know damn well, ye silly woman, that ye're no ta be doing any housework. Ye're also no supposed ta be standin' on yer feet!"

"Oh, Patrick, pipe down," Sara scolded. "You may be my doctor, but you are not my warden. I do everything I can sitting, but some things must be done on my feet."

As Patrick turned to Tommy, Madison had the feeling a lecture was going to take place and thought this would be the perfect time to excuse herself. "I think I'll take this opportunity to see about our dinner and fetch the plates and table things." As Madison walked back to the house, she could hear Patrick reading the riot act to the expectant father for allowing Sara to be on her feet and do anything even remotely connected with housework.

"Wow, I'm sure glad he isn't my doctor," Madison said to Agatha as she walked in the kitchen door.

"Aye, he's a bonnie bruisin' lad. Takes his patients seriously, does our Patrick." Agatha picked up a large wooden spoon and resumed stirring a pan of gravy bubbling on the stove top. "His concern for Sara is well deserved. Ye see Tommy and Sara have been wed boot three years now. When they first wed she was wi child faster than ye can say the deed. Aye!" Agatha chuckled. "The neighbor hens were sa busy countin' on their fingers and whisperin' amongst themselves. Silly auld woomen. Tommy's a big strappin' lad and was no' a young boy when he met and wed Sara. Stands ta reason he'd be plantin' his seed fast as it took him ta blink it off. But it didna take. Ta make the long story short, they lost the babe. Tommy was devastated and blamed himself fer a poor job, and Sara hurt because she thought she let her man doon. Time passed and she went back ta England ta live wi her mother." Agatha turned down the burner, banged the wooded spoon on the side of the skillet and went to the refrigerator to retrieve the salad. She set the large bowl on the counter and began tossing the greens without another word.

"Well?" Madison said. *She does this on purpose,* she thought. "Then what happened?"

"Oh, well, nay a body could understand why Tommy let her go wi' out a battle. He wasna in verra good shape fer weeks. He tended the grave and made a poor try of resumin' his life wi' out Sara. After a while the family, especially Ian, made the lad go after her. When he got to England she was verra sick. Her mother's doc didna think she'd live. Said it were complications from losin' the babe, and poor medical care. Damned English fool! If ye ask me, losin' that babe, just broke her spirit. Poor sweet lass. I donna think she *wanted* ta live. But that Tommy-lad stayed wi her day and night. Talked ta her and *sang* ta her! And if ye'd ever heard that lad sing? Whew! Tis enough ta wake the dead! Promised her if she'd come home wi him, they'd make another babe tha' would be big and strong. He talked ta her 'til he was near hoarse, until she came to."

Agatha stopped talking again and Madison was ready to strangle her. *I'll try another tact,* she thought.

"So I guess Tommy and Sara stayed on in England and saw the appropriate specialists until she was able to conceive. That's wonderful. Leave it to the English!" She smiled.

Agatha slammed her wooden spoon and fork on the counter hard enough to rattle the dishes in the cabinets.

"Is yer name Danaher or Mountbatton?" she thundered. "What di ye mean, 'leave it ta the English'? Poor medical care, my pa's goat's ass! NAY! They didna stay in bloody England. He brought her back ta Scotland and glad she was ta be here. Patrick was here by then and she doctored wi him. He gave her pills and some instructions ta follow. Between Patrick and Tommy and the good air o Scotland, they made her healthy again. Aboot nine months ago, Patrick told the couple they were ta have a babe! English specialists! There's no a thing in this bloody world the damned English can do fer a body that we Scots canna! And ye better get tha' in yer—" Agatha stopped her tirade when she realized she was being baited. She saw the wide grins on the faces of Madison and Lizzy, and couldn't help laughing out loud herself. "Oh, ye devil, lass! Ye had me goin' on all eight cylinders then!" Agatha picked up the bowl of salad and headed out the door. Lizzy poured the gravy in a dish and headed for the door herself.

"She's right, Maddy. I thought for a minute there I could see steam comin' oot her ears!" Lizzy chuckled.

"She tells a story better than anyone I know, but dragging it all out of her is like pulling teeth; however, I'm not sure the same method will work twice," She chuckled and held the door open for Lizzy, then called for the men to collect chairs and take them out to the table. While they retrieved chairs, Lizzy and Agatha brought out tablecloths, plates, glassware, and utensils to set the table. After hearing some of Sara and Tommy's history, Madison understood Patrick's scolding of the couple. So when Sara offered to help with the table, Madison thanked her kindly but told her to stay seated.

After the table was set, Madison asked Tommy and Patrick to help bring out the food. It took Patrick and Tommy several trips to and from the house before they had all the heaping bowls and platters carried to the table. While the food was being transported to the table by the cliff, Madison went up to her room and brought down a small-upholstered wing-backed chair. Tommy met her halfway down the stairs and reached for the chair.

"If you'll take this out to Sara, I'll help Patrick with the rest of the food."

"Ye're a thoughtful lass." Tommy smiled. "Ian's done well fer himself."

Tommy took the chair and trotted out to his wife. Madison watched as Sara mildly protested the need for such a "lovely chair to be brought outdoors," but eased her heavy bulk into the cushiony softness. Tommy leaned down and placed a loving kiss on the top of her head. "I only

carried the thing, darlin'. Maddy was the one who sent it out fer ye."
How lucky those two are, Madison thought to herself.

The meal was a wonderful affair. The yard was filled with laughter. Stories were told of Ian and Tommy as young boys, and Patrick and Lizzy shared some moments of their youth. As dinner was winding down, Madison realized she hadn't thought once about Adam and the possibilities his freedom threatened. She felt renewed with joy and warmth and new friendships. When it began to get dark, Tommy picked up his wife and carried her into the house, while Patrick, right behind him returned the wing-backed chair to the master bedroom. Once Sara was seated on the sofa, Madison and the rest of her guests began to clean up. Madison stood at the kitchen door and looked out toward the empty table. *What a wonderfully delightful evening,* she thought. Once again she was barred from the kitchen duties, so she sat with Sara in the living room.

"I may not be able to cook, but I can clean," she mumbled under her breath as she sat down on the sofa.

"Oh, don't mind them too much." Sara laughed. "It's just the way things go here. When a guest comes for dinner, especially Agatha, they push you out of the way and do for themselves."

"Yes, well where I come from the host cooks and cleans up." She looked over at the group in the kitchen as they cleaned and laughed together, and decided to just go with the flow. She leaned back into the sofa and turned her attention back to Sara. "When is the baby due?"

"Next week. Thank God!" She laid her hand on her belly and rolled her eyes. Both women laughed.

When all her guests were gathered and seated comfortably in the living room, Madison went to the kitchen, and brought back a bottle of red wine and six stemmed glasses. Everybody laughed when she handed one of the wine glasses to Sara, filled with milk. The next three hours were filled with more laughter. More stories were offered and shared as though the six people had known each other all their lives.

When Sara yawned, Tommy stood. "Well," he said, "tis time ta be on our way. I need ta get me wife in bed. Come along there, lass." He leaned down, scooped up his wife in his arms and started toward the door when Madison's phone rang. At the late hour, everyone knew it could only be one of two people. The once boisterous assembly fell silent and watched as Madison answered the persistent ring.

"I hope you enjoyed your dinner party, Madison," Adam baited. "It was kind of you to bring out the chair from your bedroom, though I'm not so sure I would have forced the expectant mother to eat outdoors in the damp air. Of course, it's not like you had much choice since that house has no table. And a good hostess such as yourself, would never allow her guests to sit on the floor." Adam began to laugh as Madison's face drained of color. Tommy set Sara back on the sofa and walked straight to Madison. "I must commend you for finding the large picnic table on the side of the house, my dear. See you soon." Adam ended the call and Madison dropped the phone on the floor. She looked into Tommy's eyes and grappled with the fear that wracked her whole body.

"He's here," she whispered. "He found out where I am and he's here. He saw me. Tonight, and all of you here with me. He's been in the house." Tommy laid his hand on her arm. She backed away and stood in front of the fireplace. He moved toward her again.

"Don't come near me," she warned. She was scared and beginning to panic. She knew that just being there with her was putting everyone in danger.

"Madison." Tommy's voice was low and soft. He knew she was terrified. When Lizzy started for Madison, he waved her off. "I'm here ta help ye, lass. Believe me no' a thing will happen ta ye." He came within arm's reach of her and stopped. "Now then, can ye tell me what the blackguard said?" Madison turned toward the fireplace and began to shake with fear and tears ran down her face.

"He said he would see me soon," she choked.

"And how di ye come ta the conclusion he was here and saw all of us?" Patrick asked from across the room.

"He knew about the chair we brought down for Sara, and he knew which room it came from. He knew that we ate on the picnic table and where I found it. He also knew the reason for eating outside was that there is no a table in the house. Now, how would he know all that if he wasn't here somewhere?"

"You're coming home with us," Sara said as she tried to stand.

"Oh no I'm not!" Madison whirled around to face them. "I will not put you or your family at risk. Any of you. I think you should all go home." Madison went upstairs and sat down on the bed. Tommy appeared in the doorway thirty seconds later.

"Ye are family now, lass. And in case ye've forgotten, I'm Chief Inspector here in the Isle. Leave me to do me job. We dinna like foreigners scarin' the bejesus oot o our citizens." He came into the room and pulled up a chair and sat down in front of her. Easing his hands over hers, he continued to speak quietly, but firmly. "I agree tha' ye shouldna come ta me house. However, ye're no ta be alone. If he has seen ye all together, ye'll stay together. I'll no' have him use one of us ta get ta ye, Maddy. I have no' enough men to protect ye all separately. So along wi Patrick, Lizzy, and Agatha, Sara and I will be stayin' too." Madison watched as he stood and transformed his demeanor from teddy bear to professional cop.

"You can't, Tommy. If for no other reason, Sara is nearly ready to deliver. She shouldn't be in the middle of this turmoil.

"Well, now, can ye think o a better thing for her than ta be marooned in a comfortable house wi her doc, then?"

"Yes!" she sniffed. "To be marooned in a hospital with him." She stood and walked to the window and searched the darkness. Standing on the dark of her bedroom she could see the land and the shape of the mountains in the distance, both comforting and unnerving at the same time. Although she would be able to see if anything was moving around outside, she would now assume every movement was Adam. *God I've brought this to Ian and his family,* she thought to herself.

"I'll be callin' Ian, then. Ye'll be wantin' ta speak wi him after." The sudden sound of Tommy's voice jolted her out of her thoughts.

"No." Her voice was solid and controlled. "I don't want you to call Ian."

"He wouldna thank me fer keepin' him in the dark. He wouldna thank ye either, Maddy lass."

"I know that." Madison turned from the window to face Ian's brother. "What's more, he'll be madder than hell with me. But telling him would only make matters worse. For both of us. He can't leave now. He's nearly finished. He'll be home in a day or two. There's no point in making him feel he has to rush home a few hours before he would be coming anyway?" She took a deep breath and straightened her shoulders. "So what's our next move, Chief Mackay?" Tommy smiled at her and walked to stand by her at the window. Madison raised her eyes to his and he pulled her into his arms. It felt nice to be held by someone.

"Are ye goin' ta follow me orders from now on, then?" he asked. She could hear his smile now even if she were bundled in his arms and couldn't see it.

"Aye, I willna disobey," she mimicked and leaned back and looked up into his eyes "within reason." Both of them laughed as they turned and walked out of the room.

Back down in the living room with the rest of the group, Tommy borrowed Madison's cell phone to call, his brother Alex and fellow officer.

"Sorry ta drag ye from yer wife, Alex lad, but I need ye oot here ta Ian's place. Aye. Now, and call Donny and ask him to come too. I dinna ask ye what yer clock says. Call Donny and both o ye get oot here! And Alex, bring yer sidearms. It's a bloody good thing Donny came home a few weeks ago for a visit." Tommy ended the call and turned to the group. "Well, now, Donny and Alex will be here soon, and since Sara and I are stayin', there's really no a reason fer all of ye ta stay. So like the lassie said, ye should all go home."

"Well, I'm stayin', Thomas Mackay! Just settle it in yer brain right now," bellowed Agatha.

"I'm not going anywhere," echoed Patrick.

"I'm sure as hell no goin' home!" Lizzy chimed.

"Lizzy," Agatha said wide-eyed, "since when do ye ha a mouth on ye?"

Tommy put his arm around Maddy's shoulders. "There's some ye donna give orders ta unless ye do it ass backwards." He grinned.

That night Sara and Madison took the master bedroom, Lizzy and Agatha the guest bedroom and the men camped on the sofas downstairs. Alex and Donny arrived after the woman had gone to bed. Tommy assigned them to watch the outside of the house from different angles to make sure nobody could sneak in unnoticed.

Madison couldn't sleep. She sat up most of the night looking out the window and pacing. She sat in the window seat with Julie and watched land bathed by light of the full moon. Scotland was a magical place. She didn't know if the land was more beautiful in the glow of silver moonlight or in bright sunshine. The sea mist collected on the blades of grass and the leaves of the trees and sparkled like millions of tiny diamonds. How she wanted to take a walk in this wondrous sight. Madison had always enjoyed walking at night, and since being here she had been able to do so. *Until now*, she thought to herself.

Her gaze was torn from the window and the land beyond when she heard Sara stirring. Madison decided she had better go to bed and try to get some sleep. She crawled in the massive bed carefully so as not to disturb Sara and lay on her side. Julie leaped onto the bed curling in next to her.

The next morning Madison was the last to wake. She sat up in bed and took in the splendor of her window view, then threw back the covers. After she was showered and dressed, she went downstairs to find the house was flooded with people. *Ian definitely needs to add on some more rooms,* she thought to herself as she surveyed the dormitory that used to be a living room. "And a table," she said aloud as she noted Sara and two men she'd never seen before sitting on the sofas eating breakfast.

"Danny! Yer awake," Patrick said from somewhere in the kitchen.

"Madison," Tommy said, walking to where she stood on the stairs. "I'd like ye ta meet Alexander Mackay, one of me best officers and Donavan Mackay, home for a visit."

Madison came down the last few steps and looked at the two new men who were standing side by side behind the sofa. "Nice to meet you." She turned to Tommy. "Cousins?" she asked, smiling.

"No, ma'am brothers," answered Alexander, although with his accent it sounded like 'mum'. "And please call me Alex."

"I thought only the Queen was called 'mum.'" She grinned.

"This is Scotland, girl. No' England. We can call a body wha' we want," Agatha called from the kitchen.

"I call her 'Danny' cause we Irish have ta stick together!" This from Patrick and they all laughed.

"In any case, Madison or Maddy will do. Or 'Danny,'" and she bowed toward Patrick. "Wow, Ian was right when he said he was related to the police." She smiled looking at Tommy and Alex.

"Ah, ye still ha two more brothers ta meet, lass," Donavan said as he came from behind the sofa with his hand outstretched. "Donny."

"SIX!" Madison was speechless. "Your poor mother gave birth to six babies."

"Nay, six *boys*," Alex smiled. "After Ian, our mother gave birth ta two more babes, our sister Bridget and then came Emily. There be eight of us all tagether."

"Jesus Mary and Joseph," Madison sighed.

"So, when might ye be given Ian a wee bairn o his own, then?" Donny asked.

Madison's eyes widened but thankfully Tommy spoke up.

"Next week," he said sarcastically as he smacked the top of Donny's head. "Dinna Mother no' teach ye ta keep a civil tongue? Now ye've both had yer food, back ta yer posts," Tommy demanded.

Civil tongue, is it? Madison thought remembering the "pumpin'" remark Tommy had made in his office. She went to the kitchen and after toasting a bagel and filling her travel mug of coffee, she picked up her purse and briefcase and started for the door.

"And where do ye think yer goin'?" Agatha interjected.

"To work, in case you've forgotten I have a business to run, and that means I have to go to the office. I have people to hire and—" The entire room began to object at once. "HOLD IT!" Madison shouted. When the din died down Madison continued. "I have given this a lot of thought. I came here to open a hospice and I am not going to let anything keep that from happening. Especially Adam Gilmore! Now you are all welcome to come along, and since Lizzy is an employee she *should* come with me." And with that she turned and walked out of the house. After she got in the car she sat and waited to see how long it would take for the house to empty. Not to her surprise, everyone came out of the front door in single file. Lizzy was the last and she locked the door behind her.

Tommy, Alex, and Donny came to the driver side window of the Wagoneer and waited for Madison to lower the window.

"We're worried boot ye, lass, and Ian will ha our heads if anything happens ta ye," Tommy said.

"I understand, but like I said, I have a job to do and besides, I can't allow myself to become a prisoner in my own... in Ian's house. Besides if I sit there all day waiting for Adam to show up, I will go insane. I need something to keep my mind occupied. I thank you all for taking such care of me. Ian is so lucky to have a family like yours."

"Thank ye, lass," Alex said. "I will ride wi ye and Donny can follow in his car. Tommy, ye should get Sara home so she can rest a bit." Alex crossed in front of the Wagoneer and opened the passenger door.

"Donna worry, Tommy lad," shouted Donny from his car. "We'll take good care o Ian's lass!"

Everyone got into their vehicles and appeared to go their separate ways. However, Tommy didn't take Sara home. He drove her to the hospital, bought her the latest Romantasy book by her favorite author, Cadmi Ó'Cléirigh, and parked her on the sofa in Patrick's office. Agatha rode with Lizzy to the office, while Patrick went to the hospital for his rounds.

Once at the office Madison got straight to work, calling the newspaper running ads for nurses, social workers, chaplains, and certified home health aides. Even though Samuel had given her the okay to hire marketers, Madison decided to handle marketing herself for right now. She was glad to have the work to keep her busy and grateful she wasn't alone. Alex and Donny lounged by both doors to the office and Lizzy was on the phone all day calling hospitals, nursing homes, and assisted livings to let them know about the new hospice in the area.

Madison received a total of three phone calls all day. One from Samuel to see how she getting along, and one from Dean, expressing his displeasure for "inviting Samuel to interfere in their personal life."

"Dean, if you call me again, I swear to God, I'm going to file charges against you for harassment! Make an appointment for yourself with an analyst!" But the last call was from Ian.

They talked for a long time, about his filming and his brothers. She told him how much she was enjoying Alex and Donny. She told him about her dinner party the night before, at least most of it. She said she only wished she had met Sara and his brothers under different circumstances. She mentioned the picnic table and the fact that the house had no table for occasions when they might have guests.

Thankfully Ian did not ask if there were any more phone calls from Adam. And since he didn't ask, Madison didn't feel the need to tell him.

By late afternoon, Madison was running out of things to do and decided it was time to go home. She told Lizzy she should go back to her own house and have Patrick stay with her.

"I would, but Patrick is puttin' in a double shift at the hospital."

"Well, then stay with Agatha." Lizzy looked hurt. "I'm sorry, Lizzy, but I don't like putting you in danger by being out there with me at night. I'm sure Agatha will be glad to have your company. Besides, the house isn't big enough for all these people. And nobody is getting any rest. Alex and Donny will be out there with me, so I'll be perfectly safe. And I'd feel better if I knew you were safe too." Madison moved toward her friend and put her hands on top of Lizzy's shoulders. "I thank you very much for caring about me, but I need you to look after yourself too. Just being with me might be putting you in danger, and I wouldn't forgive myself if something were to happen to you or anyone else for that matter." Madison gave Lizzy a big hug and sent her and Agatha on their way with Donny following them home. Madison and Alex drove back to the house where they found Tommy and Sara waiting.

After a light dinner, Madison went for a walk along the beach with Alex and Donny looking on. Now she knew how Ian must feel when he goes anywhere. Never really alone, always having someone watching you. How she hated it and Adam knew how much she hated being watched. When it began to get dark, she came in and decided to go to bed and since Lizzy, Agatha, and Patrick were no longer in the house, Sara and Tommy could have the second bedroom. Although that still left Donny and Alex on the sofas.

The next week was filled with work and more work. Madison got a lot of response to the ads she'd placed in all the papers. Lizzy took care of setting up interviews with Madison and filing all the resumes in order of qualifications and desirability. Madison had three interviews by appointment each day and allowed for drop-ins. She had

Lizzy interview applicants for the CHHA positions. Madison was very pleased at the way Lizzy handled herself with the applicants and the way she managed the office. She decided that she was going to hold off on hiring someone to run the office and see if Lizzy would be interested in the job on a permanent basis.

On Thursday Madison got a call from Ian saying that the filming had been concluded and that he was going to grab the first flight out and be home Friday morning. Madison had not received any more calls from Adam since the picnic and was wondering if maybe he realized she had so much protection and he wasn't willing to risk his freedom. *Not likely,* she thought to herself. Madison had taken the opportunity to get to know some of Ian's brothers and learn more about Ian. She was told stories about how he was young and cried when his father made him sell his pig to the butcher. And how hurt he was when Alexandra broke off the engagement.

Madison went to bed that night knowing that she was going to see Ian the next morning and was finally going to be whole once more. Even though she was surrounded by police, she still felt uneasy and the knowledge of Ian's return made her feel safe and warm. She slid under the sheets and waited for Julie to burrow under the covers before turning out the light and going to sleep. She lay in bed looking at the ceiling and a smile came to her lips as she closed her eyes and drifted off.

Chapter Twenty-Three

A s Ian packed his bags to go home, he couldn't shake the niggling feeling that something was wrong. His packing became more an exercise in cramming and stuffing than tidy placing to save space. Frustration was creeping up on him because clothing shoved into bags didn't fit as well as clothing neatly folded and placed in the bags, and his heart was beginning to race. He had called and arranged for Tommy to meet him at the Inverness Airport when his plane landed, and he was anxious to get out of the hotel suite and be on his way. With his jaws clamped tight, he finally managed to get all of his belongings stuffed into the bags and the bags zipped closed. He made a quick scan of the suite to make sure he hadn't forgotten anything, then checked his watch. It was 3:30 p.m.

"Bloody Hell!" he bellowed, snatched up his bags, and stormed out the door. He had used the hotel's auto-checkout system the night before. All he had to do was let the driver load his luggage into the limo, and get to the airport. While he rode to Kennedy International, Ian thought about the "wrap" party being held that evening. There was usually some kind of party thrown by the producer or the studio or even the actors after filming was completed. Often, actors would stay in town for a day or two after filming was finished to make sure they weren't needed for re-shooting any of their scenes. However, Ian could not and would not wait any longer to get back to Madison. She was in trouble. He knew it. He could feel it. She needed him with her, and he needed to be with her. He was going home, just as fast as he could get there.

"Where's the damned Concorde when ye really need it?" he grumbled to himself. He knew he should use the hour drive to Kennedy for sleep, but the nagging feeling in the pit of his stomach wouldn't allow it. Ian looked at his watch again. It was 3:50 p.m. He rested his head on the back of the seat and forced his eyes to close.

"That would make it almost nine o'clock at home," he said aloud to himself. "I could call Maddy. She should be on her way to bed by now unless she's still at the office." He cringed at the thought of her leaving the safety of the house to go to her office, but he knew the Lusta branch of Tender Care Hospice was important to her and wouldn't abandon it, and if he was thinking straight, he wouldn't want her to.

Ian's worry and frustration was due in part to the phone call she got from Adam the day of her picnic. What he really wanted to do was wring her neck for not telling him about it herself. Ian had been calling Tommy every day to check in, and it was from Tommy that he learned of Adam's call. Ian understood that she got Tommy to promise to not tell him what had happened the evening of the picnic. But Tommy was never a very good liar and he was never able to lie to Ian, not even over the phone. Besides, Tommy knew Ian trusted him. Ian had trusted Tommy with Madison's safety, and Tommy wasn't going to betray that trust because of some silly female idea about not wanting Ian to worry. He felt that Ian had a right to know what was going on at home. Tommy also knew that Ian would worry less if he knew what was happening, and that Tommy and his brothers were on top of the situation.

Ian opened his eyes and looked out of the tinted car window. They were nearing the airport. He reached for his cell phone and dialed his Maddy.

"Hello" came Madison's sleepy voice over the airwaves.

"Maddy, me darlin', how are ye?"

"Ian?" Her voice was much more alert now and Ian smiled.

"Aye, luv, did I wake ye?"

"Oh no... no... well, sort of. I'm in bed, but... I guess I dozed off."

"How was yer day?"

Madison scooted down into the covers and smiled at the sound of Ian's voice. "Okay, I had some more interviews today for nursing and social workers."

"Have ye hired anyone yet?"

"Aye, Lizzy brought on two aides, and I hired the chaplains, and one nurse."

"Are ye still plannin' on offerin' Lizzy the job ta run things fer ye, then?"

"Uh-huh. Monday as a matter of fact. I hope she agrees to take the responsibility. She has the right kind of heart for that position. Perfect type casting." Madison smiled and then yawned. "Sorry about that." She giggled. "I guess I was asleep. When are you coming home?"

"I'm on me way ta the airport, as we speak, darlin'." He grinned. She sounded soft and warm, and he wished he was with her. "I should be landin' in Inverness at one o'clock tomorrow afternoon."

"Okay, I'll meet your plane."

"Nay, Tommy has already arranged ta meet me flight." Ian winced as he prepared for her reaction.

"What?" her voice was deflated and hurt. "Why?"

"Because ye donna have ta work tomorrow, and I donna like the idea o ye leavin' the house anyway until this maniac is locked up or dead. I donna much care which. Actually, I think I prefer dead."

"Ian!" Madison said in shock.

"What?"

"Shame on *ye!*" she laughed.

"Trust me, luv. Shame is no' wha' I'm feelin' at the moment. Listen darlin', I have ta go, we're here. I luv ye and I'll see ye tomorrow, and Madison?"

"*Aye, luv,*" she crooned in her best impression of him.

"Donna let Alex oot o ye're sight, I donna want anything ta happen to ye."

"Okay, I promise. I love you too, Ian."

"How could ye help it? I'm a totally luvable bloke!"

Madison put her phone on the bedside table and scooted farther down into the bed. She took Ian's pillow and hugged it to her breast. *He's coming home,* she thought to herself. *He's finally coming home to me.* She turned out the light and snuggled under the covers holding tight to Ian's pillow.

The next morning Madison woke completely rejuvenated. Ian would be home today, and that made her whole world look brighter.

For the first time in a week, she only had one other person in the house with her. Tommy and Sara had gone to the hospital to see Patrick. Sara's due date had passed and so far the baby apparently wasn't ready to make an appearance. Alex went home to rest and spend some time with his wife. That left her and Donny to their own devices. Madison was thrilled. It was almost like having her life back to normal. And Ian would be home today! She threw back the covers and raced to the shower. When she was dressed in jeans and an old shirt of Ian's, she went downstairs to find Donny sipping tea in front of the window in the living room. He looked so much like Ian standing there, that Madison stopped on the stairs and to take a second look.

"Good morning." She smiled brightly as she stepped on the last stair tread.

"Good morn." Donny turned to face her. "Ye're in a good mood. Must ha slept well, then."

"I slept great!" She walked into the kitchen and began setting out the bag of bagels and the toaster. "Would ye like a bagel before we start?"

Donny turned to follow her into the kitchen and stopped in midstride. He looked at her with suspicion. "Start wha'?"

"Work, of course." She pulled out two bagels for the each of them and began to cut them down the center

"WORK?" Donny boomed. "Are ye a bloody machine or a wooman? Ye've been at tha' bleedin' office every day since ye've been back. Ye do know tha it's Saturday do ye no?"

"I know what day it is, and don't yell at me, Donavan Mackay." He backed off as soon as Madison acquired the Agatha Stuart tone in her voice. She backed away from the counter and indicated her attire. "Open your eyes, man! Do I look like I'm dressed for the office?" He remained silent as he took in the old jeans and ratty shirt that was obviously one of Ian's discards. Madison frowned waiting for a response. When none came she continued. "The answer is 'no,' Donny. The work I was referring to was gardening." She held back a laugh as she watched the different expressions play across his handsome face. First came surprise, then confusion, but the last was the best. Pure dread!

"Gardenin'?" Shoulders slumped; Donny sat down on the stool. He remembered when his ma used to make him pull weeds from her flower garden. *I hate the job,* he thought. Julie hopped up onto the counter and plopped herself in front of Donny staring at him. "What?" he asked the white fur ball. He never could understand cats.

"She wants you to pet her." Madison placed his bagel in front of him and gave Julie an affectionate ruffle behind the ear. When he made no move to pet the cat, Madison finally called attention to it. "Why, don't you like cats?"

"Donna know, I prefer dogs. Is she goin' ta stay there all day, then?"

Madison smiled. "Yep! 'Til you give in and succumb to her charms, she will follow you everywhere and never leave you alone. She is apparently determined to make you like cats. This one anyway. Now finish your breakfast and let's get started." Madison slathered her bagel with cream cheese and smiled as she watched Donny try to ignore Julie while said cat stared at him and purred. They spent the rest of the meal in silence.

When they were finished, Donny dutifully followed Madison out to the shed where she'd apparently stored what appeared to be half a nursery of plants for around the front porch. His hopes that he was there only as an observer or even in an advisory capacity, were dashed when Madison handed him the shovel.

"Here, and the tree is on the other side of the shed," Madison said with a big broad smile.

"Tree?" he questioned as his eyebrows rose nearly to his hairline. "Ye do realize, do ye nay, that I'm a professional police officer? I'm no' a gardener." Madison's only response was her cheery smile as she led him to the middle of the yard. He grumbled to himself as he began to dig a hole for the young tree. "PROFESSIONAL police officer. I do na do gardens, and I'm tay auld ta pull weeds!" When the tree was in the ground he stood back and realized what kind of tree he had planted. The Silver Birch was native to Scotland, he always thought they were very pretty trees. When Donny turned to let Madison know he was finished with the task she had given, his eyes were met with her accomplishment.

The flower beds that rounded the front of the house, which had been bare since the house was built, were now full of color and life. She had planted wave petunias in several shades of pink and purple. There were small red tea roses with silver moss interspersed for ground cover. Every four feet she had planted blueberry bushes. At either end of the beds were small evergreens. Madison stood and surveyed her efforts. She was very pleased with the effect she'd created. She turned toward Donny and smiled.

"I'm no' so sure how well those will stand up ta the weather here," he said as he walked toward her. "But they sure make the house look bright. I'll give ye that. The place doesna look so sad now."

Madison smiled. She knew he wasn't exactly thrilled about her morning work plans, which made her doubly appreciative of his grudging compliment.

"Thank you, Donny! They do make the house look happier, don't they? I don't know if they will thrive here either, but I like to plant flowers and play in the dirt." She laughed at his dumfounded expression and then looked at the Silver Birch he had just planted. "Oh that looks beautiful! You did a lovely job of it. It's perfect! That should fare well there. Silver birch is native to Scotland, you know."

"Aye. So I've heard." He ducked his head to hide the grin spreading across his face. They both turned as a delivery truck pulled to a stop in the driveway.

"Are ye plannin' on plantin' more plants, then?" Donny asked, hoping against hope she would say no.

"Yes, as a matter of fact," she said over her shoulder while she strode toward the truck. "I ordered a few things online before I left for the states last. But I wasn't sure when they would be delivered. This is great! Perfect timing!"

"What are they?" Donny followed along behind her.

"Well, I have a Russian Olive Tree and a Red Maple—"

"More trees?!" He groaned and Madison laughed. *Apparently cops don't enjoy working in the dirt,* she thought and walked to the driver. She checked the contents of her order and signed the clipboard manifest, while explaining to the workmen where to place the trees for planting. As they unloaded the massive trees, Donny cringed and rubbed his back in anticipation of how he was going to ache by evening. He was trying to dream up ways to talk Alex into coming back out to take his place for the afternoon, when Madison laughed.

"Oh, Donny, don't look so worried! We're not planting these ourselves. They're too big. These men are professionals. They will be doing the plantings." His face was the perfect picture of relief before his forehead wrinkled and the glare reached his eyes.

"PROFFESSIONALS is it? THEY are professionals! And where were THEY two hours past when I was up ta me armpits in dirt and the sweat o me brow?" He descended on her like a bull. She laughed out loud and backed up several feet raising her arms in front of her, her hands palms up.

"Now, it wasn't so very difficult, was it? And you did a beautiful job! And in years to come you can gaze out at that lovely tree and say to everybody that will listen that you were the one who planted it with your own two professional-officer-of-the-law hands!" She had to stop and laugh again, while he found her joy infectious and joined in. "All I need from you now, is to help me decide where to place them. I want to be able to see them from the house, but I don't want the view of the bay blocked."

"Does Ian have any clue what he's in for wi ye, lass?" Donny sighed. He stood back and looked around the yard toward the cliff. He had placed the Silver Birch to the far left of the house. He knew something about Red Maples and figured it could go on the far right of the house. There, it would be seen from the kitchen and by anyone coming up the drive to the house. However, he had no idea what the other tree was.

"It's a Russian Olive Tree," Madison explained "I wasn't sure if they grew here or not so I ordered it to be shipped here from a nursery in Michigan. It should grow to about twenty-five or thirty feet tall with a spread of twenty or thirty feet. They're really lovely trees and have a soft scent in the spring and early summer"

"Well, Ye could put it here." Donny walked up and stopped about twenty feet from the front walk.

"But won't that block the window?"

"Nay, just move the tree ta the left 'til ye have it in the right spot." Madison bowed to Donny's suggestions and gave the directions to the men to go ahead and plant the trees. He and Madison took this opportunity to sit on the porch and watch as the large trees went into the ground. With his attention to Madison he studied her while she watched the men with enthusiasm. "Ye seem to be makin' some permanent changes ta the place. Are ye plannin' on stayin here, then?"

The question was not exactly a shock to Madison. She was beginning to wonder when someone was going to ask. And yet she had no answer. She wanted desperately to never leave this place. She loved it here, the land, the people and more than anything else this was Ian's home. She had begun to think of it as her home too, but she didn't answer. She just smiled and returned her attention to the workmen in the yard.

After the trees were in the ground, Madison and Donny ran hoses out to each tree and turned the water on to a light stream. They unrolled Madison's new soaker hoses and placed them at the edge of the flower beds and turned them on.

"We should let the hoses run for about twenty minutes," she announced. "How about some lunch?"

Chapter Twenty-Four

They went into the house, and Madison got busy opening cupboard doors and refrigerator bins. She checked out the pantry. She took plates out of the cupboard, and set them on the counter while Donny sat on a stool and watched. He had already heard rumors of Madison's culinary skills. Thirty minutes later when he returned from the yard after cutting off the water flow to the new plantings, Madison had decided they should go to the village for lunch meat. Donny laughed and agreed, but only after he made her promise she wouldn't try to make a detour to the office.

"Okay, FINE!" was all Madison would say on the subject. He knew full well what that phrase and tone really meant and decided not to press the issue. They drove Ian's Wagoneer with Madison behind the wheel and set off for the village. On the way, Donny's cell phone began to ring.

"Aye?" Madison chuckled as he answered his cell. *Whatever happened to "hello"* she thought. And glanced over at him in the passenger seat.

"Donny, I just got a call from Ian, his flight has been delayed. He willna be getting in until after three now." Tommy paused and continued. "Ye mightna mention this ta the lass, she'll just get upset."

"Well, I'm gonna have ta say something. She's in the car wi me."

"Ye left the house!" he bellowed. "Why the bloody hell di ye do tha'?"

"We're hungry, mon! And we all know of her lack of kitchen skills. Bagels and the gooey white cheese may be passable first thing in the morn, but I willna survive on tha' lot! We're only goin' ta the pub."

Donny glanced at Madison and felt a few seconds of remorse for his remark concerning her cooking skills, *but truth was truth,* he thought. "She's no alone, Tommy, and I'm wearing me sidearm if it's needed."

"Donny," Tommy sighed, "her ex-husband has been sighted on the Isle. We havena been able ta nab him yet. He must know we're on the look fer him. He's bein' real slick. I donna think ye should be leavin' the house now."

"Does Cook know aboot this?" Cook was the nickname the brothers had given Ian when he was working at the restaurant after he got out of school. The nickname didn't bother him until he was fired. Since then Ian had cringed every time he heard it, so Donny was pretty sure he would not have told Madison about it.

"Aye, he knows. He's likely got his teeth ground ta the gooms by now. Keep yer guard up, lad. I've told Alex ta high his arse oot ta the house, and I want ye ta turn round and get yers and hers back there now!"

"Aye. How's Sara?"

"Waitin! Bless her sweet heart." The tone in Tommy's voice softened when he thought of Sara in the hospital. Probably scared and wishing he could be with her. "Patrick has her in hospital. He's goin' ta give her one more day. If the babe doesna make an appearance by the morn, Patrick says he's goin' ta 'induce labor.' He'll keep me posted, and I'll do the same wi ye."

Donny disconnected and told Madison to pull over to the side of the road.

"We need ta go back ta the house, lass."

"Why?"

"Tommy, says he ha sent Alex back, and he's there waitin' fer us. We're goin' back." Madison pulled off to the side and made a sharp U-turn toward Ian's house.

"Wait a minute," Madison said after a few moments of silence. "Why is Alex coming back? Tommy said he was just going to have you there unless—" The Wagoneer slowed as Madison released pressure on the accelerator pedal. Donny watched the color drained from her face and he grabbed the wheel when her grip slipped off.

"Pull over, Madison, and put er in Park," he ordered and did as she was told. When the SUV was safely stopped, Donny unbuckled his seat belt, swung out of the vehicle, walked to her side and opened the door. He crooked his finger under her chin and pulled her gaze to his.

"Nothin' will happen ta ye, lass. Me brothers an me willna allow it." A single tear dropped from her eye and he pulled her from the car and gathered her into his arms. "Why do ye no' get in the passenger side? I'll drive from here."

Madison looked up and nodded. On the way back to the house, Madison was silent and Donny was grateful for it. He didn't want to tell her any more than she had already guessed. She still wasn't aware that Ian's flight was delayed. Tommy had told him not to tell her, but he knew she would be watching the clock until Ian walked in the door, especially now. He felt she should be aware of what was going on, but not until they were back to the house, and Alex was with them.

When they pulled up to the house, Alex was already there and waiting in his car. The three of them got out of their cars and went inside. Madison went directly to her room without a word to Alex or Donny. Alex had only been ordered to return to Ian's, Tommy had wasted no time with explanations, so Donny filled in the details after Madison went upstairs. It was well after 4:00 p.m. when Madison came down from her room.

"Where is Ian?"

"Huh?" Donny looked up from his tea and sandwich.

"Verra cleverly put, me lad." Alex frowned and moved to Madison. "Ian's plane was delayed and willna land 'til three."

"Okay, but it's almost five now. Where is he?" Just then Madison's cell phone came to life. "Hello?"

"Maddy, me darlin how are ye?" Ian's voice sounded rushed and breathless.

"Fine, where are you?" Madison's voice, however, was weary and tired.

"Inverness. We were delayed in New York. Tommy and I will be at the house no later than seven o'clock." The phone went dead, and she stared at it before slipping it in her back pocket.

"I guess there is some sort interference, the signal was lost." Something wasn't right. Madison could feel it. Outside the sun was going down steadily. Donny went out to take a look around while Madison and Alex turned on the lights in the house.

"I think I'll sit upstairs on the balcony for a while," she said.

Alex nodded and watched as she climbed the stairs and disappeared into her room. He was proud of her for the way she was handling all this. She had to be scared, for herself and for Ian. Reports of Adam Gilmore were less than glowing. Alex went to the kitchen and made himself a sandwich while he waited for his brother to come back into the house.

After Alex had eaten he looked at his watch. It was almost six, and Donny had been outside for over an hour. Alex walked to the window and scanned the yard. The sun was down but the twilight enabled Alex to see clearly. However, there was no sign of his Donny. Alex checked the view from all the first-floor windows, when there was no sign of his younger brother, Alex second-checked the lock, and went upstairs.

As he walked in the room he immediately noticed Madison on the balcony with Julie in her lap. As he approached Julie sat up and meowed at him, drawing Madison's attention from the view to him. From the balcony, the view of the backyard was clear all the way to the mountains. If Donny had been back there, she would have seen him

"Hi," Madison said quietly.

"Hi." He smiled down at her. "Ha ye spied Donny? Has he been back here yet?" Alex asked casually.

"Oh yes, he was back here a while ago and looked around. Didn't find anything, though."

"Ye can see everything from up here," he commented, but he didn't feel as relaxed as he sounded. *Donny should be back inside by now.* Suddenly Julie shot straight up into a standing position. Her ears were flat on her head and eyes were slanted almost shut. The fur near her rump spiked all that way up her back and her tail frizzed. Alex drew his sidearm when Julie's normal soft purr gave way to a guttural growl. Alex thought briefly that he wasn't aware that house cats growled like that., and motioned for Madison to get off the balcony and back into the room. He indicated the far side of the bed and told her to get down on the floor. Alex and Madison waited, but no one came through the door.

"Why don't we go and look?" Madison asked.

"Stay where ye are and donna leave the room." He closed the balcony windows and locked them. He made a check of the closet, and bathroom, making sure the room was secure, then headed for the door. "I'll be right back. Keep the door closed. Lock it behind me," he said and left the room.

Madison sat on the bed, with Julie still very much alert and agitated in her lap. Suddenly there was a gunshot from downstairs and a loud crash.

"Oh God!" Madison's hands flew to her mouth as she stood up. She waited to hear something else, but all was silent until her cell began to ring. She reached for it in her back pocket and felt nothing. It must have popped out of her pocket and now she had no idea where it was. She knew it would be Ian. *Just stay where you are,* she thought, *once he realizes I'm not going to answer, he'll know something is wrong and come right away.* She could hear someone climbing the stairs and hoped it would be Alex or Donny. There was a scratch at the door and Madison started toward it when Julie began to hiss and growl. Madison looked at the door realizing Julie wouldn't hiss if it were Alex or Donny, and began to back away.

She searched the room frantically for a means of escape. She eyed the balcony, but the drop was too far. The fall alone would kill her. *Adam,* she thought, *it's Adam outside the door.* She grabbed Julie and opened the windows to the balcony and put Julie out on the floor first. She was about to go through the window herself, when the bedroom door smashed open, and there stood a man she would never have recognized, but for the eyes. Adam had vicious and cruel eyes when he dropped the mask he showed to the world. Hard steel hatred rushed at her from them as it had years ago. Madison made a dash for the balcony windows, but Adam was too fast. He seized her arm in a viselike grip and dragged her back into the bedroom throwing her up against the armoire. She slid to the floor dazed from the hard hit and looked up at the man she knew was going to kill her.

He walked calmly to the balcony windows and closed them, then turned the locks. *Julie,* Maddy thought. She looked at the man in her room but couldn't recognize the face. Only the eyes and even they had changed somewhat. They were harder, angrier, and held her with a lethal gaze. He had changed physically, very tanned, his shoulders seemed broader and more muscular, and his chest looked almost massive. Madison started to move to her feet when she was seized again and brought face-to-face with this stranger.

"What's the matter, Madison?" he baited. "Don't you recognize your own husband?" Madison tried with all her might to pull away, but Adam was too strong. He backed her up and slammed her against the armoire again, holding her there with his hand on her throat. "I guess it's difficult for you to remember that you have a husband since I notice you've taken your name back and *thrown, mine, away!*" with each word, his grip on her throat tightened. "It's good to see you again, *Dear Wife.*" His free hand began to roam her body. "Time certainly has been good to you. You're ripe!" He emphasized his perusal by pinching her nipple. Madison began to whimper with pain. She could vaguely feel blood wetting her hair at the back of her head and her brain was getting foggy from lack of air as he continued to tighten his hold on her throat. But her whimper only encouraged Adam.

"Ahh! I see you've missed my touch, haven't you, my love?" he said and slipped his hand under her shirt. He pushed her bra above her breast and began squeezing and twisting her nipple in some sort of odd rhythm that matched his speech pattern, between his callused fingers. "We were always so good together, my dear. Weren't we? You were always so responsive, and I was so commanding." As his attention was centering on her body, his hold on her throat lessened. Her mind began to clear as air rushed into her mouth or nose or whatever. "Does this feel good? Or this?"

"What did you do to Donny and Alex?" she demanded.

"Oh don't worry about them dear." He moved his mouth to her ear and whispered, "They won't be interrupting us."

Ian and Tommy turned into the drive leading to the house. Ian was becoming more, more agitated. Madison always answered her phone. Tommy had not been able to reach Alex or Donny for at least an hour. Once the house came into view, Ian noticed all the lights were on and both cars were in the drive. Tommy pulled up next to Donny's Jeep and turned off the truck. As Ian opened the passenger door, he saw Julie running around from the back of the house.

"Julie!" Ian called and the furry cat stopped and meowed at Ian. He ran to her and scooped her up. "Something's wrong, Tommy. Madison never lets her oot at night." Julie wiggled out of Ian's arms and raced to the door. Ian and Tommy were after her on the run. The door was closed, but the lock was broken. Alex was on the floor, blood pooling underneath him. Ian knelt beside his brother. "He's been shot!" He checked for a pulse, which was faint but steady. Tommy got his cell phone and called Patrick. While he spoke briefly to Patrick, he drew his sidearm and released the safety.

"I donna have time to explain," he whispered. "I need an ambulance at Ian's now! ... Huh? ... Nay, it's no' Madison. Alex has been shot. We haven't found her or Donny yet. I dinna know how bad. He's layin' in his own blood. Just get here." Tommy hung up the phone put it back in his pocket. "Ian," he whispered. "Find Donny."

"Nay, I'm goin' ta find Madison."

"NO!" Tommy's harsh whisper stopped Ian in midstride. "I've got one brother down already, maybe two. Don't ye dare make it three! Now go look for Donny." Ian turned toward the front door and was stopped by Tommy's next whispered words. "Ian. Take the lad's gun." Ian bent and retrieved Alex's sidearm. Released the safety and checked the load, then left the house in search of Donny. Tommy began to make his way upstairs slowly and as quietly as he could.

Adam's hands were all over her, his mouth was on her neck. Madison was crying and trying desperately to get away, but the more she fought the rougher he got.

"Oh yes, baby. Struggle! You know what it does for me. Are you getting wet?" Madison was able to raise her leg enough and thrust her knee up into his groin. The breath whooshed from his mouth as she broke free and rushed toward the door, but as Adam went down he grabbed for her ankle and pulled her down with him. She fell hard and could feel her brain beginning to cloud. Just outside the door came another shot and Madison froze. *No!* she thought, *NO!*

"Ah! Your lover, no doubt!" Adam was struggling for breath to return after her blow. "He's come to save his whore, just as I thought he would. Don't worry, sweetheart, my partner has taken care of him." Adam was now on top of her holding her throat again. "I told you we wouldn't be disturbed. And soon I'm going to cum!" he chuckled at his own sick humor.

"Get off of me, you disgusting son-of-a-bitch!" she choked out. Madison brought her hands up and raked her nails down the side of his face. Adam screamed out in pain. He grabbed her wrists and backhanded her as hard as he could.

"Now, that's the kind of the fight I want from you." He dragged a piece of rope from his pocket, bound her wrists together and tied her to the leg of the footboard. Once she was secured Adam tore her button-down shirt open, exposing her to his view. "This looks a little odd, don't you think?" He laughed. One breast had been freed from her bra earlier, and he reached down and pinched her again more savagely than before. "But we can fix it can't we?" And he drew a knife from his back pocket, slipped it under the center of her bra and pulled forward. "I see you still wear the love marks from our marriage encounters." He pressed his shin across her ankles and began to cut away her jeans.

"I have been waiting for you a long time, baby." He finished with her jeans, and she was almost completely naked. She tried to knee him again, but he was ready and blocked her. "Ever since I was taken from you. THAT will never happen again. Do you hear me, MADISON!" he yelled. "I'm going to make love to you now. I'm going to fuck you until you bleed! And then I'm going to fuck you some more! Until I'M satisfied. Did I ever tell you that I never much cared if I satisfied you? DID I?" He was getting louder and more stimulated. The louder he screamed the bigger he could feel his erection getting. "This is working well for me, baby. You could always do it for me, with your mewling and whimpers. But you liked to have me inside you, didn't you? No matter how you fought and protested. I knew it and so did you." He had to release his fly as his erection was becoming painful trapped inside his pants. "You know, it's a little sad. This will probably be our last time together, my sweet wife…. Well, look what you've done for me once again!" He sat back and admired what he understood as his proof of virility. "Can you see this? No? Too bad. It's magnificent!" He leaned down close to her tear-streaked face and brought his knife to her throat. He lowered his voice then and pressed his lips to her cheek. "I can't live without you, Madison. And I won't allow you live without me."

Chapter Twenty-Five

Ian had wanted to argue with Tommy about going directly to Madison, but Tommy was the cop and knew his business. It was better to let Tommy do his job the way he knew it should be done. Ian raced out the back door to the shed, but Donny wasn't anywhere near it. He looked up to Madison's room and saw the windows to the balcony were closed and the bedroom lights were on. He strained but couldn't see anyone in the room. Is Tommy there already, he wondered. Ian ran around to the front of the house, but still found nothing of Donny. A terrifying thought came to him as he looked toward the cliff. He made a mad dash to the fence overlooking the cliff and scanned the beach below. Nothing. To make sure the beach was deserted, he ran down the stone steps, his heart racing.

"Please don't let Donny be lying in a heap down here," he said as he reached the bottom and stepped off into the sand. He ran the length of the beach but still saw no sight of his brother. He stood at the edge of the water and tried to see as much as he could, but night had fallen and he was unable to see anything. Suddenly Ian heard a gunshot. The sound vibrated and echoed off the wall of the cliff, but he knew it came from the direction of the house and his heart stopped.

"Maddy." Ian turned, retracing his path to the stone staircase. Falling twice over rocks that dotted the sandy beach, he finally reached the steps and grabbed the iron railing. He scaled the steps two at a time. When he entered the house, he stopped at Alex's unconscious form, lying on the floor. He released his breath, grateful something was going well. Alex was still alive.

"Hold on a bit longer, laddie," he whispered.

Ian rounded the sofas and began his assent to the second floor, but came to a dead stop halfway up the log stairs. He blinked at the sight that met his eyes. Tommy was lying on the floor. A gunshot wound in his shoulder. Standing over his second unconscious brother was Donny, gun in hand. Ian slowly moved up the stairs a little farther, but then his brother turned the gun on him.

"Donny what the bloody hell do ye think ye're doin?"

"Don't come any closer Ian," Donny warned.

Suddenly there came a scream from the master bedroom. Donny turned his eyes toward the bedroom door for a second, and Ian made a furious rush toward his brother knocking him over. He burst through the door instantly spotting Madison tied to the bed leg on the floor. Rage that Ian didn't realize existed, filled his entire being. He didn't have time to think or gauge his reaction, and neither did the man pinning Madison with his body. Ian thrust his booted foot as hard as he could into Adam's midsection, sending him crashing against the armoire. In the process, Adam was knocked partially unconscious. Ian picked up the knife and sliced through the ropes binding Madison's wrists. Ian helped her to stand, and she pulled her shirt together and tugged up her jeans to cover her exposed body. Ian was about to gather her to him when he was knocked over the head with the butt of Donny's gun. Madison looked at Donny, her eyes wide with shock.

"Donny what are you doing?" She screeched as she knelt down to Ian.

"I told you I had a partner," Adam said as he stumbled to his feet. "Well, here he is. Who better to have on my side than a cop?" Adam snatched Madison by the hair and yanked her to her feet. He crushed her back to his chest holding her with one arm, and Madison watched in terror, as he raised his other hand, pointing his gun directly at Ian's head.

"NO!" Madison screamed and was able to divert the gun away from Ian's direction. The shot was fired and broke the window. Outside they could hear sirens blaring. Adam tightened his grip on Madison and turned toward the doorway.

"Kill him," he ordered Donny as he started to leave the room. He didn't get far. Ian was on his feet. He slammed his fist into Donny's face and threw him headfirst into the dresser. Donny was older, but Ian was always faster and stronger. Bright red blood oozed from Donny's nose as he slid to the floor as Ian charged after Adam.

Adam had dragged Madison to the bottom of the stairs by the time Ian reached him. He grabbed the back of Adam's shirt and yanked him backward onto the stairs. Madison stumbled free and retreated to the fireplace.

Ian looked down at the man he had hated ever since he had learned what Adam had done to Madison. He had wanted to get his hands on him for months. This man had ruined Madison's hope for happiness for years. He had raped her. He had beaten her senseless. He had caused her to miscarry her child and then left her hemorrhaging on the floor with no hope of help and walked out the door. Ian knew she had agonized for years over the possibility of never having children of her own. And now, here he was, in Ian's house with the express purpose of hurting Madison again. All of this ran through Ian's brain like a fast train and Ian wanted to kill Adam with his bare hands.

Adam watched emotion racing across Ian's face and took advantage of the lull in movement to raise his gun toward Ian, but Ian was too quick. He kicked the gun out of Adam's hand sending it flying, where it landed at Madison's feet. Madison watched in horror as Ian and Adam fought. Adam landed a solid fist in Ian's jaw causing Ian's lips to break open. Ian picked up the stool and smashed it over Adam's head. Adam went down giving Ian the chance to regain control of the battle. He grabbed hold of Adam's shirtfront and began his attack again. He slammed his fist into Adam's face again and again until Adam's face was a bloody mess, and Ian's knuckles were ragged and covered with blood. Madison couldn't tell if the blood on Ian's fists was his own or Adam's.

Madison saw Julie run down the stairs toward the two men and Madison scurried over to grab the cat from harm's way. Just as Madison picked up her cat, Adam kneed Ian in the groin, and staggered to the other side of the room picking up the gun. Adam fired a shot toward Ian and just missed. Madison screamed and ran toward Adam trying to knock him off balance. However this gave Adam the opportunity to get hold of her again. Holding her arm behind her back and pressing the tip of the gun barrel to her temple She was his prisoner once more.

"Well, what will your lover do now, *wife*?" Adam's face was bleeding badly, and his blood was running down onto Madison's cheek.

Ian struggled to get his breath. His face full of rage. "Let her go, ye sick twisted bastard!" he demanded.

"Now, is that any way to talk in the presence of a lady?" Adam moved the gun to the side of her jaw and forced her head to turn toward his. "You really must learn to choose your studs with more care, my dear." He sneered, then turned his attention back to Ian. "No, I don't believe I can accommodate you. After all, the slut is my wife, and a wife's place, you know." He lowered his eyes and looked into hers, then bent his head slightly and forced her lips to his. Ian immediately made a move toward the two of them, but Adam was watching him. "Don't move or I'll splatter her brains all over the walls of your cozy whorehouse! I swear to God." Ian stopped in midstride. "That's what I thought." Adam chuckled. His belly hurt badly, and he couldn't get the taste of blood from his mouth.

Both men turned their attention to the stairs as Donny limped down. He had a large cut across his forehead, and blood was still running from his nose. He walked calmly toward Ian and stopped in front of him. Ian didn't know what hit him. Donny reached back and sent his fist directly into Ian's face. The punch came with such force that Ian landed flat on the floor. The front door flew open, and the place was flooded with cops.

"That's far enough!" Adam shouted. "Stay right where you are. If anybody comes any closer, I'm afraid I'll just have to kill her!" he said, jamming the pistol back in Madison's temple. Donny drew his gun and backed to where Adam was standing with Madison. "Here take her," he shoved Madison to Donny who placed his gun on her temple. "I want a clear shot to the stud here." Adam raised his gun to Ian's head and two shots were fired. Madison shrieked in horror and fell to the floor. She crawled to Ian on her hands and knees and found him bloodied, but otherwise uninjured.

"Oh, Ian." She wrapped her arms around his neck. "Thank God! Thank God!" she sobbed.

"I'm okay, luv. Did he hurt ye?" He had tears in his eyes as he held her slightly away from. His eyes devouring her face for any outward sign of damage. "Are ye all right?" Her lips were swollen and there were mean purple bruises forming on the sides of her cheeks. "The fucking bloody bastard!" he said as he pulled her tightly to his chest and surrounded her with his arms. "I dinna know what I would do if I lost ye." He held her as tight as he could and still allowed her room to breathe.

Madison wiggled around in Ian's embrace and took his face in her hands bringing his lips to hers in a tender kiss. Ian turned her in his arms and his arms encircled her front. They saw Adam's lifeless body on the floor and standing over him was Donny, his gun still drawn.

Ian didn't have time to speak to Donny, and he was too tired and sore to take him on physically. He assumed the police would deal with his brother for his part in all of this.

The paramedics rushed through the doors and began giving needed medical attention to Tommy and Alex. They whisked Ian and Madison out of the house and into one of the squad trucks to tend their multiple scrapes and cuts.

"Nothing we can really do for those bruises on yer face, Miss Danaher. They'll have ta fade on their own," one paramedic admitted to Madison. "But if ye'll hold this pack ta yer mouth, it should help the swellin' ta go doon fair quick."

Ian was being tended to by one of the others, they obviously were aquatinted.

"I dinna know fer sure, Mac, but me guess is that ye might need ta have yer lip stitched a bit. But dinna worry," he chuckled, "the scar willna make ye less appealing ta the lassies on the big screen." He stuck steri-strips onto Ian's face and covered them with a gauze patch. "I donna think ye've broken any bones in yer hands, but they're a fair mess ta be sure. Some of these cuts go fair deep. Ye may need a stitch or two there too. We'll take ye in and the doc can decide about the sewin' if there's a need. Do ye feel well enough ta travel ta Lusta, then?"

One of the paramedics walked up to the back of the truck and handed Madison a fresh pair of jeans and a T-shirt to replace her torn clothing.

"The American cop over there in the FBI jacket wants us ta drop Mac and Miss Danaher at Tommy's office fer some questions, Brian. Would the injuries need the doc first or can they wait a wee bit?"

"We'll be goin' ta hospital first ta see aboot Miss Danaher's injuries." Ian spoke before Brian had the chance. "Ye can tell the American FBI we'll get to Tommy's as soon as we take care of her, and I check ta see if me brothers are goin' ta live." Ian's tone let him know that refusal was futile.

Ian and Madison road to the hospital in the squad truck. On the way, Madison changed into the clothing she'd been given, and then Ian held her in his arms. At the hospital their injuries were pronounced minor. Ian did in fact need two stitches on his cheek. Madison felt guilty that she was the cause of his face being permanently scared, but the nurse said the tiny scar would make him "devilish handsome on the screen!"

"He'll be like Harrison Ford!" she announced. "All the lassies will be forever wonderin' how he really came by the wee scar." She finished with the slight bandaging, and proclaimed him ready for the next round. His hands were cleaned, treated and bandaged. The doctor affirmed that Madison's lip wouldn't need stitches but warned her to leave the fresh dressing on for a couple of days.

"Try to sip soups for a few days, lass. I believe yer mouth will heal fine, but don't do a lot o laughin'. As long as ye don't stretch yer lip much, I think ye'll do fine." He smiled down at her and patted her swollen face softly. "Yer bruises will heal too, soon enough. I'm sorry I have no magic cream to hide the coloring, but I dinna think ye'll be feeling much like sitting for a portrait fer a few days anyhow, will ye? Now ye're head is another story. I'll be puttin' a couple of stitches back here," he said while the nurse began to snip hair away from her head wound. "But they will heal too. Keep yer head dry for two days and yer own doc can remove the sutures in seven to ten days."

After all the suturing was completed and Ian and Madison were allowed to leave the treatment cubical, Madison was given a soothing salve for the rope burns on her wrists and they went upstairs to ask about Tommy and Alex. Patrick assured them both that the brothers injuries were serious but not life-threatening. Alex had lost a considerable amount of blood, but he would recover.

"Tommy had to be sedated to assure that he would remain in bed and in hospital. He got a tongue lashing from Sara he won't be forgettin' for a while, I can tell ye!" Patrick chuckled. "He'll be fine. And Sara will make sure he does what he's told. He and Alex are in the same room. Ye can call on them in the morn or later this evenin' if ye've a mind. Are ye both doin' all right? Did ye get tended to downstairs?"

"Aye. We've been stitched and patted. I'd be happier if I could take Maddy home and put her ta bed. She's no' had a verra good day, but the American FBI are here, and we've been asked ta go ta Tommy's ta give statements."

"Tommy told us some of what happened, but he wasna too clear in his mind. He kept cursing Donny. I didna hear it all before I had to sedate him."

Ian frowned. "Aye. None of it is too clear. We'll be back later, Patrick." It hurt to think of his brother going bad. Ian wanted to smash his fist into Donny's face again. He didn't know how they would be able to explain to their mother when the time came, and it would be soon enough. His head was buzzing with questions. One, of course, was what had happened to Donny. His heart ached with the knowledge that his brother could betray the family and himself. *Why?* was the one word that kept ripping around in his brain.

When they reached the front door of the hospital, there was an FBI man waiting for them.

"Mr. Mackay? Miss Danaher? I'm Agent Malone. I'm to escort you to chief Mackay's office. Agent Thompson has some questions and would like you both to sign statements." Agent Malone ushered them into a waiting SUV and drove them to Tommy's office. He drove into the alley behind the row of buildings before Ian had a chance to explain about the size of the one Lusta street. Ian was surprised the man seemed so familiar with the local necessity. The SUV stopped behind the office and the back doors opened for Madison and Ian to climb out of the vehicle. They walked in the back door and immediately became aware of how packed the small room was. Ian recognized none of the men and women in the room. A tall woman approached them.

"I am Special Agent Thompson," she said. "Federal Bureau of Investigation. I need to ask you a few questions about what happened tonight." She ushered them both to the desk in the corner. They sat on one side while she took the chair behind the desk.

"Special Agent? FBI?" Madison echoed as she sat down on the edge of the chair seat.

"Yes FBI," replied Agent Thompson.

"Isnna Scotland a wee bit out of yer jurisdiction?" Ian interjected.

"Yes, but we have approval and assistance from your government to come for this case," Agent Thompson stated as she acknowledged, grudgingly the man in the three piece suit standing off to the side of the room. He nodded back, smiling at Ian and Madison. "Now, about tonight," Thompson continued.

For the next few hours Madison and Ian were asked question after question about the events leading up to the death of Adam Gilmore. They learned first that Adam had not in fact been released but had escaped from prison.

"But I received a letter from my attorney notifying me of his parole." Madison scooted farther to the edge of her chair.

"The letter was a fake, Mrs. Gilmore. Your husband—"

"Please." Madison cringed. "Don't call me that! Adam and I were divorced over ten years ago. I've legally reclaimed my maiden name."

"I apologize, Miss Danaher. Your ex-husband. Adam Gilmore escaped from prison several months ago. He and four other inmates escaped together. The other four were caught almost immediately, but he slipped through the fingers of the New Jersey State Police."

"I don't understand why the FBI are involved. Adam didn't commit a federal crime by escaping from a state prison." Madison was confused.

"He did when he shot and killed a federal judge, Mrs....er, Miss Danaher. If I might continue? Gilmore went to your attorney's office apparently to discover your whereabouts. By the time the local police arrived answering a call about shots fired, everyone in the office was dead. Including a federal court judge Henry W. Goldfinch, who was the brother of your attorney, George G. Goldfinch. We've learned that the judge and his brother had a standing lunch date every Wednesday. We can only assume the judge was in the office for his lunch date with his brother. Gilmore killed every staff member in the office and then lifted office stationary in order to send you a letter telling of a granted parole. We haven't figured out why he would warn you that he was free. Can you give us an idea of why he might want you to be aware that he was out of prison?

Madison shook her head, but said nothing.

"Why was she ne're informed of Gilmore's escape from prison?" Ian growled. "If he killed a US federal court judge, didna any of ye think her life might ha be in danger?" Between Madison's injuries and his own, not to mention the injuries of his brothers and his anger with Donny, Ian was ready to do battle again with somebody, and at the moment, he didn't really care who.

Agent Thompson cleared her throat. "I can't answer for the Jersey State Police, Mr. Mackay. Apparently it just slipped through the cracks." She looked at Madison. "When we realized you had not been contacted we sent agents to your office and your secretary told them where you could be found. That's when we brought in Agent Mackay."

As soon as Thompson mentioned his name, Donny walked through the door wearing a dark jacket with FBI in large gold letters printed across the back, with the federal emblem sewn to the front like everybody else's. His face wore the bruised effects of his physical battle with Ian, and he walked as though his midsection felt the way his face looked. He strode gingerly toward Ian and Madison. Ian stood immediately and scowled at his brother.

"What the bloody hell is he doin' walkin' around free?" He glared at Donny. "Why is he no behind bars where he... Agent Mackay?" Ian turned to Agent Thompson. "Somebody better be tellin' me what's goin' on and fast!" he bellowed.

Donny stopped about ten feet from his brother and spoke to Thompson.

"Have ye no told them yet o me involvement?" Donny asked, never taking his eyes off Ian's rage-infused face.

"I was about to when you walked in. I'm afraid they're still under the impression that you are a bad guy and in league with Adam Gilmore."

"Ye shot yer own brother!" Ian bellowed.

"Ian?" Madison reached up and touched Ian's arm.

"Only in the shoulder." Donny shrugged. "And only because I needed ta make it look good. It nay would have happened ha Tommy just stayed down after I hit him over the head."

"Did you shoot Alex too?" Madison asked in a meek voice.

"No, Adam shot him when he came in the door. I wasna in the room then. I was outside callin for back up." Donny turned his attention to Madison. "I am sa sorry if I hurt ye. I'm also sorry I couldna stop it sooner, me back up was verra late in gettin' ta the house." He glared at Thompson. "He wasna ever supposed to get that close ta ye."

"Do ye mean ta tell me ye used her as BAIT!" Ian bellowed again, then crossed the ten feet separating the brothers and planted his fist in Donny's jaw. All the agents in the room came to their feet in an instant, but were waved away by Donny.

"STAY BACK!" he told his fellow officers. "Nice shot, but I wish ta God ye'd quit hittin' me! Aye, we used Madison as bait. I'm sorry aboot that too, lassie. But we werena havin' any luck gettin' Gilmore any other way. I couldna tell any of ye o me involvement because I knew Adam was watching ye. And since I was yer brother, he was watchin' me too. I needed him ta think I was wi him all the way."

"Mackay!" one of the men said to Donny, "both your brothers are fine."

"So what are ye? FBI? Ye told us ye were a police officer in..." Ian asked as he struggled to control his anger as Donny cut him off.

"Nay, no exactly FBI," Donny hedged. "I work wi them from time ta time and have a badge, but I'm no' FBI. 'Tis a wee hard ta explain. Let's just say, I know a lot o people in high and low places. I go where I am needed. I always work undercover." Donny moved closer to his brother and rested his hand on Ian's shoulder, "I'm sorry I canna tell ye any more than tha'. I promise ye tha I ne're meant any harm ta yer lass or our brothers."

"Does Tommy or Alex know about your involvement?" Madison asked as she stood and took Ian's hand.

"Nay, no one did. I ha worked verra hard no' ta allow anyone ta know wha I've been doin' wi me life."

"I take it this is why ye have always refused ta take a permanent spot wi Tommy and Alex," Ian said as he brought Madison's hand to his lips.

"Aye, 'tis."

"Were ye always plannin' on killin' the blackguard, then?" Ian asked.

"Nay, the plan was ta arrest him and take him back ta prison. It would ha worked too had ye no interfered and set yerself ta be a hero." Donny scowled.

Ian dropped Madison's hand and moved even closer to Donny. Madison was afraid of more fists through the air so she stepped between them.

"Children!" Donny and Ian both looked down at her in question. "Can we deal with this without the use of testosterone?" Donny backed away a few feet and Madison continued. "Personally I am more than pleased to find out Donny is still one of the good guys. Aren't you, Ian?" she asked.

"Aye," he agreed grudgingly.

"Good! Are we finished here?" she asked Thompson. "I would like to go to the hospital and see Tommy and Alex and then go home to bed. It's been a very long day. I hurt and I'm tired."

"Yes. We're done for the time being, but I'm afraid you won't be able to go back to the house for a couple of days—"

"Why the bloody hell no'!" Ian interjected, cutting Thompson off.

"Ian," Madison warned warily.

"I know this is upsetting for you, but we need to complete our investigation. We'll collect all the evidence we will need to insure the case is wrapped up tight and there are no lose ends. We'll dust for prints and photograph the crime scene. Reconstruct what happened in the house. When we're satisfied with our investigation, you may return to your home."

"Wha' can ye get from the house. The son of a bitch is dead," Ian muttered.

"It's procedure, Ian," Donny said quietly. "Come on I'll take ye ta see the guys." He took ahold of Madison's elbow and led her out the door with Ian close behind. The three of them piled in Donny's Jeep and drove off to the hospital. The trip from the station to the hospital took forty minutes, all of which were spent in silence.

Once they arrived Madison suggested that she go into the room alone first, so she could give the brothers the information about Donny. There was no doubt in anyone's mind that Tommy would be boiling angry with Donny and by now had told Alex all that happened at the house. Going in alone would give Madison the opportunity to explain the real situation before Donny had to face the oldest brother. Ian and Donny both agreed to her idea and left them alone while she went into Tommy and Alex's room.

"Hi there," she walked quietly into the room, Tommy and Alex were staring. "Are you guys okay?" she asked the men.

"Aye, lass, we're fine," Tommy said, "in a manner o speakin'."

"How are ye?" Alex asked as he tried to sit up.

"Oh! Don't do that!" She rushed to his bedside and placed her hand on his shoulder. "I'm okay. Alex, do you know who shot you?"

"Donna know who he was, I assume 'twas that Adam fella. Why?"

"Because she's wantin' ta know if Donny wasna the bastard who shot ye as he shot me!" Tommy bellowed

"Well, not exactly." Madison smiled as she pulled a chair between the two beds and sat down.

"I dinna believe Donny would shoot ye on purpose," Alex said, for what was apparently not the first time.

"Oh no, he actually meant to shoot him," Madison said as casually as if they were talking about the weather. "You see Donny was apparently working both sides of the field." She then frowned. "Now, that isn't what I meant." She scratched her forehead and continued. "You see Donny was working with Adam—" Madison frowned again at the expression on Alex's face. "No no, that isn't right either." She looked at Tommy as if to ask for help with the explanation. "This is not as easy as I thought it would be and I'm screwing up everything and only making matters worse!"

"Nay lass, it couldna get much worse. Just say what ye ha ta say and be done wi it," Tommy sighed.

"Donny is one of the good guys. He's some kind of undercover cop, but we can't ever tell anyone. Maybe I shouldn't have told you, but you can't spend the rest of your lives thinking he's a bad guy and shot you on purpose. Although, he did shoot you on purpose. But he didn't really want to shoot you!" Madison leaned back in the chair and heaved a sigh. "Listen to me. In a nutshell, Adam was never released from prison, he escaped. The letter I got was a fake and then the FBI got involved because he killed a federal court judge. When the FBI learned Adam had come here, they contacted Donny to go undercover and worm his way into Adam's confidence." When Tommy still looked skeptical Madison went on. "See, Donny's job was to make Adam believe he was so angry with his brothers…. It was never supposed to go as far as it did, but Donny's back up was late…. He had to hit you over the head, Tommy! Don't you understand?"

"He SHOT me!" he bellowed and pointed to his shoulder.

"Only because you wouldn't stay down after he hit you. Apparently when he went outside, he called for backup, but they didn't get there in time. Adam was never supposed to get as close as he did and all of this was never supposed to happen."

"Do ye mean ta tell me, our Donny, our BROTHER, used ye, our younger brother's lass, who we were supposed ta be protectin' as BAIT!" Tommy roared.

"Yep! 'Fraid so. Now you understand!" Madison smiled. Relieved that the brothers finally had the big picture. Everything was going to be alright.

"Why in hell are ye smilin', then?" Alex asked.

"Hey, I'm just glad he's not the bad guy!" Madison laughed. Then the door to the room opened and in walked Ian with Donny behind him. Ian went directly to Madison drawing her out of the chair and into his arms, before turning his attention to the two brothers in the beds.

"How are ye feelin'?" Ian asked the two of them.

"Fine," they said in unison.

Tommy turned his attention to Donny. "When I can ge oot of this bed, so help me God, I'm goin' ta thrash the liven daylights oot o ye."

"Does tha' go fer ye too, Alex?" Donny asked.

"Nay, ye didna shoot *me*." Everyone in the room turned and looked at him in astonishment and then all eyes returned to Tommy. Madison was the first to start snickering, then came Ian. After a few tense seconds all the brothers were laughing.

Chapter Twenty-Six

Madison and Ian stayed with Agatha Stuart for five days while the FBI and Tommy's deputies gathered all the evidence they needed to finalize their investigation on the Adam Gilmore case. Agatha fussed over both of her guests like an aggressive mother hen. Maddy had never had a mother to care for her and although her injuries were comparatively minor, she found comfort in Agatha's protective ministrations. Maddy worked in the office in the mornings but was bustled off to Agatha's for lunch and ordered to rest in the afternoons. She visited Tommy and Alex during their two-day stay in the hospital and also Sara and the new baby in the maternity ward.

Ian ordered new glass for the windows in the master bedroom, and the front door, and built a new stool to replace the broken one he smashed over Adam. When the FBI and Tommy's deputies had finished their work and released the house as an official crime scene, Ian called in a cleaning team from Inverness to clean up and polish the floors; removing all evidence of the gunfire and subsequent bloodshed that had taken place there.

Agatha was a generous hostess, and her home was more than comfortable, however Maddy and Ian were happy to return to their own house where Ian could take care of the repairs and they could be alone again. Madison worried that she would never feel safe again, but when she walked into the house for the first time after that horrific night, her concerns melted away like an ice cube in front of a roaring fire. She and Ian had fallen in love within those walls and she felt the warmth and love envelope her as soon as she walked through the door. She felt only joy to be home, in the house she wanted, with the man she loved. Adam was gone for good, and nothing was ever going to threaten her again.

Ian offered to have a new bed made, but Madison wouldn't allow it. That was the bed where they had made love for the first time. She wasn't going to let Adam win even that much. She did however ask him to make a few changes to the house.

"Will you add on another guest bedroom? Since this all started, I have come to realize that the house needs just a little more sleeping room. We could also stand to have a table."

She laughed. Ian walked up behind her, and wrapped his arms around her, pulling her back snugly against his chest.

"I wasna plannin' on havin' overnight guests anytime soon, luv." Ian chuckled while he nuzzled her neck and nibbled on her earlobe.

Maddy giggled while gooseflesh raised all over her body. "I want to have guests. I love you and I want to share our love with the whole world!"

Ian continued his possessive assault on her neck while turning her in his arms.

"Aye, but maybe we could share in the daytime." He murmured before capturing her lips with his own. Careful not to add damage to her already bruised face, he lifted his head and rested his chin in her hair. "It's good ta be home again," he breathed, "and alone wi ye." He chuckled. "Agatha is a dear lady, but five days o unsolicited orders and opinions is aboot all I can deal wi at a time."

"Do you know," Madison said, looking up into his face, "that is the first time in my life I've ever been 'mothered'? it was a whole new experience for me. Actually, it was kind of nice."

"Ye just wait until me mother gets ahold of ye." Ian laughed and hugged her close. "She'll mother ye like nobody could."

Madison tightened her arms around Ian's waist.

"It is good to be home together again, isn't it?" she sighed. Every time he heard Madison refer to his house as "home," Ian felt a warmth course through his entire being. "Hey!" she continued, "did you see what we did while you were away?"

"Nay. Ta be honest I havna had time ta really look at anything. When I was here, I was lookin' for damages that needed repair. What am I lookin' fer?"

Madison took him by the hand and led him out into the yard. She showed him the trees she had had planted and the flower beds she and Donny had plotted and planted. She told him of her plan to plant flower beds around the base of all the tress and plant flowers out back.

"And ye say Donny was oot here digging wi ye?"

"Well, yes. Of course, he wasn't real excited about the project, but he was a huge help, and I think he actually enjoyed himself, although I'm sure he would never admit it. Besides, we had to do something to pass the time while we waited for Adam to be caught."

"I'm no' so sure it wouldna ha been a better idea fer ye ta ha stayed in the house while ye waited," Ian mused.

"Oh, *darlin'*, don't be cross with Donny. He was a big help to me. He kept my mind occupied and that kept me from being so scared and worried. Besides, it's not like I gave him a lot of choice. It was either come out with me or let me be out here alone, and he wasn't about to do that."

"I'll no' waste me time bein' cross wi him, luv, but I will tell our mum how much Donny enjoyed helpin' ye wi yer garden chores. She'll be delighted ta hear this bit of news." He laughed.

Later that week Sara and the baby were released from the hospital. Tommy was overjoyed to have them home. Now life seemed complete. His younger brother was still one of the good guys, his other brother had a sweet lass who seemed to be as deeply attached to Ian as he was to her. Alex and Tommy's gunshot wounds were healing nicely. They were both gaining back their strength, and Tommy was bringing his own Sara home with their new baby girl Isabella Sara Mackay.

Ian drove over to Tommy's late in the afternoon to say hello to Sara and meet little Isabelle. He wanted Madison to accompany him, but Maddy felt Sara would have enough people in the house on her first night home and opted to wait for a day or two before she visited.

Not long after Ian left for Tommy's, Madison received a phone call.

"Samuel," Madison answered, beaming, "I'm so happy to hear from you."

"Madison, what is going on over there?"

"Well, the office is fully staffed and Lizzy has agreed to take over as office manager. We've had three patient referrals, and it's beginning to look like we're going to get more referrals. I think we're actually off and running. Of course it'll take a little more time to—"

"I'm not talking about the office." Samuel tried to calm his voice. "I'm talking about you and the murder of your ex-husband."

Stunned, Madison's knees went weak and she sank down onto the sofa. "Murder?" she repeated dully.

"Well, yes." Samuel was confused by her reaction. "The media have been talking and writing about nothing but the murder of Adam Gilmore for over a week. About how everything happened at your Mr. Mackay's house."

"Murder," she said again. *My God* she thought, the media is calling it murder? "Samuel, I didn't know the media was involved."

"Madison, haven't you read the papers or at least been online or any social media outlets?"

"We don't get a paper here and I have been too busy to get online."

"Maddy girl, are you alright?"

"Yes. I'm a little banged up and bruised, but nothing serious. I'm fine."

"Why didn't you tell me he was out of jail?" his voice was full of concern. "I could have done something to help you!"

"I didn't know he was out until… Samuel, there was no murder! Adam wasn't murdered. He was shot and killed by the authorities. I don't know what else to say to you…. I came back here, and I had police protection so there was no need, I thought, to have to say anything to you."

"It's okay." Samuel's voice had taken on a soft calming tone. "Take a breath and just tell me what happened."

Maddy did take a deep breath and leaned back against the sofa. When she began to speak her voice was more calm as she related the facts to the owner of her company.

"I apologize for not calling you or Margaret," she said. "I should have, I know. To be honest after it was all over, I was really too shaken to talk about it and the authorities assured us that it wouldn't become a media event. I never dreamed you would hear until I had a chance to tell you myself." She cleared her throat. "The night before I left to return to Scotland Adam called me. He said he had been released—"

"He called you?"

"Yes. He said—"

"How did he get your number?"

"He said he got it from Dean."

"Blast!" Samuel took a calming breath himself. "Go on."

"Well, he wasn't released. He escaped. When I got back here, there was a letter from my attorney informing me of his parole. I was concerned that he was free, but at the same time I was glad I was out of the country. I didn't think he would know where I was at first. Then things snowballed. We learned the letter was a fake. Adam was denied parole and escaped from prison. He killed my attorney, the office staff, and a federal judge who was in the office at the time. Apparently, it would have been up to the state to apprehend Adam, but because he shot and killed a federal judge, the FBI became involved…. Samuel, what is the media saying?"

"It's pretty bad, I'm afraid. They're turning it into a real circus. I don't think this is going to be very good for your young man either."

"Just tell me." Her voice was tired and defeated.

"I think it would be better if you read some of the articles yourself. There will have to be some damage control on our side too. So far we've made no comment other than our collective concern for your welfare."

"Damage control." She closed her eyes and sighed. "Oh, Samuel, I am so sorry about all this."

"Don't be, it's unfortunate, but it's not your fault. Besides the important thing is that you're safe."

"Thank you, Samuel. Let me review what's being said, and I'll get back to you first thing tomorrow morning." They broke the connection and Madison turned on her computer and went online.

She didn't have to look for headlines. They came up on her screen uninvited. The top story of the day and related news on the same topic.

"MURDER AT ACTOR IAN MACKAY'S HOME IN SCOTLAND"

Another headline read:

"ACTOR INVOLVED IN SCOTLAND BLOODBATH"

There were several articles. All with the same type of sensational-grab-you-by-the-throat headline. She tried to read them all. Most of the articles gave the basic facts: "Ian Mackay, up and coming Scots film star, recently coming to the attention of American audiences. Madison Danaher, American businesswoman, originally from Philadelphia, more recently MacKay's live-in companion." And "Adam Gilmore, ex-husband/escapee from New Jersey State Prison. "Some mentioned Adam's "cold-blooded murder of a Federal Court Judge along with the murders of the judge's brother, a Philadelphia attorney, and his office staff."

Some of the articles mentioned the new hospice Madison had established in Lusta. Some mentioned the press conference announcing the new Lusta office prior to her trip abroad. Some articles were accurate enough to include the fact that Adam had murdered a

Federal Court Judge before his death in Scotland. One or two of the reporters had treated the episode as a straight news story, but the majority had treated it as a sensational scandal. Movie star, ex-wife, jealous ex-husband triangle. One reporter even suggested that Adam, when learning of his wife's affair with a film actor, had been released from a local jail by a sympathetic friend on the force, to fly to Scotland in an attempt to win back his wife's affection. All articles told of "Adam and Madison being alone in the upstairs bedroom for an unspecified amount of time, before Ian's brothers, (all members of the local police force) rushed into the house and blew Adam away in a blaze of gunfire."

Each article was accompanied with photos. It had to be easy to get hold of pictures of Ian. Even photos of Adam wouldn't be difficult. Some of those went way back to his first trial. He looked so young. But she had no clue where they could get photos of her. One was a still from the press conference, but one was taken when she was in high school. *My townhouse,* she thought, *they've been in my house! Good God!*

The longer she read the more her heart sank. Samuel was right. Not only was this damaging for her, but for Ian and his family as well. She closed her computer and sat staring out the window across the room. *I brought this to them,* she thought to herself. *I brought this mess to Ian and his family. Donny is an undercover agent if that became public knowledge he could be in serious danger.*

Julie chose that moment to leap into Madison's lap.

"Oh, Julie," she sighed, hugging the purring feline close to her chest. "What have I done to him? To his whole family? Tommy was shot. Alex was shot. Sara could have lost her baby. Ian's face is battered and bruised. This kind of publicity could destroy his career. What should I do? What can I do?" Julie nuzzled Maddy's chin. Madison and Julie stayed in the chair together while Madison ran scenarios through her mind trying to come to a decision about what her next course of action should be. Finally, she rose from the chair, placed Julie on the desk, and shoved her computer into its case.

"The best thing, I think, Julie, is for us to get the hell out of here. We should leave. If I stay here, my very presence will continue to cause damage to Ian's career and his family. And I should go before anything else happens." Julie looked up at Maddy and meowed. "Oh, we'll be back. Don't worry about that. We'll go back to Philly and take care of damage control there. Eventually, things will die down, and when the gossip sheets find a new target, we'll be back. We won't let Adam ruin what we've found here forever. But for now, we have to go." She gave a halfhearted thumbs-up to her furry friend and headed toward the stairs.

Driving home from Tommy's house, Ian was almost euphoric! He was a brand-new uncle and Tommy and Sara had asked him to be Isabelle's Godfather to boot. *Being a Godfather is important stuff,* he thought to himself as his chest swelled with familial importance and pride. He wished Madison had come with him to see the baby, but he knew she was still recovering from her own injuries and shy about being seen so battered.

Ian pulled his Wagoneer up to the house and walked through the front door. As he stood in the doorway, he was surprised not to see Madison sitting at the desk or on the sofa working. He heard movement up in the master bedroom and took the steps two at a time, in a hurry to share his new family status. But when he entered the bedroom he was not prepared for what he saw. The bed was covered with suitcases as was every other available flat surface in the room. Clothing and accessories littered the chairs and empty hangers hung from the doorknobs. Madison was folding shirts and placing them in a bag.

"Wha's goin' on, luv?" he asked softly.

Madison turned and looked into Ian's face. She knew her decision was not going to be well received.

"Ian, I think it will be best if I go back to the States for a time."

Ian felt as though he had been punched dead center in the stomach. He leaned against the doorframe, and Madison could see a multitude of emotions running across his face. She could guess what he was thinking.

"Ian, please don't misunderstand my reasoning." She moved toward him and placed her hands on either side of his face, looking deep into his eyes.

"Why are ye leavin' me?" Ian choked.

"Oh, my darling, I'm not leaving *you*! Listen, come here, and sit down." She removed two bags from the bed so they could sit down together. "I'll explain. Okay, I got a call from Samuel today."

"Yer boss?"

"Yes." She took a deep breath and continued. "He called to talk about what had happened here."

"How did he...?" Ian trailed off as the realization hit him.

"That's right, the press got hold of it and it's been turned into a media circus. I went online after getting off the phone with Samuel and there are photos of you, Adam, and me. Ian, this could be very damaging if we can't put a stop to it. Think! Forgetting your career and my work. What about Donny? What would happen if the press got his picture, and splashed it all over the internet? It could mean his life!" Madison stopped and took a breath. "I think it might be better for me to go back to the States for a while. I'll do what I can to put a stop to all the publicity. Once one of us makes some kind of statement, I don't know. None of us have talked to the press. Your agent can make a statement to the effect that I only rented your house. That we hardly know each other. I don't know. Just a brief statement of the true facts."

"Ye want my agent to tell the press that we dinna know each other?"

"Yes! ... No!" She got up from the bed and walked to the windows. "I don't know." Her voice was worn and defeated. Ian came up behind her at the windows, and wrapped his arms around her.

"Lass, I willna have me agent lie ta the press or anyone else aboot our relationship. I luv ye. Ye luv me. I do'na care if the world knows it. They will have ta know aboot us sooner or later, and I'll no' lie aboot it."

"Ian, this is such a mess!" Tears dripped from Madison's cheeks and dropped onto Ian's arms. "And I brought it here to you. Maybe if I leave, the mess will go with me and leave you alone."

"Maddy luv, ye canna do this on yer own. It's like ye said, this includes all o us. We will all deal wi it." Ian turned her in his arms. He brushed the tears from her cheeks with his thumbs and then placed his hands on either side of her face gazing into her eyes. "And ye dinna bring the trouble wi ye. Ye canna take responsibility for the actions o a madman. Please, luv, do'na leave." Madison could see his eyes were getting misty. "We can handle this together. Here, I'll help ye put yer things away."

"Ian, more than anything, I want to stay here with you forever, but I need to go back and try to salvage what reputation I have left. Not only for me, but for the company too. I promise you, I won't be gone long, but I have to do this."

"When do ye leave?" he asked with his eyes cast down to the floor.

"I don't really know, I got off the phone with Samuel and came up here almost immediately."

Just then Ian's cell phone rang, and he reached in his pocket to retrieve it.

"Aye."

"Ian you rogue!" his agent's voice bounded over the airwaves. "What the hell have you been doing since you left the set in New York?"

"Victoria?" Ian winced and turned away from Madison. "Look, this is no' a good time fer me right now, can I call ye later?"

"No! You most definitely cannot! And mind your brogue. Have you seen the papers?"

"Nay, but we have been made aware of them. Why?"

"WHY!" she laughed. "The best writers in Hollywood couldn't have dreamed up anything as awesome as this! And think of all the free publicity, man!"

"Victoria, I canna talk ta—"

"I've taken advantage of the opportunity, and set up a few interviews for you. Say, do you think you could get your Madison Danaher to come to them with you?"

"YE DID WHAT?!" he bellowed. He began pacing around the room while Julie scurried to get out of his way. "Ye ha' no bloody right ta do tha!"

"Ian, your accent," Victoria interjected.

"Never mind me bloody speech, woomon! Ha' ye no heart? Me brother was nearly killed! Madison was nearly beaten ta death! Most of me family was in mortal danger. And a bloody bastard died right here in me livin' room!"

"Ian, don't be over dramatic." She sighed. "Everyone is fine and healthy, aren't they? And your 'bloody bastard' was on the FBI's top ten most wanted list, wasn't he? So what's wrong with using this to your advantage."

"I dinna know wha ye ha planned, but cancel it now or I'll find meself a new agent!" He hung up and threw his phone out the bedroom door where it sailed over the railing and landed with a clatter as it hit the hardwood floor below. Ian walked through the doorway and stood with both hands resting on the railing. Madison joined him there and they stood staring down at the broken mess that littered the living room floor. Before starting to descend the stairs. "You know," she said as she placed her hand on his back, "there is not a land line phone in this house."

Ian looked down at her and chuckled. "She wants me ta use this as a publicity stunt," he growled.

"Ian, she can't," she breathed.

"I know, and I told her I willna do it. Madison ye canna leave now, ye just canna."

"I could try to handle as much as I can from here, but Ian, I would have to go back at some point to deal with this firsthand. I think it's better to do it now before it gets worse."

"I do'na want ye ta go, luv." He gathered her in his arms and held her tightly. "We can deal wi things from here together."

"I don't want to leave you either, but I have to do this. And I promise, I won't be gone long." She looked up from his chest and into his eyes. "I love you. You know that. I want to be here with you. But this is important too and it needs my attention now. So I have to finish packing and find out how soon I can get a ticket back to Philly."

"So ye're goin', then?" he said as he backed away and looked down at her. "And it doesna matter wha I want or wha I think is best fer the two o us."

"Ian, I told you I *have* to go. I don't want to. Please try to understand. I can't think of just you and me. I have to consider Samuel and the company I work for. Samuel has been good to me. He trusted me and had faith in me. I can't just leave damage control solely on his shoulders. The reputation of the company he built can be damaged by this affair and I'm inadvertently responsible. You have to try to understand that."

"I dinna want ta try and understand. Yer place is here, wi me, no' in Philadelphia wi yer boss."

Madison was stunned one more time in the same day. "Ian, what is the matter with you? You're being unreasonable."

"Ye're the one bein *unreasonable*. Do ye no' realize if ye go runnin' off, the press will use it? 'LIVE-IN COMPANION FLEES SCOTLAND film at eleven.'" His frustration led to shouting.

"Ian, first don't yell at me. Second I—" It hit her, Ian had quoted one of the articles. *He knew!*

Chapter Twenty-Seven

"You did see the papers! You knew what was happening and you lied to me!"

"Nay, lass. I dinna see anything. Alex canna do anything but sit in bed and play wi his tablet. He saw the items online and told Tommy. Tommy told me about the articles a couple of days ago. I dinna lie ta ye! But I dinna want ye upset, and I knew ye would be when ye got wind o the stories. I was afraid ye'd want to cut and run." He walked toward her, but she backed away. "Do ye understand why ye should stay here wi me and we can see this thing through tagether?"

"You lied by omission! And of course I would have been upset, but I at least would have known that the story was out there. I could have called Samuel and talked to him sooner. I wouldn't have sat here totally oblivious, or have the owner of the company I work for call to ask what the hell was going on!" She turned and started up the stairs. She stopped halfway up and turned to face him. "And I don't give a rat's ass what the press thinks about my going back to the States. I do, however, care about you. But you have to understand that my *job* is at stake here, as is the reputation of the company I work for and I can't just stand idly by and let it fall apart."

"Fine, then," Ian said, throwing up his hands and heading for the door, "go back." He grabbed his coat and stormed out, slamming the door in his wake.

"Ian!" Madison yelled and ran down the stairs and out the door after him, but she was too late; he was gone. Her shoulders slumped as she walked back in the house and slowly closed the door. She dropped onto the sofa and replayed in her mind the events of the afternoon ending with her argument with Ian, and began to cry. Julie, sensing that the storm was over or at least had reached a lull, came out from under the sofa, and climbed onto Madison's lap.

"What the hell happened here?" Madison sobbed to the cat. "How could everything come to this? Why can't he understand?"

"*Rrrrreow!*" Julie nuzzled Maddy's arm

"I'm doing the right thing for all of us, aren't I?"

"*Rrrrrreow.*"

"Well, why can't he see that? Why is he being so unreasonable? He's never behaved like this before. And he should have told me what was on the news as soon as he knew about it. He was wrong!"

"*Rrrrrreow!*"

"He was trying to protect me, but he was still wrong. But it was kind of sweet too." By now her tears has ebbed and she leaned her head back on the sofa. "Well, we'll go back and clear all of this mess up, if we can, and then we'll come back home. We may be unemployed by the time we get here, but we'll be back." She gave Julie a hug and reached for her phone.

For the next half hour, Madison made plane reservations for her flight to Philadelphia, arranged for Shawn O'Conner to drive her and Julie to the airport, and made a brief call to Margaret to arrange transportation when she reached Philly.

"I'll want a car to take me home first so I can drop off my bags and Julie, but I'd also like for you to arrange for one to take me home at the end of the day. I'm not totally up to par yet and I'm already tired, so I'm not sure I'll feel like driving once I'm done at the office."

"No sweat, boss lady. I can have a car put at your disposal for the full day. I'll handle it. And let me welcome you back ahead of time? We've missed you around here."

"Thanks, Margaret."

"Were you badly injured? Maybe you should rest when you get home and come to the office in a day or two."

"No, my injuries were minor. I don't look very pretty, but I'm okay just terribly tired. I'm fine. And I think I need to be in the office as soon as possible. Is Samuel in? Can you put me through to him?"

After Madison, spoke briefly to Samuel, she returned to the bedroom to finish her packing. She tried to organized her thoughts concerning what needed to be done from a business standpoint to minimize the negative publicity and she interrupted her packing periodically to jot down ideas. But she wasn't making much headway with either her packing or her thoughts concerning the publicity problem. Her mind was being crowded by thoughts of Ian.

She supposed all couples have little misunderstandings, maybe they were just due for one. But Ian had left so abruptly.

"Slamming doors isn't the way to solve anything, Ian," she said aloud. *When he gets home, we'll sit down and talk through this if it takes all night,* she thought.

She eventually finished her packing and carried her bags downstairs, setting them by the door. Then she showered, pulled on jeans and one of Ian's button-down shirts, made a fresh pot of tea, and sat of the sofa to await Ian's return, but he didn't came home.

As dawn broke behind the mountains, there was a knock at the door, waking Madison from a sound sleep. She rose from the sofa and saw Shawn Conner standing at the door and his Rolls Royce parked in the drive. She opened the door and motioned toward her bags.

"Ye havena much time, lass, ta be makin' yer flight," he said as he took in her odd attire and then grabbed the first of her bags.

"Yes, I'll be just a moment." She turned and raced upstairs to the master bedroom. *Maybe he came in late and didn't want to wake me,* she thought. But she knew even as she thought it, that Ian would have woken her if he had come home. The bedroom was just as she had left it the evening before. The bed was neatly made. Nobody else had been in the room.

"I guess that says it all." She sighed aloud and walked out of the bedroom.

Madison placed Julie her in her carrier and draped her purse strap over her shoulder. She hoped the large pair of sunglasses would hide the worst of her bruised face including her puffy eyes, which were now moist with fresh tears.

"I'm ready," she told Shawn when he returned for her last bag and Julie's carrier. She followed Shawn out the door, and when she turned to lock it, she held the keys in her hand, trying to decide if she should just leave them under the mat. Looking down at the mat by the door, she fisted her hand tightly around the key ring and jammed it into her pocket.

Shawn held the door for her, and once she was settled, he placed Julie's carrier on the seat beside her and shut the door. As they drove away from the house, Madison didn't look back out of fear that she would toss responsibility out the window and turn around. *I'll be back,* she told herself.

During the drive to Inverness International she called to make Lizzy aware of her trip to Philadelphia.

"You'll be in charge, of course, while I'm gone. You have my cell number and the number at the office in Philly. If for some reason you can't get hold of me, talk to Margaret. She usually always knows where I am and can generally handle any problem that might come up as well as I can, but things seem to be running smoothly here. I don't anticipate any problem you can't handle."

"I appreciate yer confidence in me, Madison. How long do ye think ye might be gone this time?"

Madison blinked tears onto her cheeks. "I don't know yet. It might be…. It depends on how things shape up. Lizzy, I have to go." Madison hung up before Lizzy could say any more. Madison leaned her head against the back of the seat, closed her eyes and let silent tears course down her face.

"Ian, what the bloody hell is wrong with ye?" Tommy bellowed.

Ian had been ranting and raving ever since he stormed out of the house the evening before. Now it was morning and he was pacing and his head was throbbing.

"Wha' do ye mean wha's wrong with me? Should ye no' be askin' *her* tha' question?"

"Ian, sit down" came Sara's voice from the hallway. When Ian still didn't sit she became more insistent. "Sit down, damn you!" Both men turned and looked at this tiny gentle woman who never raised her voice, and because of this, Ian sat as he was told. "Good, now, if either of you shout one more time and wake my daughter, so help me I'll wipe the floor with both of you." Sara came into the room and stood with her hands on her hips scowling at her husband and her brother-in-law. "Ian, I believe you're being a jackass?"

"I'm being... nay, I'm—"

"Be so kind as to allow me to finish." She spoke softly. "You know, I never thought of you as the Neanderthal type, but you're doing an excellent imitation in this instance." She sat daintily in the wing-backed chair across from him and sighed.

"Wha'?" Ian was stunned. Sara had never talked to him that way and he couldn't believe it.

"Well, what would you call your behavior? Since you blew in here last evening, are you interested in the one term that has been repeating over and over in my mind?" When nobody else spoke she continued.

"'Throwback.' However, since the sun rose, I believe you've actually digressed to Neanderthal." Ian looked flabbergasted and crushed at the same time. She lowered her head and brushed imaginary lint from her robe to hide her smile. The room remained silent and when she was confident she could paste her schoolmarm expression back on her face, she went on.

"Madison is recovering from physical injuries, brought on by an emotional and physical trauma of the worst kind imaginable. Now she's been made aware that her life is being broadcast over the internet, the news, and social media as well as the supermarket tabloids. Not to mention, of course, your career, and embarrassment to your family. On top of all that, her job and career might be in serious jeopardy. A job we all, and you especially, know she loves and is extremely passionate about. It must have taken an enormous personal courage to travel to a different country, *ALONE,* to accomplish what she has with the hospice in Lusta."

Ian opened his mouth to speak, but closed it again when Sara raised her hand and closed her eyes. When silence continued, so did she. "Yes, she could have sent someone to do the job, and it might have been less of a hassle for her to do so, but the fact remains, she didn't send someone else. She came herself to make sure the first hospice in the Highlands was set up professionally and with the best possible regard to the local physicians and residents. She brought not only hospice but good will to Lusta by using local labor and goods to set up the office. She's done an exemplary job of it. The office is working and the local people adore and respect her. I imagine it's also quite a feather in her cap with the gentleman who owns the company. He trusted her and had faith in her ability and she didn't disappoint him.... Until now. in *her* eyes, of course.

"And what happens when she's afraid it's all going to come crashing down around her head? Does the man she has fallen in love with and who professes to love her, support her? Does he respect and understand her in her desperate time of need when she comes to him and says, 'my darling, I love you, but I have to be gone for a few weeks to fix this, and I'll be back,'? Does he pull her into his arms and say, "I love you too and I understand totally. I'll miss you like the very devil, but I'll be waiting for your return'? He does not. He first informs her she's *incapable* of handling the situation on her own and in addition, her place is with him? Being the little woman leaning on her man."

"I didna—" But before Ian could say more, Sara raised her hand again.

"And when this declaration of his lack of faith in her inability to solve said crises without him to hold her hand and bottle feed what needs to be done, don't achieve the results he's looking for. Does he put his macho card on the back burner and ask her what she wants to do? No, he resorts to shouting and slamming doors upon his exit from the premises. Yes...." She squared her shoulders, raised her chin, and looked down her nose at Ian. "Yes, I would say 'Neanderthal' fairly covers your behavior. Or jackass, take your pick."

Ian slumped back into the sofa, defeated, and confused. He wasn't ready to give up his frustration and anger, but he was certainly more contrite than he was twelve hours ago when he arrived. Sara couldn't help feeling sorry for him, but she wasn't ready to give up yet. She rose from her chair and went to sit beside him on the sofa.

"And in the end, dear laddie, you might have done the one thing you were trying to avoid, and driven her away."

"Ye've done a fair job o tellin me what a louse I am, Sara. Do ye have an idea o wha' I might be doin' ta repair the damage?" Ian's voice was quiet and somewhat deflated. He'd never thought of himself as a "throwback" either, but according to his sister-in-law, he had become one. He had no idea he'd succeeded in hurting Madison when all he wanted was to protect her.

"Go to her, Ian. Tell her you're sorry. Tell her your love for her and your desire to make things easier, made you act like a bloody fool. And ask her what you can do to help her." While Sara continued to advise Ian, the phone rang, and Tommy got up to answer it.

"Hello? Lizzy, me darlin, how are ye ... She what? ... When? ... She was? ... Thank ye, Lizzy ... Aye, we'll tell him ... Nay, dinna worry." Tommy hung up the phone and turned toward Sara and Ian. "I dinna know wha' ye said that did it, laddie, but she's gone."

"Gone." Ian shot up from the sofa and ran out the door.

Sara and Tommy stood arm in arm at the door watching Ian's SUV screech out of the drive.

"I thought 'desperate need' was a wee bit over the top, lass." Tommy smiled as he watched Ian's brake lights flash around the turn. "But I ken he dinna notice. And by the way, I believe it's 'STAND by her man' no' 'lean on' him."

"To coin my future American sister-in-law, *me darlin'*, 'whatever.'"

Ian raced home hoping Lizzy had been wrong. Maybe she just misunderstood. Maybe Madison said she was planning to leave, but hadn't gone yet. *She has to know we can work this out,* he thought. *She has to be waiting for me to come home to apologize.* However, when he got to the house there was no sign of her. He took the stairs two at a time, but the closet was empty. Even Julie was gone. He searched the house, but there was no note. The only thing left to show that she had ever been there was a teacup by the sofa and her lingering scent. Ian went back to the bedroom and fell across the bed dragging Madison's pillow to his face and breathed in. He could smell her shampoo. He had to get her back, but how. *She's angry and needs time,* he thought. He felt his own anger start to flame again, but just as quickly, it died, and a desperate feeling of loss took its place. *I'll get her back,* he thought. *I just have ta reason out how ta go aboot it.* As Ian lay there thinking, he drifted off to sleep.

Chapter Twenty-Eight

Madison walked through the boarding ramp and into the terminal of Philadelphia International and scanned the gate area, searching for her driver. There was a rather large crowd of people milling about. Some waiting to board flights, some saying goodbye and some, like her, looking for their ride. It didn't take long to spot the sign with her name inscribed in bold black letters.

"Hello, I'm Madison Danaher." She held out her hand to the uniformed driver when she reached his side.

"Yes, ma'am. It's nice to meet you. My name is David and I'll be your driver for the next few days. This way, please." He gestured toward the baggage claim signs. "If you would like to wait for a few minutes in the privacy of the car, I'll collect your luggage."

"Thank you very much."

"Shall I take this one as well?" he asked, referring to Julie's carrier.

"Oh no. I think she would be much happier with me." David nodded his agreement and began to lead Madison toward baggage claim. "Excuse me, David. Did you say you would be driving me for the next few days?

"Yes, ma'am," he said as they maneuvered their way through human traffic in the terminal causeway.

"I think there has been a misunderstanding. I live here and have my own car. I won't be needing you after today," she said as she swung Julie's carrier out of the way of an oncoming briefcase.

"No, ma'am. No mistake. I'm to drive you for the next several days due to the possibility of harassment from the press?" Madison's only response was a grim expression that caused a crease between her eyes.

They reached the shiny black stretch limo waiting at the curb outside the baggage claim area. David helped Madison into the back and placed Julie's carrier on the seat next to her, then he strode purposefully back into the terminal to retrieve her luggage.

Maddy rested her head on the back of the seat. The car was roomy and well appointed. There was ice in the bucket and the beverage tray was stocked with soda and beer along with selections of stronger drink if she so desired. David seemed nice and definitely knew his job well, but she missed old Shawn and his Rolls.

While she waited for David and the luggage to return, she went over in her mind, what she and Samuel should include in her statement to the press. She should be truthful without allowing herself to get involved in some kind of discussion about her relationship with Ian. She closed her eyes and the crease between them reappeared.

"I don't even *know* what our relationship is now," she muttered aloud. "What a mess!"

The ride from the airport took less than an hour, so when the limo turned onto Madison's street, she hadn't truly had enough time to prepare herself for what met her eyes. There were news trucks from every major television network jamming up the street leading to her condo. Madison sat up straight in the seat and stared out the blackened window.

"Oh my God," she said. "How do I get into my house?" Her front lawn was a mass of humanity, all armed with cameras and microphones.

"Do you have a back door, Miss Danaher?" David asked when he had lowered the partition between the front seat and the passenger section of the car.

"Not unless you have a rope ladder in the trunk." She grimaced.

When the car came to a stop in the driveway, the reporters and photographers surrounded the car, jamming their cameras against the glass in an effort to get photographs of the passenger or even better, *passengers.* Questions were shouted randomly at the unmoving limo. Madison was totally unprepared for what she would face when it came to the press.

"I had no idea it would be anything like this?" she said.

"If you'll give me your keys, Miss, I can get you into the house faster, but I'm afraid we'll have to run for it." Madison dug in her purse for her keys and watched as he made his way around to her side of the car through the maze of flashing bulbs and people with cameras. He opened the car door and reached for Julie's carrier. As Madison exited the car she felt David wrap his arm around her waist and spoke into her ear. "Stay close and keep up with me," he said, and he propelled her up the short walk and into the house.

When the door was firmly closed behind them, Madison let the air whoosh from her lungs. She hadn't realized she had been holding her breath since leaving the safety of the car.

"Thank you. You must have been through this kind of thing before? You seem like a pro." She smiled.

David handed her Julie and smiled back as Madison placed the carrier on the floor and released her kitty. "I can't say for whom, but yes, I have dealt with these matters a time or two in the past." He stood in front of the door with his hands clasped behind his back.

Madison took a moment to really look at him. He was tall, but not as tall as Ian. *Will I compare every man I meet from now on to Ian?,* she thought. *Yeah, I guess so,* she smiled. David had a very large frame and looked bulky as though he spent every spare minute working out in a gym somewhere. He wore a mustache, perhaps to soften his chiseled features. His black hair was longer than most drivers, was pulled into a ponytail at the base of his neck. Actually, he looks more like a professional bodyguard than a limo driver, she thought, or a hit man with brown, teddy bear eyes.

She was staring at him, and David began to feel a little nervous under the scrutiny.

"If you would like to freshen up a bit, Miss, I'll drive you to your office, unless you would rather stay in for the rest of the day."

Madison snapped out of her reverie and glanced down at her attire. She was still wearing her jeans and Ian's button-down shirt.

"Oh, yeah, I guess I'd better...." She didn't really want to change. She felt closer to Ian somehow with his shirt next to her skin. She clutched the shirt front and then smoothed her hand down the buttons. "And yes, I definitely want to go to the office. I won't be a minute. Excuse me." She took her oversized purse upstairs and walked into her bedroom.

When she entered the master suite, she remembered the last time she had been in this room, and tears welled in her eyes. Madison missed Ian and the home she had shared with him. She felt as though her heart was breaking while she was being torn between her responsibility to Samuel and the company and her loyalty and love for Ian. She dropped her purse on the bed and headed for the bathroom to turn on the shower, then chose a light weight black silk business suit to wear to the office. Julie was sticking close to Maddy's side during the preparations for showering and Madison tripped over her while she was moving back and forth between the closet and the bathroom.

"Julie, please stay out from under my feet." She begged as she picked up her feline friend and placed her on the counter beside the bathroom sink. Madison stripped off her clothes and stepped under the hot stream letting the water massage her body. Her body was still sore and bruised from Adam's assault. Her eyes were puffy from the tears she'd shed in the past several hours, and she was so very tired. Madison couldn't remember ever feeling this tired before in her life. She could never seem to get enough sleep. *Stress,* she thought. *When this is all over, I'll take a real vacation.*

When she finished showering, she wrapped herself in a towel and wiped steam from the bathroom mirror. Her eyes were red as well as puffy and she soaked a cloth with cold water and held it to her eyes.

"I look like I've been on an all-night binge!" she told Julie who had curled up on the counter. She dried her face and patted the skin around her eyes with witch hazel. Examining her face in the mirror she heaved a sigh and returned to the closet. "Well, that's the best I can do for now. It'll just have to do." She finished drying herself off and dressed. She toweled her hair, ran her brush through it and gave it a fluff with her hands. When she was dressed, she slipped her feet into black leather pumps and hurried downstairs.

David was still standing point, at the door. Maddy smiled at him, "I'll just put down Julie's bowls and then I'm ready," she said.

"Yes, ma'am."

Julie followed Madison to the kitchen and leaped to the counter while Maddy set out food for the cat. She glanced back at David. *If he had pointed ears and a long nose, he would look like a German Shepherd,* she mused while filling a second bowl with water. She gave her friend a pat and returned to the living room. Swinging her bag onto her shoulder, she took a deep breath.

"Well, are ye ready?" she asked, then was struck by her own words. "'Ye'?'" she mumbled. David turned to the door to hide his smile.

"Yes, ma'am. Let us away." Again he wrapped his arm securely around her shoulder and led her through the mob stationed outside. Madison's heart raced while the cameras clicked and microphones were thrust near her face. Questions were shouted and answers demanded. She was being touched and shoved. Someone grabbed at her jacket and she heard her pocket rip. David got her to the safety of the car and slammed the door shut. He shoved his way through the crowd to the driver's door, slid behind the wheel and locked the doors. "While you were upstairs, Miss Danaher, I took the liberty of phoning ahead to your office. Building security is going to block off the garage entrance." He threw the car into motion and drove right through the mob of reporters.

"Be careful not to hit anyone," Madison called from the back seat.

"Don't worry, ma'am, if they don't want to be hit, they'll move."

Madison laughed at the comment. "You know you don't have to call me 'Ma'am.' Madison will be just fine. By the way where did Margaret find you?"

"Who's Margaret?"

"My assistant. She's the one who hired you."

"Sorry, ma'am. I don't know the lady. I'm with Feddsey."

"Feddsey? Who the hell is Feddsey." She sat forward in the seat, her eyes on the back of David's head.

"Feddsey Associates. We're a national group. We drive and protect celebrities, governmental officials. Mostly government people when they travel. My job is to keep you safe and protected until the press gets tired of you and goes on to harass the next media victim. I'll be with you night and day, ma'am, until this nightmare of yours is over."

"I've never heard of your company. I wonder how Margaret knew of it." She slid back against the seat back and looked out the window. "Feddsey," she repeated. "Feddsey?" Then she chuckled. "Drivers with an attitude." And she finally found a reason for a genuine smile. "I like that."

"Yes, ma'am. You can relax, ma'am. You're safe with me, ma'am. You're family now, and we protect our own." David glanced at her in the rearview mirror and hid his smile. "There's a Wi-Fi and a monitor if you want to stream a movie in the back there, ma'am, if you're interested. It will take about forty-five minutes to get into the city."

Madison turned on the monitor, pulled up the movies and looked through the stock. She paused when she recognized one of Ian's films. *One way or another*, she smiled to herself and selected. Leaning back into the seat, closing her eyes and waited to hear the sound of Ian's voice.

'*David*' heard the music as the credits rolled across the screen and raised the partition window giving his passenger her privacy. He reached for his headset so his call would not be overheard by Madison and punched in speed-dial on his cell phone.

His grin widened from ear to ear when the call was answered.

"I hear ye've made a mess of things in yer life, laddie. I was just wonderin' how much longer ye were goin' to depend on yer brothers ta pick up the pieces!" He chuckled.

"Donny! Where are ye? Are ye still in Philadelphia? Madison is—"

"At the moment, I know more aboot the lady than ye do, little brother. I've got yer lass in the back of me big black limo. I'm her driver-slash-bodyguard." He could hear the breath whoosh from Ian's lungs over the six thousand miles that separated them.

"How did ye know?" was all he said.

"Tommy rang me last night after ye left his house. Then I got an earful from our Sara. She says ye behaved like the ass I always knew ye were when ye were trailin' after the rest of us as a kid."

"Is she alright?"

"Aye. She's worn out and could use a good rest, but she's a fine bonny lass. She'll come through."

"I'm a wee bit surprised she let ye near her. She's that angry with yer's truly."

"She doesna know who I am. After speakin' wi Sara, I dinna know if ye had blundered the whole family into yer fight wi her. So I'm traveling incognito. She thinks I work for a company who protects dignitaries in times of stress." He chuckled.

"I'll be there as soon as I can get a flight—"

"Stay where ye are, lad, take care of yer end, and allow her to take care o hers. I'll ring ye after a while." Donny tapped End on his phone with a satisfied smile, continuing the drive from Cherry Hill to Madison's office. He was very familiar with the Philadelphia area, and was glad he was already there when Tommy phoned him with the events of the past thirty-six hours. Even though carting Ian's lass around wasn't what he thought of as an intriguing assignment, it gave him the opportunity to get to know her better. *Thank God she doesna know who I am,* he thought to himself. Although she couldn't be that upset with Ian, because from what he had heard of the video music, she was watching one of his brother's films. The drive to Madison's office was uneventful. It was late morning and traffic was minimal.

When the car stopped and Donny turned off the motor, Madison tore her gaze away from Ian and his movie to look out the window. They were inside the garage of her office building and Donny came around and opened the car door for her.

"Don't worry about a thing, ma'am. There are no reporters or cameras here in the garage. We have a clear path to the elevators. And I'll be with you round the clock in case any of them get past security," he said as he closed the door.

"Thank you, David. Really, though, you don't have to call me—Wait a minute. You mean to tell me that you're going to follow me everywhere I go?" She looked horrified and embarrassed.

"Well, not *everywhere*, ma'am, but most places." He took her elbow and led her to the elevator. "Come on. Put on a brave face for your boss." They stepped in and waited 'til the doors opened again on Madison's floor.

Margaret was stationed at the elevator when the doors opened.

"Madison!" she exclaimed and threw her arms around her friend and gave her a huge hug. "I am so glad to see you. Security called from downstairs and said you had entered the garage, so I waited by the doors. I wanted to be the first one to welcome you back"

The three of them walked swiftly into Madison's office and shut the door behind them. Madison took off her big sunglasses and Margaret sucked in her breath. Donny's hands clenched behind his back. He wished he could get his hands on Adam Gilmore one more time for what he'd done to Ian's lass.

Madison saw the expression on Margaret's face. "Oh, Margaret, don't worry about me. I'm fine. The bruising looks much worse than it really is." When her assistant wasn't quite convinced, Madison continued, "Believe me, I've looked much worse." She took a deep breath "Okay," Madison said, taking her seat behind the desk, "what has been going on here and what can we do to put a stop to it."

Chapter Twenty-Nine

"**Y**ou can start by apologizing to me." Madison shifted her gaze to the door where Dean Michaels stood with his hand still holding the doorknob. He was wearing jeans, a T-shirt and an angry expression. Donny had never met Dean, but recognized him from Ian's description and immediately moved closer to Madison.

"Dean, and what are your talking about?" *And why are you dressed like that*, Madison thought. She remained seated and leaned back in her chair giving him the message that he wasn't worth her time.

Dean came farther into the room and glared at Donny and Margaret. He jerked his head toward the door. "You two are excused!"

Donny raised his eyebrow and Margaret looked at Madison.

"No," Madison said. "This is *my* office, Dean. You don't dismiss anyone from my office."

"Fine!" He came closer to the desk. "First, you let Samuel into our private life, and then you shack up with some foreign gutter-rat in that Godforsaken country—" He didn't have time to finish the rest of his sentence.

"Now you wait just a Goddamn minute!" Madison warned and stood from her chair. She walked around to stand in front of her desk. Her eyes fired sparks at the handsome man standing across from her. "First, how *dare* you! We *never* had a relationship. Ever! The idea of a relationship with you makes my skin crawl. Secondly, don't ever refer to Scotland that way again. It's a beautiful country and one that I've chosen as my own and come to cherish. And last, and most importantly, that 'gutter-rat' is the man I love. Not you! He doesn't operate in some dream world that exists only in his own mind. He's a man. A *real* man.

"As to my bringing Samuel into our so-called personal life, we never had a personal life. I would have to be just as sick and crazy as you obviously are to even *consider* entering into a relationship with you. Now, go directly into your office and immediately call for an appointment with the closest shrink you can locate. You crazy, sick, twisted son of a bitch! And get the hell out of my office before I have you arrested!" She turned and retraced the steps to her desk chair.

"Arrested! For what?" Dean started to advance toward her, but Donny stepped into his path.

"For endangering my life, and the lives of others." Without giving him a chance to speak Madison went on. "You told Adam Gilmore where to find me and gave him my phone number."

"I most certainly did not. I spoke to a Jason Danaher."

"You're a fool, Dean. That was Adam you spoke with, which is bad enough. But aside from the mess you created, you really had no idea who he was. You had no right to give out any information about me to anyone. What I should do is have you fired."

"You did!" he shouted.

Madison was shocked, and took a moment to recover. "I did not!" And she took Sara's best English School Teacher stance.

"Yes, you did, you called Samuel and told him to fire me, and he did."

"No, she did not," Samuel said softly from the doorway. Dean turned and watched as the elderly gentleman closed the door quietly and walked to stand beside Madison. "I fired you because you gave out personal information of an employee to a total stranger causing what might become irreparable damage to her and to the company. And because you have proven yourself to no longer be an asset to this company," he said as he turned back to Dean. "And by the way, you're trespassing. Kindly leave of your own accord. It would be embarrassing not only for you but for the company, should I have to resort to having you bodily removed by security."

Dean stood rooted to the floor and Donny stepped closer to him.

"Mr. Goldblum and Miss Danaher have requested that you remove yourself. I'll be more than happy to assist you with your departure if you prefer."

Madison choked back a giggle after hearing his polite offer to help Dean leave her office. It was remarkable how much better she felt having told Dean exactly how she felt. She was embarrassed that Samuel heard, but she still felt some of the weight lift.

After Dean closed the door behind him, Samuel turned to Madison and surveyed her face and the bruising. He then asked if Margaret wouldn't mind leaving them alone for a while.

"Of course, sir. If you need anything just give me a buzz," Margaret said as she closed the door behind her. Samuel motioned Madison toward the wing-backed chairs and they both sat down. Donny stood at the closed door with his hands behind his back.

Madison spoke first. "Samuel, I want to say again how sorry I am about all this."

"Don't worry about it. This wasn't something you planned." He spoke so softy and with such compassion Madison felt like Poppy had come back to life and was sitting in the chair next to hers. "I'm sorry Dean was still here. I assumed he would be gone before you came in today. Now all we have to do is hold a press conference and give them the straight facts and go from there. Do you have any idea how your Mr. Mackay is going to handle the situation?"

Madison lowered her eyes to the floor and spoke through held back tears. "I don't know what he is planning to say. I know his manager wanted him to use this as free publicity exposure, but he refused." She could feel her control slipping again. "How about some coffee or tea." She stood and walked to her wet bar. She filled the coffeepot with water and began opening the cabinet doors in search of coffee.

"Madison, why don't you come back here and sit down." Samuel stood and waited for her to return. Donny standing guard at the door noticed how good Madison's boss was with her, and began to understand more why she needed to come back here and fix the problem firsthand. He was also becoming increasingly angry with Ian's behavior regarding Madison's need to return to Philadelphia. "Tell me," Samuel began after Madison took her seat again. "what happened with you and your young man."

"Oh nothing. Don't worry about that, Samuel. We have enough to deal with right here and now." Madison straightened her back and squared her shoulders "So when do we have the press conference and what are we going to say to them?" It was obvious to Samuel and Donny both that she didn't want to talk about Ian so Samuel dropped that part of the conversation.

Donny became quickly aware that Madison was completely safe here in her office. He figured while Madison and Samuel had their meeting this would be the perfect time for the errands he needed to do.

"Excuse me, Miss Danaher ma'am, if it's okay with you, I have a small errand to take care of. I'll be back within an hour."

"Certainly, David." Donny reached for the doorknob but stopped when Maddy spoke again. "And, David? Thank you." He smiled at her and she caught a glimpse of something familiar, but dismissed it.

"Yes, ma'am." And he was gone.

"'Miss Danaher ma'am?" Samuel asked. And they both laughed.

Madison and Samuel spent the next three hours going over what the statement would be to the press and the date and time for the meeting. Madison looked down at her watch, it was only three o'clock, but she was exhausted and decided to go home for the rest of the day. She opened the door to her office and nearly walked smack into Donny standing guard on the other side of the door.

"Do you want some company tonight?" Margaret asked as she gathered up Madison's things.

"No, you're very sweet, but I think I would like to be alone tonight. Thanks anyway." Madison turned toward her door and looked more closely at Donny and couldn't figure out who he reminded her of. "Besides, I won't be alone, will I?" she eyed Donny. "David here has been instructed not to leave my side 'til this whole thing blows over." She narrowed her eyes and concentrated, *something about him. Something in the eyes,* she thought, *or the mouth.*

"Really, by whom?" Margaret asked as they walked to the elevator.

"That's part of the service you get when you hire Feddsey, ma'am." Donny guided Madison into the elevator car and the doors closed. Margaret stood looking at the closed elevator doors.

"Feddsey? Who's Feddsey?"

They rode the elevator in silence. Madison leaned against the wall and began to feel light-headed. As the car descended, Madison began to sink to the floor. Donny caught her before she hit the floor.

"Maddy, are ye alright, lass?"

"Yeah, I'm fine, I don't know what happened I just got—" Madison now realized his accent was different. "You're Scottish!" She stood immediately and backed away from him. Donny straightened and said nothing. "Who the hell are you!" she shouted. The doors opened and Donny moved out into the garage, but Madison did not follow.

"Ma'am, we're on the correct floor."

"Stop it! If you're going to lie at least use your own accent." She crossed her arms and leaned against the wall of the elevator. "I'm not moving from this spot until you tell me who the hell you are." Donny didn't respond. "Look, Bub, I'm in no mood to fart around. Now spill it!"

Donny sighed and decided maybe the next several days would be easier for both of them if she knew who he was. After all, she had a right to know that she wasn't being looked after by a total stranger. "Alright, I'll tell ye, after I get ye ta yer house safely." He offered her his hand and she looked at it for several seconds before deciding if he wanted to hurt her, he had already had plenty of opportunity. She didn't take hold of his hand, but exited the elevator.

Madison was surprised when he opened the rear door to a silver Lincoln Town Car.

"The stretch wouldna fit into yer garage, ma'am, and I thought it will be easier to drive straight in as opposed to running the gauntlet."

"'Ma'am,'" she repeated, but slid into the back seat.

On the way back to her townhouse Madison tried to think of all the people she had met in Scotland. *Not one of them looked like this David guy.* This had to be someone she had met *or was he a friend of someone she knew? Maybe he was related to Old Shawn Conner and driving was a family tradition, but why would he lie about where he was from?* she wondered. *Course he didn't really lie,* she thought, *I never asked him where he was from.* Donny raised the partition window and Madison called Lizzy at home and asked her how everything was going.

"Everything is goin' fine. The referrals we go' while ye were here have been brought on the service. Patrick ha given us three more and his doctor friends are plannin' on given us some. Madison, Agatha was askin' fer ye today," Lizzy said quietly.

"Tell her I'm thinking of her and miss her." Madison took a deep breath. "Has anyone else been asking for me," another breath, "doctors, nursing homes?"

"No, Madison, Ian hasna been here or called. I'm sorry." Lizzy wanted to cry for how defeated her boss sounded.

Madison's heart broke all over again. "No that's okay. Listen I have to go and you need to go to bed. I'll call you tomorrow during the day so I can talk to Agatha." Madison ended the call and silent tears dripped from her lashes. "Damn you," she said aloud. "Damn you to hell and back, Adam Gilmore! And damn you, Madison Danaher, for being so emotional. What's wrong with me?"

When the car slowed to turn into her drive, she looked out the window. Thankfully, the reporters had diminished by half. There were only twenty or so on her lawn. Donny punched the button on the garage door opener and then again to bring down the door when the car came to a stop inside the garage. Madison didn't wait for Donny to come around and help her from the car. She swung open the door and went directly into her townhouse from the garage without a word to her mystery driver. Donny was able to get in the house just before she shut the door and locked it. It didn't take him long to notice her red-rimmed eyes and know that she had been crying again.

"Are ye alright, lass?" he asked quietly.

Madison dropped her purse on the kitchen counter and turning to face Donny, crossed her arms over her chest and glared at him. "Okay, spill it!"

"Why do we no' go into the living room and sit where we can be comfortable."

"Fine." Maddy walked into her living room and flopped down on the sofa. She looked around the room, "I hate this room." She folded her arms over her chest again and scowled at the TV set. Julie hopped up on the sofa and curled into Madison's lap.

Donny followed behind her and sat down on the other end of the sectional. Julie stood and walked the length of the sofa until she reached Donny, then sat on his lap and purred. He looked at Madison and decided now was as good a time as any and began to speak.

"Maddy, are ye sure ye want to know who I am?" she said nothing, so he continued. "Maddy, look at me." She turned her head to him and watched as he, removed contacts revealing green instead of brown eyes, tugged off his mustache, and took off his long black wig to reveal a full head of blond hair. Madison stood and looked at him with wide eyes and an open mouth.

"You son of a bitch!" She laughed as she threw a pillow at his head. Donny reached up and knocked the pillow out of the air before it hit him and stood.

"Are ye angry?" he asked cautiously.

"Angry? Hell no!" She leaped to him and threw her arms around his neck, kissing his cheek. "I'm so glad to see you! But wait I don't understand. I'm not under investigation, am I?" She pulled away from him and they sat back on the sofa.

"Well, ye know after the FBI had cleared ye and Ian to go back to the house, they went back to Philadelphia. I had ta come with them and tie up the ends. I was supposed ta go back home tomorrow, but Tommy called me this morn and told me of the troubles between ye and Ian. He asked if I wouldna mind hangin' around ye 'til this was over."

Madison sat still for a moment and took in all of what Donny had said, but there was one thing still that she didn't understand. "Why the disguise? Why not just come as you are and tell me who you were?"

"That's the way Tommy wanted it. He said ye dinna leave on good terms and was afraid if ye knew who I was ye would refuse to let me near ye." Donny began to fidget and stood up.

"But why?"

"Well, Tommy dinna know how ye'd feel aboot the rest of the family after Ian had behaved like such an ass."

Madison laughed. "Is that what Tommy said?" and she laughed again. "Well, so now that I know who you are. Let me show you to the guest room and we'll get you set up for your stay." Madison got up from the sofa and walked upstairs with Donny trailing behind her. Her mind was racing with thoughts of Ian and his attitude when he stormed out of the house the other night. She was so confused and wanted so much to call him.

As they walked into the guest room, Madison began to laugh. She hadn't been in the house for so long she didn't remember about all the boxes. She had been basically using the room as a storage room ever since she moved in. Donny climbed over the boxes and found the bed, in pieces, in the corner. Madison leaned against the doorjamb and surveyed the room.

"Well, the room needs to be set up anyway. And since we can't really leave the house, why don't we get to work?" She entered the room and started opening boxes.

"Ye seem to have a knack for gettin' me ta be doin' housework. First the gardenin', now tis decoratin'." Madison laughed again—it felt good for a change–then continued with her unpacking.

After several hours they had the guest room and her office unpacked and set up. Madison stood back and took in their progress and was pleased with the way the two rooms had shaped up.

They trooped down to the garage and brought in all the bags from the trunk of the car. They took their bags to their rooms and began to unpack. Madison cleared two bags and then decided she was too tired to do anything further without rest. She set the remainder of her bags on the floor and lay across the bed. She was asleep within minutes. Donny checked on her when he finished unpacking. She was sleeping, so he went downstairs, took out his laptop, and set himself up in the dining room. He checked his email and refused all jobs for the next several weeks. He decided after this last job he pulled with Adam Gilmore and the FBI that he needed a break. He'd begun to think he should settle down and raise a family. He'd started to envy what Alex and Tommy had, and now what Ian had found with Madison. Julie jumped up on the table and demanded attention.

"Yer a sweet girl," he told the purring kitty. "Do ye think she's plannin' on sleepin' the night away, then?" He looked at his watch and it was eight thirty. It had been three hours since he had checked on her. Donny picked up Julie and went upstairs to check on Madison one more time before going to bed.

When he entered her room, he noticed that she wasn't in bed. Donny put Julie down on the bed and walked to her sliders and peered out to the balcony. *Nope,* he thought, *not there.* Then he heard noise in the bathroom. His eyebrows came together as he recognized the sound.

After a while she came out and saw Donny sitting on her chaise lounge petting the cat. "Are ye feelin' okay, Maddy girl?"

"Yeah, I think I'm just so tensed up about everything that has been happening over the last few weeks that my body can't take it. That would explain the dizziness, the sleepiness."

"And the upchuckin'?" Donny, like his brothers, was not one for subtly.

"Yes, and getting sick." She smiled and sat down on the bed. Donny was looking at her through the corner of his eye.

"Do ye normally get sick when ye stressed, then?"

"No, come to think of it. This is the first time. But then this is the first time I have ever dealt with this kind of stuff." She stood up and felt light-headed so she sat back down.

"Do ye think ye should call a doctor and see if ye might be comin' down wi somethin'?" *Like pregnancy,* he thought.

"No, it'll go away." She could feel the dizziness subsiding, so she got up one more time and reached for her bags to continue unpacking once more.

Oh the hell wi it, Donny thought. "Madison, if ye donna mind a wee bit of a personal question."

"Course not, ask away." She stopped midstride and turned to him "Unless you're planning on making a *"pumpin"* comment like your brother did the first time I met him."

Donny had heard about Tommy's comment and laughed. "Nay, lass, but now ye mention it my question is o that nature."

"Go ahead." She walked into her closet with clothing from her bag.

"When was yer last...?" He cleared his throat. "...monthly?"

Madison was startled by the question and began to laugh. "My what?" Then she understood and poked her head out of the closet. "Donny, I'm not able to have children."

He sat straight up alarmed. "Why no'? Since when?"

Madison came out of her closet and stood in front of Donny. "Since I was married to Adam. I had a miscarriage because of one of his rampages. The doctors told me after that it would be impossible for me to have a child. Now, please no more questions. I'm going to have enough of that tomorrow," she said, referring to the press conference.

Donny kept her company while she finished unpacking and they went downstairs. After ordering a pizza, they spent the rest of the evening watching TV and saw news reports on Madison, Ian, and Adam. Most of everything that had been broadcast so far had been mere fabrications of the truth. Madison was horrified when pictures of Ian leaving the house in Lusta flashed over the screen. *My God,* she thought, *they even got to the house.* That wonderful, secluded house was now all over the news. Donny finally flipped off the TV and announced that they should retire for the night.

"Ye have a big day ahead, and ye need yer rest." He paused at his door and reminded her that when they were out in public, he was going to have his disguise on. Madison bid him good night and she closed her bedroom door. She stripped off her clothes and put on her nightgown. After taking all the throw pillows off the bed, Madison slid under the covers and fell fast asleep.

Chapter Thirty

Thanks to Tommy and his team, Ian was able to get to and from his house without being hounded by reporters. The land across the road, bordering Ian's property resembled a full-blown convention. Media trucks from nearly every television network in the British Isles and the United States appeared to be dug in for the duration. But the long drive leading to the house itself, kept all but the most adventurous at bay.

Madison had only been gone for one day, but to Ian it might as well have been months. The house seemed bereft without her physical presence. He felt some relief knowing Donny was looking out for her in Philadelphia. However, Ian wanted to be the one protecting her from the media and the stress brought on by Adam's appearance in Scotland. He wasn't sure he truly understood why Donny wanted Ian to stay away, and it was a great struggle for Ian to comply with Donny's wishes. He was frustrated, lonely, and confused. His frustration was beginning to burgeon into anger. He wanted to do something to make things right for Madison and for himself, but he had no idea what that something might be. In all of his thirty-five years, he had never felt at such a loss for a plan of action.

Since he broke his phone the night he and Madison argued, he was now using his spare. He was able to transfer all his information from the broken phone to the spare including any and all messages. His voicemail box was filled to capacity with frantic calls from Victoria. She had even left idle threats to drop him as a client if he didn't get back to her. For Ian it wasn't much of a threat. Victoria had become almost a liability, and he was getting tired of her nagging. "I can always be a chef again." He chuckled. "Maybe I'll open my own restaurant in Edinburgh." He stood looking out toward the cliff and visions of himself walking along the beach hand and hand with Madison tumbled into his mind. "I have to do something!" he said and ran his hand through his hair. He turned from the window and, grabbing his keys and jacket, headed for the door. *Maybe Lizzy has heard from her,* he thought as he climbed into the Wagoneer, punched the ignition, and turned the SUV toward Lusta and the hospice office.

Ian parked behind the office and walked in the back door. He hadn't been in the space since Lizzy had taken over, but as he looked around the room, he could see Madison's touch all over it. Her presence poured from every inch of the delightful office. He could see Lizzy sitting at the magnificent desk and knew it was the one Madison had gotten for her. *She's right,* he thought, *Angus Jamison is an artist.* Lizzy looked up from her desk and saw Ian standing in the back doorway.

"Ian Bryce Mackay!" Ian and Lizzy both turned toward the bakery doorway. Agatha stood with her hands on her hips and a vicious scowl on her face.

"Agatha?" he said sheepishly.

"What the hell do ye think ye're doin' here?"

"Agatha?" was all he could seem to get out of his mouth.

"I should give ye a sound lashin'. What the hell is wrong wi ye!"

"Agatha."

"I'm well aware of me name, laddie. Now be so good as ta answer me question. Wha' are ye doin' in Lusta?" Her face was red and he didn't think it was related to the heat of her ovens. When Ian just looked at her she continued. "Have ye lost wha' wee brain the good Lord gave ye?" she waited. "Speak, ye daft boob!"

"Alright!" Ian shouted back at her. Then lowered his voice. "Ha ye heard from Madison then?" He walked a little farther into the room and looked from Agatha to Lizzy. They both just stared at him, and his shoulders slumped in defeat.

Agatha shook her head from side to side with disgust. "Ian, ge' in here!" she bellowed and turned back to her kitchen.

With his head bowed, Ian followed and sat on one of the stools around the butcher-block island in Agatha's kitchen. "Might I ha a cuppa?" he asked.

"Hell no!" she growled, but her heart began to soften when she read his discouraged body language. She reached for the steaming kettle on the stove top, poured a mug of tea, and plunked it soundly on the counter in front of him. "Laddie, I dinna think I've ever been more disappointed in ye than I am at this minute." She crossed her arms over her chest and stared at him.

"Wha' was me first clue?" he mumbled.

"Watch yer sassy tongue, young lad, or I'll use me bread paddle across yer arse."

Ian rested his head in his hands and tried to massage the headache that had been building since the day Madison told him she had to go back to Philadelphia. "I dinna know wha ta do."

"Go after her" came Lizzy's quiet voice from the doorway.

"And do ye no think that's just what I want ta do?" he snapped as he turned his attention toward her.

"Dinna be growlin' at her, Ian Mackay," Agatha warned. "She's no' the one who fucked up!" Ian jerked his head back to Agatha. He had seen her upset with him a time or two in his life, but she rarely punctuated her anger with *that* much color. He was trying to remember when he had last seen her this enraged and drew a blank. "Apologize this minute."

"I'm sorry, Lizzy. I'm just... I'm sorry."

Lizzy went farther into the kitchen and sat on one of the stools. She took one look at his bloodshot eyes and rested her hands gently over his encircling his mug. "It's okay. Might I ask ye again? Why do ye no' go after her?"

Ian kept his eyes focused on his mug. "That's wha' Sara said too. I was plannin' ta get the next flight, but Donny said ta stay where I am."

"And what's that young bucko got ta do wi it?" Agatha asked as she sat on one of the stools.

"He's wi her in Philadelphia. Chauffeur. Bodyguard. Runnin' interference wi the press."

Agatha all but slammed her mug on the countertop, drawing Ian's attention from his tea back to her face. "I dinna give a rat's rump wha' Donny Mackay wants. He's no' the one who should be wi her in the first place. She's yer responsibility. Ye can hire a driver if ye dinna know how ta make yer way aboot the countryside. But it should be ye who chases after interference and lookin' after the lass's body. Ye're ta go after Madison right this verra day."

Ian shook his head. "Nay, Agatha. I hate like the devil ta say it, but I think Donny might ha the right o it this time. Mayhap she'll be less besieged by the press if I'm no' around givin' them coal to toss onta their fire. It might be better fer her if I stay away from her for now."

"Blast yer eyes! Ye're a bloody fool!" Agatha boomed. "I'm gettin' me bread paddle—" And she rose from the counter. Lizzy reached for her arm and pulled her back onto the stool.

"Agatha, sit doon!" Lizzy ordered, then turned to Ian. "Have ye thought clearly aboot wha's best fer Madison?"

"I've been thinkin' aboot nothing else. I'm no' sure I know wha's right anymore."

"Her question was, are ye thinking o wha's best for Madison. Or are ye thinking o yer own name, boyo?"

"AGATHA!" Lizzy screeched.

"She's a right ta ask, Lizzy." He turned saddened eyes toward his old friend. "I do ha a name o' sorts, Agatha, and I'm wonderin', if she ha been involved wi anyone else when Gilmore was killed; would she be facin' what she's facin now? Me presence in her life right now could only be makin' matters worse fer her."

"Are ye oot o' yer mind?" Agatha bellowed. "Ye should ne'er ha let her go ta Philadelphia alone in the first place. In her condition, she needs ye wi her. I ne'er heard such clap-trap come oot 'o yer mouth "

"Nay, I'm no oot o' me mind, and would thank ye ta no beller at me any longer, Agatha. I've no need ta hear it." Ian stood abruptly and turned toward the door when he stopped suddenly. "Wha' condition?"

"Ye are daft." Agatha decided, exasperated. She looked at Lizzy, but the anger was gone from her watery blue eyes. "Men! Did ye e'er know o a dumber lot?"

"What condition, Agatha?" Fear shot through Ian's heart as he lunged back toward the counter again. "Wha's wrong wi Maddy?" He rested his balled fists on the countertop and drilled his eyes into those of the old woman.

Agatha smiled up into Ian's terrified face and reached up to gently press her palm to his cheek. "She's wi child, laddie."

Ian's face drained of color and he began to feel light-headed. He took a step back and leaned against the doorframe for support, staring. "Nay, she canna be. She's unable," he whispered. "The doctor told her she's unable ta conceive."

"Doctors!" Agatha sniffed. "Wha do they know? They're the same buggers who told our dear Sara she was goin' ta die. They told her she couldna carry a wee babe ta term and look at her now. Healthy and wi a brand-new babe in her arms." She turned her eyes to Lizzy and patted her hand. "Our Patrick is a fine lad, lass," she stated with reassurance, "and he'll make an active energetic husband and a good da ta yer babes, but aboot babes and who the good Lord will give them to? Like all men, he doesna know dick!" Agatha lifted her mug and took a sip of tea while Lizzy and Ian stared at her silently. Finally, Ian sat down on the stool he had abruptly vacated only moments before.

"She dinna *tell* ye she was goin' ta ha a babe?" he choked.

"Nay, she dinna ha ta. I'm still a woomon, contrary ta wha ye may think. All I have ta do is look at her." She peered into her cup and mused aloud. "She mayna even know herself, if she's been told she canna conceive." She shook her head. "Men!" she said. When Ian stood and walked slowly to the doorway leading into the office, Agatha spoke again. Her anger was completely gone now. Only love and an ache for both Ian and Madison could be detected in her voice. "Ian, ye need ta go ta her. I dinna care wha' Donny lad said. He may think he's telling ye the right way of it, but tha lass, she needs ye wi her. Now. She's dealin' wi forces she has ne'er had ta deal wi before. And havin' feelins she may no' even understand.

"Maddy needs yer love and strength around her." She stood and moved to Ian laying her weathered hand on his arm. "Go ta her, laddie. It doesna matter how things were when she left. And it doesna matter if ye think ye'll bring more trouble down on her. Ye love each other and ye'll weather the troubles together, whate'er they are. She needs ta be wi ye and ye need to be wi her. And the wee bairn she carries in her belly needs both o ye."

Agatha's words sent pictures running through Ian's brain like a locomotive in high gear, and he had to shake his head to make them stop. He looked down at Agatha and then back to Lizzy and made his decision. Without another word he wrapped the old woman in his arms and gave her a hard squeeze, then kissed her smartly on the cheek and was out the door.

"Where is he goin'?" Lizzy asked as she heard the back door to the office close.

"He's goin' ta get his family! And aboot bloody time too!" Agatha sniffed and dabbed the corner of her apron to her eye before lifting a bowl of bread dough off the shelf over the stove.

Madison woke that morning and stared at the ceiling. Julie was curled up in a ball on her chest. She sighed and began to stretch causing the sleeping fluffy ball to squeak. There was a knock on Madison's bedroom door.

"Come in," she yawned.

Donny opened the door and peered in. Seeing that Madison was sufficiently under the covers, he entered the room, and smiled down at her. "Good morn, how are ye feelin?"

"Fine I suppose. I have to have my photograph taken numerous times, and give a speech to the press about my personal life and endure a lot of prying questions from people who have no right to ask them in the first place." She sat up and pulled Julie to her heart. "Under the circumstances, I guess you could say I'm in top form. How do I look?" Her hair was bunched at the top of her forehead and because she hadn't bothered to remove her makeup before climbing into bed, her mascara was smudged under her eyes. Donny rubbed his index finger over his chin and looked at the floor. "Never mind!" She smiled, noticing that Donny was already sporting his disguise. "How about you?"

"Fine. I have ta say, last night was probably the best night's sleep I've ever had. If ye're no' careful ye might be havin' a regular houseguest. It's a good bed ye've got in yer spare room." Donny sat down on the edge of the chaise lounge and looked at his watch. "Ye might want to start gettin' ready ta leave fer the office." Madison scooted back down in the bed and pulled the sheet over her head. Donny chuckled as he walked over and gave a slight tug on the covers.

"I heard you!" Madison giggled from under the sheet.

"Aye, I know ye did, and if ye dinna get a move on, ye're goin' ta see me from me belt to me ankles if I have ta haul ye out of the bed over me shoulder."

With a firm grip on the covers, Madison stuck her head out and gaped up at him. "You wouldn't dare!"

"Aye, lass. I would." He was smiling, but his face was determined.

"I believe you would." She sighed as she through back the covers, padded to the bathroom and turned on the shower. "Donny?" she called after him.

"Aye?" he answered from the hallway. He was examining his face in the decorative mirror hanging on the wall. Making faces at himself while trying to recreate the exact expression that had convinced her he would do as he'd threatened. *Whatever it was, I'd like to get it down. I might want to use it again,* he thought.

"Do you want to stop at the WAWA down the street and get some breakfast sandwiches?"

"Nay, I've made some eggs and bacon already. Get dressed and come doon and eat." Donny smiled and walked down to the kitchen and filled Julie's food and water bowls. When he heard the shower kick off and was confident that Madison would be down soon; he started the coffee. Glancing out the window, he saw the reporters were still on the lawn and was glad he had decided to use the garage from now on.

Donny heard his personal cell phone in the other room and strolled over to answer it. "Aye?"

"Donny lad, how are ye?" Tommy's voice boomed over the airwaves.

Donny was alerted immediately because Tommy said he wouldn't call unless it was absolutely necessary. "Wha's the matter?"

"Oh, no a thing. Relax, laddie. I thought I would touch base wi ye and see how our lass is holdin' up."

"She's a bonnie strong lass, Tommy, but I dinna know how much more she can deal wi. She has a press conference today. I feel fer her. She's such a private person and that privacy has been invaded and will be aired on the evenin' news." Donny sighed. "Have ye heard from Ian o late?"

"Nay. I havena seen nor heard from him since his blow-up with Maddy. I did hear from Agatha, though. Said he stopped by Maddy's office early this morn."

Donny smiled. "I'll bet she gave him a sound lashin'."

"Aye! Tha she did. She wouldna be Agatha Stuart if she wasna tongue lashin' somebody aboot somethin!" Tommy laughed. "Stick close ta Maddy today. I ha a feelin she'll need someone ta lean on after the blasted thing is over."

"I know." Donny looked toward the stairs and saw Madison on her way down. "Thanks fer the update." And without another word Donny stuck his phone in his jacket pocket and gave Madison his full attention. She was dressed in a burgundy silk suit with her chestnut hair swept into a dignified French roll. She wore almost no makeup and a simple pair of diamond stud earrings. "Are ye ready to eat before leavin'?"

Madison looked at the breakfast Donny had prepared and suddenly felt nauseous. She couldn't understand it. She loved breakfast. *Must be more nervous about the press conference than I thought,* she said to herself. *Thank God it'll all be over today.* "No I don't think so. Just some tea and we can be on our way."

Donny looked at her queerly as she passed quickly by the counter where the breakfast plates sat. *She wanted me to go out to get something for breakfast, and now she doesn't want anything,* he thought. *And she's drinkin' tea instead coffee.* "Ye're no' hungry, lass?"

"I think I'm just nervous about the press conference. Once all this is over and everything goes back to normal, I'll be fine." She poured some tea for herself and offered some to Donny, but he already had a cup of coffee. She turned off the stove and sat to sip her tea, nudging the plate of eggs and bacon as far away from her as she could.

They sat companionably while Donny ate and Madison nursed her tea. When it was time to leave, they loaded their dishes in the dishwasher. Madison wiped the counter, and gave Julie a hug, noticing that Donny had already filled her food and water bowls. He opened the door leading to the garage and locked it behind him. Madison sat in the backseat and Donny behind the wheel. He locked the car doors and pushed the button that raised the heavy garage door. When the garage door opened, the reporters stationed in the drive came alive "like a swarm of locust," Maddy mumbled. Donny put the Lincoln Town Car in reverse and glided through the maze of reporters.

Chapter Thirty-One

Madison used the drive into the city to go over in her mind what she was going to say to the press in a few hours. She only hoped her statement would put an end to all the reporters and publicity that she and Ian were getting.

Ian, God how she missed him. She hadn't talked to him since they had had their argument the evening before she left Scotland and so badly wanted to talk to him. She knew he was against her decision to come back to the States, and he was angry when he slammed out of the house. She hoped that after thinking it over he would realize it was something she had to do. It had only been two days, but he might have calmed down by now. She also hoped that he was having an easier time with all of this than she was. It suddenly struck her that she and Donny had almost avoided talking about Ian. *I'll call him tonight*, she decided. *I have to know what he's thinking.*

"Oh shit," she muttered, and remembered him tossing his cell down the stairs where it smashed all over the floor. She sighed and closed her eyes and leaned her head back on the headrest. Mental pictures of her and Ian standing by the fence overlooking the bay flooded back to her.

When the car came to an abrupt halt, she was jolted from her reverie. Madison sat forward to see why they had stopped. To her dismay the entrance to the underground parking garage was blocked by reporters and photographers.

"Why can't they leave me alone long enough to get from my house to my office?" Madison exclaimed. "For God sakes they're going to get their statement. Isn't that enough?" She was exasperated

"I could drive over a couple o them. That might make them move out of the way." Donny looked in the rearview mirror and smiled at her. He wished he could do that very thing. How many times during his years in law enforcement had he wished the same thing. "The public has a right to know, ma'am." He repeated the line that had become a standard joke.

"I have come to hate that line," she said. "The public doesn't have a right to know about my personal life. How would those reporters feel if I started asking them about the intimate details of their lives? On camera."

"Dinna worry, lass, here comes the cavalry." Madison looked up the street when she heard sirens coming toward them." Donny turned slightly and winked at her. "If ye'd like, I might be able to nail at least one of the buggers before the cavalry arrives."

Madison knew Donny was trying to lessen her stress with humor. Not wanting to discourage his efforts, she responded. "Why, Donny, I had no Idea you were that hard up for a date." They both forced laughter and Maddy looked out the window in time to see the reporters being forced to move aside. As a path cleared, Donny pulled the Lincoln down into the garage and parked in Madison's spot.

Not waiting for him to open the door for her, Madison got out of the car, and headed toward the bank of elevators as soon as the car came to a stop. Donny waited with her in silence as the doors opened and they both entered the steel box that would take them to her floor.

Donny watched as Madison wrung her hands together and began to fidget with her clothes. "Dinna worry, Maddy girl; yer goin' ta be just fine." He rested his hand on her arm to quiet her fingers. "Ye're a strong bonnie lass, and I've been proud o ye. I've been in law enforcement many a year, and I've yet ta see a lass handle trouble wi as much strength as I've watched ye do it. Ian would be proud o ye too, if he could be wi ye."

Madison looked up at Donny and gave a weak smile. She squared her shoulders and straightened her back as the doors opened. She wasn't surprised to see Margaret waiting for them. They said hello and walked quickly to her office. Once in the safety of her office Madison drew her first free breath.

"Is Samuel here yet?" she asked Margaret as she handed over her coat and briefcase.

"Yes he came in about ten minutes ago. He wanted me to tell him the moment you arrived."

"Well, I'm here, so let him know." Madison walked behind her desk and sat down. "Oh Margaret, can you get me some chicken soup from the café` ?"

"Sure, aren't you feeling well?"

"No not really, it's probably just nerves but soup always makes me feel better."

"Okay. I'll let Mr. Goldblum know you're here and call down for some soup." Before closing the door Madison thanked her.

As Madison shuffled papers around her desk, Donny strolled around the office and stopped at the wall of windows that overlooked Philadelphia. A while later, the door to Madison's office opened and in came Margaret with soup and to let Madison know that Samuel would be in to see her before the press conference. Madison thanked her once more and removed the lid from the warm container. She hoped that once this fuss was all over, her stomach would go back to normal, but it wasn't long before she had to excuse herself and get rid of what little soup she had eaten. When she returned from her bathroom, Donny was looking at her like a concerned father.

"Ye know lass, I'm no so sure ye should wait 'til after all this is over ta go have a checkup." He watched as she sat on the sofa, leaned back and closed her eyes. She looked so pale and worried. *Damn ye, Ian,* he thought, *ye should ha come wi her in the first place. Stubborn, ass!*

"Donny don't frown, you'll get wrinkles." She smiled up at him. "Besides, it's just nerves. Believe me when this is all over I'll be just fine."

"When do ye plan on goin' back to Scotland, then?" The question was out of his mouth before he had time to think about it. Thankfully, Madison didn't have to answer. The door opened and in walked Samuel.

"Samuel," Madison began to stand when he motioned for her to stay where she was. Thankful to remain seated, she continued. "How are you?"

"Fine!" However, he noticed that she didn't look exactly fit. "We will all be better when the building is free of these dreadful reporters. Have you your statement ready?" He was all business this morning and Madison was grateful for the focus it gave her.

"Yes, I have it. By the way, how long are we going to allow them to ask me questions? And is there a way to let them know that I will not answer anything too personal?"

"Well, my girl, unfortunately this whole issue is personal. We can't limit what they ask, but you can certainly limit what you answer. But in the interest in saving you as much grief as possible, we will only allow ten minutes of questions after you have given your statement." She actually looked a little green around the edges and he leaned over to pat her hand then took on the role of father figure. "Don't worry, girlie; it'll all be over soon and no matter what, you will be protected by me and the company as a whole." He stood and walked to the door, but before exiting, he reminded her to be ready in an hour. He then looked at Donny. "Take good care of my girl." Donny nodded and Samuel shut the door as he walked out.

An hour later Madison and Donny stood outside of the conference room door. The press was packed inside the room like sardines listening to Samuel give the lead-in to her press statement.

"I can't believe they can care this much about someone's personal life," she whispered to Donny. "You would think the president had just been caught with his pants around his knees in the ladies room at Bergdorf's."

"Aye, lass," Donny whispered. "Or at least handing out cigars at the main entrance."

"That," Madison chuckled, "was a different president."

When Samuel announced Madison would be taking questions for no longer than ten minutes after making her statement, Madison recognized her cue. She took a deep breath, squared her shoulders, straightened her back, and walked into the room. As she came through the door, there was a thunderous roar of questions. Each one more outrageous than the one before. The reporters as a group would have blocked her route to the podium had it not been for Donny physically shouldering their way to the front of the room. Maddy took her place behind the podium and gave Donny her most confident smile. *You're the Chief Operating Officer of an international company,* she told herself. *Don't let them push you around.* She stood quietly saying nothing until the noise died. Then she surveyed the press core and began to speak.

"Ladies and Gentlemen, I have a very short statement, and then as Mr. Goldblum has already told you, I will open the floor for ten minutes of questions.

"First allow me to thank you for attending today. As some of you may be aware, I went to Scotland six months ago to initiate a branch office for Tender Care Hospice. We have done very well and have begun to take on patients.

"During my stay there, I've been renting a house from Ian Mackay. Mr. Mackay and I have become close.

"Adam Gilmore and I were divorced more than ten years ago. During those years he had been confined in the New Jersey State Penitentiary. Two months ago Mr. Gilmore made a successful escape from incarceration. Mr. Gilmore committed multiple murders after escaping the penitentiary making FBI involvement necessary. He unfortunately met his death while trying to escape capture by the FBI and other law enforcement agencies in Scotland. During that escape attempt, Mr. Mackay, some of Mr. Mackay's family members, and myself sustained injuries.

"That concludes my statement. Questions?" Madison had barely finished when a swarm of questions flew at her. She remembered few of the reporters from her last press conference, and none of the faces were familiar, so she just nodded to one face in the front of the pack

"Isn't it true that during your stay in Scotland you became romantically involved with Ian Mackay?" the reporter asked.

"As I said, I rented a house from Mr. Mackay and we have become close." Madison selected another.

"Isn't it also true that your divorce from Gilmore was because your husband was savagely abusive?" shouted a woman from the middle of the room.

"My ex-husband was not the best of men; however, I don't think the particulars of my divorce are relevant." She selected another.

"When will you be returning to Scotland?"

She should have been prepared for this one, but for some reason unknown to her, she wasn't. "My travel plans are as yet uncertain."

"Do you plan to attend the funeral of Adam Gilmore?" the next reporter asked.

"No, I will not be in attendance."

"It has been rumored that one of Ian Mackay's brothers is an FBI agent, can you confirm?"

"I was never privy to information about the Mackay family." She then gave Donny a small twitch of her finger. Donny took the opportunity to lean to Samuel and suggest the questions end.

"Last question," Samuel announced, and Madison felt instant relief and chose one more reporter.

"What is your relationship with Ian Mackay since Gilmore's death?"

"I've already stated—" Maddy began.

"Isn't it true that Gilmore went to Scotland when he heard of your affair with Ian Mackay?"

"Excuse me?"

Before she could answer, the questions shot at her rapid fire.

"Do you plan to continue living with Mackay?"

"Why didn't Ian return with you to the United States?"

"I d-don't...," Madison stammered.

"What kind of an effect do you think your affair with Ian will have on his career?"

"What does his family think, now that your affair is out in the open?"

"Mr. Mackay and I are—"

"What does your husband's family think of your affair with Ian Mackay?"

"He's not my—"

"Did you love your husband?" this from a tight skirt and fried hair.

Donny, by then, had wrapped his arm around Madison's shoulders and was again shouldering their way from the room while the questions bounced off the walls and camera lights bright and ugly followed them through the doorway.

"He's not my husband." she was saying almost to herself as Donny led her down the hall and into her office, shutting the door behind them. She sank slowly down onto the sofa and sat with her hands limply in her lap. Donny stood by the door for a moment before joining her, pulling her into his arms.

"Do'na worry, lass. It's all over now." He didn't have time to say more. There was a brief knock at the door and Samuel came in.

"How you holding up?" he asked as he sat in one of the winged back chairs.

"Not bad, I... I had no idea they would be so vicious. Samuel, I'm so sorry about all of this. I was so sure if we made a calm civilized press statement; that we could clear everything and put an end to this mess." She rose and walked to the window behind her desk. "It's not over is it? They weren't interested in hearing the facts. They're like a pack of wild dogs that have come across a carcass." She returned to the sofa and sat facing Samuel. Donny made a move to leave the two alone.

"There is no need for you to leave, son. You've been an enormous emotional support for Madison and a good friend. You have every right to remain where you are." Neither Madison nor Donny was surprised by Samuel's assumption, so Donny stayed seated. "So, my dear, when would you like to go back to Scotland and your young man?"

Donny couldn't help chuckling. "You seem to have the same question as everyone in the world right now."

"To be honest, Samuel, I haven't given it much thought. I think it would be a good idea for me to stay put for a while. I mean, yes, the press conference is over, but there will still be a lot of press around. If I leave now it could only make matters worse. Don't you think? They would very likely follow me back to Lusta. That in itself would be a disruption to the office, and could destroy what we've managed to achieve there with the doctors and hospital."

Samuel leaned forward and studied her face and smiled. "I think you have given this more thought than you would like to admit. You'll have to go back sooner or later, you know. I'll need you to be 'hands on' for a while, until we're confident the office is running smoothly. And even after, you might have to make the trip quite often, I'm afraid. However, I won't press you for an answer right now." Not saying any more, he patted her hand knowingly and left the room. Madison sighed as she walked behind her desk and sat down. Apparently she planned to work for a while, so Donny took the opportunity to go for a walk and make some phone calls.

A few hours later, Madison leaned back in her desk chair and stretched her arms over her head. She felt a little better. It had been a productive afternoon and she was satisfied with what she had been able to accomplish despite the rocky beginning to the day. She decided it was time to pack it up and go home. She turned off her computer and sorted through some papers to add to her briefcase. As she grabbed her coat and headed for the door, Donny came in and they both laughed. Apparently they had both come to the same conclusion.

"Are ye ready ta call it a day then, lass?"

"Yes." She smiled and spoke to Margaret as they passed her on the way to the elevators.

"Get some rest tonight, Madison. Each day will get a little better," Margaret said as she, too, was reaching for her jacket.

It was past six o'clock when Donny pulled the Lincoln into her garage. Madison got out of the car and unlocked the door to the house. Donny was still waiting by the car when Madison turned around.

"Aren't you coming in?" she asked.

"Nay, I have to run one more errand. Go ahead and lock the door behind ye. I'll return later. Get some rest, lass. Ye deserve it. And ye might eat something. Ye've had nothing in yer stomach but a wee bit of tea and soup." Madison smiled and shut the door.

She waited for a moment before going upstairs. She went to her home office she and Donny had set up earlier, and put down her briefcase. She thought about checking her email but decided she had had enough and needed to go to bed. She closed her laptop and left the room. Julie was under her feet as Madison turned on the light by the bed and sat down.

"Hi, sweetie, how are you?" She picked up her furry friend and began to scratch behind her ear. "Well, I don't know about you, but I'm beat."

Julie meowed in response. "What'll it be? Dinner or bed? Why don't we make it a very early night and just go to bed?"

"I could no' agree more" came a male voice from the doorway.

Startled, Madison stood abruptly and was captured by deep emerald green eyes. She blinked because she couldn't believe her own eyes.

"Ian?" she breathed and brought her hands to her mouth as her eyes began to tear.

Ian crossed the room in two paces and drew her into his arms. His eyes also welled with tears and he didn't trust his voice. Finally, he pulled back to look down at her. Her vivid aqua eyes were swimming with tears that puddled and coursed down the sides of her face. Ian reached into his pants pocket and drew out a kerchief that he used to blot her cheeks.

Madison started to speak, but Ian pressed his finger to her lips. "Shhh," he whispered. "Ye're okay, luv. Ye're okay. Everything is goin' to be okay, now." And he held her gently but firmly in his arms.

"Ian," she breathed. "Ian. Thank God!"

Ian closed his eyes as his body relaxed. This was what he had been waiting for. This was what had been nagging at the back of his mind for the last three days. She had left Scotland despite his objections. The sudden understanding came to him at the same time as did reassurance. He had been scared. Physically afraid he was losing her, or had lost her, but he hadn't. She loved him. It was in her eyes when she looked at him and in her touch as she clung to him. *I've been a bloody stubborn fool,* he thought to himself, *I should ha come wi her. I should ha been at her side at her press conference.*

"Thank ye, Agatha!" he breathed.

"What?" Madison drew back her head and saw matching tears welling in Ian's eyes as he grinned at her. He gently touched his lips to hers and then brushed the kerchief under her eyes again.

"I had a chat wi Agatha this morn." He chuckled while trailing his lips down her throat.

"Agatha?" Maddy sighed. She loosened her grip on his neck and leaned her head back to give him better access.

"Mm-hmm." He pulled her more tightly against his body and recaptured her lips with his own. Hers were even more sensual than he remembered. Madison secured her arms around his neck again. Her heart was racing and her mind was running with questions, but right now all she cared about was Ian. *Here* with her. She felt butterflies in the pit of her stomach and her legs actually seemed to be getting weak.

Ian broke the kiss and looked into her face. "Maddy, I love ye so verra much. Nothing is real until I can share it wi ye." Looking up to him, she could see his red rimmed eyes, and the dark circles from worry and lack of sleep. She brought her fingers to his unshaven cheek and smiled through her own tears.

"You make me strong, Ian. And weak at the same time. How is that possible?" she whispered.

He laughed out loud and scooped her up into his arms with a flourish. "Because ye luv me!"

"Yes," she breathed into his mouth. "I do that." And she kissed him deeply.

"Now ye're makin' me weak," Ian whispered when she finally broke the kiss. He laid her on the bed and settled himself beside her before gathering her into his arms again. His breath was warm as he pressed his lips to her neck while his hand roamed under her silk blouse. "Nice shirt," he said.

"Uh-huh." Madison let a small moan escape.

"Would look good on tha chair." And Maddy could feel his lips stretching into a grin as he worked his way to her earlobe.

"Mm-hmm," she reinforced and stretched her body along his.

"Yer pants are nice too." Ian ran his hand over her firm bottom.

"Mm-hmm." She smiled.

"We'd likely be more comfortable under the covers."

"Think so?" she giggled and snaked her fingers into the waistband of his jeans.

"I'm no a teenager, lass, and ye're drivin' me crazy!"

Madison leaned back and looked him square in the eyes, raising her brows in mock outrage. "Are you suggesting I sleep with you, sir?"

"Eventually, madame." He grinned and took her lips with his. When he finally pulled away, he rose from the bed and helped her up. They stood together and made a ceremony of removing each other's clothing. Savoring exposed skin while each garment fell to the carpet.

When they stood with nothing between them but the moonlight streaming through the shear curtains at the glass doors, Ian raised his hands to either side of her face. His eyes were serious and she could detect remnants of despair.

"I was afraid, luv." He spoke so softly she could barely hear him. She started to speak, but he moved his thumb over her lips to still her voice. "I was angry when ye left, but it was no' true anger. It was fear. I dinna realize it until I heard ye come in the door a while ago. When ye were wi me, I could deal wi whatever came. When ye left, I was lost and I think I was afraid I was losin' ye too. 'Tis as simple as tha'. Me stubborn streak is me worst enemy. Ye may as well know it now," he said, trying to smile.

Madison lifted her arms about his neck and pulled him close to her. "Oh, Ian! I was afraid too. I wanted to call you, but I was so worried that you were still mad at me. Everyone has asked me when I'm going to return to Scotland, and I didn't know what to answer." She leaned back and gazed into his handsome face, the tears welling in her eyes once more. "I was afraid I had destroyed what we had by racing off full steam, the way I did. And I didn't seem to have any control—"

"Shhh, lass." He gathered her to him again, pressing her face into his chest, he buried his hand in her hair and closed his eyes breathing in the scent of her. "We're no' destroyed. We're fine. Everything is goin' ta be fine." He dropped his hand to her back and rubbed up and down.

"And mayhap we're both a wee bit too stubborn." She laughed a bit and sniffled. He reached down putting his arm under her knees and lifted her onto the bed. As he settled himself above her, she placed her fingertips on his mouth.

"We are fine now, aren't we?" she said.

"Maddy, I luv ye wi all me heart," he said against her lips. "We'll allow nothin' to destroy us. We share the same breath. The same soul." He pressed his lips to hers before seducing her tongue with his own. He was tender and demanding at the same time.

Ian laid seductive kisses on her neck and trailed them down her throat. He passed her collarbone a settled on her breasts. Madison arched her back as the pleasure Ian gave washed over her body like a warm gentle rain. When it seemed to Maddy that her body couldn't be more consumed with joy, Ian brought his lips back to hers.

"Tell me," he begged.

"I love you, Ian," she breathed. "Please take me."

She was ready for him and cried out her ecstasy when he entered her smoothly. Her hands floated across the sleek expanse of his back feeling his muscles tighten and ripple as his trusts became more powerful. Madison grabbed at the bed sheets and arched her back as their momentum built. She exploded her orgasm as Ian threw back his head and cried out her name while his own orgasm consumed him.

Ian collapsed on top of her breathing heavily, then rolled onto his back pulling her into his arms. They lay there in silence. Exhausted. Each with their own thoughts, and each, silently thanking Agatha Stuart for her interference. Madison snuggled closer to Ian and stretched her arm across his chest. He drew her fingers to his lips and pressed his lips to them before pulling the covers over them and drifting into the first restful sleep he had had in days.

Chapter Thirty-Two

Madison woke the next morning feeling contented and rested still nestled in Ian's arms. She tipped her chin up and smiled, he was still sleeping soundly. She gently ran her fingertips down his cheek, the three day growth of beard was kinda sexy, but Madison also noticed that in addition to the dark growth, he also had dark smudges under his eyes. *He hasn't been sleeping any better than I have,* she thought to herself. Trying not to wake him she slid out from under the covers and headed to the shower.

As the spray of the hot water coursed over her body her thoughts trailed to the press conference. She cringed at the prying questions and the enthusiasm with which they were hurled at her. With no regard for her feelings or anyone else who was affected. The fact that one of those lives was a celebrity was the cherry on the top for the scummy ass puranas that have the nerve to call themselves real journalists.

"They don't want to report what happened or why," Madison muttered aloud. "I don't know why they bother asking questions at all, if they're going to make up their own answers. They're not interested in reporting the news. They want sensationalism. Some mean nasty little story; they think is going to make people salivate over their Danish and morning coffee." She wanted to hug herself as the term "victim" crept into her brain, quickly replaced by anger. "I won't be Adam's victim and I won't be trampled by the press." She stated as she soaped up her bath poof ball and applied it to her body. "Where are the Walter Cronkite's of the world when you need them? Probably buried under twelve tons of yellow tabloid journalism!" she grumbled. "Trapped. Without air to breath and gasping for—"

"Is this a private conversation or can anyone join in?"

"IAN!" she half laughed, half screamed as Ian stepped in under the spray closing the glass door behind him. He took her soapy wet body in his arms and pressed his lips to hers as the warm water sluiced over both of them.

"Ye're a wee bit slippery, Luv." He grinned when he released her lips and looked into her eyes.

"Aye!" she laughed. "And *ye're* dripping water into my eyes."

"A thousand pardons, *my* lady. Pray, wha can I do ta make amends?" he grinned.

"Stop talking." She purred and slid her arms around his neck.

When the water began to turn cold, Ian turned off the faucet and stepped out of the shower reaching for a towel.

"Yer cape, me lady." Ian held Madison's towel open as she stepped into it. He wrapped the soft white fluffy bath sheet around her dripping form and pulled her in close to his body. "I'm hungry." He leered.

"Ian, you're insatiable!" she laughed.

"Fer breakfast!" he defended. As he gently held her in the fluffy white terry cloth fabric he was reminded once more about the baby Agatha believed Madison was carrying. *Should I ask her about it,* he wondered. *Should I just tell her of Agatha's suspicions instead,* he thought. She looked so pale and worn. *Maybe I should just beat aboot the bush,* he decided. "How are ye feelin' luv?"

"Better now that you're here." She placed a peck on his cheek and walk back to the bedroom where Ian followed. "Speaking of which, why are you here?" she asked as she stepped into the closet.

Ian retrieved a towel from the bar and wrapped it low around his hips. "Am I ta understand that ye didna want me ta come?" He arched his eyebrow with feigned offense and looked after her.

"Oh God no!" she emerged from the closet with her hand to her chest. "I merely asked, because of the way things were between us when I left Scotland."

Ian leaned against the wall and looked at her. "Aye, I've been wantin' ta speak wi ye aboot that." He scrubbed his hand through his hair trying to find the right words. "I owe ye an apology, lass. I fear I overreacted a wee bit. I should ne'er ha spoken ta ye the way I did. Ye have a job and because of what happened it was in jeopardy. I know ye needed ta come here, and do wha'ere ye could ta fix wha'ere damage was done ta yer company." Ian took a deep breath and continued. "I guess I was afraid if ye came back ye might no ever return."

"What?" Madison breathed, she couldn't believe what she was hearing. She stood in the doorway of the closet wearing black denim jeans holding a red cotton shirt in her hand. "You thought—"

"Let me finish luv. I know, the idea shouldna ha entered me mind, but after what ye had just been through. What we had all been through. I thought tha maybe…" He shrugged his shoulders and walked to the bed and sat down. "I ha been thankin' God tha I hadna lost ye when Adam had ye in the house. Ye dinna ken wha went through me brain when I realized he had ye prisoner in there. Then when ye were safe again and we finally could go back ta our home together, ye announce tha ye're leavin'. I guess I went a wee bit looney." Ian looked up and captured her questioning eyes. "I wanted ta come after ye when I got back ta the house and ye were gone."

"Why didn't you?" Madison whispered.

"I didna return ta the house until the morn. Then I got a call from Donny. He told me he was here lookin' after ye. I said I was comin, ta get ye, but he told me ta stay away."

"Why would he do that?" Madison pulled her shirt on over her head as she walked over to sit beside Ian on the bed.

"He felt; if I came before the press conference it would only make matters worse fer ye and the company. He said tha ye were gettin' a lot o support from Samuel and the people ye work wi." Ian raised his hand and brushed a lock of hair away from Madison's eyes. *She looks like an angle* he thought to himself.

"How did you know about the press conference?"

"Donny told me Samuel had set one up fer ye when ye got back. He said tha Samuel felt it was the best way ta clear up the rumors in one shot and—"

"But if Donny told you not to come here, why did you?"

"Because I couldna be away from ye any longer, luv. And as I said before, I was afraid ye wouldna return once ye came back ta yer own city and friends and yer job here."

"Ian, I love you. I never planned to stay away." He pulled her into his arms and held her tightly. "I admit, our disagreement scared me. I wasn't sure how we could get passed the things we said ta each other." She tightened her arms around him. "I missed you so much." she breathed, then drew back and looked into his eyes.

"I was afraid too," she said. "I was so happy to learn my chauffeur was Donny, when he finally dropped his disguise. It made me feel closer to you somehow. Like we still have a connection."

Ian pulled her back into his embrace and pressed his lips into her hair. After a few minutes Madison chuckled.

"You should have seen him when we arrived at my building. He was like John Wayne chasing off the bad guys!"

"The next time ye'r in need of the cavalry, lass, I'll be wi ye." Ian murmured. "From now on, we deal wi the press together."

After a few minutes Madison pulled back and looked into his eyes. "I saw on the news; the reporters were all over the house. What happened with them?"

"I called Tommy and he had them removed from the property." He smiled devilishly

"How?" Madison grinned and wondered if she *really* wanted to know.

"Tommy just asked them *politely* ta leave. Now do ye want ta tell me aboot the press conference?" He watched as Madison stood and walked to the window.

"It was awful. I gave my statement and I thought that would be enough, but as soon as the last question' was called for, they bombarded me. They wouldn't even let have time to answer one question or accusation before the next ones were thrown at me. They wanted to know what kind of effect our *affair* has had on your career. What my *husband's* family thought of the affair. Whether or not I loved my *husband*. They wanted to know if it was true that my *husband* came to Scotland because he found out about my affair. I don't think they even cared if I answered or not, they were so busy throwing mud at me." Madison pounded her clenched fist on her thigh, stood and stalked across the room. "He was not my *husband!* Don't those people know the meaning of the word divorce?"

Ian could see she was getting worked up again and he could feel her frustration. He stood and crossed the room to stand behind her. Leaning over, he drew her against him. "I'm sorry ye had ta go through all this, luv."

"It's not your fault." Madison rested against his chest and put her hands over his arms wrapped around her. It felt so good to be near him again. "But Ian, we do have to talk about your career. What will this kind of publicity do to your career? What kind of effect will it have on you?"

Before he could comment, they heard a door downstairs open and Ian was immediately alerted.

"Don't worry it's probably Donny coming back from, well actually, I don't know where he went. He dropped me off here last night and said he had an errand to run and I haven't seen him since. Do you suppose he is just now getting back? Does he know you're here?"

Ian looked back at her and shook his head. He took hold of Madison's shoulders and told her to stay in the bedroom, then turned to leave the room.

"Where you go, I go." She stated flatly and taking his hand, she followed behind him down the stairs. But they could see no sign of Donny or anyone else for that matter. Ian suggested Madison stand near the door while Ian checked out the kitchen. Just as Ian disappeared around the corner, suddenly the basement door opened and Donny walked through it with a basket full of clothes.

"Donny." Madison sighed with relief. "And I thought we were finally finished with the cloak and dagger stuff! Are you just getting in??"

"Aye, I had something I needed ta take care of" Noticing Madison staring at the basket in his arms Donny continued. "I hope ye do'na mind I had some o me laundry ta do."

"No. Of course not. Help yourself." Madison's attention moved to the kitchen. Donny, following her eyes, saw Ian standing in the middle of the room wearing nothing but a bath towel holding a cast iron frying pan in his hand.

"Well, and I see Prince Charmin' has arrived, wearin' his suit of armor and weapons for battle." He grinned "Are ye plannen on fryen me ta death, lad? Is tha how tis done on the big screen, then?"

Ian looked down at the item he held in his hand. "Nay, on the 'big screen' we use big guns. Would ye be interested in some big eggs?" Ian asked weakly and laughed as he and his brother embraced.

Madison smiled and went to her purse to retrieve her ringing cell phone.

"Hello?"

"Hi Madison, it's Samuel. How are you holding up?"

"Better now. Thank you."

"You're welcome, I wanted to check. We were all worried."

"Worried?" Madison questioned. "Why?"

"Well, it's not like you to just not show up for work."

"Oh my God!" Madison said, realizing; Ian's surprise arrival blocked everything from her brain. "Samuel, I am so sorry. I'll get dressed and come in right now." She rubbed her forehead, mentally kicking herself.

Samuel chuckled. "No don't do that. Yesterday was a tough one. You could use a couple of days to regroup. Take sometime to rest and relax. We'll see you bright and early Monday morning."

"Are you sure, because it won't take me long to get ready and come in."

"Positive. Get some rest, and on Monday we can talk about your return to Scotland."

"My return?" Madison never thought of herself as dumb or slow witted but she couldn't seem to get a hold on anything today.

"Yes. I assume that your young man will need to be getting back to his career before too long a time and when he goes back he'll want you to go with him."

"Well, we haven't really talked about..." Madison smiled and looked at Ian "How did you know Ian was here?" She was always baffled by Samuel's uncanny ability to always know what was happening in her life.

"Call it intuition. Get some rest and I'll see you Monday."

"Thank you, Samuel." Madison smiled. She walked to the kitchen and watched from the doorway as the two brothers talked to each other and laughed together. Never having had siblings, she enjoyed the banter between Ian and his brother. To be part of a family must be wonderful, she thought. For the first time since she had been back in the States, she felt at peace. She had no idea how much she really needed Ian around her. She felt stronger and with the brothers there in her kitchen, almost like she was in a small way, part of a family. Madison dropped her phone back into her purse and cleared her throat as she entered the kitchen to join the men.

"Who was on the phone luv?" Ian asked as he circled his arms around her. The need to protect her seemed even greater than before, since

Agatha's announcement. *How do I handle this,* he thought to himself. *She could be carryin a life inside her. A wee babe tha she and I made together. She might be a mother and I might be a father.* Ian could feel his heart swell with pride and warmth. *I donna care if it's a girl or a boy,* he thought. *Truth be told, a bonnie lass would be nice. Tae many lads in the family now. Of course if tis a laddie we could name him after me da.*

"Ian!" came Madison and Donny's voice in unison.

Wha?" Ian started. Embarrassed that he was caught woolgathering.

"See, I told you he wasn't listening to me." Madison laughed "He's been off in la-la land. What were you thinking about?" she asked.

"Thinkin' aboot?" Ian questioned. Realizing he couldn't tell her the truth, "Oh ,tis o nay import." Madison and Donny kept looking at him, so he said the first thing that came into his brain "Victoria threatened ta drop me as a client."

"WHAT!" Both Madison and Donny bellowed.

"Aye. She's verra put oot wi me as I wouldna allow her ta use the Adam thing as a publicity stunt." Madison's face blanched and her mouth dropped open. This was something he hadn't planned to tell her, but he guessed it didn't really matter much now as he had already made a decision. "Like I said, it doesna matter. I've been thinkin' of gettin' meself a new agent anyway."

"No you weren't," Madison said. She couldn't believe how cavalier he was being about this.

"Aye I was," He looked down a her and smiled "I didna tell ye?"

"No." She was exasperated.

"Oh, well I meant ta. So...." He clapped his hands together and started opening cabinets "what would ye both care ta ha fer yer breakfast?"

"Pants." Donny chuckled.

"Wha?" they all stood still as Ian finally looked down at his attire and realized he was still wearing the now sagging wet towel. "Oh." He grinned. "Aye. Good idea." He bussed Madison her on the lips as he breezed past her heading for the stairs.

"By the by, laddie, how did ye get in here wi'oot alertin' the press?" Donny followed behind to the bottom of the stairs.

"Maddy gave me a set o keys some months ago." Ian called from the bedroom. He came to the top of the steps while zipping his jeans." I ha the car drop me a couple o streets away and walked ta the back yard, and leaped over the fence 'in a single bound' like we movie heroes tend ta do," he said as he made an exaggerated display of sucking in his stomach while puffing out his furry chest. "Then I snuck inta the garage through the back service door like a snake." He chuckled.

"Did ye call fer a cab at the airport, then?"

"Nay. We big screen heroes always travel in Limos."

Ten minutes later, Donny watched in awe, as his brother made his way around the kitchen preparing what promised to be a magnificent breakfast. Madison couldn't dismiss from her mind what Ian had said about Victoria. Dumbfounded by his announcement. But rather than pursuing the issue, she decided to set the dining room table, and get a load of laundry together. The agent issue was something they could talk about later.

While Madison was out of the room, Donny took the opportunity to ask his little brother what the real reason for his sudden appearance in the States was.

"Before I answer, I ha a question o me own." Donny nodded and Ian continued. "How has Maddy been feelin' o late?"

"She's been upset and nervous! Wha' did ye think?"

"Nay, I ken that. I mean, *physically*." Ian wanted to come right out and ask if his brother thought Maddy might be with a child, but it seemed like a betrayal to discuss such a personal matter behind her back.

Donny thought for a moment then answered, "Aye she hasna been feelin' quite the thing lately. She's no' been able ta keep her meals doon. And she hasna been eatin' much other than some kind o watery soup. I asked her aboot it once, but she thinks it's nerves." He looked at his brother and his original concern returned in force "Are ye thinkin' there might be something wrong wi her then?"

"Agatha says Maddy's wi child." To Ian's surprise Donny had no reaction to the information.

"I thought so meself, but when I asked her if tha might be the cause o her troubles, she told me she was unable."

"Aye," Ian agreed, "She told me the same thing a long time ago. And I told Agatha she was wrong, but Agatha said I was a damned fool and she is ne're wrong."

Donny chuckled. In his mind, he could just hear Agatha Stuart telling Ian what a damned fool she thought he was. "Are ye plannin' ta tell yer lass aboot it?"

"Who Madison?"

"No, the Queen Mum." Donny said sarcastically "Aye, who do ye think?"

"I do'na know." Ian sat down heavily on a stool by the counter. "I would like ta, but I dinna know how. It's a verra difficult subject fer Maddy. She wants a wee babe sa badly, but the doctors say no. I dinna want ta cause her more pain. Mayhap ta get her hopes in the air ta be crushed." Ian was quiet for a moment. "Wha do ye think?"

Donny was honored that Ian would ask him for his opinion where his personal life was concerned. "I dinna ken either, but ye might start by askin' the lass ta wed ye."

Without saying a word Ian reached into his pocket and pulled out a small box embroidered in the Mackay tartan and handed it over to his brother. Donny opened the box and winking back at him from inside was a ring with a large emerald cut diamond nestled between perfect baguettes on either side of the main stone. Donny looked at Ian.

"I bought it when I was in New York ta finish shootin' the picture. I knew then tha I dinna want ta live wi' oot her. Unfortunately, there's no been a good time ta pop the question." Ian took the ring box back and slid it into his pocket. "And now I'm afraid she'll think the only reason I'm askin' is because o the babe."

The room was quite for several minutes before Donny spoke. "Aye. It's a tough dilemma, and I'm no the one ta be givin' advice. Our mam is the one who would know wha' the answer is fer ye, laddie." He looked at Ian and felt he'd somehow let his brother down. "Ask the lass ta wed wi ye, lad, and worry aboot the bairn after." He advised resting his hand on Ian's shoulder.

Over the next few days the three of them rattled around in the house together. Madison worked from her computer, but rested and slept a good deal of the time. Donny finished up paperwork that filled his briefcase and made several calls to his FBI contacts. Ian followed through with his plan for a new agent and made several phone calls of his own. The days were restful and relaxed for all of them. Ian took on the role of chef and the evening meals were a joy for all three. Donny and Ian regaled Madison with stories of their childhood. Brother against brother and brothers banded together against an outsider. Madison was enthralled with the stories of the MacKay family. And once again wished that she had siblings with whom she could share a past.

The media, who at first continued to camp outside Madison's house and her office, finally began to dwindle, and then disappeared completely at the first sign of the next big story, when they scrambled off to harass some other victim. On Monday morning when Madison backed her Wagoneer out of the garage, she was relieved to find her yard empty and the tree lined street, quiet. She went to work every morning and returned home in the late afternoon to Ian and Donny. They shared Ian's gourmet dinners and then she and Ian retired to Maddy's bedroom, which became their private sanctuary.

Samuel wanted Madison to go back to Scotland in a month's time to pick up in the office where she left off. He was interested in expansion and wanted Madison to start making inquiries in that direction.

Madison of course was delighted at the prospect of going back. Even though she had Ian with her, she missed the home they shared and the office she had spent so much time and love building. She was also becoming very home sick for the people she had become so close to, and who she had come to think of as her small family.

Donny announced at dinner one evening that he would be leaving in three days for a new assignment. He couldn't give Ian or Madison any details about the job or even tell them where he was going, which made the separation harder. No one knew the particulars of Donny's work, but since the involvement with Adam Gilmore, they all knew his job could be dangerous. However Donny seemed to like his work and he was eager to get started on the new assignment.

Three days later Donny left, and Ian and Madison had the townhouse to themselves. Madison continued to have trouble keeping her meals down and despite Ian's pleas, refused to see the doctor.

"Maddy luv, how long has this been goin' on?" Ian asked

"Not long." She shrugged "I think it's a combination of the travel. Getting the Lusta office set up. Then of course there was Adam and then the media blitz. A lot of stress in a short period of time." She looked into Ian's worried face and smiled "Don't worry. Soon everything will go back to normal, and I'll be fine." She picked up her purse and briefcase and headed to the door for the drive into the city and her office. They gave each other a hug and she got in her car and backed down the driveway. Within a few seconds, she slammed on the brakes, threw the gear selector into park, leaped out of the door and raced into the house heading for the bathroom. When she came out of the downstairs powder room, she looked weak and drawn. Ian was leaning against the counter holding a bag of soda crackers. Neither of them spoke. Madison smiled at him wanly and took the bag of crackers as she headed back out to her car.

On her drive into Center City, she went through her mental rolodex of everything she wanted to get accomplished during the day. When she reached the office she parked in her reserved spot a few steps from the elevator. On the ride up to her floor she went over everything she had been through the past few months and wondered if she was indeed due for a break. As the doors opened to her floor she was surprised to see Samuel standing there.

"Samuel." she smiled "Going down?"

"Nope." His smile was broad and warming "I'll walk you to your office." He took her by the arm and led her through the outer maze of desks and cubicles.

Once inside her office Madison took her things to her desk and turned her attention back to Samuel. "Okay, what's up?"

Samuel laughed and sat down on the sofa. He motioned for her to join him. "You have done an excellent job with the Lusta office, Madison. I realize we spoke briefly of this earlier in the month, but as you know, over the last week or so, we've had a number of inquiries come in from other council areas in Scotland concerning interest in additional hospice offices.

"I'm thinking the time is right for expansion, and I think you're the one to head this kind of project. So, when you get back to the Lusta office, I'd like you to begin looking into other council areas. You have the list of those interested that's being updated on a daily basis. I'd like for you to get started on that as soon as possible. And of course with the added responsibilities, I was thinking you would need a new title to go with the position. How does 'Chief Executive Officer of European Operations' strike you?" Madison was stunned. She didn't know what to say and just stared at him. "Don't stew, girlie. You don't have to answer now. Give it some thought. Talk it over with your young man" He got up and walked to the door, but before leaving, he turned to her. "I knew you'd go a long way when you hired on here fifteen years ago." And with that, he went out of her office and closed the door behind him.

"Holy shit!" Madison breathed. She didn't doubt she could do the job, but it was a huge responsibility. "'European Operations'" she repeated, then clamped her hand to her mouth and dashed to the bathroom. When she emerged from her bathroom, weak and drained, she poured a cup and hot water from the hot pot on the credenza and dipped an herbal tea bag into the cup.

For the rest of the day Madison worked at her desk, making phone calls and clearing up details in preparation for her return to Lusta. At three thirty in the afternoon, she noted the time on her computer. Her stomach seemed to be under control, and since she hadn't eaten all day, she grabbed her purse, told Margaret she would be back in a half an hour, and went to the café in the building. She ordered soup and ginger ale and a coke for Margaret, "to go", deciding to return to her desk, and work while she ate. *Not that I would be able to keep anything down,* she thought.

On the ride up in the elevator, she thought about Lizzy and Patrick. She missed them and wondered how their relationship was progressing. "If I haven't been able to shake this bug by the time I get back, I'll go see Patrick." She mused aloud.

Margaret wasn't at her desk when Madison reached her office, so she set the soda near Margaret's calendar and went through her door. The sight of Ian sitting behind her desk with his feet propped up greeted her when she walked though the door.

"Ian!" she grinned

"I came ta see ye luv," he stood and crossed the room to her "Are ye surprised?"

"Yes, and what a lovely surprise!" Ian leaned down and took her mouth with his ever so tenderly. Madison felt her knees turn to rubber, and pulled away from Ian's lips. "Let me put this down before I drop it."

"Well lass," Ian stroked an imaginary mustache and leered at her "I no realized I was tha good a kisser."

Madison reached up and patted his cheek. "*Dinna let it go ta yer head, Laddie.* The cup is hot." She walked to her desk and set the Styrofoam cup by the phone along with her can of soda.

"Wha ha' ye got there?" he inquired although he knew exactly what it was.

"Just a little chicken soup. I've been so busy all day and haven't had time to..." but she caught the expression Ian's face. "Yes, yes. I know. And if I haven't shaken this bug by the time we get home, I'll go see Patrick when we get back."

"Aye. Tis a good plan. And I can see ye've given the situation a great deal o forethought. T'would be a verra pleasant fifteen hour flight fer ye; makin' yer way up the aisle o the plane ta toss yer cookies in the vibratin' chemical toilet."

Madison opened her mouth to speak, but couldn't come up with a worthy response. So she said nothing. When she looked back toward the container of soup, she noticed a small box embroidered in Mackay Tartan resting in the middle of her desk. "What's this?" she asked and crossed to stand behind her desk

Ian walked closer "Open it." Heart beating in his throat, he'd never been so nervous as he watched Madison pick up the delicate box and gingerly opened the lid.

Her eyes brimmed with instant tears, and she sat down in her chair before her knees let her down completely. She looked at the brilliant stone and then back to Ian. His eyes locked with hers as he stepped around the desk and knelt beside her chair. Resting his hands on the chair arms, he swiveled her chair toward him.

"Madison Danaher," his voice welled with emotion "I think I ha' luved ye since the moment I saw ye standing on me beach. Ye walked inta me life wi yer cat and yer bonnie smile and yer winnin' ways. I do'na want me life if I ca'na have ye in it. I ne'er want ta be wi'oot ye." He lifted his hand to wipe the rolling tears from her cheek. "Will ye do me the honor of becomin me wife, lassie?" He looked into her eyes and they were as bright as the stone he had given her. She stared at him but remained silent. "This is where ye say yea or nay, Luv."

"Oh," she sniffled. Cushioning his face between her hands and she brought her lips to his. "Yes," she whispered. "Yes". She then drew back and looked into his eyes again. "Yes" she repeated. Ian stood, pulling her up with him. He encircled her with his arms, and took her mouth again with a building need that he knew would have to be postponed until later.

"Besides," he broke the kiss. "Ye've already bed me. It's only right tha ye make me an honest man and wed me!" he laughed, and without warning, scooped her up in his arms and twirled around the room. Remembering her weak stomach he stopped and placed her on her feet. Taking the ring from her, he slid it on her finger, then turned her hand over and pressed his lips to her palm. "Lets go home, Luv."

"I don't know if I can wait til we get to Lusta." She giggled.

"Home for me is where er're ye are." Ian breathed as he pressed his lips to hers again. He held her in his arms for a long embrace until their breathing returned to normal. Then they turned out the lights to her office and walked arm in arm to the elevator.

Chapter Thirty-Three

Madison and Ian especially enjoyed their privacy that evening. The townhouse was quiet with just the two of them. Ian prepared a delicious dinner, and they ate side by side at the table in the dining room. While they ate, Madison related Samuel's plans for her.

"And will this promotion no' create more work fer ye?" Ian asked. He couldn't help thinking of the baby she might be carrying.

"Well, yes. It will. It would also mean I would have to travel some. Mainly around Scotland, but that would be in addition to the regular trips back to Philly too." She mused. She seemed to be thinking out loud rather than explaining the new responsibilities to Ian. "I suppose in time, I could staff-out some of the travel and the workload, but in the beginning, I'm afraid most of it would be on my shoulders...," her voice trailed quietly.

"Aye. 'Tis quite a promotion he's offerin' ye. A CEO ye'd be. O European Operations. Ye're good at yer job, Maddy girl. I'm proud o ye." He smiled. "And will ye make Lusta yer headquarters, then?"

"What?" Madison took her eyes from her plate and looked up at Ian. "What did you say?"

"I said, darlin', tha' I was verra proud o ye."

"Oh! Thank you. It's been quite a ride, these past fifteen years."

"Ye worked fer the company while ye went ta school did ye no'?"

"Yes. I went to work for them when I was nineteen."

"Ha ye done much travelin' over the years, then?"

"Some. Not a great deal." Madison was silent for a few minutes. "When I suggested we open an office in Scotland, I never dreamed Samuel would send me to get the office started." She smiled at the memory. "I was flattered with the responsibility and thrilled at the prospect of going. It's one of the countries I've always wanted to visit but never had the time."

"And why did ye choose Scotland fer yer first overseas venture."

"I've read a great deal about the country over the years. Medical care is excellent. It's mostly rural, and the hospice concept is perfect in rural areas."

"I'm glad ye came, lass." Ian smiled and reached for her hand. Madison looked from her plate into Ian's green eyes.

"Oh, so am I! Who knew I'd meet my knight in shining armor." She grinned.

"Sometimes me armor isna wha' it should be," he said, and they both laughed. "Have ye given any thought ta the kind o weddin' ceremony ye'd like ta ha? And do ye wish ta be married here where yer friends can attend the festivities?"

"No. I haven't thought about it. After all, I've only been engaged a few hours. But as long as you brought it up, Ian," she said, nudging away from her plate, pulled one leg up underneath her bottom and turned to face him. "I'd like to be married in Lusta. I have so few close friends and no family. You've become my family. You and Agatha and Lizzy and Patrick and your brothers and Sara." Suddenly Madison's face paled and her eyes widened. "Ian, I've never met your mother or your sisters! What if they don't like me? What if they would want you to marry some lovely Scottish girl? Does your mother even know you're interested in me?" Then her pale face became a mask of horror. "What will she think when she learns I can't even cook?"

Ian's expression was pure joy as he gazed at the woman sitting next to him. "So ye wish ta be married in the Highlands, lass?"

"Ian!"

"Maddy, luv. I've nay doubt the first question they'll be askin' is why ye would even be wantin' me in the first place! And then they'll give ye a list of reasons why ye shouldna." He squeezed her hand gently when the look of near fear remained in her eyes. "Ye're no marrin' me mother or me sisters and brothers. Ye'll be wed ta me." Madison opened her mouth to speak, but Ian pressed his finger to her lips. "First, me mam will luv ye on sight. Mam has the gift, she'll see right off tha ye're a keeper, and will fall in luv as soon as she claps eyes on ye. Me sisters will nay doubt be overjoyed ta ha an audience fer all the tales they'll be wantin' ta tell aboot me. Second, what parent would no' be happy when her son brings home a 'nice Irish Catholic' girl? I just wish me da was still alive ta meet ye. Third, me mam can teach ye anything ye've a wish ta learn in the way o cookin' and would nay doubt enjoy the teachin' no end. Gives her a chance ta show off. Fourth, Mam and Sara are verra close. Sara is like mam's own daughter, and she's English! And finally, Aye, they all know I'm interested in ye. Like as no, by now they know more aboot us than we do."

Madison looked down at their joined hands on the tabletop. "Parents want grandchildren, Ian," she whispered.

"When we're ready, lass, we'll give her grandchildren."

"Ian, I—"

"When ye're ready, we'll adopt them. We'll buy them. If we ha ta. We'll buy a dozen of them!" he laughed. "We'll keep me mam sae snowed under wi bairns, she'll ha ta build another house ta keep us all at Yuletide." He reached up and wiped a tear that dripped onto her cheek. "We'll ha a babe, Maddy. As many as ye want. And we'll spoil them and paddle them, and dress them and worry aboot them and yell at them. And they'll be ours, because we'll luv them. Do'na worry aboot that."

"Yeah," Madison sniffed. "We'll have so many, I'll scream to get out of the house, just to have ten minutes of peace and quiet." Madison smiled.

"Aye, lass," Ian whispered before he leaned over and pressed his lips to hers.

Later that night as Ian slept soundly beside her, Madison lay awake thinking about the new job and all the responsibilities that went with it. *A lot of travel,* she thought. It wasn't so much the travel around Scotland that she thought about. She would have to make regular trips back to Philly to keep up with the offices in the United States. Board meetings. Marketing meetings. Staff meetings. She wondered if she would spend as much time in Lusta with Ian as she spent on planes and in the car. She wanted the job. She wanted the promotion, but how could she handle the commute and still find time to be with Ian. And children! She wanted a family almost as much as she wanted Ian. A family of her own, and to make her little family part of the larger one. How could she do all of that. She sighed and took a steadying breath. *I guess I'm like all the other career-oriented women I have ever read about,* she smiled to herself. *I want it all. A home, a family, a husband, and the career with a title.* Her decision made, she snuggled closer to Ian and closed her eyes.

As Madison sat behind her desk early the next morning, she wondered how she was going to break the news to Samuel. She didn't want a half-life, if she and Ian were going to make a successful marriage, changes would have to be made. She loved Ian and she loved Scotland. She wondered if Samuel would accept her decision. He had been very good to her over the years. He had confidence in her and she had never let him down before. *Will he think of this as a betrayal?* she asked herself, and like magic, there was a knock on the door and Samuel strolled in.

"Hello." Madison smiled. She watched as he came through the door and moved toward the seating area in the center of Madison's office. Settling himself in one of the wing-backed chairs, he motioned for Madison to join him. "Samuel," Madison started as she sat on the sofa across from her boss and friend. "I have something I would like to discuss with you."

Samuel smiled and nodded his head, giving her his full attention.

"Well…." She cleared her throat. "I was wondering how you would feel about a transfer?" She held her breath and watched as he appeared to mull the idea over in his mind.

"No." He smiled. "I like it here. I think I would rather stay."

"What?" Baffled Madison shook her head. "No, I meant me. How would you feel about a transfer for me?"

"Oh well, I would miss having you in the office every day, but if you feel you need a change, I think it's a fine idea. Now, let me think." He rested his chin in his hand and thought for a moment. "How about one of the California offices? They're nice and most of them are fairly large." He looked at Madison's confused expression and tried again. "No, huh? Okay how about one of the Texas offices. The weather is rather hot in summer, but not much snow during the winter months."

"Um no, Samuel, that's not what I had in mind," Madison stammered. "I was hoping I could transfer to the Lusta office permanently."

"Oh." Samuel was laughing inside and was exceedingly proud of himself for being able to keep it from showing. He knew that his Madison would eventually want to live in Scotland. *After all*, he thought, *that's where her husband would be.* Mustn't say *that* out loud, he cautioned himself. He was pleased about her relationship with the handsome Scot, it had been a long time since he had seen her so happy. However, the realization that she would no longer be here within arm's reach, made him feel a little bereft. Here was a young woman he had thought of as a daughter for so many years, and now he was faced with the prospect of losing her. Not just to a man, but to a country. *There's really no decision here*, he thought to himself as he looked into her face. *It's time to let her go.* "You want to live in Scotland, then? Well, I guess

I shouldn't be surprised. You're going to live there with your young man?"

"Samuel, I'm going to do more than live there with him. I want you to be the first to know." He watched as her smile grew from ear to ear, pure joy beamed in her eyes. It warmed his heart to see her so happy "Ian and I are going to be married." Samuel clapped his hands together and stood to take her in is arms for a fatherly embrace. They stood for a long while until Samuel finally broke free and sat down on the sofa with Madison beside him.

"Well, well!" he laughed as he took both of her hands between his. "Maddy, I'm happy for you both. This is wonderful news! Yes it is! You must come to the house and bring your young man, so Angie can meet him. Come and we'll have dinner." He patted her hand and looked into her eyes. "Of course you can transfer to Lusta, when would you like to make the move?"

"Well, Ian wants to leave yesterday." She laughed with relief. "But I told him I had to wait until you could let me go."

"You tell him you can't leave until Angie has had a good look at this eager young buck who wants to take you away from us!" He squeezed her hands again between his and grinned at her. "I'm truly happy for you, girlie. It's been a long difficult road for you at times. You deserve all the happiness you can find." He sniffed and reached into his pocket to draw out a snowy white handkerchief, which he brushed briefly under his nose, then cleared his throat. "Well, we'll be busy working out the logistics for the next couple of days. Until the transfer is a done deal you'll have to come back every few weeks or so."

"Yes. I assumed I would be making several trips back to Philly for a while until things are settled. I'm not going to give up the townhouse or the car. As often as I'll be here, it would make things more comfortable for me."

"I think that's a sound idea. You can always sell it. No hurry to do it now."

Just than Madison's cell phone came alive with the music she had designated for Ian's calls and she ran to the desk to answer it. "Hello Ian. ... I'm with Samuel now. Can I call you back? ... Yes, I told him." Maddy chuckled. "He's delighted. He's very happy for us." She was silent for a few minutes while she listened to Ian. "You want me to do *what* before we leave?!... Oh, Ian, I told you I was going to see Patrick... I realize I've been having an issue... I don't care if I throw up on the plane... No, I have a doc here in Philly. Yeah, see you when I get home. ... Yes." She smiled. "Me too." She tapped end on her phone and looked back to Samuel who was smiling. "Ian wants me to go to the doctor before we leave to make sure there isn't anything seriously wrong with me." She sat back into her desk chair and sighed. "I told him that I was going to see Patrick when we got back." She had to admit it was a good idea, she really didn't relish the idea of putting her face in line with the chemical toilet of the plane mid flight.

Samuel took the cue and rose, moving toward the door. "Well, call your doctor and get the appointment. Come to think of it you haven't had a physical in over three years. You might want to give a copy of the report to Samantha Matthews in Human Resources for your file"

"What?" Madison asked.

"I happen to know she has been bugging you for a new physical for your file and you need to give her one." Samuel smiled and reached for the door handle pausing for a moment to look back at her "How about you and your young man come to the house tonight for dinner?"

"I have a better idea, why don't you and Angie come to my house and Ian can whip us up a big elaborate festive dinner." Samuel nodded his agreement and grinned at her as he left her to make her phone calls.

Madison called her doctor first, fully expecting to wait several days for an appointment, but her doctor had a cancellation the next morning, and Maddy signed up for it. Then she phoned Ian to make sure he was interested in making a celebration dinner for the two couples.

"Aye luv, it'll be nice ta cook fer a crowd." Madison could hear the excitement in Ian's voice. "What time were ye expectin' them ta arrive?"

"You know what, I never asked." Madison giggled "I'll call you back when I talk to Samuel. Oh and Ian, I have an appointment for tomorrow at 9:00 a.m. So if you want to, you can make flight arrangements to go home."

"That's good, lass." Ian let out a breath of relief. "Would ye like me ta go wi ye?" he asked.

"What?"

"Well, it's just tha' ye hav'na been feelin' sae good in the last few weeks. Mayhap there are some medications ye'd ha ta pick up at the pharmacy and I could do tha fer ye while ye trod back ta yer office, if ye feel like goin' back once ye've seen yer physician."

"Oh, yes, well, it's not necessary, but—"

"Ye're me intended now, lass. Ye should get used ta the idea o me lookin' after ye." Ian cut off her refusal. Madison swiveled her chair around to gaze out the window, her eyes beginning to tear at his thoughtfulness. *What in hell is the matter with me? The bad stuff is over, and I couldn't be happier and so what's with all the waterworks?* she thought to herself as she reached for a tissue.

When he completed his explanation, she continued with a goofy smile glued to her kisser. "*But,* if you'd like to come, everything is more pleasant when you're with me."

"Aye!" they both laughed and said their goodbyes.

Madison and Samuel decided on an eight o'clock dinner, and after talking briefly to Ian again, she worked steadily the rest of the day, clearing up as much business as she could before leaving the office. On her way through Philadelphia late that afternoon, her thoughts were of the house in Lusta and how happy she and Ian were there. She thought about her office and all the friends, "Correction," she said aloud—"My

Scots *family!*" She grinned as she turned onto the entrance ramp of I-295. "Life is sweet!" she said.

Madison was so happy she felt she might burst at the seams. She had wanted to call Agatha and Lizzy to let them know about the engagement, but Ian thought it would be more fun to tell everyone at once when they could make the announcement in person. She decided he was right, and she did want to be able to see everyone's faces when the news was broken. She drove the rest of the way back to the townhouse with the windows down and the radio blaring.

Ian spent part of the morning surveying the pantry and freezer to see what he would need to make dinner. "Everything," he chuckled. "Me Lady isna one fer cookin'," he said to Julie who was perched on the counter watching his every move.

Later in the afternoon while he went about the kitchen preparing the celebratory dinner, he was silently congratulating himself on getting Madison to the doctor. *Now she would be told if she is in fact carryin' a babe, and I know she would believe her physician,* he told himself. *It's good tha' I'm goin' wi her. She might be needin' me arm ta catch her if she nearly passes out when the doc tells her the good news.* He heard the garage door open and knew Madison was home. Ian hoisted himself up on the counter and pulled Julie onto his lap while waiting for Madison to enter the house.

As Madison pulled into the garage she had the same urgent feeling to run to the bathroom. *God! What is wrong with me? This "bug" seems to be hanging on forever,* she thought as she pushed the door to her Wagoneer open. She shoved her key into the door to the house and made a beeline for the powder room. Ian watched her race through the door and recognized her destination. He was aware of her embarrassment each time she made this rush to the bathroom, and decided to stay put, allowing her entry into the kitchen to be made without explanations. Soon, he heard water running in the sink and the whine of her electric toothbrush.

"Good thing she'll be goin' te see the doc in the morn, huh?" he murmured to the purring kitty in his lap. The powder room door opened, and Madison emerged. She looked pale and drawn. *"Don't just sit there, ye buffoon,"* he could almost hear Agatha scolding him. *"Get the poor lass some herb tea."*

"Don't look at me like that," Madison said as she rounded the corner and saw Ian and Julie sitting on the counter looking at her with pity. "I'm fine. There's not a damn thing wrong with me. I just can't seem to completely shake this bug. It's getting better, though."

"Aye, lass, I can see you're feelin' much better." She and Ian exchanged looks. "Okay, luv," Ian chuckled as he hopped off the counter with Julie now in his arms. "Why don't ye take a lie down on the sofa fer a bit and I'll bring ye a cuppa tea?"

"Good idea," Maddy mumbled and headed to the living room sofa.

"When is yer appointment?" he called while he poured fresh tea into a mug and went to stand behind the sofa where Madison was sitting with her head resting on the back of the seat. He handed over the mug and kissed Madison on the forehead.

"Tomorrow morning at nine." She rested her free hand on Julie's back when the cat leaped onto the sofa and curled next to Madison. "So *Master Chef*, what's on the menu for tonight?"

Ian puffed up his chest with pride. "I thought we'd start wi' a Caesar salad. Then, Aberdeen Steak with mushrooms in a burgundy wine sauce. Fer dessert: Key Lime Pie."

Madison winced at the very thought of food in any form, but shifted her weight and tried to look up at Ian. "That sounds wonderful, but there's only one problem."

"What?" he could guess that anything edible was not at the top of her priority list at the moment.

"I don't think you can get Aberdeen Steak here in the States."

"Oh, well, aye. At least no' at the market ye've got here, but that's okay. I purchased filet mignon instead. The pieces willna be as big, but the taste will be just as fascinating."

"You've already done your shopping?" Madison sighed in relief.

"Aye, luv. I figured ye'd want ta relax a wee bit when ye got home. Drink yer tea. Mayhap ye'd like ta go up and stretch oot on the bed a while before it's time fer the guests ta arrive."

Madison started to assure Ian that she was fine and didn't need to rest, but she had to admit even to herself that she was drop-dead tired. She smiled gratefully at Ian, took her mug, and went up to the bedroom. Ian stood where he was behind the sofa and watched a weary Madison climb the stairs. "By ten o'clock tomorrow, lass, ye won't be feeling sae bad," he whispered with a grin.

Chapter Thirty-Four

Two hours later Ian went to the bedroom and woke Madison to let her know she had about an hour to get ready for dinner.

"Only an hour?" She shot out of bed and ran to the bathroom to start the shower. "Ian why didn't you wake me up sooner? I'll never be ready in time."

"Donna worry, luv," he said as he sat on the edge of the bed to watch as she ran around the room. "Samuel called and wanted to know how formal tonight would be and I told him 'jeans and a T-shirt.'"

Madison poked her head around the corner and looked at Ian in dismay. "You told the owner of my company and my boss to wear *jeans?*"

"Aye." Ian was amused by Madison's bafflement.

"It's not how I pictured him dressing." *I don't know if I've ever seen Samuel dressed in jeans,* she thought to herself. "It does make the evening much more casual and relaxed, though."

"Precisely." Ian walked to Madison, still standing just inside the bathroom door and kissed her cheek. "Which is why I told him jeans. This should be a relaxed evening wi two couples. It's no' a dinner meeting, luv. So take yer shower and come doon and help me."

"Help you?" Madison's hand froze on the shower faucet. "Ian, you want me to help you cook?"

"Nay, luv, but definitely!" he said as he rubbed his belly. He ducked in time to evade the folded towel Madison threw his way. "I may be a

'*Master Chef*,' but tha' doesna mean I know which side of the plate the napkin goes on." He chuckled and left the room.

A half hour later, Madison came downstairs, and began setting the table. At eight o'clock on the nose, the doorbell rang, and Madison went to receive her guests.

She opened the door and there was Samuel wearing jeans and a blue button-down shirt tucked in. It was the first time Madison could ever remember seeing Samuel this casually dressed. She had seen him in khakis and a polo before, but never jeans. He looked sophisticated and yet, comfortable. Samuel's wife, Angie, was petite at five foot one, thin, and very attractive. She, too, was in her early sixties with casually styled soft silver hair. Angie had gently smiling hazel eyes with flecks of gold. You could always tell when she was distressed with her husband because her eyes went very dark. However, tonight they were bright and sparkled with pleasure. Madison always thought Angie was the spitting image of the fairy-tale grandmother who lived on a farm and baked cookies, but could be equally comfortable in a boardroom wearing a Dior suit.

Madison welcomed them into the house and showed them into the living room. There she made the introductions with Ian.

"Are you the young man who the press was hounding our poor Rosey about?" Angie asked as Madison introduced them.

"Angie," Samuel warned and nudged his wife in the side with his elbow.

"Rosey?" Ian chuckled as he looked at Madison who was so embarrassed she wanted to crawl under the table and disappear.

"My nickname is Rose and Angie has always called me Rosey."

"Oh." Ian smiled and turned his attention back to Angie. "Aye, I'm the one the press was 'houndin' yer Rosey aboot." He took her hand in his and bowed. "And I do apologize fer any inconvenience or stress it may ha' caused ye." As Ian kissed the back of her hand, Angie blushed and lowered her eyes.

"Oh, you're a charmer! No doubt about it." was all she said.

"I'm Samuel," he said as he extended his hand to Ian. "It's a pleasure to finally meet you. And I understand congratulations are in order."

"Aye!" Ian wrapped his arm around Madison's shoulder and drew her close to him. "The lady said yes."

"Rosey, you're absolutely glowing, dear. There's something about you.... Are you doing your hair differently?" Angie asked as she drew Madison with her to the sofa.

"Thank you, Angie, but no, I'm not doing anything different with my hair." Madison chuckled.

"Well, love certainly agrees with you."

"I'm very happy. Can I get you something to drink before we have dinner?"

"I'll have Johnny Walker Red and tonic," Angie answered causally. Still trying to figure out what was different about her Rosey.

"With a twist?" Madison asked as she noticed Ian's wince.

When Angie agreed, she, too, saw Ian's expression. "Don't knock it, until you've tried it, young man. My doctor recommends tonic water for my leg cramps." Then Angie grinned conspiratorially. "And if I flavor it with a little Scotch, we're both satisfied."

Madison laughed and asked Samuel what he would like.

"Red wine," he replied and winked at her as she smiled.

"Ian?" Madison asked.

"I'll have red wine also, luv." Ian turned to Samuel and then looked back to Madison as she walked into the kitchen. "Samuel, would ye excuse me please?" Samuel nodded and took Madison's place on the sofa next to Angie.

Ian followed Madison to the kitchen and began to help with the drinks. When he saw she was going to pour herself the same as Angie, Ian suggested that maybe she should have red wine or plain tonic instead.

"Red wine or *tonic water*?" Madison repeated. "What planet are you on?"

"Well, yer stomach hasna been the best and I donna think Scotch should be your first choice. Water would be better, but I do'na think a *small* glass o red would hurt ye any."

While Madison and Ian were in the kitchen Samuel and Angie talked quietly together in the living room.

"There's something different about our Rosey," Angie stated firmly. "I just can't put my finger on it."

"She's happy." He took her hand in his and smiled. "What else? It's nice to see, and she deserves it. Although, since she's been back, she's had some kind of stomach problem. She's been sick often, and has been eating mostly soup at the office, when she eats at all. I'm glad she's going to see her doctor in the morning. It must be a worry for her young man. But she certainly looks healthy this evening. Must have passed whatever it was."

Ian and Madison returned to the living room with the cocktails. Samuel offered a toast to the happy couple and soon they adjourned to the dining table where Ian served the first course of the meal. The room was full of lively conversation and laughter. Madison was reminded of the evenings she had spent with Ian's brothers and Sara, Agatha, Lizzy, and Patrick.

When Ian served the main course of filet mignon on a bed or sautéed mushroom with a burgundy wine sauce, Samuel's eyes grew large with appreciation.

"My boy, you are a gourmet chef! This looks delicious and smells wonderful!" he said, devouring his plate visually.

Ian and Madison laughed. "Funny story, Ian studied to be a gourmet chef. That's how he got into acting as a career." Madison beamed at Ian.

"You studied to be a gourmet chef and that's how you became a movie actor." Samuel held his fork in midair and looked across the table at Ian. "*That* sounds like the lead-in to an interesting story." He put the fork into his mouth and savored the taste of Ian's culinary talents. "Excellent!" he proclaimed.

Ian and Madison smiled at each other as Ian accepted the compliment. Madison raised her wine glass, and silently toasted Ian.

Angie had been quietly pondering her own thoughts during the conversation and it finally dawned on her what was wrong with Madison, or what was right depending on how you looked at it.

"I'm so happy for you, Rosey." Angie reached over and pressed her hand over Maddy's. "You've got so many beautiful times ahead of you."

"Thank you, Angie." Madison grinned at the older woman. "Life is suddenly so full of promise and exciting experiences."

Angie laughed out loud. "You have no idea, my dear! Truer words were never spoken!" she winked at her husband who turned a pale shade of pink and they all laughed.

"Yes, so many things to look forward to." Samuel smiled at both Ian and Madison.

"What kind of plans have you made for your wedding?" Angie asked. "I'd be happy to help in any way I can."

Madison flashed Angie a wide grin. "We have made some initial plans. Nothing is written in stone yet, but we'd like to be married in Scotland. Ian has a very large family, and it might be a hardship for all of them to get to the States. My side of the guest list is rather small, as you know." She looked from Samuel to Angie. "Would you both be willing to come to Lusta for our wedding?"

"Absolutely!" the older couple said in unison. Madison beamed her pleasure at them.

"Thank you both," she said and then turned her attention to Samuel. "I'd like to ask a favor of you, Samuel."

"Anything, my dear."

Maddy took a deep breath. "It would mean a great deal to me, if you would stand in for Poppy at the wedding."

Samuel had to clear his throat because of emotion welling up in his chest. "I would be truly honored to stand in for your father, and give you away in marriage, Madison."

Madison felt Samuel's emotional pull and equaled it with her own. Her eyes began to well, and Ian reached for her hand, and then raised his glass.

"I think this calls fer a toast," he said. "Ta Maddy and her small but very special American family, and all those we love, now and in the future."

The rest of the evening was festive and comfortable. Madison talked about Ian's house and the Lusta office and the people she had come to care about. They talked about the wedding. Angie offered to go over early to help if Madison needed her. And Madison picked Angie's brain for wedding suggestions.

"It's a little difficult to decide on some issues until you've decided whether you want a church wedding or a less formal ceremony in your home," Angie suggested.

Ian and Samuel talked about the hospice office in Lusta briefly, but Samuel was interested in hearing about Ian's career. Ian told him how he went from gourmet chef to a film career. Samuel was fascinated. By eleven o'clock, Madison was beginning to tire. Angie noticed first and announced that it was time for she and Samuel to leave.

"Samuel, Rosey needs her rest," she said. "It's time to go." She took Madison's hand, and headed toward the door. "Samuel tells me you've not been feeling so well lately. I'm glad you're going to see your doctor tomorrow. I'll be interested to hear what she says. Go to bed now, dear and get your rest." Turning to Ian, she patted his cheek. "You're a fine chef, young man. Dinner was divine! Now take good care of this little girl."

She knows, Ian thought to himself.

After Ian and Maddy waved their goodbyes and closed the door, Ian scooped Maddy up into his arms and headed toward the bedroom.

"To bed, lassie!" he laughed.

"Ian! I may not be able to cook, but I can clean up! We can't just walk away and leave this kind of mess," she protested.

"Nay, luv. Ye get yerself into bed and I'll do the cleanin' up. It'll take me less than five minutes. I've only to rinse the dishes and load them inta the machine. I'll be up before ye get yer hair brushed." And with that, he deposited her inside the bedroom door and hurried down the stairs.

True to his word, he returned to the bedroom while Madison was doing her nightly hair brushing.

He stripped down to his boxers and stretched out on the bed with his hands behind his head on the pillow.

Maddy glanced at his reflection in the mirror. "You look very pleased with yourself." She smiled.

"Aye," he replied. "It was a good day and a better evening. Angie and Samuel care a great deal aboot ye, luv. I'm glad they're goin' ta be part o our weddin'. Come ta bed, *'girlie,'*" he laughed.

Maddy grinned and climbed into bed snuggling beside Ian as he wrapped his arm around her, pulling her close. "Close yer eyes and sleep the sleep o the angels, luv. Tomorrow we start the beginnin' o the rest o our lives tagether."

Chapter Thirty-Five

The next morning Madison and Ian got dressed and headed into Philly. Ian was as jittery as a squirrel on caffeine, and Madison was calm as a lake on a windless day.

"What is the matter with you?" Madison asked after she had seen Ian go through every compartment in the front seat.

"Wha'? Oh, no a thing, luv. Why do ye ask?"

"Because you seem like you're about to hurl yourself right through the windshield!" she laughed. "Relax. I'm fine and Lara will give me a clean bill of health and probably some meds for this flu bug, and then we can go back to the townhouse and get ready for our flight home."

Ian smiled at her while taking a deep cleansing mental breath, deciding to calm himself down before he blew the whole thing. Twenty minutes later, Madison pulled into the parking garage of her building.

"My doctor's office is only a few block away," she explained to Ian. "We can walk. Believe me it will be a lot faster than trying to maneuver a car around the city."

"Aye." Ian nodded as he slid out of his seat in the Wagoneer. Madison was right, the walk wasn't a long one, and with the mild weather, it was a pleasant stroll to her doctor's office. Ian wasn't at all prepared for the types of office buildings doctors preferred in Philly. They were high-rises and what looked like penthouse apartments. *I bet Patrick would luv ta have an office here*, he thought to himself.

As though Madison was reading his mind, she said, "Patrick would hate this." She chuckled at Ian's expression as they made their way through the revolving doors. "'A doctor belongs with his patients,' he always says." Madison laughed. The two of them got in the elevator and she hit the button for the twenty-third floor. "Used to be a gentlemen's agreement in Philly," she continued, "Nobody would put up a building in the city that was taller than William Penn, but I'm not sure anyone pays attention to that now days."

Ian looked at her like she had lost some of her reason. "William Penn must have been a man of significant physical stature." He smiled kindly.

"No, I don't think so…"

"How are you feeling, luv?" Ian asked with nervous concern as he took her hand in his. Madison turned and glanced at the look on Ian's face and burst out laughing.

"There is a statue of Penn on the top of City Hall in Old Town. He was the founder of Philadelphia. And for many years new buildings weren't built any higher than the top of his statue. But I suppose due to the need for office space and the lack of land; office space took precedence." She squeezed his hand. "And I feel just fine. Honestly, right now I feel, pretty good." She smiled. "Whatever this bug was must be passing, finally."

They reached the correct floor and walked directly into the most sterile room Ian had ever seen in his life. The walls, carpet, and furniture were all different shades of white. He stood in the middle of the room while Madison signed herself in, and marveled at all the uninviting furniture and magazines. Madison came back and they both took seats next to each other.

"Not even the pictures on the wall cheer it up," Ian whispered to her. Madison stifled a laugh. Ian was used to Patrick who made everything warm and inviting. They waited for about ten minutes before the nurse invited Maddy down the hall to the exam room.

Madison rose and asked if it was all right if Ian came back with her.

"Of course it is," the older nurse said. "It's nice to see some husbands aren't as bad as mine." Madison and Ian exchanged looks and smiled as they followed the nurse to the exam room. "Have a seat on the table there, dear. Now what is the reason for your visit?" she asked as she strapped on the blood pressure cuff and began to pump all the feeling out of Madison's arm.

"To be honest I was going to wait until I got home and see my doctor, but Ian has made a good point." Madison said, wincing, as it didn't seem the cuff could possibly get any tighter.

"Where are you going? 120/80, perfect!"

"Scotland." Madison smiled

"Oh? I lived there for a spell, didn't care for it much," she said as she scratched in Madison's file. "Are you having any problems or is this routine checkup?"

"I've been battling some sort of bug lately. I can't seem to keep anything down. Although I do feel better today."

"Is there any chance of pregnancy?"

"Nope, 'fraid not," Madison answered.

"Well, I'm sure the doctor will run some tests and have you shipshape in no time. Sit tight and she'll be right in." She winked at Ian, and closed the door behind her.

"Did ye see that?" he whispered to Madison.

"Maybe she's a fan," Maddy whispered back.

"Why are ye whisperin'?" he realized.

"Why are you?" Maddy chuckled.

Madison and Ian sat and looked at the walls and finally Ian stood and walked over to the counter and started looking at all the tools of the trade.

"Ian, what are you doing?" Madison whispered.

"Just lookin'." Ian turned and arched his eyebrow at her. "Why *are* we whispering?"

"I don't have a clue!" she giggled.

"That's what I like to have in my office, happy people!" announced Dr. Lara Michaels as she sailed through the exam room door, followed by her nurse, Jesse. "Well Madison, It has been quite a while, hasn't it?" scolded Dr. Michaels.

"Yes, it has." Madison squirmed then turned to indicate Ian. "Lara, this is my fiancé Ian Mackay."

"Your fiancé! Congratulations to you both. Hello, Ian. It's a pleasure to meet you," she said as she shook hands with Ian and took Maddy's hand with her other. "This *is* exciting news!" She looked more closely at the tall handsome man. "Ian Mackay. I've seen your films, Ian. Count me as a fan!"

"Thank you, Dr. Michaels. I'm happy to meet you also and I appreciate your recognition of my work," Ian said, slipping into his Americanized accent.

"Are wedding plans already in the works?" she asked.

"Yes," the couple said simultaneously. Ian moved nearer to the exam table and slid his arm around Madison's shoulders.

"We haven't set a date yet," Madison said, "but it'll be soon. We're going to be married in Scotland and we'd like to leave in the next few days. But I've been having issues with my stomach and it was decided that I should b e check before flying out of the country. "

"Well I thinks that's wise." Dr. Michaels repeated just as her nurse Jesse handed her Madison's file. "Well lets have a look here." She eyed them both and then opened the folder in her hand. "Okay, you need a physical, and you've been having some nausea." Dr. Michaels mused as she scanned Jesse's notes in Maddy's file. "Let's see. 'No chance of pregnancy,'" she read then closed the file and reached into one of the drawers and handed Madison a plastic cup. "Why don't we get a urine sample to rule out urinary tract infection and start from there."

Madison stepped down from the exam table, taking the cup with her while Lara held open the door. Before going out of the door herself, Lara looked back at Ian and raised her eyebrow. Ian shrugged his shoulders, but the best he could muster was a rather weak grin.

When left alone in the exam room, Ian exhaled a nervous breath. He rubbed his hand through his hair, and then shoved both hands into his back pockets. *Agatha was right,* he chastised himself. *I should ne'er ha kept her suspicions from Madison. This is startin' to get complicated and if she ever finds out that I knew or suspected a babe.... Agatha was right, Ian Mackay, ye're a—.*

Madison returned to the exam room with Dr. Michaels close behind carrying Maddy's file, silencing Ian's inner tirade.

"Your weight is fine, your blood pressure is excellent, ears clean, pulse rate good, everything looks fine. We just need the results from the urine sample, and I can get you out of here." Dr. Michaels went on to semi-lecture Madison on the infrequency of her annual visits, until the nurse came back with the results from the test. The doctor looked over the results and back to Madison. "I thought you said there was no chance of pregnancy?"

"There isn't," Madison said confused.

Hmmm, Lara thought to herself. *This is an interesting dilemma. She looks clueless and he looks like he's about to go in to convulsions.* She looked back to Madison.

"I can't get pregnant."

Here it comes, Ian thought to himself. He could hardly sit in his seat. He wasn't sure now if he was excited or petrified.

"Who told you that?!" Dr. Michaels boomed.

"My old doctor. After the miscarriage." Madison was getting really nervous "Why? What's wrong?"

Dr. Michael's sat down on the bench next to Madison and laid her hand on top of Maddy's. She spoke with the calm gentle voice. "There's nothing wrong with you, sweetie. You're healthy as the proverbial horse." She smiled "But I feel it's only fair to suggest that if you're planning a formal ceremony with an expensive wedding gown, 'soon' *would* be the best course of action, unless you're interested in continuous alterations. You're going to have a baby, Madison."

Ian could hardly sit still. He carefully looked over to Madison to see her reaction to the news. Her face was priceless, she was pale and stunned.

"No," she whispered, "there must be some mistake. I—" Her voice cracked and broke. "I was told I was no longer able to have children." She looked at Ian and tears welled in her eyes.

"Well…." Dr. Michaels stood and took Madison's hands in hers. "I'm sorry you were told that, you shouldn't have been. You have been *able,* more than likely, for years. In the past," she said, moving to sit on her rolling stool and continued to counsel, "when a woman has had some sort of major trauma resulting in a miscarriage, some docs have told the patient she couldn't, or *shouldn't* have children. The idea being that this eliminates emotional distress if the patient tries unsuccessfully to conceive again and creates tremendous joy if she does conceive." She waved her hands briefly in a gesture of dismissal. "But then there are still some docs who consider themselves right up there on the same level as the almighty. Some even higher for that matter. However, I always considered that kind of reasoning ludicrous and even dangerous. Reason being this particular instance.

"I'm so sorry that doc told you what he did. You have thought for years you were unable to have children and I imagine, considered yourself *broken.* I believe a patient deserves to know exactly what their health situations are. In any case in the nine or ten years you've been my patient, I've never found any reason to consider your abilities to conceive in question. Again, I'm sorry you were told otherwise. I wish I had known of this before now. I could have cleared up the misconception a long time ago."

While Lara Michaels spoke to her, Ian had moved to sit beside Madison on the exam table. Dr. Michaels stopped and looked at the couple sitting side by side clasping hands, and her face broke into a huge smile. Three pair of eyes welled with tears and an overwhelming emotion filled room. Lara pulled a box of tissues from the counter and, after taking one herself, she passed it to Ian and Madison.

"Well," she sniffed, "I can only assume from the looks on your faces, that this is happy news for you both?" she asked rather than stated.

"Are you sure there wasn't any kind of mistake?" Madison asked sheepishly.

"No, my dear, no mistake." The doctor smiled., "But let's do an internal exam to see how far along you are." She stood and faced Ian. "Why don't you step out into the waiting room and once the exam is over, the nurse can bring you back in." She handed Madison a gown. "Here, get undressed and put on the gown. I'll be back in a few minutes." Ian followed the doctor and nurse out of the room while Madison began to undress and put on the cotton gown.

Thirty minutes later, Madison was dressed, and she and Ian were sitting across the desk from Dr. Michaels in her office.

"Congratulations! You're about nine weeks along. How does it feel Mom and Dad?" Dr. Michaels smiled.

"Can she fly?" Ian asked.

"Well, not physically, but she can get on a plane if that's what you mean." Both Ian and Madison looked at the doctor and all three of them started to laugh. "Yes, I give you a clean bill of health and you may fly. You'll have to make regular appointments to see either me or another doctor Madison." she warned.

"Oh don't worry about that. I have a wonderful doctor in Scotland." Madison said as she stared dreamy eyed at Ian.

"Oh, yes. You mentioned that you were going to be married there." Then remembering something else, she added, "You're not really far along enough that you need to worry about flying."

"Will Maddy be needin' any pills or vitamins or maybe something fer her stomach?" Hoping there was something that would make the flight easier on her.

"Yes," she smiled and eyed Ian. "Do you come from a large family, Ian?" In her estimation he didn't seem quiet as shocked as Madison did.

"What? Aye. I mean, yes, I do. I have five brothers and two sisters."

"So you're not exactly in the dark about *family* life." Now it was Ian's turn to look more closely at Dr. Michaels.

"Nay." He smiled. "I have a rather large extended family as well, with many good friends of wise intuitive counsel."

"I see." Lara grinned. "You're a fortunate man in many ways."

"Aye," he agreed quietly and relaxed somewhat.

"Well, you better get a move on. You have lots to get done." She looked at Madison. "And pretty soon you won't be allowed to fly." She gave Madison a script for prenatal vitamins and medication to help with the nausea, then sent the new soon-to-be parents on their way.

Chapter Thirty-Six

Madison and Ian walked back to the parking garage, holding hands. Ian could hardly contain his excitement on more than one level. Dr. Michaels must have realized that he at least suspected Madison's pregnancy, but hadn't told her of his suspicions and thankfully wasn't adverse to letting his secret slip by. Ian was relieved by her apparent understanding and also that his and Agatha's suspicions were correct. *A wee babe,* he thought. *Maddy's child, and mine.*

Maddy however seemed to be in a daze, ever since she received the news. *A baby,* she thought. *I'm going to have a baby. Ian's baby, and mine.* She unconsciously pressed her hand gently over her belly. As they approached the car, Madison stopped short.

"Wha's wrong, luv?" Ian asked as he moved back to where she stood.

"Ian, I'm going to be a mother," she breathed, her hand resting on her belly.

"Aye, luv," he answered and drew his fingertips down the side of her cheek.

"And you're going to be a father." She looked up into his eyes.

"Aye, luv." He took a deep breath. "And how do ye feel boot tha'?" he asked.

"Well, I'm stunned," she said as she walked past Ian and toward the car. Ian trailing behind. "Furious, giddy, happy, and I think a little scared."

"How do ye mean furious?" he asked, hoping to God she didn't mean with him. *Although,* he said to himself, *she didna know I suspected it before she learned of it.*

"Well, Lara was right. For years, I *have* thought of myself as broken. I believed I was unable to have children. And yeah, that makes me furious. At myself for not having the balls to question the original doc and at the doc for being such a prick." She stopped and with her hand on the door handle of her Wagoneer, she turned and looked up into Ian's face and her eyes began to well up again. "And now, the anger is so quickly gone because, low and behold I find that not only *can* I have children, but that I *am going* to have children. Yours and mine. It's a lot to take in, Ian, after all these years of sadness and doubt and guilt over what I always felt I could have avoided in some weird way." She glanced toward the elevator. "I should go to work."

Ian placed his hands on her shoulders and turned her to face him. "I dinna know why some physicians are good and some are nay sa good, luv, and I canna deny that I'd like ta get me hands on the one who told ye wha' he did. I'm sorra ye felt broken all these years. Ye shouldna have. Havin' babies is a gift some get and some do'na. Those that ca'na are nay broken. I'm no' a religious man, but I dinna think yer life is meaninless if ye can no' have babes. I feel there are babies out there fer those who really want them. If ye canna have yer own, ye go oot and find them and make them yer own. Everyone's life has meanin' and purpose. We mayna always know what tha purpose is fer a while, but we figure it oot sooner ere later. As fer ye thinkin' there may ha been some way fer ye ta avoid wha' happened ta ye, tha's just plain wrong.

"What could ye ha done ta avoid bein beatin'?! And dinna feel bad aboot bein a wee bit scared. I'm feelin just a bit scared meself, but I've nay doot our parents had the same feelins when they first became pregnant. Me mam always said, it's like 'on the job training and ye're not sure ye've got the right of it until ye've had six or eight wee ones!" He slipped his arms around her and pulled her close to him. "But ye're right aboot one thing, darlin. Ye're goin' ta have our babe. We're no' two anymore. We're three. You, me, and the wee one ye're carryin' wi'in ye. Half you and half me. Half-Scot, half-Irish. Wha' a combination. He'll nay doot have a voice as loud as the devil and a temper ta match!" And he scooped her up in his arms and whirled around with her. "Now, what's this blather aboot going ta work?" He laughed.

"Ian!" Madison laughed. "Put me down! What if someone came down here?"

"And wha' if?" Ian nuzzled her neck. Madison crooned at the heat Ian was generating, then glanced toward the elevator again. She smiled and nibbled at his earlobe.

"We have to make plans for the trip home, get things organized," she whispered into his ear.

"Aye, lass," he moaned. "But tha's no' the way... I'm beginning ta make me own set o plans!"

"Ian, put me *doon*!" she giggled. "Besides, I'd like to tell Samuel the good news. Wanna come with?"

"Aye, I would." He set her on her feet, then bent down and kissed her lips long and soft. "Are ye sure ye're willna be doin' any work while ye're up there?"

"Ian, I'm pregnant not, crippled. Don't baby me." She stopped and looked down at the floor and back to him. "I'm pregnant." She repeated in awe, and then laughed out loud and stated in a strong loud voice that echoed through the cavernous parking garage, "I'm PREGNANT!" She threw her arms around Ian's neck, and he twirled her around a few times before placing her feet firmly on the ground again.

Even though most of the office knew Madison and Ian were an item, it was still a shock to see him walk through the doors, with her. Every now and then there was a small blurb in the newspaper about the two of them and speculation as to whether or not they were still together. The office staff was aware that Ian was in town again, but basically that was all they knew. And when Ian was visiting the office, the younger female staff tended to visit the soda machine in the outer office more often hoping to catch a glimpse of him. So far no announcement had been made as to Madison's new position in the company, but rumors were circulating at a high rate.

They rounded the corner to her office and stopped at Margaret's desk so Maddy could give her assistant a few instructions, then enclosed themselves in Maddy's office. Ian relaxed on the love seat and Madison sat behind her desk. Margaret checked flights and reported dates and times while Madison checked her calendar and made notes of appointments and meetings to clear up her schedule. Forty-five minutes later there was a knock on the door and Samuel walked in.

"It's good to see you again, my boy," he said as he shook Ian's hand, then turned to Madison. "Well, how are we feeling this morning?" Samuel asked as he took one of the chairs across from Madison's desk, while Ian sat in the other one.

"*We* are feeling good. I have a good bill of health from the doctor, and I can fly back home now. I have emailed a copy of the physical report to HR. Everything is wonderful, just couldn't be better." She smiled and leaned back in her chair.

Samuel knew there was more to the story for a number of reasons. One, Angie had confided in him her suspicions that Madison was pregnant. Secondly, Maddy was beaming. She appeared to be supremely happy and bursting with information, she obviously couldn't wait to share. He leaned forward "Spill it, girlie."

Madison was excited and had looked forward to telling Samuel the good news. Now, suddenly she felt almost awkward and shy and wasn't quite sure what to say. She looked to Ian for help. Seeing her discomfort, but knowing that Madison wanted to be the one to tell Samuel about the baby, Ian walked over to her and took her hand in his. They both stood and faced Samuel.

"We have had some verra good news," Ian said slowly.

"I'm pregnant!" Madison blurted out.

Samuel fell back into his chair and his eyes began to puddle up. Madison's awkwardness became concern immediately as she broke from Ian making a beeline for Samuel.

"Are you alright?" Madison questioned.

"Alright?" Samuel choked. "I'm better than 'alright! I'm delighted! I am so happy for you." He looked up to Ian. "Both." He took hold of each of Madison's hands. "I'm so very happy for you both," he said gently to Madison.

"Thank you, Samuel," she whispered.

"I'm wondering...." He hesitated a second then went on. "Since your father is gone and you have no family of your own... would you allow Angie and I to think of your child as our grandchild?"

Madison grinned and the tears dripped onto her blouse as she looked around to Ian.

"We would be honored ta ha ye be grandparents ta this child," he said, smiling broadly, "and ta the other eleven ta follow him!"

The three sat and talked for a little longer; then Samuel rose from his chair saying he must call Angie to give her this wonderful news. He shook Ian's hand, congratulating him again and reached for Maddy's hand. "Life is going to change for you now, girlie! The best of it starts from this hour on. And it will only get better. You've been waiting a long time. Enjoy every millisecond." He squeezed her hand slightly and left Madison and Ian alone.

Ian took a handkerchief from his pocket and blotted Madison's eyes and cheeks, then wrapped her in his arms. "I would have ta guess tha' Samuel is pleased wi our news." He grinned. "Now give me the medication papers yer physician wrote fer ye and I'll ha them filled while ye wrap up yer business here." He planted a kiss on the top of her head and was out the door.

When Ian came back from the pharmacy Madison was still working.

"Time ta go, luv," Ian cooed. "Ye've been here fer almost two hours. Tha's long enough. We ha only the rest o today and tomorrow ta pack sae we can make our flight Wednesday morn." Madison smiled and rolled her eyes as she followed Ian's suggestion and cleared off her desk.

They stopped by Samuel's office to say goodbye.

"You take very good care of yourself, girlie," Samuel said as he held Madison in a long embrace. "Make sure to call when you land and let us know when the wedding will be so we can make our flight arrangements." They hugged again and then Madison and Ian left. Samuel watched the door close behind the younger couple with "their whole lives stretched out before them. Marriage, children, a family of her own for Maddy-girl," he breathed aloud. "Good for them!" He turned to reach for the phone and then changed his mind. Instead, he took his suit jacket from the closet, turned out the light as he sailed through the door, told his assistant he was taking the rest of the day off, and went home to be with his wife.

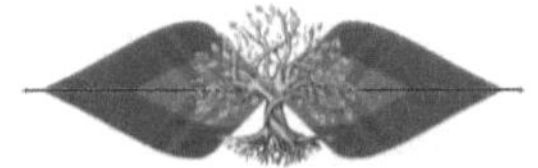

Madison and Ian spent the rest of that day packing and closing the townhouse for what looked to be a very long time. Julie, now all too familiar with the signs of a trip on the horizon, was forever under Madison's feet and getting tripped on in the process. Ian, fearful that Madison might fall, suggested they lock the cat in the bathroom. However, Madison told him, no. She placed Julie on the bed and sat with her until the cat lay down and went to sleep. At six o'clock, Ian announced they had finished for the day and it was time to eat dinner and relax.

"But we have so much more to do!" Madison stewed.

"Aye, and we ha all day tomorrow ta finish." He took the clothing items she was holding and placed them in her open bag on the bed, zipped it shut, and then set it on the floor. "It's time ta ha' a meal now and fer ye ta get off yer feet fer the rest o the evening." At Madison's expression, Ian held up both hands in semi-surrender. "I'm no babyin' ye, luv. I realize ye're no crippled, only pregnant." He grinned. "But there's nay use in gettin' yerself all tuckered oot either. We ha tomorrow ta finish and it's been an exhaustin' day fer both o us. Besides, Herbie's hungry!" he said, rubbing his flat belly.

Madison laughed, unable to resist his logic or "Herbie's" need.

They changed into their pj's and sat in front of the TV. Ian suggested delivery from her local pizza parlor, and Madison had to admit, she was starving, and in reality she was ready to sit and relax. So they ordered a large with mushrooms, onion, green peppers, pepperoni, sausage, and broccoli on half, and plain cheese on the other. The order nearly made Ian sick to repeat over the phone.

"Good God!" he groaned when he finished making the order. "I dinna know how ye're goin' ta look at tha mess, le alone eat it."

"I'll loan you one of my nausea pills if you need it."

When the pizza came, Madison and Ian sat on the sofa and watched old movies while curled in each other's arms. Both of their cell phones rang but neither was answered. They decided that night was for them and whoever called would call back, or leave a message.

Much later, Ian looked down to see Madison had fallen asleep. He turned off the TV and very gently so as not to wake her, carried her to the bedroom and gingerly put her under the covers. When he was satisfied she would not wake, he went back down to the living room. Two remaining slices of pizza sat in the box. He collected the pizza box, glasses and napkins and went to the kitchen.

Sitting down on a stool at the counter, he put in a call to Agatha. While he waited for her to answer he took a bite of Madison's disgusting pizza. *Hmm, this isna quite as bad as it looks,* he thought. *Good*

God, maybe I'm pregnant too! And with that, he dropped the slice into the box and tossed the box in the trash.

"I've go dough risin' and it's just aboot ready ta slip inta the oven," Agatha said when she picked up the call. "This better be important!"

"Agatha, hello." Ian chuckled. Some things and people never change.

"Well! Ian, laddie! Are ye home, then?"

"No, Agatha. We're still in Philadelphia, but tha's wha I phoned ta tell ye. We're leavin' here day after tomorrow and—"

"And did ye tell the lass she's wi child? She dinna figure it oot before ye arrived, did she? Ye did tell her, did ye no?"

"Agatha. Will ye pu-a-lid on it and let me say wha' I called ye ta say?!"

"Aye, lad. Ye do'na need ta get yer panties in a twist."

"I dinna tell Maddy tha' ye suspected she was wi child. I thought it best ta figure the lay of things fer a day or so first. We've been ta see her physician this morn, though, and it's as ye said. We're goin' ta have a wee babe."

"Well, I already told ye tha', Ian laddie. Ye dinna need ta pay a physician ta learn it."

"Agatha!" Ian was fast losing his patience. *Aye, some people and things ne'er change,* he thought. "I donna want ye ta mention the babe. Let Maddy tell ye herself." He warned.

"Are ye telling me ye havena told the lass tha' ye knew she was wi child?" she scolded.

"Nay, I havna told her, and I dinna want ye ta tell her either." Ian's voice lowered. "I will, but I ha ta wait fer the right time."

"I'm sure ye ha yer reasons, laddie," Agatha grumbled, "but it doesna make a lick o sense ta me."

"Well, believe me, I ha ta do this me own way. And if it makes ye feel any the better, I'm beginnin' ta think ye knew the right o it in the first place. I just didna want her ta think... I feared she might think... I wanted ta ask her ta wed me before she knew... I did'na want the babe ta be the only reason ta wed."

For the luv o' God, Agatha thought. *young pups are looney!* "Well, laddie, in me day, it was reason enough, but I suppose I can see the way ye were thinkin." *With everything but yer brain,* she thought silently. "And did ye ask her ta wed wi ye, lad?"

"Aye. I did."

Agatha waited but Ian said nothing more. "Well, are ye planning ta tell me what the lassie said or are ye no?"

Ian laughed for the first time since he had placed the call. "Aye. She said yes, Agatha, ye old darlin'! She said yes, and when we get back home there'll be weddin' plans ta make. I'm sure she'll look ta ye fer help."

"Acourse, I'll help wha'er'er I can."

"Agatha, I have a favor ta ask o ye," Ian continued.

"Anything, laddie." Her voice softened. She knew of Ian's broken engagement years ago and she knew, too, how hurt he had been. Although at the time, Agatha was glad to see the backside of that hellion when she walked away from Ian, she also realized how afraid he might be of losing Madison.

"Can ye talk ta Sara? I want Maddy ta meet the family, but I do'na want her ta be overwhelmed on her first day back home. So can ye ask Sara ta talk ta everyone and see if we might give the lass a couple o' days ta rest up from the trip before the brood bombards her?" Ian took a breath. "I plan ta phone Sara meself in the morn, but if I do'na get the opportunity, if ye can just give her a heads-up, I'd appreciate yer help."

"Verra wise, me laddie. And ye needna phone her at all. She'll be comin ta the shop first thing in the morn. Some o the loaves I ha' risin' are fer her and Thomas. However, I'm thinking ye willna be able ta keep yer mam at bay fer more than a day." She cackled. "She's near ta havin' her bustle in a twist already since ye saw fit no' ta take the lass te meet her afore this."

Aye, Ian thought to himself. Tommy had already mentioned their mother's growing impatience the last time the brothers spoke. "I'll do me best. Luv tea ye, Agatha. See ye soon." Ian hung up the phone and turned out the lights, before heading upstairs to bed.

He wasn't exactly surprised to find the bed vacant when he walked into the bedroom, and because of her stomach upset the last weeks, he looked toward the bathroom first, but it was dark and apparently vacant too. Hoping she had not overheard his conversation with Agatha he looked in the second bedroom and then found her in her office sitting at the computer.

"What are ye doin?" he asked as he walked through the doorway.

"I thought I would email Lizzy and Patrick to let them know I was coming home." She turned to smile up at Ian. "You have no idea how difficult it was not to tell them all of our news, but I want to see their faces when we tell them." *She's glowin',* Ian thought. *She is so beautiful.* All he wanted to do was hug her. *And a few other things,* he chuckled to himself.

"Well ha ye sent yer email then?" he asked.

She looked back to her screen and clicked on her mouse then back to Ian. "Yep." She smiled.

"Good! Now off ta bed wi ye." He waited while she shut down her machine before offering her his hand, then they walked to the bedroom together. Ian was right, it had been an emotionally exhausting day and it didn't take either of them long to fall into a deep restful sleep.

"God damn that bloody clock!" Ian bellowed Wednesday morning, as he raced around the room looking for his other shoe. "The blasted thing was ta go off two hours ago!"

"Here it is," Madison sang out. "It was under the bed." She handed Ian his shoe and gingerly pushed Julie into her carrier. "I don't know why you wanted to get up so freaking early in the first place. We're already packed, the flight doesn't leave until 6:00 a.m. and the car won't be here for another hour."

Ian slipped on his shoe and began to check his carry-on bag to make sure he had Madison's soda crackers and prenatal medications.

"Well, ta be honest, me darlin', it hasna been so easy ta wake ye o late, and I wanted the extra time." He smiled and kissed her on the forehead, then took the bags downstairs. When all the luggage stood waiting by the front door, Ian helped Maddy put clean bedding on the bed and carried Julie's carrier downstairs, then called up to Maddy. "Ye'll check the doors and light timers, will ye no?" he said. "I'll be back in a few minutes." Not wanting to keep any perishables in the house, they had thrown out anything that would spoil. However, knowing that Madison would be hungry, Ian took the Wagoneer to get some breakfast sandwiches from the WAWA down the street. Returning at the same time as the limo, Ian parked the Wagoneer in the garage, locked the house and helped Madison into the car. Madison placed Julie on the seat across from them and cheered when Ian presented her with a WAWA sausage egg and cheese on a croissant.

After their hour ride to Philadelphia International Airport, Ian, Madison, and Julie took their seats in first class section, and waited for the next stage of their lives to begin.

Chapter Thirty-Seven

As a very sleepy Madison stepped off the boarding ramp into the terminal, she was thrilled to see Shawn Conner's sweet old face. *Seeing Shawn at the airport is an integral part of the "coming home" experience,* she thought to herself. Still clutching Julie's carrier, Madison and Ian made their way through the airport until they were finally seated in Shawn Conner's black Rolls Royce. Madison relaxed into the soft leather upholstery and slept most of the drive, while Ian sat and looked out the window wondering how long he would be able to keep his family at bay. He wanted to have a few days at home alone with Maddy before the family got involved, but he knew Agatha was right when she said he wouldn't be able to keep his mam away for very long.

Not realizing that he, too, had drifted off to sleep, Ian was surprised when the car stopped in front of the house.

"Maddy, me darlin'," Ian whispered, when her eyes fluttered open, he continued, "Yer home, lass." He watched her come fully awake and grinned with warming pleasure as her eyes grew wide and bright as she jolted up. She looked through the window to see the house basking in the moonlight.

"Ian," she breathed, "isn't it beautiful? Just sitting there waiting for us. Sort of like an old friend." She was so overjoyed she almost started to cry. Not wanting to wait for Shawn to open the door, Madison clasped the handle and pushed open the door to the car. Ian grabbed Julie's carrier and followed Madison up the walkway toward the front door.

She automatically reaching into her pocket to retrieve the keys she refused to leave behind. Ian noted that she used her own key and not the one kept under that potted plant, *even then, she never planned to stay away.* She had told him as much, but seeing her use her own key finally cemented it into his brain. He watched as Madison walked slowly into the house, suddenly she stopped and looked toward the fireplace and then back to Ian.

"I' home!" She threw up her hands and ran to Ian's embrace. "Home, engaged to be married to the man I love, and pregnant with his child." She looked up into Ian's eyes. "Oh, Ian, I have never been so happy in my life." He bent his head and kissed her softly on the lips.

"I need ta help Shawn wi the bags luv. Why do ye no go and turn on some lights so we do'na trip ov'er ourselves." He handed Madison Julie and he left to help Shawn. She did as he asked and turned on some lights.

As the men were bringing in the last of the luggage, she began to get Julie's water, food, and litter box ready for her. Madison thanked Shawn for picking them up, and he was on his way. She opened Julie's carrier and let her free, they both watched as Julie sniffed the air to make sure it was safe. She apparently remembered the place, for she meowed at the two of them before going after her food and water.

"Do we have to mess with all this tonight?" Madison asked, sighing as she looked at the number of bags in the entryway.

"Nay, luv." Ian took her hand and led her upstairs to the bedroom. "We do'na have to mess wi the luggage tonight." Madison giggled as Ian closed the bedroom door.

The next morning Madison and Ian woke at the same time. While Madison took her shower, Ian brought up the bags. With her shower finished, Ian took his while she began to dress. After the battle of the bathroom was done, they both took their respective bags and began to unpack. Already noticing that they no longer had enough closet space in the master bedroom.

"Well, I'll ha ta expand the upstairs tha's all," Ian said as he looked at the now highly overcrowded closet.

"Oh, Ian, no." She sat on the edge of the bed. "That will change the house. I don't want you to change the house."

"The house will have ta deal wi some changin', luv, wi the wee babe comin." He smiled and walked out to the balcony to survey what needed to be done. "Aye, we can finish the wraparound porch ta come ta the back of the house, then build an extension ta the closet on top of the roof of the porch. Then..." He walked to the doorway of the guest room with Madison following amazed by his sudden jolt of building frenzy. "We can keep this as the guest room after the babe is old enough ta be on his own. Since we'll already ha the extension on the back o the house fer the closet, we can extend tha' ta make another bedroom on the back fer the tike later."

"How would *he* get to the room?" Madison asked warmly.

"We would build another walkway like the one here."

"This all sounds wonderful, but I think we need to get unpacked, eat, and take it from there." She smiled and walked back to the bedroom to finish the unpacking. Even though she didn't want Ian to make any changes to the house, she knew he was right, and they definitely needed more closets. Suddenly she remembered that she had not called Samuel to let him know they were here.

"Do'na worry luv, I called him while ye were sleeping in the car on the way here." He kissed her forehead and made his way down to the kitchen to fix breakfast.

An hour later Madison came down with Julie trailing close behind. Ian was cooking an amazing breakfast and Madison had to admit she was starving. "Humm," she exclaimed, smelling the delicious air in the kitchen. She sat on one of the stools while Ian placed a cup of decaf tea in front of her. "Thank you, but where's my coffee?"

"Nay caffeine, lass, until ye have talked ta Patrick." He smiled and placed a plate of gourmet scrambled eggs, sausage links, sourdough bread, butter, and jam.

"Okay, then give me your phone and I'll call him," she said as she began to glom the food down.

"Nay, we're goin' ta ha a day or so ta ourselves before we go and see friends and family." Ian sat on the other side of the counter and began to eat his meal.

"Ian, I just had a dreadful thought." Ian looked up from his plate at her. "What is your mother going to say when we tell her about the baby?"

Confused Ian thought then admitted, "I do'na know." He paused in thought again before saying, "Maybe 'finally.'" Ian chuckled

"Ian." Madison was getting annoyed. "We're not married."

Now understanding her predicament. "Maddy, darlin', Me mam willna care a lick aboot us nay bein' wed before the babe was conceived. All she'll care aboot is tha' we're gettin' wed and tha' yer gonna give her another grandchild."

"Are you sure?" Madison asked.

"I'm positive." He picked up her hand off the counter and brought her knuckles to his lips. "Now eat yer breakfast." They finished with their breakfast and did up the dishes. Afterwards, they went for a walk around the grounds and Ian showed her everywhere he had plans for expanding the building. They spent the rest of the day curled up on the sofa listening to the radio and talking about their future together. Once the clock chimed five in the evening, Ian made dinner. Madison had been tired, and after they cleaned up the dinner mess, they went to bed for the night. This time, however, Julie was able to get into bed with them.

The next morning no matter what Ian tried, Madison was determined to go to the office and see how everything was.

"I want to see Lizzy and Agatha," Madison explained as she finished putting on her shoes. "Besides, you can tell by my attire I'm not planning on going to *work*." Pointing to her jeans and T-shirt. "I would also like to see Patrick so I can start to have my coffee again." She placed a fast kiss on Ian's lips and sailed out of the bedroom. "Are you coming?" Madison asked from the bottom of the stairs.

"Oh aye." Ian came down to greet her at the stairs and placed a more thoughtful kiss on her lips. "Are ye sure ye wouldna rather stay here and do some other extracurricular activities?" he asked as he began to kiss her neck

"Ian," she breathed, "you're not playing far."

"Aye." He smiled against her neck "I know." He placed another kiss on her lips as he drew her to him in an embrace. "I ne'er play far when I'm faced wi stayin here wi ye or goin' oot ta see people," he said against her lips before dipping to her neck again.

Not wanting to give him the upper hand, Madison did the only thing she could think of. "Ian," she whispered, "when do I get to meet your mother?" Well, that stopped him.

"Me *mother*?" Ian straightened up and looked down at his soon-to-be wife and began to laugh. "Alright, luv, we can go."

"Thank you." Madison smiled and walked toward the door. Before she could grab the door handle Ian's hand was already there.

"But I intend ta finish this later," he promised, his emerald green eyes now very deep with lust and desire. She smiled and Ian opened the door, and they were on their way to the village.

Ian pulled his Wagoneer behind the building and Madison barely waited for the SUV to come to a complete stop before she was out. She walked through the back door and saw Lizzy hard at work at her desk, Patrick not so surprisingly nearby on the phone talking to, she assumed the hospital. Madison could also smell Agatha baking through the door that was always kept open. She had no idea she had missed these people so much. She was home and was thrilled to be so. She took another step forward and wanted to wait until Lizzy was off the phone to make her presence known. However, her cover was blown.

"Danny!" Patrick exclaimed. "I have ta let ye go." He shoved his cell phone in his pocket, raced to Madison and gathered her up in a big brotherly bear hug. "It is so good ta have ye home." Patrick let her go so Lizzy could hug her.

"Oh, Madison, it ha been sae lonely wi oot ye here," Lizzy said as she hugged her.

"Well, tha' doesna say much fer the good doc here," Ian laughed

"Maddy, lass" came Agatha's voice from the doorway of her bakery. Madison smiled and walked to her open arms. "It's good ta ha ye home where ye belong. And yer lookin' wonderful ta boot," she said as she held Madison at arm's length. Ian gave her a warning stare and the older woman winked.

"Thank you." Madison smiled

"She's right, Danny, ye look ta be beamin'. What's the news?" Patrick asked.

"Well...." Madison smiled and walked back to Ian, who wrapped his arms around the front of her. "Ian and I are going to be married." This gave the group a great cry and applause. "There's more." She looked up at Ian to get approval. He nodded and she looked back to her friends and continued. "We're going to have a baby." Well, this brought everyone to the couple, and hugs were being handed out like candy. In the meantime, none of them noticed that the front door had opened and Tommy and Sara walked into the scene.

"What seems ta be happenin' here?" Tommy bellowed and then saw Madison and Ian. "Maddy, me darlin' ye've come home at last." He strode over to her and scooped her up into his arms and kissed her smack on the lips. "How are ye doin' brother?" he asked, looking at Ian.

"I will be fine if ye put her down." Ian smiled. Tommy did so and the two shook hands while Sara and Madison shared hugs.

"So what seems ta be all the excitement?" Tommy asked.

"The're gettin' wed and havin' a wee babe," Agatha blurted out. Ian looked down at her. "Ah, come off it, laddie. I'm happy."

"Would now be a good time to let Madison know about the party?" Sara asked.

"What party?" Madison asked and looked at Ian.

"Well, luv, the rest o the family wants ta meet ye, and we thought tha' a party would be a good time ta meet and announce the engagement."

"When is it?" Madison turned to ask Sara, who seemed to always have the answers.

"Tomorrow afternoon at Evelyn's."

"Tha's me mam," Ian explained.

"Wait, you're going to introduce me to the entire family tomorrow afternoon at a party?"

"Aye," the group said in unison.

"Okay." She smiled and hugged Ian who was relieved.

Everyone huddled around Agatha's butcher-block island with tea and danish while they shared in the small celebration. Ian and Madison filled them in on what happened with the press and what they didn't get from the papers. Madison told them all more about Samuel and how he and Angie were going to come for the wedding. About Samuel giving her away and he and Angie taking the role of grandparents to the baby. They all remarked on not hearing from Donny in a while but they knew they wouldn't unless something bad happened. After the group had their fill of tea and sweets, they all met back at the house and shared a casual meal, that Ian, of course, cooked.

"Nothing fancy Ian, Just burgers and dogs," Madison requested. While cooking, Ian related to Tommy and Patrick his plans to expand the house to make more room for the family. And of course, as brothers do, Tommy had some of his own suggestions. Ian smiled and listened to everything his brother said before there was a knock on the door.

"I'll get it," Madison sang out and opened the door to see Alex on the other side. "Alex!" she exclaimed.

"Maddy Girl!" Alex picked her up and whirled her around.

"I only wish me brothers were as happy ta see me as they seem ta see you." Ian smiled as he walked to the door to greet his brother. "How ye doin', Alex?" Ian extended his hand and Alex yanked him in for a hug.

"Good, littl' brother." Alex released Ian and slapped him on the back before entering the house to join the others. Alex apologized for his wife's absence, but she was off with their mam prepping for the party to introduce Madison to the family. Ian and Madison relayed their news and Alex was thrilled.

"If I had known tha' we would have had e'eryone here tonight we wouldn't have had any need for a party tomorrow," Ian said to Madison as they walked back to the kitchen "I'm sorry we're no' gettin' our night alone, luv," he whispered.

"Oh, Ian, as much as I would want to be alone with you…" She looked into the living room at everyone she knew and loved. People that she had made her own family. "…I wouldn't have passed this up for the world." She smiled and gave Ian's arm a slight squeeze before calling to Patrick to come into the kitchen.

"Patrick, I was wondering if you would be my doctor?" Madison asked.

"I would be honored ta be yer doc." Patrick smiled.

"Good." Madison clapped her hands together, looked at Ian and back to Patrick. "Can I have coffee?"

"Tha's me girl," Ian laughed and gathered her into his arms. "One-track mind she has."

"Donna think it's a good idea to stop cold turkey; however, it would be wise to cut way back until yer no drinkin' any." Seeing the disappointment on Madison's face, Patrick laughed "Sorry ta be the giver a bad news, Danny." Patrick kissed her on the cheek and the trio joined the group in the living room. They enjoyed each other until the sunset and crickets began to sing. Ian noticing the time getting later suggested that they call it an evening. After they said goodbye, Ian and Madison did up all the dishes from the indoor barbecue. Madison looked at the clock.

"Ian, it's after ten o'clock," she said as she sat backwards on the sofa, looking to Ian who was still in the kitchen.

"Aye luv, we should be gettin' ta bed." He turned out the last of the lights and walked to Madison on the sofa, took her hand, and led her to the bedroom. "Remember what I said before we left ta go ta yer office this morn?" he asked as he closed the door and once again Madison giggled.

As Ian drove the Wagoneer over the narrow curving Highland roads, Madison became more and more anxious about meeting his mother. He had tried to reassure her that her fears were groundless.

"No matter what," Ian said, "me mam will love ye." She had heard this ten times if she heard it once in the last few days. And today was no different. "How could she nay luv ye? Ye're a sweet bonnie lass," he stated and reached for her hand.

How does he know what his mother will or will not like? Madison thought to herself. "How many future mothers-in-law have you met for the first time, Ian MacKay?" she muttered.

"Oh? I'd hav ta guess mayhap, at least a couple dozen." He ruminated as he released her hand and rubbed his chin. "Just turn on the charm, lass. It always worked fer me." He laughed, but sensing Madison's discomfort, he recaptured her hand and gave it a loving squeeze. Madison couldn't help an escaping giggle and began to talk herself into a more relaxed state of mind until they turned into the drive of his mother's house.

House, *hell,* Madison thought, *this is an estate!* her mind screamed. The house was a mammoth three-story mullioned-windowed stone structure ruling the landscape at the end of a very long gravel drive. Ian drove the Wagoneer through the tunnel of mature silver birch that bordered on either side of the lane leading up to the house. Madison could see a large property between the breaks in the trees. The deep green manicured lawn seemed to stretch out for miles, and what she could see of the landscaping would put the White House to shame.

The SUV pulled into the circle car park in front of the house, and slowed to a stop. Madison was relieved to see smiling familiar faces waiting to greet them. However, there was a face that she of course did not know. *Oh God,* she thought.

"Tha's me mam.," Ian said, pointing her out. *Be calm,* she said to herself. *She has to be wonderful; she raised Ian, Tommy, Donny, and Alex. She can't be obnoxious or snotty if she produced such wonderful men.* Madison's smile faded slightly. *Unless they got all their values from their father.*

Evelyn MacKay was short in stature, maybe five foot, if that. Her thick silver hair was cut in a stylish bob and almost sparkled in the sunlight. She wore jeans and a flannel shirt that looked to be three sizes too big for her. She stood between Alex and Tommy, creating somewhat of a whimsical picture: this tiny woman between two giants. Maddy's smile returned to full measure. *How in the hell did that woman give birth to those men?* Madison thought to herself. And then the two women locked eyes and Evelyn's face was bathed in a warm, welcoming smile.

Ian turned off the ignition and fairly leaped from the Wagoneer. As Madison opened her door, she watched Ian round the front of the car making a beeline for his mother. He picked her up, whirled her around and placed her back on the ground before bringing her over to meet Madison.

"Mam, this is Madison Danaher." Ian grinned. "Maddy girl, this is me mam, Evelyn Mackay."

"It's nice to finally meet you Mrs. Mackay." Madison extended her hand. Evelyn took it in both of hers.

"No need to botha with the 'missus' stuff. You can call me mom, or *'mam,'* as ma sons do. Or if you would prefer fora now, you can call me Evelyn. That would do as well." Her smile was angelic and her voice; like a song. And she didn't appear to have the strong Scots accent, Madison noticed, but she had an odd mix of accent that was difficult to place. "And it's wonderful to finally meet you too. Ah have been afta Ian for quite a while now to bring you up here." She took Madison into her arms and gave her a warm, inviting hug.

"If I'd known, I would've made the trip sooner." Madison smiled. She was listening for a slight brogue on a couple of words, but didn't hear much. And assumed Evelyn didn't live here year round. *I can't place the accent,* she thought. "You have a beautiful spot here," Madison said.

"Thank you! It was ma husband's family seat. They built tha house hundreds of years ago but tha walls did not faira so well against the winds, and Steven restored it. Come on in, honey, and meet the rest of tha brood." She hooked her arm around Madison's and the pair walked up the massive stone entry steps disappearing through the large Redwood double doors. "Ah hope you'll excuse ma dress mode. Ah had planned to spruce up a bit befora y'all arrived, but once tha clan descended, time got away from me."

Ian and his brothers, each smiling broadly, followed as Evelyn led Madison through to the back of the house.

Walking along beside Ian's mother, Maddy marveled at the old architecture, ceilings were vaulted and covered in the finest carved wood. The floors were gleaming polished stone.

"Back in the day," Evelyn said, "they put straw on the flooras and dried grasses. They had to be changed every day because sometimes tha horses and cows lived in tha house with the family just to help with heatin' in the winta months. Ah don't even want to think what that was like!" she chuckled. Each room was very large and included at least two fireaplaces big enough for a full grown man to stand in. There were tapestries on the walls and paintings of who Madison assumed to be ancestors. She wasn't sure if the building qualified as a mansion or a castle. There seemed to be room after room, tastefully filled with antiques, and wondered if the house was ever going to end. Then suddenly they entered an enormous open space. The two end walls each held a giant fireplace, but the back wall was nothing but floor to ceiling windows.

"This was tha great hall," Evelyn explained. "All official family ceremonies and most of tha meals were held hera. We've held formal balls in this room in mora recent yeas, but it does get drafty in tha winta. Steven did his best, but all this glass and the wind..." The brothers recognized this as nervous chatter, but Madison only noticed the massive group of people milling about on the back terrace and stopped dead in her tracks staring out the windows. *Holy shit!* she thought.

"I apologize for tha horde, ma deah." Evelyn said rather sheepishly. "Ah had no idea thera would be so many people hera. It's not exactly what Ah had planned," Evelyn explained as she drew her arm around Madison's shoulder. "But when word got out that Ian was bringin' his fiancée, everyone and their third cousin came to get a look at you and welcome y'all to tha family." She smiled. "Ah considered tossin' them all out on theira butts," she mused as she eyed the crowd through the windows, "but the Scots are a stubborn people. They'd only break down tha hedges to get back in." She sighed. "In the long run, it's just as well to brave tha clan all at once and get it behind you." She took both of Maddy's hands in hers and gave them a light reassuring squeeze.

Madison smiled weakly and then seemed to pick up on what Evelyn had said earlier. "Fiancée. How did you know Ian and I are getting married?" Madison was stunned.

"Oh, Ah know everything, dahlin. Tha marriage," Evelyn's smile got bigger "The baby. Oh you sweet child, Ah am so happy about tha baby!

You have no idea. Hell, until Tommy and Sara had their little girl, Ah wasn't sure Ah would evea have *any* grandchildren. Now Ah'm gonna have two! This is so excitin!" She hugged Madison again and wrapping her arm around the younger woman's waist, pushed open the doors to the terrace, and urged Maddy forward.

Ian's sisters, Emily and Bridget were the first to greet Madison as she stepped through the glass doors with Evelyn. Emily was a younger copy of her mother, petite and pretty with delicate features, and the same inviting smile. She welcomed Maddy to the family with a generous hug. Bridget was much taller and had the most gorgeous red hair. Her eyes were green like Ian's and she was fair skinned. She was breathtakingly beautiful. Both girls had the same open personality as their mother, and Madison felt an instant kinship with them. *I am actually going to have sisters now,* she thought. *And brothers.* She surveyed the mob on the terrace and lawn. *And apparently a clan*, she chuckled to herself.

Finally, Ian stepped between his mother and Maddy, placing his arm around both of their shoulders. The three made the rounds together as Madison was introduced to one family member or close friend after another. Madison's brain was swimming with names and familial connections. Everyone was gracious and welcomed Madison expressing wishes for a happy future with Ian. There was laughter and teasing and slaps on the back for Ian and cheek bussing for Maddy. They were all overjoyed about the marriage and the news of the baby. To Madison's surprise not one batted an eye at her being pregnant before marriage. Even though Ian told her no one would care, she hadn't really believed him. She should have. This was a group who loved children and didn't seem to care when, where, or how many were born to join their clan.

Chapter Thirty-Eight

Congratulations were the order of the day, and questions were shot from every direction. When was the weddin' goin' ta take place? Where would it take place? Is the Great Hall no' where old Angus and Mary Ferguson, were married? Who was comin' from Madison's family? Would her siblins be attendin' from the United States? How many siblins did she have? Had she chosen a gown yet? Would it be a large weddin' party? One interesting old fellow who looked like he was out of some kind of time warp, sported a thick gray beard, a bushy mustache, rather long muttonchop sideburns, and was wearing a kilt. He even stepped back taking a long admiring look at Madison's form and grinned as he announced to those nearby that she had "Bonnie hips fer the birthin' o wee bairns!"

Madison was beginning to feel slightly overwhelmed when Evelyn came to her rescue.

"Thank you, Uncle Lasta. Ah'm sure that's a great comfort for Maddy. Okay, folks," she said to the group they had been talking with. "don't bombard tha poor girl." She took ahold of Madison's arm like a protective mother. "She and Ian and will be married a long time. You can hold the rest of your questions fora a latea date. Right now, Ah think tha lass here needs sustenance." She steered Madison toward the buffet tables.

"Uncle Lasta?" Maddy questioned in a conspiratorial voice.

"Alistaia Mackay. To be honest, Ah'm not sure if he's an uncle or a forty-second cousin twice removed. Ah tend to lose track afta a certain distance in lineage." She looked back over her shoulder at the milling mob. "Thera are so many of them, you know. Ah gave up tryin to keep straight how they all fit in yearas ago. As long as Ah've been part of this family, he has always been called 'Uncle Lasta.'" She shrugged. "It works fora me." They reached the extravagant buffet tables, and each picked up a plate. Madison surveyed the offerings. She had been to many buffets for large groups during her years with Tender Care Hospice, but she had never seen a spread like this one.

"I hardly know where to start," she commented.

"Ah don't know why I evea botha with a caterer. Nobody comes to one of these things empty-handed," Evelyn mused as she filled her plate. "Oh, and by the way, dea, Ah heard Ian refer to you as Maddy, Ah hope you don't mind if Ah do the same?"

"I would be delighted." Madison smiled at her future mother in-law as she began to make her own choices from the offered array.

After they had both mounded their plates to capacity, Evelyn and Madison set off together and found a nice quite spot under an elm tree somewhat removed from the large group.

"Whera *were* y'all plannin' to have the weddin?" Evelyn asked as she cut into her steak.

"Well, to be honest, we haven't really had a chance to talk about it." Madison took a bite of her roast beef. "But I would *like* to have it in front of the house on the cliff with the ocean as the backdrop." She smiled as she looked off into the distance.

"Y'all may not have talked about it," Evelyn laughed, "but y'all sure have been *thinkin'* about it, you sweet thing."

Ian was standing with Tommy and Sara looking across the lawn at his mother and Madison laughing together, and he began to relax. He knew his mother would like Madison. She had all the qualities Alexandra had lacked. *Mam never really cared much for Alexandra,* he thought to himself. *Why didna I see what Mam did from the start? Youth,* he mused, and then his eyes rested on his Maddy. *She's warm, caring, and always thinkin' o other people before thinkin' o herself. God, how I luv tha lass!*

Not realizing that Tommy was asking him a question Ian moved toward Madison and his mother. Tommy recognizing his brother's intentions put a restraining hand on Ian's arm and pulled Ian back to him and Sara.

"Leave them be, laddie," he advised.

Sara laughed. "Yes, Ian. They have to get to know each other, and they can't do that if you're hovering." She looked back to her husband and smiled. "This reminds me of when you brought me here to meet the family. And I bet you were the same way."

"Aye, me darlin." Tommy smiled. "I was at tha'. Ne'er wanted ta let ye out of me sight. *Especially* wi our mam." Tommy looked in the stroller to check on Isabelle and saw she was awake and gurgling. "Ah, come here ye wee faker. Come and see yer uncle Ian." Tommy picked up the little girl and handed her to Ian. "Ye can divert his attention and get him inta the da mode."

Ian smiled broadly and accepted his niece with pleasure.

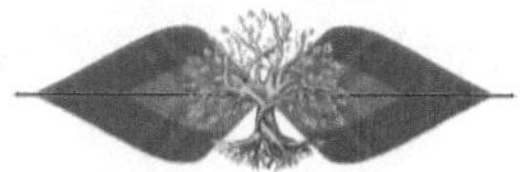

"I hope you won't mind if I ask where you're from originally. You're accent is quite a bit different from Ian's and I'm going nuts trying to place it," Madison said.

Evelyn chuckled and her face turned a little pink. "Acourse Ah don't mind you're askin, dahlin. Ah was born in Chalston, Noth Carolina. Ah'm afraid my accent gets a bit thicka when Ah'm nervous. And then ma family can't even undastand what A'm tryin to say." Evelyn took a sip of wine and a deep breath.

Madison was almost speechless. "You were nervous?" Evelyn nodded her head. "About all these people?" This time Evelyn shook her head. "Not about meeting me? Surely!"

"You sweet thing!" Ian's mother reached across the two plates resting on the table and patted Maddy's hand. "Of course Ah was nervous about meetin' y'all! Ah've seen too many bride and mothas-in-law meetins get off on the wrong foot and afta that, you may as well just give it up, suga!" She looked softly into Maddy's eyes. "Ah didn't want that to happen to us. Ma boy loves you, Madison Danaher, and it's obvious to anyone with half a brain that you love him. He's happier than Ah think Ah've eva seen him, so Ah'de come to care deeply fora you before we even met. Ah'm hopin y'all can come to care fora me too." Tears began to well in two sets of eyes as the women looked at each other across the table.

"I've never had a mother," Maddy said quietly. "I think I'm going to like finally having one."

"Whew!" Evelyn sighed and offered a soft chuckle. She scarfed up two soft paper cocktail napkins from the holder on the table and offered one to Madison, who laughed as she accepted it. They both dabbed at their eyes and laughed again together.

"Was Ian's father traveling in the States?" Maddy asked to open the door to Evelyn's past.

"No, dahlin. Ah met Ian's daddy when Ah came with ma mama and daddy to Scotland on Holiday. Ah met him and fell smack in love on the spot! He was a handsome laddie, Steven was. Acourse ma daddy was against ma havin' any kind of relationship with him."

"Why?" Madison asked as she leaned back into her chair.

"Simple!" Evelyn raised her eyebrows. "Ma family had money and Steven's didn't! Fara from it! Just between you and me, Ah think ma daddy brought me hera in the first place to find me a titled husband. He neva actually said so initially, but we spent weeks goin' to all kinds of comin' out parties in London before comin hera. We met some folks who had invited us to spend some time at their Scottish estate. That's why we came out hera in the first place. Daddy met Colum MacGrega at one of those comin' out parties and they became fast pals. MacGrega had a boy and Daddy had a girl. Perfect! MacGrega had money and Daddy had money. Even betta!"

Madison was fascinated. She sat with her fork poised over her plate.

Evelyn stopped her story for a moment and looked at her audience of one. "You know, baby girl. That food isn't goin' to do you or that baby you're carryin one bit of good unless you put it in your mouth."

"Oh, right. Sorry. Please, go on." Maddy loaded the fork with, she had no idea what, and stuck it in her mouth.

"Ah met Steven at a party MacGrega threw at his estate, and like I said, that was all it took." She laughed at the memory. "One look at him and Ah was hooked fora life. We had several dances together and we strolled onto the ver-randa." She drew out the word and winked at Maddy. "Daddy noticed acourse and asked his best pal who that young man was. The MacGregas are some kind of distant relation to the Mackay's. Ah'm not real sure what tha relation is. Ah'm not even sure they know. But Steven was in school with Malcolm and they were friends. MacGrega, the fatha, knew who Steven was and explained the relation of tha Mackay's and the MacGregas as best he knew. 'Steven is a fine lad,' he told Daddy, but didn't have a farthin' to his name.

"And *that's* all Daddy needed to know. Ah really don't know what Daddy and MacGrega had worked out between them, but Daddy told Mama that thera was to be nothing goin' on between his daughta and that Mackay fella. He told Mama and eventually me that his 'only daughta betta not be gettin' any idea about' … what was it he called them? Oh yes, Ah betta not be gettin' any 'ro-mantic ideas' in my head about maself and 'that *paupa*'" Evelyn laughed again, pressed her palm to her breast, and took a deep breath. "Acourse *I* was sixteen and determined to prove that Ah could make ma own decisions about the rest of ma life. Steven and Ah met as often as we could manage in secret.

Then Daddy and *Ah* had a huge row when he announced that he had betrothed me to Malcolm MacGrega. Now, Malcolm was a nice boy and Ah did like him, but Ah sure as hell wasn't goin' to marry him!

"Then Ah think Daddy and MacGrega, the fatha, had an even bigga row because Daddy said he'd have to talk me into goin' through with the marriage." Evelyn stopped talking for a minute and smiled at her own thoughts. "MacGrega figuaed a daughta should have betta discipline. He thought Ah was 'bein stubborn.' Imagine a Scott accusing someone else of bein' stubborn!" Evelyn rolled her eyes toward the heavens.

"*Ah* think Ah told Daddy that he could send out invitations to tha whole world if he wanted to. He could fit me out in some fancy weddin' gown and spend a damned fortune on food and flowers, but when the minista asked me if Ah'd '*take this man,*' Daddy might just as well start takin' bets and make a second fortune, because Ah'd say '*NO*' and Ah'd say it loud and clear. Oh ma goodness! Daddy was so angry! Ah thought he was goin' to have a stroke! He thought he could bring me round to his way of thinkin'. Ora maybe MacGrega thought I would come round. Ah'm not sure. Anyway, we stayed on for close to a month. But then Ah think Daddy and MacGrega, the fatha, had another row about ma stubbornness and lack of discipline. One mornin' Daddy just announced we were leavin'. Ah sent a note to Steven by messenger tellin him Daddy was takin' me back to America. Steven came that vera aftanoon and asked me to marry him."

"And you said yes," Madison stated.

"No."

"*No?*" Madison breathed

"Daddy learned Steven was coming to see me. Apparently, the lass Ah sent with ma note, had scruples, and she told Daddy. So he waited and watched. Daddy heard Steven propose and stepped in. We all had words then. Ah told Daddy Ah was goin' to marry Steven. Daddy threatened to charge Steven with contributin' to the delinquency of a minea."

"You were sixteen?"

"Yes. Ah didn't want Steven to get into that kind of trouble. He was workin' his way through graduate school. He didn't have money fora attorney's fees. So Ah cried and yelled, but Daddy wouldn't budge. Steven yelled and threatened Daddy. Ooooo! It was a ho-rrific scene." She shook her head. "In the end, Steven said we'd find a way. But Daddy was a nasty old brute. He dragged me kickin' and screamin into the house. Then MacGrega came out and ask Steven to leave."

"But you somehow managed to get together."

"No, not then. The staff had us packed up in an houra and we left that vera day."

"What did your father try to do to keep you and Steven apart?"

"He didn't just try, dahlin. He succeeded." Evelyn shook her head. "For two long yeas anyway. He packed me off to boardin' school in France. Ah wrote to Steven and told him where Ah was, but never heard a word from him. Ah was in *agony* for the next year and a half. When Ah graduated, Ah learned that Daddy had made it perfectly clear to the head mistress when he enrolled me, that Ah was to have no contact with Steven Mackay whatsoevea, and all ma lettas to him were confiscated. He neva got any of them." Evelyn took a deep breath and looked over at Madison. "Are you sure you want to hear all of this? Ah hadn't intended to go on for so long... I hadn't intended." Madison giggled at Evelyn's correction in her accent and nodded her head vigorously.

"Please go on. I really want to hear the rest," Maddy encouraged.

"Mercy, Ah haven't talked about this in years! Well, afta graduation Ah went back to Charleston, but Daddy and Ah didn't get on too well tagethea. And when I went away to college, I went as far away from Daddy as Ah could and still stay in the United States." There was a kind of sadness in her eyes when she spoke of the estrangement with her father. "Then the summa after ma freshman yeara...." Her expression changed to one of excitement and delight. "...Ah took a trip to London with ma best friend and anotha doram-mate. One of the girls was doin' some kind of paper foar our sophomora yea and the otha just wanted to see the Beatles. Ah can't rememba now, who wanted what. Ah, acourse, was hopin to find Steven somehow. One weekend, we came to Scotland to see the sights. We hired a car and drove all over on these terrible roads, and believe me, baby girl, if you think the roads are not so much now, you should have seen them then! We came to a village where therea was a crowd, so we stopped to see what was goin' on. It was an auction. Some huge tract aland was goin' up for public sale. We stood around and watched the biddin'. Then suddenly Ah recognized a voice. Ah scanned the faces until Ah saw him."

"Steven!" Maddy breathed.

"Yes, dahlin. Steven. He was biddin' on the land. He had gotten grand in those two years since we had seen each otha. *Ah* watched him until he finally won the bid and had his land. *This* land, honey." She smiled and looked to Madison sitting with her elbows on the table and her chin resting on her fists, hanging on every word. "When the thing was ova, Ah waited at the edge of the crowd, hopin' he would see me, but he didn't. Ah talked to the auctioneer and asked about the man who had won the bid and learned Steven had become a builda and was makin' quite a name foar himself."

"That evenin' Therea was a party at oura hotel. Ma friends and *I* decided unattached girls were always welcome at a big party so we dressed to the teeth and went. Acourse Ah knew Steven was goin' to be attendin' too. The auctioneer told me about the party when Ah talked to him earlia. When we entaed the hall, Ah spotted Steven right off. He looked so handsome in his tuxedo. Ah had attended that kind of function before because of Daddy's business and so Ah was used to minglin' with people Ah didn't know, and had no interest in evea seein' again." She chuckled. "So Ah made the rounds until Ah found some bucko who knew Steven."

"How did you find out he knew Steven?" Madison was fascinated with the entire story.

"Oh, suga, that's easy. You make small talk. Where you'rae from. How long y'all been in town. What you've seen since youra arrival. Ah had been to an auction! See? Eventually youa goin' to run into someone who knows the guy who won the bid!"

"And you did!"

"And Ah did. So this fellow said he knew Steven and finally got round to introducin' us." She paused to laugh and shook her head. "Steven was very polite and accepted the introduction, but acted like he had neva seen me before in his life!"

"He didn't!" Madison said baffled "What the hell was wrong with him?"

"He was hurt, baby girl. Apparently the reason Ah neva got any lettas from him was the same reason he neva got any from me. Daddy and the head mistress of the boardin' school Ah was attendin'. She confiscated his lettas as well as mine. Steven thought since Ah was so young, that Ah got over him just as quickly as we had fallin' fora each otha. Actually it didn't take long to figure it out. One question did it for both of us: 'why didn't you write to me?' Pretty simple. We left the party and went to a small café in Inverness and talked. Then we went to his place, and *talked* until dawn." She wiggled her eye brows and winked. "He asked me again to marry him, and acourse Ah said yes." Evelyn leaned back in her chair smiling and looked to the sky. "We went back to ma hotel and Ah packed up ma things, wrote a note and left with Steven. We were married the followin' day." She smiled and picked up her fork. It had been a personal story and Evelyn had relaxed little through the telling as had Madison due to listening.

"What did your parents say?"

"We called them a few days lata. Ooooeee! Daddy nearly had an ap-oplexy!" She drew out the word. "But what could they say? Ah was eighteen then. Ah was of legal age and it was done. Daddy neva forgave me. He never spoke to me again and he cut me right outta his will. However, Mama was happy fora me. She liked Steven and she knew Ah'd be happy with him. Probably because Steven and Ah chose each other. You see, baby girl, my parents' marriage was arranged by their parents. Mama barely knew Daddy when they were betrothed. And they only saw each otha at arranged events, so she didn't get to know him much betta during the courtship. She didn't *really* get to know him until afta they were married and by then, she didn't like him at all! Daddy was a propa Southern gentleman, but he was also a bully. As long as you did what he wanted and behaved like a propa lady, he just loved you to pieces. But buck and he wouldn't have it. No sir, he would not have it!"

"Did you ever get to see your mother again? After you were married, I mean?"

"OH! Ma gracious yes! Mama has a fairly large family all ova Carolina. She'd go to visit them and so would *I*. But Mama didn't come to Scotland until afta Daddy died. She loved it here. I always wished she would come to live with us, but she said 'the last thing Steven needs is his motha-in-law livin' in the next room'. *And* she was *comfortable* in Chalston. She had friends and activities and acourse a big family. We visited her and she us. When Daddy died, he left everything to her, so she was well fixed. Acourse he made her promise that when she died she wasn't to leave one nickel to that 'ungrateful daughta' of theiras. And Mama promised him she would do just as he asked, but acourse, she didn't, bless her sweet heart. She said we both earned every nickel he had." Madison's mouth dropped and Evelyn laughed. "Said she'd like to laugh right in his face when she walked through the pearly gates, but she didn't think she'd see him there!"

Madison laughed too and they were both startled by Ian's voice, "If ye two donna come back ta the party people are gonna start talkin'." He smiled as he helped the two women to their feet. "What were ye talkin' aboot?"

"Your mother was just telling me how she met your father." Madison smiled as she hugged his frame

"She was, huh?" Ian smiled at his mother, "And how did ye like the tellin'?"

"It was spellbinding! A fantastic story!" Madison laughed. "It would make a great novel."

"It's a bonnie tale, I'll grant ye." Ian smiled at his mother and the three of them laughed as they strolled across the lawn to join the larger group.

Madison and Ian spent the rest of the day at each other's side accepting congratulations and answering questions. When the daylight began to fade, Evelyn announced that Ian and Madison had better get a move on so they could get home before the night was done. An hour later the pair was on their way back to the house on the cliff.

Madison, eyes closed, head on the headrest, and sighed. "Ian, you have a wonderful family."

"I was hopin ye'd like them, darlin', cause ye're gonna find they're no' likely ta leave ye alone for any length o time." Ian pulled the Wagoneer into the driveway and noticed a car parked by the house. "Who in the hell could tha' be?" Ian boomed. When he got close, he recognized the jeep. "Donny!" Ian exclaimed and he and Madison leaped from their vehicle as if it had teeth and hurried into the house.

Stretched out on the sofa, fast asleep was Ian's older brother. Madison rounded the sofa and gently awakened him.

"Donny?" Madison called gently, as he turned his head to look at her, she saw the bruising on his cheek and eye. "Oh my God! What happened to you?"

"Maddy darlin'." Donny rose from his comfortable position and gave Madison a hug and a peck on the cheek. "How're ye feeling?"

"Forget me, what happened to you?" Madison gingerly touched his face and saw Ian coming from the kitchen with an ice pack.

"Here." Ian handed his brother the cold bag and watched as Donny held it to his face. "Answer the lady. What happened?"

"Nothing much, I'm fine and on holiday." He looked at Ian. "I'm sorry I couldna get here for the party. I tried." He shrugged and looked back to Madison. "So what's new?" he grinned.

Knowing they would get no answers from him until he was ready, Madison and Ian told him their news of the marriage and the coming baby. Ian knew Donny was already aware of his and Madison's news, but was proud of the way his brother simulated surprise. Ian wondered who the actor of the family really was. Madison told Donny about meeting his mother and "The Clan Mackay".

"So it was a big do, was it? How did ye like our mam?" he asked.

"Ah thought she was a perfect dahlin!" Maddy laughed, and so did Ian and Donny, although the extra facial movement made the badly bruised Mackay wince.

"Aye. She is that. The Carolina comes out strong when she gets excited or nervous."

"Aye!" Ian chuckled. "Remember when we were young lads?" He turned to Madison and his grin covered his face. "We'd be in trouble for something and our mam would be givin' us hell. Half the time we dinna know what the devil she was sayin'!" The brothers laughed and for the next hour, Maddy was regaled with stories of the young boys and their mother. Eventually Ian noticed the time and suggested they all retire and start fresh in the morning. He retrieved Donny's bag from beside the sofa, and watched his brother gingerly inch his way up the stairs and decided to talk to him in the morning about a career change. They said good night at the guest room door and Madison suggested Donny take a hot shower and pile into bed.

Ian and Madison snuggled under the covers hearing the guest room shower kick on and knew Donny had taken Madison's advice.

"Ian, can you talk to him about getting out of, whatever his job is?" She sat up and leaned against the headboard and continued. "It's dangerous. I don't know what else has happened to him over the years, but just since I've known him, he's been shot, he shot Tommy, he's been clunked severely on the head, and now here he is and somebody has beaten him to a bloody pulp!" She pulled the covers up to her waist and smoothed them down firmly with both hands. "I just don't think his career is a very healthy one."

"I know, luv, but I canna do anything more than offer advice. Any decisions have ta be his own." Seeing she was about to protest, Ian continued. "However," he added, holding up his hand. "I've already made up me mind ta talk wi him in the morn aboot joinin' Tommy's force." Madison snuggled back down under the covers into Ian's arms.

"Thank you, '*dahlin.*'" She giggled and she drifted off to sleep. Ian lay there for a long time looking at the ceiling and back to Madison. He was happy here with her. Not to mention he had his whole family around him now that Donny was back. *Aye, I do need to speak ta the lad about his job*, he thought. But he also knew he had been right when he told Madison that in the end, the decision would have to be Donny's. Finally, Ian too drifted into sleep.

The next morning Madison woke to find she was alone in the large bed. She rose slightly and reached for her nausea meds, a can of ginger ale, and soda crackers that had become morning ritual. She smiled at the thought of Ian making sure she had what she needed to start her day. She opened the can of soda, swallowed the pill and leaned back into the pillows to nibble on the crackers. She reached under the bed for her book and read a few pages, waiting for the meds to have time to get into her system. Twenty minutes later, she headed for the shower. Before going downstairs, she made the bed, dressed, and tidied the bedroom. She heard Ian in the kitchen, when she reached the main floor of the house, but didn't hear Donny. *Must still be in bed,* she thought to herself as she entered the kitchen, where Ian was cooking up a storm.

"Mmm, smells good." Madison smiled as she took her place at the counter. Ian handed her a cup of tea and went back to work. "You know," she said. "I don't know if it's your cooking, my imagination, or the baby, but these jeans are beginning to be a bit snug. I'm thinking it might be time for a size adjustment." She grinned. Ian looked at her and smiled. His green eyes loving every inch of her face. "Donny still asleep?" she asked as she took a sip of the tea. *Tasty,* she thought, *but it's not coffee.*

"Nay, he went ta see our mam," he explained as he gave Madison a plate piled high with pancakes, eggs, sausage, and toast. "I told him I didna think he should be goin' until his face at least was more healed, but he wouldna be swayed." She watched as he piled his plate the same as he had hers. She could tell by his body language he was agitated.

"Ian, is something wrong?" Madison asked.

"Nay, why?" he stated as he shoved food in his mouth.

"Hungry?" she asked.

"Aye."

Now she was getting irritated. "You argued, didn't you?"

Ian took a deep breath, laid down his fork, and looked at Madison. "The lad has nay interest in quittin' the... the... whatever it is he does. He's '*happy*' doin' what he's doin'. He '*likes*' the danger part of his job. There's 'no reason' for him to change. It 'shouldna bother anyone' tha' the job could get him killed." Ian stabbed his fork into the pancakes again. "The discussion went downhill from there."

Madison left her stool and put her arms around Ian in a consoling embrace. Ian was very upset by the conversation with his brother. It hadn't gone as he had originally thought it would and the end result left Ian frustrated.

"I'm sorry it didn't go well, my love," she soothed. "But you said yourself that it had to be his decision. We both knew that. But you put into words what everybody has been thinking and it can't hurt for Donny to hear the words. He's been doing this for a long time, and he obviously knows what he's doing. Maybe he just never thought of his job in terms of how it affected those who care about him. And now you've pointed it out to him. Let's hope that when he gets off by himself, he'll think about the things you said. Was he as angry when he left as you seem to be?"

"Aye. He was hoppin' angry." Ian sighed.

"Well, then, maybe what you said to him were things he had already said to himself and your confirmation could just have enforced what he already knew to be true. He cares about you, Ian, and he cares about what you think. He could have gone to Tommy's last night or Alex's, but he came here." She returned to her stool at the counter. "That has to count for something." She took Ian's stilled hand in hers and tilted her head so she could look into his face. "He's on holiday now and he's got four weeks to think about what you said. He's made it this long because he's smart and knows when to take cover. He's smart enough to make the right decision. I think he'll leave the business sooner or later. We'll all just have to hope he chooses to do it sooner." She smiled. *Business,* she thought to herself, *sounds like I'm talking about the Mafia.* "Did he say when he was coming back here?"

"Nay." Ian looked up from his plate at Madison. He could see in her eyes she didn't believe a word she had just spoken, but she wanted him to feel better. And he did. *Amazing the power this woman has over me,* he thought to himself. "Just tha' he wanted to see our mam and tha' he would be back."

"Then he can't be too angry with you if he had already made up him mind to come back when he left." Madison placed a kiss on Ian's lips and ran her fingers through his hair. "I love you" was all she said. It was all she had to say. Ian rose from his stool, took her in his arms and kissed her long and lustfully.

When he finally pulled his lips from hers, he whispered. "What would I do wi'oot ye, lass?" Madison swallowed and took a breath to regain her balance.

"Ye'd grow ta be an embittered old man with a paunch, warts on yer ass, and ingrown toenails." She frowned wrinkling her brow and trying hard not to smile. Ian looked into her eyes and laughed out loud.

"Ye're undoubtedly right. Sae I may as well stay wi ye. There's nay another womon in the world would be wantin' me in that shape."

"Aye," she crooned and pressed her lips to his again.

Chapter Thirty-Nine

In the month that followed, Madison was busy at the office during the day. Most evenings she sat with Ian, Agatha, Sara, and Evelyn making wedding arrangements. Ian and Donny worked out their differences over Donny's career choices. Ian agreed that Donny's career choice was his to make, and Donny said he would consider Ian's concerns. Madison had successfully and begrudgingly become caffeine free and Patrick assured her that she and the baby were doing very well.

Plans for the wedding were going along well too. They settled on a date and Madison called Samuel to give him and Angie plenty of time to make their flight arrangements. Evelyn opened her home to any guest that would be arriving for both families. When Madison protested that it was a lot to take on, Evelyn responded with jokes about "Southern hospitality." "It's not as though Ah don't have the extra room." She laughed. "Ma house has seventeen bed chambahs. I can only sleep in one of them at a time, dahlin!"

Madison was going to have the dream wedding she had always wanted. The ceremony would be held outside in front of the house by the cliff. They arranged for a marquee in case of rain. Sara knew of a trustworthy florist, and suggested that Lizzy would probably know what printer would be best for the invitations. Ian and Madison decided on what they wanted the invitations to say and then she turned that job over to Lizzy. Evelyn insisted on using her caterer for the reception, but Agatha was adamant that only *she* could make a wedding cake that was "fit fer human consumption."

Madison and Ian decided against having a bridal party. "Ye canna choose four or five oot of two hundred wi'oot creatin' a big hew and cry!" Ian was adamant.

"Yes, somebody always gets their feathers ruffled because they were left out," Madison agreed, knowing all too well that if they had a bridal party, it would likely get out of hand.

"But y'all should have at least a small group of attendants, don't you think?" Evelyn urged.

"Evie, I told ye months ago, these two wouldna e'er go in fer one of yer big elaborate dos, but ye wouldna listen any better than ye're listenin' ta them now," Agatha argued.

"Well, ah know, Aggie, but that was way back when the press was givin' them so much trouble, and Ah just assumed that once all that hoopla died down they'd—" The room suddenly got very still as Evelyn stopped speaking and she and Agatha looked at each other and then over at Ian and Madison. Agatha glared at Evelyn.

"Ye've a mouth as big as Loch Ness, Evelyn Mackay!" Agatha grumbled. She looked over to Ian. "If ye're expectin' me ta apologize fer tellin' yer mam that ye'd fallen in luv wi the lass here, ye'll be disappointed. Ye're a damned fool if ye thought I wouldna. There's no' a breathin' soul in Lusta nor half the countryside that didna know ye'd talk her inta weddin' wi ye."

Ian grinned at her, but his smile faded when Madison asked, "And the baby?"

"Just as soon as I knew aboot it!" Agatha stated and Ian's smile returned.

"Well," Madison sighed. "At least we got to make the announcement ourselves at least once." Ian took her hand in his and grinned at Agatha and his mother.

In the end, Ian and Madison agreed to have a best man and maid of honor. Ian chose his oldest brother Tommy and Madison chose to have Lizzy next to her during the ceremony.

Evelyn told Madison that Ian's sister Bridget had mentioned she would like to sew Maddy's gown if she would allow it. Madison was thrilled with the offer. Immediately after, the talk ran to fabrics, style of the dress, and fittings. Madison, Lizzy, and Bridget met at Evelyn's on a regular basis for fittings. Ian's other sister Emily, Madison learned was also handy with a needle, and volunteered to help Bridget with the dresses for the bride and her maid of honor.

Madison and Ian were very busy for the next few weeks. Maddy was going to the office on a daily basis, much to Ian's dismay at first, but her nausea began to subside, and the baby was growing well. Several scripts for new films were coming to Ian and he was reading and marking each with a yes, no, or maybe. But the wedding was uppermost in both their minds. The invitations arrived, were addressed, and mailed. Maddy chose a soft hunter green satin for Lizzy's dress, which Bridget designed in the same style as Madison's.

As the wedding drew closer, Ian, not Madison, was getting more and more jittery. At one point Madison sent him to "go and play" for the day so she could get him out of her hair. When she and Lizzy went for their fittings the next afternoon, Evelyn asked her how Ian was holding up.

"I'm not sure!" Madison laughed. "I thought the bride was the one who's supposed to go ballistic. But in our case, it's the groom. Ian always seemed so calm to me, but he certainly doesn't seem that way now. Yesterday I had to send him out to play with somebody. Anybody! Just so I could have some peace."

"Yes. I ah know. He came here and nearly drove me plumb out of ma mind!" Evelyn laughed. "It was charmin', really, to see the great boy with stage fright! Howeva, next time you chase him from the house? Send him to Tommy's, if you please, baby girl!" She sat back and admired the gown Bridget was fitting. "Oh ma word! Y'all are goin' to make such a lovely bride, Maddy dahlin. Bridie, you do beautiful work!" she breathed when she rose from her seat and fingered the fine stitches of the gown.

Finally three days before the wedding, guests were beginning to arrive. Madison hired Shawn Conners to pick up Samuel and Angie at the airport. She spent two hours constantly looking out the windows from the second and first floors of the house hoping to get a glimpse of Shawn's gleaming black Rolls Royce and the passengers that it carried. After a while, Ian heard Madison squeak. She came running down the stairs and raced to the front door. Ian followed and saw the car coming up the drive. He stood at the end of the walk with Madison, and waited for the car to come to a stop in front of the house.

Shawn opened the rear passenger door and Samuel got out extending his hand to his wife to help her. Madison all but ran to them. Angie was first to receive an embrace.

"Welcome ta Scotland!" Ian said as he and Samuel shook hands. "It's really verra good ta see ye both." Angie let Madison go and gave Ian a big hug while Samuel did the same with Madison.

"I am so happy to see you, Samuel," Madison smiled. "I've missed you!"

"It's good to see you as well." Samuel took her hands in his and held them away from her sides giving her the required fatherly inspection. "And you look radiant!" She did look happy. *She's positively glowing,* he thought to himself.

Angie came and took Maddy's arm in hers. "You never should have asked him to stand in for Poppy," she said. "He takes this role very seriously, you know. He'll be driving you insane before it's over." She laughed. "But I'm so glad you did. It's given him a whole new interest in life. So, show me your house, my dear."

Madison was delighted. She wanted nothing more than to show off the house that Ian had built. Ian invited Samuel to follow along with Madison and Angie, and he would be along shortly. He told Shawn to take the bags to his mother's since that was where Samuel and Angie would be staying.

"Maddy and I will take them over there later this evening." Ian shook Shawn's hand and thanked him again for making the airport run.

"Do'na worry non aboot it, Mr. Ian. Ms. Danaher and yerself ha been sae good ta me and me family over the past year. It was me pleasure." Shawn smiled and slid into the driver's side of his Rolls and drove away. Ian smiled and turned to join Madison and their guests in the house.

Ian smiled with pride watching Madison give Samuel and Angie the grand tour of their home. She was explaining what and where all the renovations were going to be when Samuel finally stopped her dissertation.

"I thought he was an actor," Samuel chuckled.

"Oh, Ian, is multitalented! He built this fantastic house himself and, as you know, he is a gourmet chef. He studied at one of the finest culinary schools in the country. He has so much talent."

"You don't have to sell us, Rosey." Angie smiled as she touched her arm. "We like him. Besides, anyone who can make you as happy as you are, is no less than perfect to us."

"I thank ye for the vote of confidence." Ian chuckled from the bottom of the stairs. Madison blushed at her rush to brag about Ian's abilities. Ian climbed the stairs and wrapped his arm around her. "It doesna get any better than livin' wi yer own fan club, does it, lass?" he laughed.

Madison continued with the full tour, including the cliff and the beach below. She told of the plans for the wedding and where it was going to take place. She told them about Ian's sisters making her gown. She told them about Evelyn. "You'll like her. She's a lovely lady. And she's from the States originally."

"We're going to be staying at her home. Isn't that what you told us?" Samuel asked.

"Aye. All the oot of town guests will be stayin' with our mam. We'll be takin' ye over there before long."

"Yes, are you tired after your flight? It's a five-hour difference. If we're keeping you here too long, just say so. If you'd like to rest before dinner, we can show you all of this at another time."

"Relax, girlie, and take a breath!" Samuel chuckled. "We're older but not arthritic yet."

"Now who's jittery?" Ian whispered. Maddy turned and looked up at him. Ian shrugged his shoulders and grinned. "Agatha talked ta our mam and I talked ta Agatha."

"Yes. If you don't want the whole county to know your thoughts don't tell either your mother or Agatha," Maddy said with a grimace.

"Ye're learnin, luv," Ian laughed, which made them all smile. Although Samuel and Angie weren't exactly sure what they were actually smiling about.

"Would you like to see the office?" Madison asked.

Samuel seeing how much she wanted to show him, said he would love to see it. And with that the four of them piled into Ian's Wagoneer. Madison pointed out areas of interest as they drove into Lusta. She told them about things she had learned during the months she had lived in Scotland. Before they got to the office, Madison pointed out Angus Jaminson's place, where she had purchased all the furnishings for the office and gave them a small account of his and Agatha's story.

"Oh, Agatha! Wait until you meet her. You're gonna love her, just so long as you can get past her abruptness." Madison smiled as they drew nearer to Lusta and the alley behind the office. Finally, they went over the bridge and Ian drove around to the back door. As he did so Madison explained; the village roads. "They weren't designed for automobile traffic, really and they're just too narrow to accept cars driving side by side. Most everyone walks everywhere anyway." Ian parked the car and the four of them got out. Madison unlocked the back door and allowed Samuel and Angie to enter first. She watched Samuel survey the room and the fixtures in it.

"This is really beautiful, Madison," Angie whispered.

"Yes, it is." Samuel turned and faced her with an approving grin. "This is an extremely inviting and warm place you've made here Madison. What's that lead to?" he asked, pointing to the door of Agatha's bakery.

"That door leads into Agatha's bakery kitchen. You see, Agatha owns the building and I leased the space from her. When we're all here, the door stays open. A multitude of wonderful aromas come from her kitchen!" She rolled her eyes heavenward. "We usually all sit there in the morning before business hours, and have tea and pastries. It has become quite a tradition. I have a full crew now of RNs, chaplains, CHHAs, and social workers. And you will be happy to know that we are now carrying a census of twenty-four patients."

"I'm proud of you, girlie." Samuel sat at Lizzy's desk and admired the handiwork. "You have done very well here, and I couldn't have picked a better place or a more beautiful one."

"It's too bad we didn't come during office hours when you could have met the staff. Of course, you'll meet them at the wedding and Lizzy is my maid of honor, so you'll meet her at the rehearsal," Madison explained. She could hear movement in the bakery and went over to knock on the door.

"Come in, lassie," Agatha sang out. "I'm workin' on me cakes, I ca'na come ta ye." Madison opened the door and saw Agatha hard at work on a four-tiered cake.

"Agatha," she exclaimed as she walked in with Ian, Samuel, and Angie following. "It's gorgeous! Is that our cake?" she asked.

"Well o course it is, ye silly lass." The cake was white with touches of green and deep blue. "Well, laddie, what do ye think?" Agatha asked as she backed away to show off her work.

"Agatha, ye know there's nay a baker in the country who can work the magic tha' ye do yerself. Come and meet Samuel and Angie." Moving aside, Ian made the introductions.

"Ah, so ye're our Madison's big boss?" She extended her hand and grasped Samuel's in a strong grip. "It's sae good ta meet ye at long last. I ca'na tell ye what it means ta me and the rest o the clan that ye sent Maddy here ta us. She has been like me own child and a breath o' fresh air ta this old place."

"You're welcome. I'm glad Madison was able to make herself a home here and have what appears to be a wonderful group of family and friends." He smiled.

"It's lovely to meet you, Agatha." Angie smiled and shook her hand.

"Thank ye, Angie, is it? Would ye all be interested in havin' a cuppa tae and maybe a pastry or two?" Agatha stated more than asked.

The five of them sat around Agatha's butcher block island and got to know each other. Samuel thought it was obvious how Madison was able to fall in love with the land and the people she had met since arriving in Scotland. Angie had been after him to retire for years and lately, Samuel had been giving the idea some serious consideration. He breathed deeply of the aromas in Agatha's kitchen. *Maybe I should retire,* he thought to himself. *Angie would love it here. Madison certainly does.* He just wasn't sure who to leave in charge of the company. He had always, more or less hoped Madison would take over when he was ready to retire. *She has learned the business from the ground up,* he told himself, *and has held nearly every position in the company except director and triage nurse, both obviously requiring the acquisition of a degree in nursing. Now, I'm not sure she'd want to be president of his company. She's going to have a family of her own now, and is living here. But I could ask,* he thought to himself. *But, of course, this isn't the time. Let her start her family and get her feet wet being European head first,* his mind suggested.

Samuel and Angie enjoyed Agatha. She knew everyone it seemed and told histories of most of them. Angie wanted to know more of Agatha's history, but before long Ian announced it was time to get started to his mother's, so Samuel and Angie could get settled.

Madison was awed by Evelyn's house each time she turned into the lane. She had been meeting Bridget and Emily here regularly for just short of a month. She always felt welcome and was no longer nervous about being there, but the house had a magnificence that nearly took her breath away. Evelyn was outside, standing at the bottom of the wide front steps waiting for the car.

"How does she always know when someone is about to arrive?" Madison wondered aloud and then looked over at Ian and they answered in unison.

"Agatha!" they laughed.

Madison made the introductions and she and Ian accompanied Evelyn as she invited her guests into the house.

"Ah'm so glad y'all could make the trip. Ah know how anxious Maddy was for y'all to be here. It's goin' to be such a lovely weddin. Has Maddy told you what the schedule is to be for the next few days? It's all so excitin'!" Evelyn was talking a mile a minute. Both Ian and Madison smiled that the lady was nervous.

"You have a lovely home, Mrs. Mackay." Angie smiled as they entered through the huge Redwood doors.

"Please, won't y'all call me Evelyn?" she said. "Afta all, we are almost family. Seems a shame to be so formal."

"Oh yes, lets!" Angie agreed. "And we're Angie and Samuel."

"Now, Ah'm goin' to take you right up to youra rooms. Ah imagine y'all'd like to get settled. Unless y'all'd care for a drink first?"

"Actually, Evelyn, I've been wearing these shoes since 4:00 a.m. this morning, and I'd like to change and wash my face."

Evelyn laughed as she and Angie locked arms and headed toward the main staircase with Samuel and Madison trailing behind. "*I* understand perfectly. Ah know what travelin' such a distance does to me. *Ah* thought you'd like to get your barins and maybe rest up a bit afta your trip."

"I'm not sure who made the conquest, but I think they're going to be fast friends." Maddy chuckled as she linked her arm through Samuel's, who smiled and patted her hand.

"Yes, I'd say so," he said.

"Youar bath is right through that doorway," Evelyn explained to Samuel and Angie as a young boy placed their bags in the sumptuously appointed bedroom. "Thank you, Brian." She wrapped her arm around the boy's shoulder and introduced him to her guests. "This is our young Brian," she said. "He's ten years old. And in his spare time, he helps me out in the garden. He knows every plant his daddy has in the ground on the place and is constantly tryin' to come up with new ones. He wants to be a horticulturist when he's old enough and we are goin' to send him to University of Edinburgh one of these days. Right, laddie?" The boy beamed up at her. "Now run along, suga, and see if youra mama has any of those cookies left for you.

"If there's anything y'all need that you don't see, just push that little button by the door." Then she turned to Madison. "Ah thought we'd have an early dinna this evenin'. Is that alright with y'all, dahlin? Tomorra's goin' to be a big day, what with the final fittin' and the rehearsal and the dinna"

"Yes, it's fine. Ian has become somewhat of a nag lately about my getting enough rest and he's jittery enough as it is without adding too many late nights to the mix." Maddy chuckled.

"Good," Evelyn said. She took Maddy's arm and headed back into the wide hallway. "We'll be servin' wine and cocktails downstairs in the library just off the main staircase in an hour or so. Y'all come on down when you are ready."

True to her word, Evelyn's kitchen staff served an early dinner. She and Angie and Samuel had become fast friends, and Madison didn't feel one bit guilty when she and Ian left shortly after the meal was over. The others had adjourned to the library for coffee and brandy before the fire that warmed the cozy room.

"You know," Madison commented as Ian turned the Wagoneer out of the car park. "I think they almost couldn't wait for us to get the hell out of there!"

Ian laughed. "Aye! I'm thinkin' me mam and your Angie wanted to exchange bits o information and compare notes. I dinna know what Angie and Samuel have ta be tellin' aboot ye, but I dinna want ta even count up the stories me mam has ta tell them."

The next morning Madison and Ian were up early.

"If I had known ye were goin' ta make me get up at the crack of dawn, lass, I'm nay sae sure I would ha agreed ta a big weddin'!" he grumbled.

Maddy stopped with one leg halfway into her jeans and looked at him. "Ian, you're always up early. It never occurred to me—" Ian scooped her up into his arms and tumbled her back onto the bed with him.

"Aye, luv," he leered, "I'm generally *up* in the morn, but I'm usually in a reclining position." He laughed as he captured her mouth.

"Do you realize you have become more—" Maddy giggled as Ian dipped his head and began a seductive assault on her neck stopping her in midsentence. "—insatiable oooooo, since we got engaged and found we were pregnant?"

"Aye, luv, I ha. Are ye complainin'?" He turned her in his arms and kissed her lustfully.

Maddy closed her eyes and was sorely tempted to phone Evelyn and forgo her final fitting when the doorbell rang. "The caterer is here with the tables and chairs," she moaned.

Ian rolled onto his back and breathed deeply. "Aye," he groaned. "Didna I tell ye tha' once me family got involved we wouldna have a minute ta ourselves?"

Madison pulled on her jeans and grabbed her blouse, buttoning up on the way down the stairs. Ian joined her on the lawn a few minutes later where she was explaining how she wanted the ceremony and reception to be set up. "Ian can tell you anything else you want to know. Hun, I've got to get to your mother's," she said as she pressed her lips lightly to his and dashed back into the house for her bag and car keys.

When she finally arrived at Evelyn's, Ian's sisters teased her and joked about the possibility of not seeing the couple for months after they were wed. Madison thought they were probably correct if Ian had his way.

"I was nearly ready to leave the house when Mr. MacGuffey arrived with his tables, chairs, linens, and things. I don't know where he's going to put all that stuff until Saturday." She shook her head.

"Don't y'all worry bout him, sweet baby. He knows what he's doin'. You won't even know his parcels are in the same council area, by this evening. The man is a veritable genius," Evelyn soothed. "Now, just step in so we can slide this up ya," she said, and as she and Bridget slipped the shimmering satin gown up Maddy's body, she began to glow. The strapless A-line style fit her form as though it had been molded to her body, with a sweetheart neckline, and a corseted bodice. Madison stood in front of the full-length mirror, admiring her reflection.

"I look like a bride," she breathed.

Bridget and Emily laughed. "I should hope ye do," Bridget chuckled. "And I havna ever seen one more bonnie."

"The gown is stunning, Bridie. You've done a beautiful job." Maddy smoothed her hands down the front bodice. "I don't know how to say thank you."

"No thanks are necessary. I enjoyed the doin'." Bridget smiled as she stood back and gazed at her brother's pretty bride. "You and Ian are goin' ta be sae happy." She turned to Emily. "Remember when we were sae afraid he'd end up with Alexandra?"

"Aye. Now tha' was scary!" Emily chuckled.

Evelyn had been sitting in a chair by the window watching the gown being fluffed and adjusted on Madison. She opened a drawer in the table by her chair and came to Madison holding a length of the Mackay tartan in her hands.

"This is my gift to you, dahlin." She straightened the length of fabric and draped it over Madison's shoulder and across the front of the gown securing it just below Maddy's opposite hip with a small pearl broach.

"Oh!" Maddy breathed. "Can I wear this? I'm not a Mackay. I wore Ian's neck scarf when I first came here, but I didn't know until later that I shouldn't have."

"Did Ian see it on you?" Evelyn asked.

"Yes, I'm afraid he did." Maddy smiled.

"And did he object?"

"Well, no. But I know now what the tartan means to the Clans." She looked at Ian's mother. "I'm not a Mackay," she said simply.

Evelyn embraced Madison and when she pulled slightly away, she rested her hands on the girl's shoulders. "You are now, dahlin. And so is that sweet baby you're carryin." She slid her hands down along Maddy's arms, took hold of Maddy's hands, and held them out from her sides. "I made this scarf for y'all to wear Saturday on your weddin' day. I'm Ian's mother. I'm a Mackay, and it's ma right to give you the tartan of the Mackay clan."

Tears puddled in Maddy's eyes and dropped to her cheeks as a smile spread across her face. Bridget and Emily each took tissues from the box on the table and passed the box to Madison and then Evelyn.

"Mama, that was the loveliest presentation I think I ever witnessed," Emily said, sniffling, and all four women laughed as they blew their noses. The tissue box was passed around again and the laughing continued for some time.

"Now, ya don't tell Ian about the scarf. It's somewhat of a surprise for him too." Evelyn warned the girls. "He'll be so proud when he sees y'all comin down the aisle wearin' his family tartan." She grinned as she swore all three of the younger women to secrecy.

Madison turned to gaze at herself in the mirror again before removing the gown. "You know what?" she chuckled. "The scarf also hides my belly!"

"That corset isn't too tight, is it, baby girl? We don't want to hurt the bairn.'"

"No, not at all. It's fine," Madison answered. She turned to Evelyn and the sisters. "Thank you so much for all of this. All my life, there was just myself and Poppy. We were all we had. So I never really knew what it was like to have a family, but you've made me feel a part of all of you, and now I know what having a family can be." She eyed the three women standing before her. "Isn't it wonderful?" she sighed.

"Ma children mean the world to me, baby girl," Evelyn said. "You have made ma Ian, so happy. Thank you for that, dahlin. And now *you* are one of ma children, and youra happiness means as much to me. Welcome to the family, Maddy." Evelyn's eyes were beginning to puddle again. Madison gathered her up in her arms as the tears dripped from her own eyes.

Emily grabbed for the tissue box again, and Bridget cleared her throat. "Ye're goin' ta ha that dress soaked if we dinna stop the tear fest." She sniffed. "Mama, help me get the lass oot o the gown now."

Before Madison broke her hold on Evelyn, she spoke very softly to her. "May I call you 'mama' too like the girls do?"

Evelyn laughed out loud. "Well, ma stars and garters, baby girl! I hope you will!"

When Madison got back to the house, Mr. MacGuffey had the tables and chairs set up and the marquee erected in place for the wedding. Evelyn had been right about MacGuffey's genius. Madison had no idea where all the linens and tableware were, but there was no evidence of it in the house and no clutter anywhere that she could see.

Lizzy and Patrick arrived along with Agatha, escorted by Angus Jamison. Ian grinned when he saw the group exit Patrick's car.

"Angus," Ian called out, "it's good ta see ye. Help yerself ta the refreshments there." He walked purposefully to where Agatha stood looking toward the cliff. "Agatha, I see ye've come wi a date." He smiled.

"What are ye talkin' aboot, ye fool? I've done nay such a thing!"

"I just saw ye get oot of Patrick's car wi Angus on yer arm." He grinned.

"I didna invite him ta ride in the car wi us. And I dinda ask him ta attend this shin-dig." She brushed an imaginary wrinkle from her dress. "Samuel expressed an interest in meetin' the man. The lass invited him. I ca'na be held responsible fer his transportation." She looked up into Ian's face. "And if ye e're again say tha' I've brought him as me 'date, ye'll be standin' in front o tha mob Saturday morn wi me boot sticking oot o' yer ass!"

"Hello, Agatha!" Madison called as she came across the yard toward Ian and the older woman. "I'm so glad you.... What? What's going on?"

"Nay a thing oot o' the ordinary, lass. Yer intended and I were just passin' the time o'day. Ye're lookin' luvly, Maddy girl." She smiled at Madison. "Ian, lad, did ye no' mention refreshments a time ago?" Ian motioned toward the array of cool drinks and cheeses set up near the porch and, Agatha headed in that direction stopping along to way to speak to the vicar who had just arrived.

"Ian?" Maddy questioned.

"Agatha came wi Angus, but until after the weddin', that's all I'm at liberty ta say." He laughed and wrapped his arm around Maddy's shoulder, leading her toward their guests.

The wedding rehearsal went smoothly. All participants learned their parts and what they were to do. Madison spoke with the string quartet to make sure the music was what they had chosen earlier. Samuel and Angie talked at length to Angus, and the vicar cautioning everyone to make an early night of it.

Late in the afternoon, all the guests had returned to their cars and started out for Evelyn's, who was serving the rehearsal dinner at her house. Madison was speaking with Mr. MacGuffey about last minute details when Ian came up behind her. He nodded at the caterer and MacGuffey picked up his notebook and headed toward his car.

"Ye know, luv," Ian cooed as he nuzzled her neck. "The bride and groom are ne're expected to show up on time ta these things." With his arms encircling her waist, Madison tried to wiggle away, but Ian's hold was too strong.

"If you think I'm going to allow your mother to make excuses for us to all those hungry people, Ian Mackay, you're crazy!" she laughed. "Mmm, God! Don't do that!" she moaned when Ian's thumbs brushed purposely back and forth under her breasts. She turned in his arms and reached up to meet his lips. "We have to go, Ian," she muttered as he took her mouth with his.

Ian tore his mouth from hers long enough to agree with the earlier warning. "The vicar was right. We need ta make this an early night," he said before taking her mouth again.

Finally, Madison broke the embrace and leaned back to look into his eyes. "Agatha says it's not proper for us to 'share a bed on the eve of our nuptials.'"

Ian quirked his eyebrow at Madison and half frowned. "Agatha Stuart came here this afternoon wi Angus Jamison as her date!" he announced.

"Whaaat? Really?"

"Aye!" he said as he took her arm and walked her to the Wagoneer. "And donna be surprised if ye see me wearin a long coat at the ceremony tomorrow, and Mrs. Stuart wi only one 'boot.'"

"What?!"

"Or I suppose I could stand wi me back ta the cliff and face the 'mob' durin' the ceremony." He grinned.

"WHAT?!"

Ian laughed out loud at Madison's confusion and pushed the ignition.

Chapter Forty

When Ian and Madison arrived at Evelyn's, the guests were gathered in the Great Hall. As the couple entered the hall, everyone turned to face them and raised their glasses in a toast to the bride and groom. Patrick came forward and handed them each a glass of wine. Maddy looked at him questioningly.

"I do'na think a glass of red will hurt the wee babe, Maddy, and I'm thinking it might do *you* some good." He smiled.

Ian raised his glass. "I'd like to make a toast," he said, and the room quieted. "Ta our mam, for lovin' our da and goin' through all she did to find him again, and raisin eight bairns in this house." He looked across the room and into his mother's eyes that he knew were bright with tears. "And ta the bonnie lass, here." He brushed away the tear that dropped to her cheek. "For endurin' all tha' ye have. And for comin' here and luvin' me and the wee babe ye carry. I'll make ye happy, luv. I'll spend the rest of me life tryin' ta make ye as happy as ye've made me," he said and pressed his lips softly to hers.

"Here! Here!" came a chorus of voices filling the Great Hall.

The evening was a festive one. As the family ate dinner they shared stories and accounts of Ian and Madison's lives together and apart. Everyone wanted to know about Madison's business and she and Samuel had the floor for quite a long time. After dinner, the group adjourned to the terrace to watch as a fireworks display light up the sky. Madison and Ian held each other and watched the rocket-like blasts shoot up into the dark, and bloom out into sparkling colors and then fade and drop to the distant ground. There were "Oohs" and "Aahhs" and applause all round for the magnificent showing. However, Sara and Tommy's baby daughter, Isabelle, didn't care for the fireworks quite as much as everybody else, and they had to leave to put her to bed.

"Why not leave Isabelle herea tonight?" Evelyn suggested. "Come for breakfast in the mornin'. Y'all can take her home afta, if you want. It's late and too long a drive for this sweet child. Go on now. Enjoy a night to yourselves. Maddy and I will take her up to the nursery and put her to bed." She laughed. "It'll be good practice for her!"

"Oh yes!" Madison smiled as she reached for the tiny baby. "I'd love to fuss over her for a while."

Sara handed her daughter to Maddy and hugged them both lightly. "The next time I see you, will be your wedding day." Sara smiled and gave Madison a kiss goodbye.

Madison and Evelyn excused themselves and took the baby upstairs to the nursery. Evelyn sent one of the maids for a bottle of warm formula, and they fed and rocked Isabelle until she dropped off to sleep. They laid her in the crib and turned on the soft tiny light in the room.

"Before long, I'll have my own child to feed and rock and put to bed," Madison said as she took one last look at the baby before she closed the nursery door.

"That's right, baby girl. And you'll never have a sweeter gift."

Ian looked up the grand staircase and watched his mother and Madison walking arm in arm down the steps. He smiled with pride and affection. *This is me moother,* he thought to himself. *And Maddy is going to be me wife. Me wife and a wee babe. We're goin' ta be a family.*

The two women joined him at the bottom of the stairs. Madison smiled as Evelyn handed her off to him and the three of them joined their guests in the Great Hall where both fireplaces had been lit and the room glowed with light and heat from the orange flames. Not long after that, there was a steady stream of goodbyes and departures, until only Ian, Madison, and the people who were staying with Evelyn were left. Ian then took the opportunity to bid his mother good night and he and Madison took their leave.

The next day was one of complete relaxation for Ian and Madison. They slept until almost noon. They talked quietly together while Madison took her nausea meds, nibbled on soda crackers, and sipped ginger ale. Ian showered first then went down to the kitchen to make brunch. After Madison showered, and did the rest of her morning routine, she joined Ian there. Both knowing this was the last time they would do any of this before becoming man and wife, they savored every moment. Tomorrow would begin a new phase of their life together. It was exciting and they had so much to look forward to, but today was special to them. Something that was surprising to them both, was that neither one was nervous. Ian seemed to have relaxed in the last day or so.

After they had eaten, Ian cleaned up the dishes while Madison stepped out onto the porch looking at the site where the marriage ceremony would take place. Neither had wanted an arbor or archway that might disrupt the view, but had given in to the idea of a marquee tent due to the number of elderly guests. The chairs and reception tables were in place. Flowers would be attached to the fencing by the cliff in the morning. Madison walked down the aisle and stopped where she would to marry Ian. She looked out at the ocean, remembering the time she stood in this very spot her first day in Scotland. Never in her wildest dream, did she ever imagine; she'd be standing in the same spot the day before her wedding to the man she loved and who loved her in return. She also remembered seeing Ian for the first time down on the beach. Wanting to relive the memory, Madison walked down the steps to the beach. When she reached the bottom, she looked back up the steep flight of stairs and like on that first day, she was almost dreading the walk back up them. She walked the beach wanting to hold on to every breeze through her hair, every chirp of the birds circling overhead. She watched, as each wave that rolled in on the rocky shore seemed to wish her good tidings of happiness. She was creating new memories to add to those she already had. At the sound of Ian's voice she turned and looked up the cliff and smiled. As if like magic, her first memory was coming back to life. She watched as he came down to her and met him at the bottom of the stairs.

"Hello," Ian smiled, remembering the day they met as well.

"Hello." Madison started to walk to him. "May I help you?"

"Actually, I was figurin' on askin' ye that question. What are ye doin' here?"

"Oh, well, I'm renting the house for six months." Beaming as he played along. "I just got in last night. As a matter of fact, I was hoping to meet the owner, so we could go over everything."

"Ah, well what's yer name?" he smiled.

"My name is Madison Danaher." Madison smiled. "I'm sorry, I don't mean to be rude, but who are you?"

"Oh I'm sorry;" He chuckled slightly, "I'm the owner from whom ye're renting."

"Oh excuse me. I didn't realize."

"Please, dinna worry. I should have told ye as soon as I got down here. But I really didna remember yer name."

"Your accent doesn't seem to be quite as thick as everyone else's."

"I was asked to practice curbing the accent." His smile was perfect. "Why don't we walk back to the house and we can talk inside where it's warmer." His grin got even wider

"Sounds wonderful." They turned and walked back up the stone stairs. When they reached the top, Madison was out of breath. "Can I help ye, lass?" Ian asked as he extended his hand to her.

"Yes, you may." She took his hand and two of them walked arm and arm into the house. They spent the rest of the day cuddling on the sofa, listening to music, and making love.

Wedding day, Madison thought as she woke. She and Ian had decided to obey some of the traditions. So at midnight Ian left their bedroom and slept in the guest room. Madison crept from their bedroom hoping to get a glimpse of Ian, but what she got was Donny sitting on a chair outside the guest room door.

"Donny?" Madison questioned.

"Good morn!"

"How long have you been sitting here?" She grinned.

"Since aboot 4:00 a.m. We talked it o're last night, the brothers and meself, and decided tha' it wasna such a good idea fer the two o ye ta be seein' each other before the weddin'. But when we got here, the laddie was already in the spare room. Sae, we're makin' sure he stays put until it's time for him ta wed ye. He's already tried three times ta get inta yer room, lass, and we all know tha' ca'na be!" Donny stood with his back to the guest room door and stretched his arms out to block the doorway in mock horror.

Madison laughed and then stopped and sniffed the air. "Coffee?" She looked back at Donny. "Do I smell coffee?"

"Aye. I believe it is." Donny grinned. "Would ye like some?"

"Is it decaf?" Ian called through the door, and Madison grinned as she rolled her eyes.

"Our mam and me sisters are here ta help ye dress and Tommy and Alex are in wi him." Donny smiled while aiming his thumb toward the guest room door."

"Did ye take yer pills?" Ian called from the guest room.

Donny kissed her on the cheek "Off wi ye." He directed her back to her room, then yelled downstairs to the cavalry that Madison was awake, and the ladies could "come up to begin wi the primpin'. And ye might bring her a cuppa... coffee!"

Madison made the bed and tidied the room while she waited for Evelyn and the sisters to come up. They arrived in the room in a flurry of activity. Evelyn held a tray of cups and pots of coffee and tea along with muffins and juice. Bridget and Emily each carried satin-covered hangers of dresses and Sara had a dress and her overnight bag.

"We're not actually moving in with you, Madison," Sara laughed.

"I'll go down and bring up our bags. If ye do'na mind, Maddy, we'll all dress here fer the weddin'." Bridget announced while hanging the covered dresses on the front of the closet door.

Emily handed her hangers to Bridget and headed for the door again. "Lizzy called earlier," she said. "Patrick is bringin' her shortly. I'll ge the bags, Bridie. Be right back."

"Here. Sit down and eat your muffin and have some coffee, dahlin. You've got plenty of time yet, and you need something in your stomach." Evelyn turned at the knock on the door.

"The laddie in there wants ta know—"

"Ma. Stars and garters! Yes, tell him it's decaf, for goodness sake! Maddy has taken her pills and he should stop all that yammerin'! Y'all tell him to straighten up and behave like an adult." And she shut the door in Alex's face. "The soona we get that boy married and you have that baby, the betta off we are all goin' to be!" Evelyn sat on the edge of the bed and looked at Madison. "You did take your pills didn't ya, dahlin? You sure don't look like you feel sick."

"Yes, I did take them, and I feel wonderful… Mama."

Evelyn beamed. "You sweet child. Well, now have a muffin and some juice and coffee. Bridie, do y'all want some more coffee or would you ratha have tea? Sara?"

"Tea, please, Evelyn."

"I'll have tea, Mama. We'll need fer Maddy ta have her shower and do all the preliminary stuff, sae Sara can do her hair," Bridget said as she slid the protective cover from Madison's gown.

"Oh!" Sara breathed. "It's lovely, Bridget. You are a wonder with a needle."

"Thank you. It did turn oot well, did it nay?" Bridget smiled when she looked back at the gown.

After Madison showered and dried her hair she dressed in her formal petticoat and sat for Sara to do her hair.

"Ian likes my hair down," she said. "Can we do it down and still have some curl?"

"Of course you can!' the three other women echoed together and then laughed.

"Why don't we pull a little up from the sides for curls at the back of the crown and the rest can fall in soft curl and wave down the back naturally," Sara suggested. "And I have some baby's breath and a couple sprigs of heather to put in the curls at the crown if you'd like since you aren't wearing any kind of veil or headpiece."

"That sounds great!" Madison grinned.

The hot curlers were ready and so was Sara. She rolled and combed, fluffed and brushed. When she had finished, she placed tiny sprigs of baby's breath and heather into the soft flowing curls at the back of Madison's shiny chestnut hair and handed her a mirror

"It's beautiful, Sara! It's perfect!" Maddy held the mirror and viewed Sara's work from all sides. "It looks so soft and natural." She set the hand mirror on the bathroom counter and took Sara's hand in hers. "Thank you. I love it." Madison glanced out the window and noticed the activity on the lawn.

"Don't worry, baby girl. MacGuffey has everything under control. The man is marvelous! He knows exactly what to do and when to do it. Now, let's get y'all into this gown."

Bridget and Emily were carefully removing the wedding dress from the hanger. Evelyn and the girls helped Madison get into her dress and sash. Madison didn't want a veil or headpiece, so Evelyn helped Sara place more of the baby's breath and heather throughout her hair. Finally, an hour later, Lizzy showed up and gave Madison her flowers to carry.

"I'm sorry I'm sae late gettin' here, Maddy, but I dinda want ta rush makin' yer flowers." She held up the bouquet for inspection. Madison looked at the flowers in Lizzy's hand. It was about the most beautiful bouquet Madison had ever seen. Mixed white and green roses, with baby's breath pocketed between the half-open blooms.

"Lizzy, it's lovely. Really stunning. Where did you find green roses?" Madison asked as she admired the work

"Oh, and that's the easy part. Ye only let the flowers sit in water wi green food colorin' in it." Lizzy looked at Madison. "Do ye like the bouquet, then?"

"Oh, Lizzy, I love it." She threw her arms around Lizzy. "Thank you so much for this."

"It is stunnin', Lizzy." Evelyn and Emily examined the flowers Lizzy had arranged into the bouquet for Madison to carry on her wedding day. "But we've no time to be cacklin'. You girls have to get into youra gowns. Come on!" From then on it was a whirlwind of activity in the bedroom as the bride and her maid of honor were helped into their gowns. Evelyn, Sara, and the sisters helped each other into their dresses. And, "Fora heaven's sake, don't sit down, girls!" Evelyn would say, often.

Patrick knocked on the door and handed in a box filled with flowers for the mother of the groom and his sisters. There were single roses for Bridget, Emily, and Sara, and a small bouquet of heather and daisies for Lizzy. When all the ladies were dressed and ready, Evelyn placed the Mackay tartan sash over Madison's shoulder and secured it with the small pearl broach below her hip.

"Now, baby girl, go down and marry ma boy and be as happy with him as I was with his daddy." And she kissed Madison on the cheek.

"Thank you, Mama," Maddy whispered.

"Mama, if ye start us all blubberin' again, I dinna know what I'll do wi ye!" Bridget sniffed and they all laughed.

"It's time to go, Madison," came Samuel's voice from the other side of the door. Evelyn opened the door and Maddy turned to smile at Samuel as he walked into the room. "You look breathtaking, my dear," Samuel said before taking her in a fatherly hug. "Evelyn, you're sons have Ian locked up downstairs. If you and the other ladies are ready, the boys are going to seat you before they let Ian out of the pantry." He chuckled.

Evelyn and the younger women went downstairs, where Tommy, Donny, Alex, and Patrick waited to escort them to their seats. Lizzy waited at the bottom of the steps until Tommy came back to retrieve Ian from the pantry and walked out with him. Then she gave Samuel the nod to bring Madison down.

Madison took Samuel's arm and he led her down the stairs and to the door. Lizzy grinned at Maddy and then went through the door to take her place opposite Tommy and Ian. Madison looked out and saw Ian and Tommy standing by the cliff next to the vicar. Ian didn't look the least nervous. He had a huge smile on his face and eyes only for her.

Samuel slid Maddy's arm through his and they began their walk down the aisle between the seated guests. When they reached the point where Maddy had a full view of Ian, she came to a dead stop. Samuel looked over at her questioningly. Her smile was still in place, but her eyes had welled. At the end of the aisle, before the cliff, stood Ian, in all his formal Scots splendor. He was wearing his kilt! She couldn't believe it. He hated kilts. Swore he would never wear one again. Promised to avoid any and all functions that required the wearing of a kilt. *He's doing this for me,* she thought to herself. Their eyes locked and Ian all but laughed out loud. "Samuel, did you know it's snowing in Hell today?" she whispered.

"Excuse me?" her escort questioned, but Madison had already resumed the slow walk.

When Samuel and Madison reached the end of the aisle, and Ian could see the full view of Madison, with the Mackay sash draped from her shoulder and down across her gown, he couldn't have been more proud. Tommy had to tug slightly at the back of his jacket to keep him in place.

"Dearly beloved...," The vicar began. "Who gives this womon to be married to this man?"

Samuel turned to look at Madison, "Her Poppy and I do," he said and leaned down giving her a kiss on the cheek, then reached around pressing his hand to Ian's shoulder before stepping back to take his seat in the front row next to Angie. Maddy handed her bouquet to Lizzy and turned to face Ian. As the vicar began to speak the words of the wedding ceremony, Madison and Ian looked into each other eyes.

"Do ye, Ian Mathew Mackay take this womon to be yeer wedded wife?" the vicar asked.

"Aye, I do," Ian said as he gazed upon Madison.

" And do ye promise...," the vicar went on.

I'll never forget how I feel at this moment, Maddy thought to herself as she listened to Ian vow his love and faith.

"And do ye Madison Elizabeth Danaher take this man to be yeer wedded husband?"

"Aye." Madison grinned. "I do."

"And do ye promise...."

Ian and Madison repeated their vows of marriage in strong clear voices that neither the wind nor the sound of the surf below could muffle.

"...the givin' and receivin' of rings."

"With this ring...," Ian said as he held Maddy's hand to slip the blue diamond set in a wide band of gold onto her finger. "'Tis the color of yeer eyes, darlin." He smiled at her.

When it was her turn, Madison slid onto Ian's finger the yellow gold band with a sparkling white gold overlay of the Irish Claddagh.

"If there be no one who can give just reason why these two should not be joined in holy wedlock, let them speak now or hereafter, forever hold their peace." He waited for a split second. "Then I pronounce them ta be mon and wife. Wha' God has joined together, let no man put asunder! Ye may kiss the bride now, laddie."

Ian looked to Madison. "I love ye, Maddy, wi all me heart."

"And I love you, Ian, from now until eternity," Madison answered with tears of joy glimmering in her eyes. Ian dipped his head and kissed his wife for the first time. The guests rose form their seats, and applauded and raised cheers as Madison and Ian walked up the aisle as husband and wife.

Epilogue

Madison and Ian sat on the picnic blanket at the back of the house and watched as their two-year-old daughter Christina and her cousin Isabelle played together.

"I love to have Isabelle here to play with Christina." Madison laughed as she watched the children trip over each other in play. "It's nice to have two children around, don't you think?"

"Aye, luv, I do." Ian leaned over and placed a kiss on his wife's lips. "How long before this one shows his head?" he asked, referring to her pregnant belly.

"Patrick says at least another couple of weeks." She looked at all the addition work Ian and his brothers had done on the house. "It's such a beautiful house, isn't it? Our house on the cliff." She smiled "It's a good thing you and Tommy had the good sense to build two rooms on the house instead of the one. I really should to go in to the office today," she added.

"Maddy, ye ca'na go ta work. Patrick told ye no more work," Ian protested.

"Ian, I am the CEO of the company and I have new offices here in the Highlands that need to be looked after. I have to do this. I don't need to be there very long." She kissed his forehead and smiled. "Besides, you have your press conference. I can ride into the village with you and while you're telling your public how honored you are for being nominated for best lead actor, I'll do my thing at the office. By the time you're finished, I will be too and I can come back home with you." She grinned at her own logistics.

"Ye think ye're verra clever do ye no?" Ian laughed.

"Ian, I am so proud of you."

"Thank ye, luv, and ye're tryin' ta change the subject." He pulled her into his arms. "I'm proud of ye too, darlin'. It took a lot of courage ta take on the responsibility of chief executive officer. I know Samuel was pleased, though, when you accepted his offer."

"So was Angie." Madison laughed at the memory. "I remember after I said yes; she literally jumped for joy, and ran to the phone to start looking for houses here in Scotland. I'm so happy they moved here to be near us and Christina."

"I know ye are, luv. So am I."

"Do you regret not going to the ceremony to accept your award?" Madison asked.

Ian laughed. "Ye're fairly sure I'll win it, then?"

"Well, of course! How could you not win? You are the best! There's no doubt in *my* mind." She laughed too.

"Ye're all the fan club I need!" He kissed her forehead and ran his hands through her hair. "Nay, luv, I do'na, regret no' bein at the ceremony. I ne'er wanted ta be in the spotlight. It's the work I like. There's no' many people in the world who actually like their work. I'm a lucky lad. I luv the work and I'm lucky ta be able ta make a comfortable living doin' the work I luv. When ye get right doon ta it, if I get the award, it will make me verra happy because it's an acceptance from me peers. That's important, but the most important thing ta me, is us." He reached for her and rested her back against his chest. "Ye and our children and our life together. Besides, if I went, I wouldna ha been wi ye when our wee babe is born. I can miss accepting that award." He pressed his lips to the top of her head and held her close. "But I ca'na miss the birthin' of our bairn.

Madison sighed. "You're such a nice man, my love." She kissed him lightly on the cheek. "I've decided to keep you."

"Thank ye, lass. I—"

"Mama?" Ian and Madison drew their attention from each other at the sound of their daughter's voice. Christina was a ball of energy. She had her mother's hair and her father emerald green eyes. Her personality was a mesh of both parents, and she was a very happy child.

"Isa stay wi Tina?" She was also beginning to pick up the brogue. Madison was thrilled with that. She only hoped she would pick it up one day.

"Why don't we call Aunt Sara and ask if it's okay? Don't forget we're going to Lizzy and Patrick's tomorrow to see the new baby."

Christina charged off at a run. "New baby, Isa!" she yelled to her cousin. Madison smiled as Ian helped her to her feet. They followed behind as the two children raced to the house.

"Sara is happy for Isabelle to sleep over," Madison relayed to Ian with her cell still at her ear, "and says she'll drop off clean clothes for her later in the afternoon." She grinned, "Oh, Sara, you don't have to do that. I'm gonna shoot over to the office and have a look see. I can pick up Isa's things then." Madison and Sara said their goodbye's and Madison turned to see Ian's frowning face. "I won't be there all day, just a peek. I'll take the girls to Samuel and Angie's and you can pick them up after your press thing. *Best Lead Actor in a Motion Picture*." She smiled.

"I'll go wi ye ta the office, and then *we* can go and meet wi the press." Ian smiled and kissed her on the forehead.

"Ian, the press doesn't want to see me!"

"What sane person wouldna want ta see such a bonnie pregnant lass?" Ian asked as he punched Samuel's phone number into his cell.

Samuel and Angie were delighted at the prospect of having the two little girls for the day. He and Angie took their role of surrogate grandparents seriously. As far as they were concerned, Christina was their granddaughter, and since moving to Scotland they had grown very close to the rest of Ian's family and thought of Isabelle as their granddaughter as well.

Ian and Madison dropped off the girls and then they drove on to Lusta. Madison spent a little over an hour checking the progress of the new office and talking with her staff there. Then she and Ian left and drove to Ian's press conference in Portree.

Madison stood to the side as Ian took his place in front of the reporters. But before he spoke, he opened his arm toward her, and she joined him before the cameras and microphones. Madison hadn't realized until then that she had become more or less accustomed to the flashing bulbs and constant yammering of the press. She stood next to Ian while he spoke graciously about his pleasure and surprise over the nomination for the film award nomination. As Ian spoke her heart filled with pride for her husband. Suddenly Madison began to have a somewhat familiar sensation. She looked to Ian and while he was picking a reporter to answer another question Madison gave a slight tug on the bottom of his shirt.

Ian looked at her. "What, luv?" he asked.

"I think Patrick might have overestimated how long before this little tike would arrive," Madison whispered and winced at the same time.

Taking the cue, Ian looked back to the press corps. "I'm verra sorry, ladies and gentleman, but we have ta go ta hospital." Ian then scooped up his wife and moved purposefully out of the building and to the car. While Ian drove to the hospital, Madison called Patrick. Thankfully, they were only twenty minutes away since Madison's contractions were four minutes apart. Ian pulled his Wagoneer to the emergency entrance and yelled for a wheelchair. Madison scowled at him, but happily took the chair. As she was wheeled in, she caught a glimpse of Patrick who was already in his scrubs.

"Well, I see ye're plannin' on makin' a liar out o' me, lass." He smiled and took ahold of her wrist to check her pulse rate. "Take her up ta labor and delivery. I'll be along shortly." he told the nurse and Madison was whisked away. Ian filled out paperwork at the counter, and then he and Patrick took the elevator to the labor and delivery floor. Ian changed into scrubs and Patrick led him to Madison's room. Ian went directly to Madison while Patrick went to the nurse.

"Her water has broken and she is dilated to ten centimeters," the nurse informed him.

"Okay, then, Let's meet the new member of the Mackay family." Patrick smiled.

Forty minutes later Madison lay in her bed holding their new baby boy. Ian sat on the side of the bed with Maddy's hand clutched in his own.

"I'd like to name him after your father." She smiled.

"Me da would love tha'," Ian choked. "Hello there Stephen Michael Mackay." He took ahold of tiny Stephen's hand and the baby wrapped his small fingers around Ian's thumb. "What stories we will ha' for ye, laddie." Ian looked back to his wife with tears in his eyes, "I luv ye, lass."

Maddy released his hand and reached up to brush the tears that had dropped to his cheek. "And I you, luv." She smiled.

Nora Weirich

Nora Weirich lives with her husband and four fur babies. Since 2007 she has worked as a Teachers Aide in her local school district. She has a ferocious love of reading. You can find her most days either in her office writing or in her favorite chair curled up with a blanket, a warm cup of coffee or tea with a her nose in a book.

Cadmi Ó'Cléirigh

Over the years Nora has fallen in love with the genre of Romantasy. When the opportunity arose, she began her penname of Cadmi Ó'Cléirigh. She is currently working on Golden Realm Chronicles.

Other Works

Nora Weirich

Mackay Series
Mackay's Cliff House (Formally Cliff House)
Dunnegan's Cottage

Cadmi Ó'Cléirigh

The Golden Realm Chronicles
Quelocand: Land of the Queens
Locbroalm: The Golden Realm(Coming Soon)

Social Media

Nora Weirich Cadmi Ó'Cléirigh